27

HOURS

THE NIGHTSIDE SAGA

Tristina Wright

Entangled Publishing, LLC
2614 South Timberline Road
Suite 109
Fort Collins, CO 80525

Entangled Teen is an imprint of Entangled Publishing, LLC.

Visit our website at www.entangledpublishing.com.

Edited by Kate Brauning
Cover design by Fiona Jayde
Interior design by Toni Kerr

ISBN 978-1-63375-820-9
Ebook ISBN 978-1-63375-821-6

Manufactured in the United States of America

First Edition October 2017

10 9 8 7 6 5 4 3 2 1

entangled teen
an imprint of Entangled Publishing LLC

To Stephen,
for believing in me even when I couldn't.
I love you

~

To every teenager who's sat on the sidelines
relegated to sidekick
or comic relief
simply because you weren't The Default

To every teenager who's wanted to be more
to be the hero
to be the love interest
to fight the monsters
and save the day

This book is for you

The first generational ship leaves Earth:
2075 AD

As these brave few,
these extraordinary few,
leave this planet for new homes amongst the stars,
they enter our imaginations, our dreams,
where they'll live forever.

- Malia Mora
Canadian Prime Minister

RUMOR

Rumor Mora feared two things: hellhound gargoyles and failure.

The first stemmed from the gargoyle attack that killed his mother when he was ten and left him with a silvery scar down his spine. The second was why he methodically swung through his blade exercises again

and again

and again.

They never knew when another attack would hit. *Always be ready*. His father's words. *Always be aware*.

Sweat rolled down his temples and his back, sticking his shirt to him despite the cooler temperatures on Sahara's nightside. His muscles burned, and his scars twinged, but he kept going, pushing through each slash, each step, each memorized movement. The twin machetes felt like extensions of his arms, their inner cores glowing red-hot along the entire blade. His boots slid through the gravel of the empty training lot. He liked the top terrace for a few reasons: it was only a few kilometers from the north city wall, it afforded him privacy for training, and the view of the city was spectacular.

Not many people stayed in the upper terraces for training. The training building was *right there* so any instructor could see them at all times. Rumor didn't mind that, if it meant fewer people around to talk to him.

Most trainees picked the lower terraces: more practice weapons, dummies, obstacle courses. Plus the lower you were, the quicker you got out when each training session was over. The main avenue through HUB2 started at the lowest terrace and cut the city in half north to south, ending at the main residential district.

Far away, lights dotted the residential towers that were staggered along the wall in enormous stair-step patterns, but they were nothing compared to the illuminated sprawl of HUB2's central district at night. It curved down below him and up again on the western side — an enormous bowl of a city stretching toward the northeastern corner of Lake Llyn. The eastern side of the avenue housed HUB2's adamantine mining operations. Every dayside, the steady thud of drills pounding into the ground filled the air like the city's own heartbeat. Right now, the drills sat silent and dark, long shadows thrown across them from the glittering lights of the city. The mag-train hummed along its elevated magnetic track around the city, ferrying HUB2 colonists who didn't care to walk from one side to the other.

Sahara's host planet cast a dark shadow across the eastern side of the HUB, the gas giant eclipsing a third of the night sky. The stories from Earth said the night sky there had been the color of the void and pricked with millions of stars. Only one moon had stamped a hole in the darkness. The sky above the colonized moon of Sahara was a jumble of blue-green nebula, Sahara's host planet (which had some long number designation Rumor could never remember), and five other moons.

From up here, the sounds of the city—the mag-train, the marines, the shouts, the automata, the traffic—all blended into a steady, thrumming white noise that helped him focus as he trained.

"Did you sleep?"

Rumor glanced at his father, who must have come out of the training facility without him noticing. "A little bit. Like six hours."

"You need more sleep than six hours." Eric Mora folded his arms, his stance wide as he watched.

Rumor hitched a shoulder as he spun around, ending the exercise with a diagonal slash toward the ground. The blade blurred as he moved, thirty centimeters of heated adamantine that cut through the blue-green light from the nearby butterfly nebula smeared across the sky.

"Drop your shoulder more when you land that hit," his dad said. "You'll be able to move into defense better if you do."

Rumor nodded. "Got it."

"Rumor."

He switched the blades off as he straightened and faced his father. Rumor had inherited Eric's wild dark curls and dark eyes, but the brown skin and the wide smile came from his mother. He knew Eric saw his late wife in their only son. The tightening of Eric's eyes always betrayed him. After all, Rumor saw his mom every time he glanced in the mirror or the scar up his back hurt. It'd been seven years, and those memories still didn't hurt any less.

Eric looked like he wanted to say something. Finally, he ran a hand through his curls and blew out a breath. "We need to talk about something."

Rumor arched an eyebrow. "Okay."

"Not now. Later. I don't want to disturb your training."

The second eyebrow joined the first. "Ohhh-kay."

Eric's lips twitched in a smile. "Stop looking at me like that."

Rumor fought to maintain the patronizing expression, but he couldn't stop the smile. "I'm probably going to head down to Padriack's after this. Maybe meet up with Jordan and Steve."

"I have to head into the office. General Stewart wants to discuss something. He said it was urgent. I'll try to meet you there later." He turned away as he spoke, his eyes narrowing at the shadowed side of the HUB, just beyond the military barracks.

"Is it about finishing that?" Rumor pointed up at the partially completed dome that would one day cap HUB2 from wall to wall. Supposedly. The project had been delayed many times for many reasons: supplies, manpower, attacks. HUB1 had completed a dome two years ago, protecting the citizens from air attacks. The HUBs were far too large for the adamantine webbing the smaller colonies used.

"I hope so," Eric said in a distracted tone. "Did you see that?"

"See what?" Rumor glanced in the direction his father faced, squinting into the darkness where the wall cut across a small set of foothills before heading south. Several guard towers dotted the edge, their guns trained out. Marine barracks lined up in organized rows, following the wall to the foothills. Most of them were dark, their occupants asleep. A handful glowed with life, shouts and muffled music seeping out of open windows.

"I don't…maybe nothing." Eric waved a hand dismissively and walked away. He spun around after a few steps, walking backward as he pointed at Rumor. "Talking. You and me. Later. I promise not to embarrass you in front of your friends."

Rumor gave him a mock two-fingered salute. "Talking. Got it." He rotated his wrists, spinning his weapons over twice as his dad walked away, frowning at the shadowed part of HUB2. Rumor shook his head. *Paranoid Dad.*

The ground vibrated. It was low and brief, but it was enough for Rumor to pause.

Maybe not paranoid?

Metal groaned. The very distinct sound of stone on metal screeched across the night from somewhere behind the training building, sending goose bumps across his skin. Rumor pressed his tongue to the back of his teeth and strained his hearing over the white noise of the city. He scanned the immediate area, then looked upward toward the nebula. The sky remained clear. HUB2 bustled on as it had before. His dad had stopped walking on the other side of the terrace, and now stared at the shadowed portion of the city.

Rumor's skin tingled as he stood perfectly still and listened. His thumbs ghosted over the hidden switches on the inside of each handle, releasing the chemicals that heated the core and made the blades glow softly. They threw orange light across the ground as he tried to hear past the music and shouting from the barracks.

A roar echoed off the mountains to the north of the wall—a little to his left. The roars never ceased to put him on edge. Even if they never came near the HUBs, he'd never get used to gargoyle roaring during nightside.

Metal groaned again, this time behind him, bending into a squeal that seemed to echo across the entire training ground.

Eric turned around, his eyes fixed on something over Rumor's left shoulder. "Son, you need to move now," he said in an overly calm voice.

Rumor flexed his fingers around the leather-wrapped handles of his blades. He inhaled a shaky breath and took a step forward, his back muscles tightening and the base of his skull prickling. Gravel behind him crunched.

"Come on, Rumor," his dad said, his focus still over Rumor's shoulder.

Gunfire erupted in the distance, the cracks echoing through the city. Rumor flinched at the first shot, hating the instinctual movement despite all his training. His heart sped, and adrenaline flooded his system.

Not again. The words whispered through his mind as he stared at his father.

"Dad," Rumor managed.

"Drop," his father ordered.

Rumor dropped.

The gargoyle launched, clawing the air where he'd just stood. It landed on the other side of him, sliding in the loose gravel as

Rumor rolled and came up to a crouch, his blades ready. The gargoyle was one of the more humanoid-looking ones—one head, two arms, two legs—except it had too-long arms and horns curling up from its hairless head. Its skin was an ashy gray color, dappled by the nebula light. He had no idea if it was male or female or if the gargoyles even had those genders. He didn't care. He just wanted it to die.

"Stupid to try to attack a HUB, asshole," Rumor growled as he rose.

"Rumor!" Eric shouted. His gun fired twice, but Rumor couldn't turn around to check on his dad.

The gargoyle clicked at him, guttural noises rolling out of its throat. It lunged, claws swiping for Rumor's face. He bowed backward and slashed at the creature's ribs. The thick hide almost resisted the heated blade.

Almost, but not quite.

Black blood oozed out of the slash, streaking down the creature's side. Rumor straightened and spun, bringing both blades down across its back as it stumbled to the side. Skin split along bone, and the creature howled.

Howls answered it. Howls reverberating all around the wall. A chorus of howls overlapping and echoing as they built in volume and ferocity.

Rumor lowered his chin and stared at the gargoyle. It spun at him again, its claws catching him across the side. Pain bloomed up his side. He brought his blade down across the gargoyle's throat. The skin split, sizzling where the heated blade touched. Hot blood spurted across his shirt and arms. It stank like something muddy and rotten.

The gargoyle sank to the ground, scrabbling at its throat as the blood pooled, a void across the light gravel. Rumor held his side, breathing hard.

"Dad!" Oh, gods, where was his dad? Was he even okay? He'd been so focused on the gargoyle, he hadn't kept an eye on his dad.

Eric stumbled to him. "Are you okay?" Sweat dampened his shirt and stuck a few curls to his forehead. Parallel scratches ran down his cheek, and his hands were spattered with stinking black blood.

Rumor nodded. An alarm wailed, and he winced away. The whine grew to a feverish pitch, echoing across HUB2 and mixing with the horrified screams of humans—of his neighbors, his friends—and the grating and clicking of gargoyles to create a cacophony of terror.

"Rumor!" His dad grabbed his shoulders and pulled him away from the corpse. Eric cursed, loudly and creatively. Rumor thought he caught the word "Hector" but wasn't sure.

"What's happening?" Rumor bent a little to protect his injury. Pain radiated through his ribs. "Where did they all come from?"

His father's answer was swallowed by deafening roars that shook Rumor to his bones.

Rumor looked at the twisted gray body of the gargoyle he'd killed. Its blood was so black, it reflected the nebula above. His grip on his blades tightened. How dare something so ugly live under such a sky? "How did they get past the wall cannons? What's happening?"

Eric shook his head. "That doesn't matter. You need to run."

"What? No." Rumor pulled himself free from his father's grasp.

"Rumor, you need to get out of here."

Screams rose in the air as shadowy figures erupted over the city wall in dark waves. The shadow of a dragon slid across the sky. Gargoyles were swarming his city. There were so many. More gargoyles than he'd ever seen in one attack. Hundreds. Maybe thousands.

The dragon landed roughly twenty kilometers away, on the eastern side of the HUB just past the darkened mining equipment. Its bulk scraped over buildings, peeling off layers of greenery from walls and destroying solar panels as it hit the ground with a roar.

Rumor had always thought the old Earth descriptions of dragons from the archives were ridiculous. Giant lizards that breathed fire and hoarded gold and stole princesses. Those were nothing compared to these. Monstrous creatures as large as those giant lizards, but with long bodies, six legs, and serpentine necks ending in a mouth that split four ways and opened like space's deadliest flower. These didn't care about gold or girls. They wanted to kill and eat and destroy anything that happened to wander across their path. They were untamable and near impossible to kill.

He'd never seen them in a city.

The dragon's head swung and smashed into a narrow red tower, knocking the upper three floors to the ground. It trampled over the rubble, heading directly for the mining equipment.

"That was Padriack's," Rumor said in a shaking voice. "Jordan and Steve were there."

"Rumor."

Rumor's stomach lurched as the dragon howled. "There's a gargoyle riding the dragon."

"What?" Eric breathed.

Rumor pointed at the cloaked figure standing between the dragon's spiked shoulder blades. "Why would a gargoyle be riding a dragon?" That would require an intelligence—a hierarchy— they didn't possess.

"Why aren't the wall guns firing?" Eric asked.

"Seriously, why is a gargoyle riding a dragon like a commander?" Rumor insisted.

An explosion flared along the western edge of the wall, followed by a domino of smaller ones that studded the entire length. Metal wall panels screamed as they tore like paper and fell.

"Dad, what's happening?" Rumor gripped his blades tighter, his wound forgotten as the gargoyles poured into HUB2. The beasts moved in unison, their clawed hands wrapped around shiny weapons Rumor recognized. They moved inward, circling the city like predators stalking their prey.

"Those are our guns. Dad, those are our guns." He couldn't breathe.

"It wasn't supposed to happen like this." Eric's voice shook. "Oh, gods. We need to warn the colonies."

Rumor shoved his dad out of the way as another gargoyle noticed them and charged. He ducked under the initial swipe and drove his blade upward into the gargoyle's jaw. The beast collapsed instantly. He yanked his weapon from the creature's skull and spun around to yell at his dad.

One of the giant wall cannons finally fired, drowning out Rumor's yell and sending large-bore ammunition into the dragon's middle legs. It howled in rage and swatted the gun off its mooring like a tiny bug. The gargoyle standing on the dragon's back wielded a giant curved blade that resembled a reaper's scythe. It pointed the weapon at the rest of the wall cannons. The dragon's long neck swiveled in the same direction, and it swatted at the next cannon in line. That cannon managed to get off a shot but missed as the dragon's jaws clamped around it. They were close enough to the training grounds that Rumor heard every crunch of the dying cannons, his bones vibrating with the aftershock of each one that managed to fire.

Organized.

This couldn't be right.

"Come on." Eric grabbed Rumor's arm and tugged him back to the training building. Inside, they ran through the open space for indoor sparring. "What's the closest colony?"

Rumor stared at the big room. With the door shut, the sounds from the city fell to a muted hum. Sparring gloves hung on the wall in neat pairs. Towels lay folded in stacks. Training dummies stood along the back wall, waiting for the next session. He shivered.

"Rumor," his dad said sharply. "What's the closest colony?"

"You already know that," Rumor said.

"I need to make sure you're with me here. What's the closest—"

"Epsilon." Of the four colonies that surrounded HUB2 like notches on a compass, Epsilon was the nearest. It was exactly twenty kilometers away, closer to Lake Llyn. He only knew that because that's where Dahlia had moved when her mom had taken the chief medical officer position there.

"Okay, we need to get to Epsilon."

"What?" No. No way was he going to run. "I can fight. We can fight. We've been training—"

"We can fight, but not here."

"Are you kidding me? We have marines!"

His dad pointed to the large front windows overlooking the bowl of HUB2. "Do we?"

Rumor stared as his dad headed for the far door to the vehicle lot. "Where are the squads?"

"We can worry about that later," his dad snapped. "Rumor, come on. We should get out of here. They're coming."

Rumor sheathed his blades and jogged after his dad, slowing as the pain burned up his side. Red seeped through his shirt. He peeled it up and grimaced at the blood running in long streaks down his side and into the waistband of his pants. "Hold up, I need a bandage or something."

"First aid kit under the counter. Should be a few tubes of knitting gel. We can find medical at Epsilon."

Rumor paused by the side counter, half his attention on the still-open door his dad had just disappeared through. He could spare ten seconds to find something to staunch this bleeding. It'd be super horrible if he passed out from blood loss on the ride to Epsilon.

He found the medical kit and opened it with a swipe of his hand across the sensor. He grabbed one of the slim silver tubes. The gel was so cold he bit back a curse as he smeared it messily across the cuts.

"Dad!" he yelled as he headed for the side door, wiping his hand on his pants.

Low, rumbling growls answered him.

Rumor froze in the doorway, his veins turning to ice at the sight of three of the most fearsome gargoyles circling his dad. *Hellhounds*. It was the name he'd given them during his research on monsters from the myths back on Earth. The painted depictions of the giant canines from the depths of hell summed up exactly what Rumor saw in his nightmares. Four legs; hunched back; long, whiplike tail. They almost resembled wolves from Earth, but their shape was exaggerated, with large talons on their massive feet and elongated jaws with oversized teeth.

"Dad," he croaked. One hellhound turned at the sound of his voice. It snarled at him, then turned its attention back to Eric.

"Rumor, go to the lot to your left and get a rider," his dad said in that same overly calm voice he'd used before. He watched the largest of the hellhounds pace. His hand rested on his holstered gun, but there was no way he could draw it in time. They both knew it. "You have to go."

"Dad," Rumor whispered, completely ignoring the sailboard lot. He couldn't take his eyes off his dad. "Don't make me leave you, too."

Eric's gaze flicked to Rumor's. "Run, Rumor. Warn Epsilon. Tell them to warn the others."

He pulled his gun.

The hellhounds leaped.

Rumor ran.

He raced past several large trucks and armored transports to the sleek sailboard wind riders. They floated a few feet above the ground, ready to soak up solar energy with their broad orange sails.

Gunfire exploded in rapid shots, several skimming the sailboard to Rumor's left.

He ignored the gunfire and snarling behind him as he slid his feet into the anchors along the polished black board. The boom was cold under his grip. He pressed his thumb to the plate along the shaft. It hummed to life when it recognized his thumbprint, and he jerked back on the boom, recklessly pulling it from its mooring and flipping around to face the fight.

A hellhound's body lay mere meters from the transports, bullet holes in its head. It was facing Rumor as if it'd run after him, but his dad had shot it in time. He swallowed bile and searched for his father, but all he saw was the trail of blood leading out of the lot.

"Nononono…" He lurched forward. The shift of his weight sent the sailboard along the blood trail that wrapped down the hill. The copper tang burned his nostrils. He coughed and gagged. Yanked the sailboard to a stop.

The blood led into the military barracks. Glass was scattered across the ground like snow. Several bodies in colony-issue recruit clothing lay jumbled together, many of them not much older than Rumor. One bloodied and detached hand clutched a tablet, mangled music still playing.

In another year, this would have been him. In his barracks for the night. No weapons. No way out other than the front door as the monsters poured in through the windows and peeled open the roof. It was nothing but a teeming mass of sharp horns and sharper claws, flayed limbs and pools of blood gathering in the scuffed mud.

Get to Epsilon. Get help.

He stared past the mangled limbs, down the main avenue, and in the direction of his home. Chills ran over him, his stomach twisting at the horde of gargoyles swarming the once-pristine throughway bisecting the city. He couldn't get back there. He couldn't find his dad, and he couldn't get to his home. His own home.

Rumor inhaled sharply and slapped at his chest in search of—there it was. His fingers curled around the familiar warped shape of the coin necklace his mother had given him.

Three humanoid gargoyles fighting over human body parts at the other end of the barracks noticed him and roared. They threw their fresh kills on the ground and raced up the hill, long legs pumping in loping strides and too-small wings giving them speed but no flight. Rumor gunned the rider, turned, and raced away.

The wall. He could get through the breaks in the wall. Go wide around to the north and hit the main road into Epsilon that way.

Get help.

No, go back for your father.

He's dead. Get help.

Nononono, he's not dead. Go back. Don't leave him.

He tightened his grip on the boom, his eyes burning with tears as he sailed faster. The rider whined as he pushed it to its limit, zigzagging down streets and between buildings. His side pulsed with pain, and his entire body trembled as he sped past gargoyles and humans fighting. Part of him wanted to jump off the board and throw himself into the fray. Take as many of the monsters down with him as he could.

A gargoyle leaped at the rider, slamming into the back and sending Rumor into a spin. He crouched and leaned into the spin, drawing a knife from his boot as he did. He slashed at the creature, catching it across the face. It screeched at him and let go, tumbling to the ground in a heap of thrashing limbs and grating noises.

Rumor stood and pulled the boom back, straightening the sailboard. His heart pounded in his ears as he neared what was left of the towering wall that protected HUB2. It was maybe ten meters away. It lay in ruins, torn and scorched all over. Curled in on itself like burned paper.

Seven meters.

The dragon roared, and over the cacophony of screeches and screams, Rumor heard a noise that felt like it came from everywhere at once. It echoed off buildings and blended with the roars around him. It sounded like a rockslide—a grating, cutting voice impossibly forming human words.

WHERE IS SHE

FIND VALA

The gargoyles couldn't speak. They didn't speak. They didn't speak.

Three meters.

They couldn't speak.

He pulled the sailboard up higher. Two buildings loomed ahead of him, their plant blankets torn and hanging.

Two gargoyles, something with horns and something with two tails, climbed each building using ravaged ivy. He couldn't pull high enough to clear it in time and avoid them.

Rumor gunned it.

The gargoyles clicked at him and leaped into the air. He yanked the board to the side, tilting dangerously. One gargoyle fell past him with a shriek. The other scraped its claws down the board itself, swiping at his ankles. Rumor slashed at it with his blade.

Its talons raked across the rear engine with a squeal that set Rumor's teeth on edge. He gritted his molars and pulled the board up hard, spinning it almost perpendicular to the moon. Then he hit the accelerator and yanked hard to the left and down, spinning them in a flip that threw the gargoyle forward.

He slashed his blade, catching the thing on the neck as it fell past him. His pulse pounded in his fingertips.

Something about the howls changed. They tilted up at the end. They synchronized. They almost…almost sounded like celebration. Without even turning back to see the city, he knew why.

One meter.

He shot through a gap torn in the wall, gripping the boom with sweaty palms, his nerves on fire while his city—his home—fell.

NYX

N yx Llorca kept two secrets: the moon spoke to her, and she was in love with her best friend.

The first secret was why she shoved more clothes into her worn messenger bag, which was already bulging with clothing, two knives, a small pistol, spare ammo, her hearing aids, an extra pair of boots, and a few keepsakes so she wouldn't forget Epsilon.

The second secret was why her stomach rolled with guilt and uncertainty.

But she wasn't going to find answers here. It was time to leave, and she finally had it all planned out. She'd spent several days watching the guard shifts and the routes in and out of Epsilon colony. Even though the main gate and the two side gates closed during nightside, the intake gate allowing water in from Lake Llyn stayed open unless there was a lockdown. And lockdown only happened in case of a direct assault—something that had only happened a handful of times that she could remember. The odds were with her.

Granted, leaving during dayside would be safer, but she wouldn't have enough time before she was missed at her job. She needed as much time as possible, and twenty-seven hours until dayside would be just enough.

It had to be.

She tied the bright pink laces on her black boots, then slipped a small knife into a hidden sheath on the outside of the left one.

Nyx chewed on the inside of her cheek as she stared at her computer tablet on the desk. She needed to leave it here. The colony could track her via its location.

But it was one of her only ties to Braeden and Dahlia. She might never see them again. Bile crept up her throat. She swallowed it back and pressed her fingers underneath her eyes to keep from crying. She'd made this decision. She had to follow through. Answers meant sacrifice.

Unless they came with her.

The thought crept up again. She'd batted it away before, because it was foolish to hope. Dahlia was happy here with her mom and her medical studies. She even had a new boyfriend. *Colt.* She wouldn't leave him. Dahlia was loyal to the end.

Nyx's lip curled. Maybe it was good she was leaving, so she didn't have to see him get to hold Dahlia's hand anymore. See him drop a kiss on her cheek as he was leaving for drills. See him grab her hips and pull her close as she smiled that blinding, beautiful smile up at him.

Or maybe just Braeden could come with her. She sighed as quickly as the thought appeared. Braeden was the colony commander's son, and on track for great things in the military. Or maybe in science. He was a genius. Something close to pride swelled in her chest.

It wouldn't hurt to ask, right?

Her fingers hovered over the messenger application on her tablet.

No.

They'd try to stop her. Maybe even tell her abuela or Braeden's moms. Then she'd lose her chance. Her fingertips tingled, and she curled her hands into fists, her nails digging into the soft material of her fingerless gloves. She just had to get to the forests, which were a little over two kilometers from Lake Llyn. Plus, it'd been a quiet nightside so far. Ten hours in, and there were zero reports on any of the news broadcasts of gargoyle attacks on humans, or even rebel attacks on colony transports. She could get to the forests in one piece. Surely the rebels who lived there would have answers. They lived among the beasts of the moon with no walls or gates or webbing.

They had to know why.

Why the ground under her boots vibrated and hummed in a language she couldn't decipher. Why it poked and tugged at her insides like a small child tapping on her arm. It was a different sort of buzz than the one she heard when her ears were tired of straining all day, even with the hearing aids. It was different from the numbness when her legs went to sleep after she sat too long with them curled underneath her. It was different from the vibrations of passing transport trucks or animals. It was a deep thrum that traveled through the ground, and it knew she could feel it. It was alive, and it frightened her.

Tonight, it felt especially chaotic. Almost…angry.

Ten hours into nightside, and everything ran as usual. Those who'd worked during dayside slept. People who'd slept during dayside worked. Swing shifts in the medical center chugged onward, overlapping with both sides. Marines patrolled the wall. Automata loped through the streets, their glistening eyes recording everything. Everyone and everything moved around outside her window as if she hadn't made an irreversible decision.

Even though her gut churned with foreboding to the cadence of the vibrations, life moved on as normal on the tiny moon orbiting a gas giant.

Nyx blew out a breath and pulled on one of Braeden's sweaters she'd appropriated. It hung off his bony frame, but it fit her curves perfectly and actually covered her hips without hiking up. She held the ends of the sleeves while she pulled on her coat. The hood covered her short blue hair. She wiped her sweaty hands on her stomach and tried to swallow past the dryness in her throat.

Finally, she unsnapped her wrist communicator and left it next to her tablet. Her vision blurred as she stared at the paler strip of skin around her forearm, and she sniffled as she pulled her sleeve down to hide what was missing.

On her way out, she paused by her abuela's room, angling herself against the doorframe so her abuela couldn't see the bag.

Reni Llorca sat in her puffy chair with a blanket that she'd been crocheting for the past month thrown over her lap. Nyx smiled at the swirl of color across the yarn. Each blanket Reni made told a story—usually something from her Hispanic ancestors back on Earth.

Nyx touched the panel on the wall to make the lights dim for a moment. Her abuela turned from her wall screen, her heavily lined, dark brown face worried. Nyx had always loved that her skin matched her abuela's exactly, even down to the almost coral undertones. They had the same hair, which they kept short. They had the same stubby fingernails that refused to grow. They had the same eyebrows, which would take over the moon if not kept tamed. One day, Nyx would sit in a puffy chair with a blanket on her lap and tell stories to anyone who would patiently listen.

Her chest tightened.

"I'm leaving for a while," Nyx signed, guilt and the tiny lie slicing across her heart like a paper cut. It was best not to worry her abuela. She was independent, and her mind was sound. She'd be able to take care of herself without Nyx.

"You going to Braeden's?" Her abuela's long fingers moved quickly, and her dark eyes narrowed.

Nyx nodded.

"You wearing your hearing aids?"

Nyx licked her lips and shook her head as she signed. "They make my ears sore. I'm fine."

Her abuela frowned, but didn't press her. "Stay alert, m'hija. When you come home, I'll tell you a story." She patted the nearly finished blanket on her legs.

Nyx smiled and blew her abuela a kiss. Her fingers formed a sign that was theirs alone, a product of shorthand developed between the only two Deaf people in a household.

Her abuela returned the gesture and faced her wall screen again.

She'd been born Deaf, but Nyx's abuelo (gods rest him) had been hearing just like Nyx's parents. When Nyx's hearing began to fade, she and her abuela had developed a method of communicating that included mostly ASL, but also the occasional made-up shorthand only the two of them knew. When her parents had transferred to HUB3 for promotions, they'd left her with her grandmother so her schooling wouldn't be interrupted.

Sometimes she wondered if they'd left her because they'd known her relationship with her abuela was better than her relationship with them.

Nyx headed out before she could change her mind, her heart breaking a little as the front door whispered shut behind her.

Outside, with the chill in the air and the nebula unfurling across the sky like a watercolor blanket, the vibrations of the moon crawled up her legs, wrapping over her hips and her belly and the swell of her breasts. It was like sinking into a quicksand of movement—she almost felt tethered to the ground by it. That if it let her go, she'd float off into the nebula and the silence of the stars.

She squatted and laid her palm on the red dirt beside the front walk, her fingers splayed wide. *What are you telling me?* she thought for the millionth time.

The ground hummed at her, speaking in a language she couldn't even begin to understand. Not without help.

She stood, brushing off her knees. Nyx hitched her bag higher on her shoulder and headed down the walkway toward the western side of the colony. As she crossed the main thoroughfare, movement to her right caught her attention.

The main gates were open.

She stopped. The gates shouldn't be open during nightside. The only way they'd be open was if Epsilon were receiving persons of importance or survivors of an attack. No transport vessels were rumbling in with supplies. No marine entourages or surprise visitors coming from the main HUB, which meant...

No. Please no. Not tonight.

The main gates faced northeast—toward HUB2. Normally HUB2 was a faint glow on the horizon, with a series of small foothills blocking a direct line of sight to their mother city.

Now...

Oh, gods.

The horizon burned. Orange and red and yellow pulsed along the ridge, flickering. Plumes of smoke blocked the stars and the nebula. Had the gargoyles actually attacked HUB2? This couldn't be another Crater Event. Had they sliced open the world and dragged an entire HUB into its gullet like they had with HUB4?

Someone grabbed her arm.

Marine.

Talking too fast for her to follow his lips.

"I'm Deaf," she interrupted.

The man gaped at her, then started overenunciating his words. "Get. In. Side." He pointed at her, then to the building behind her, and repeated it several times.

She stared at him for a moment, decided it wasn't worth it to try to explain he was being ridiculous, and pulled her arm free from his grasp. "I'm Deaf, not stupid," she signed, even though it was obvious he had no idea what she was saying. Finally, she gave him a bright smile and a thumbs-up. Satisfied, he moved away, clearing the street as he went. She flipped off his back. He'd at least know that gesture.

At the very edges of what tiny bit of hearing she had left,

an alarm blared. Every curse word she knew filled her head. Lockdown. Children rushed inside. More than a few colonists reappeared with guns or blades in hand. Lights mounted to rooftops shone straight up like beacons, beckoning people to safety.

Or beckoning gargoyles to come feast.

She shifted her weight from foot to foot, debating. She could still leave. Sneak out when survivors showed up. There'd probably be a lot of them. Wounded and scared, pouring into Epsilon seeking safety and solace. Her heart twisted. The medical center would be overrun. Dahlia and her mom would need help. Help Nyx could provide.

She wanted to scream right along with the world. She couldn't leave. Not now.

RUMOR

Rumor pushed the sailboard to its absolute limits. The hover engine bled sparks from the holes raked down its side by claws. The glowing sail flickered as the remaining solar power drained fast.

Too fast.

He wasn't sure if he'd made a clean escape from the gargoyles, or if a few still chased him. He was maybe a little less than five kilometers from Epsilon.

Five kilometers might as well be five star systems.

Rumor looked over his shoulder at the burning city, trying to pick out shapes along the roadway. His movement and the dying engines were too much for the sailboard. The nose dipped, struck a rock, and flung him into the air.

Duck head.

Twist body.

Land on shoulder.

Roll.

Pop up just fine like you meant it.

The last part of his father's relentless training failed to execute.

Rumor landed on his back, air exploding from his lungs, and stared into the nebula-bright night sky. He pressed a hand to his ribs and rolled to his side before slowly climbing to his feet.

The wrecked rider smoldered a few feet away. The base had cracked in two, and one dented engine had detached a little way back down the road, where it lay like a gleaming breadcrumb. The sail membrane hung in ragged strips. Cold whipped through his hair, throwing curls in his face and raising goose bumps up both arms.

A roar in the distance sent fear crackling down his spine, and he spun, searching for pursuers. They'd be coming soon if they weren't already hiding in the long shadows of the foothills running parallel to the road.

Every nerve in his body told him to run, but he stared at the glow of destruction of HUB2. *Run*, his mind screamed, but his eyes were glued to the devastation. His chest felt hollowed out, scraped bare, like he'd left his insides back home. Fire flickered on the horizon, blending with the brilliance of the nebula overhead until it felt like the entire sky was burning.

But the beauty and chaos overhead were nothing compared to the chaos on the ground. Nothing compared to the gargoyles, which crawled out of their hidden tunnels when night fell. Nothing compared to the thirty-seven-hour nights, during which Saharan residents hid away as best they could while gargoyles howled in the distance. Nothing compared to the waves of those same creatures who had taken *everything* from him tonight, leaving him bleeding and alone on a deserted highway.

He could sink to the ground here and wait for the monsters to get him. It wouldn't matter. He'd be just another name on the HUB2 casualty list.

To deep space with that. Go. Get. Help.

A grinding howl split the night. More howls joined the first in answer.

He ran.

Pain shot up his rib cage with every step. Blood glued his torn shirt to the skin. The dark liquid seeping through his fingers looked black against the greens and blues of the nebula light, harsh against the dark brown of his skin.

The lights of Epsilon glittered in the distance, welcoming and taunting at the same time. The gentle *whuff whuff whuff* of the spinning wind turbines overhead urged him onward, their long blades rotating in the direction he ran.

Five kilometers became four.

Power generators from HUB2 exploded, sending their dying screeches into the nebula.

Come on, Rumor, you can make it. His dad's voice thrummed through his skull. *Run, boy.*

His legs churned. Air sawed in and out of his lungs, the chill of night slicing through his chest like the fine edge of a scalpel. His breath puffed in tiny clouds, each whispering away as quickly as it formed. The road stayed empty. No transports. No marines. No one coming to help. No one running for escape.

No one left.

Growls. Heavy breathing. Closer this time. He'd definitely been followed. He gritted his teeth and pushed harder, pressing the wound in his side with his right hand and reaching for the blade strapped to his thigh with his left. The twisted remains of UV lights dotted his path, their silhouettes like scarecrows for any humans who dared to fix them each time the gargoyles destroyed them.

He focused on the looming walls of Epsilon colony at the end of his goal. The gates were open, and a shaft of amber light bathed the roadway. Rumor prayed it was because they saw him coming and not because the gargoyles had beaten him there. He poured energy into his legs, ignoring the burning in his calves.

Four became three.

Marine guards in the lookout towers waved at him, beckoning him forward with unintelligible shouts. His body couldn't move any faster, even though his instincts screamed at him to *go go go run*.

The waving turned to pointing. The light glinted off the barrels of rifles in their hands. Several guards brought them up, sighting and sweeping before they fired. The staccato of gunfire streaked through the night, the sound rattling his bones and putting his teeth on edge. Heavy bodies thudded to the ground behind him. The tingle at the base of his spine crawled up his back and down his arms, every hair on his body pricking to attention as the crashing, clawing footsteps gained on him. All he had to do was run. The marines in the towers would take care of the gargoyles.

Three became two.

One gargoyle ran directly behind Rumor, close enough he felt the vibrations of its steps. Vehicle wreckage on his left. A deep scar in the ground on his right. He exhaled through his nose, his eyes drifting shut for the next four paces, letting his hearing fill in the spaces where his eyes might betray him.

He cursed as he veered toward the wreckage. He jumped onto it, then pushed off with his left foot and twisted in the air, drawing the blade from its sheath as he spun. His thumb flicked across the barely there switch, and the black blade glowed crimson with chemical fire. It sliced into a limb of the gargoyle, cleaving through thick, stonelike hide.

The gargoyle screamed and fell back, clutching its dangling, useless arm.

Rumor took off running.

Every muscle in his back tightened, waiting for claws or teeth.

Two became one.

The open gates loomed ahead.

Twenty meters.

Fifteen.

Pounding. Wings flapping.

Ten.

Bright red bullets streaked through the sky like shooting

stars as he sprinted through the gates, which crashed shut behind him with a resounding bang.

His knees hit the ground as his adrenaline tanked. Rocks bit through his pants and into his skin, and debris stuck to his hands as he caught his fall. Pain flooded his system with a punch to his ribs that sent him down in the fetal position. His vision blurred with tears, and dust flew into his lungs with every heavy pant. He coughed and gagged.

The gargoyle hit the gate with a boom of dense body on metal, howling in frustration.

Gunfire exploded above him, and he flinched. He wished the moon would open and swallow him.

The only sound was his heartbeat.

Hands grabbed him. He hissed and jerked away, immediately regretting the reaction as pain stabbed through his side. He groaned and curled tighter, protecting his side from…he had no idea what. It just seemed like the best idea.

Someone shouted for a doctor.

Voices overlapped and cascaded, falling bells of sound that rang through his head. He caught snatches of words.

"Survivor?"

"Attacked HUB2."

"He the only one?"

"Oh, my gods, Rumor?" Another voice cracked the chaos and washed over him with familiarity. Cool hands touched his face, and his pain-fuzzy vision caught eyes as black as his own and umber skin made even darker by the white medical uniform.

"Wren?" he managed, relief sweeping through him at a familiar face. "How are you here?"

Doctor Wren Adams smiled down at him—a mother's smile filled with warmth and concern—and rolled him onto his back. "Hold still, kiddo."

She took one look at his side, her brows knitted, and ordered him brought to the medical center. Her hand found his as he was loaded onto a cold metal stretcher that bobbed in the air with his weight, and held on tight, obviously not caring about the blood and grit smeared across his palm. The pain pushed aside all his normal bristling, and he clung to her—the only familiar face in a crowd of marines and civilians.

Roars echoed in the distance, and he flinched away from them. "My dad…HUB2…gone. They're all gone."

"Shhhh, it's okay."

Rumor stared at the nebula overhead as the stretcher hummed along the magnetic path, the blues and greens and pinks swirling together like someone had splashed water on a palette of paint. Lines crisscrossed overhead, turning the nebula into checkerboard chunks he couldn't blink away. "Gargoyles attacked HUB2." He winced as the stretcher jostled him on a turn and pain shot down into his hip. "They're gonna come here… organized attack."

"You're safe," Wren said soothingly. "Did anyone else get out with you? Follow you?"

He shook his head, catching a flash of silver in the corner of his eye. Wren pressed a device to his neck and he jerked away from the sting. "No drugs. Can't go to sleep."

"Rumor, you're safe here."

The nebula sky gave way to the unforgiving steel and glass of the medical center. The antiseptic air burned his nose. The sedative curled around his bones and turned them to liquid. "Not safe anywhere. They're coming."

He thought he said that out loud, but no one responded.

Rumor hated drugs. His body would take a good long look at them, then either get high or sick. Right now, his body tiptoed along a knife's edge separating the two, tilting slowly into too high.

He blinked at the button-sized silver disk affixed to the inside of his forearm, trying to remember how he'd gotten here. The slow-blinking orange light, signaling the delivery of painkillers into his system, was hypnotic. He was fuzzy around the edges, but the pain in his side was sharp and present despite the painkillers. Rumor closed one eye, then the other, trying to get his memories to fall into place. He remembered the gates slamming shut. He remembered shouting as he lay on the ground. He remembered warm hands and warm eyes, both the color of his mother's. But not his mother. No, Mom was…she was dead. He shuddered and opened his eyes. Mom was dead—killed in a gargoyle attack when he was ten. Killed by hellhounds. Now… now Dad was dead. Right?

A trail of blood leading nowhere.

He was an orphan.

He widened his eyes, pushing his elbow against the bandages taped to his bare side and using the flare of pain to rip him out of the drug haze.

"Easy now," came a gentle voice.

"Miss Adams?"

Wren laughed as she peered at him. "You must be high. You haven't called me that since before you and Dahlia dated."

His blink took hours, his brain chugging to keep up. *Dahlia.* "No more drugs," he slurred. "Please. I can't think."

Wren tapped a stylus to the disk on his arm. The light winked out, and she peeled the disk from his skin with long nails the color of the blue sun. She brushed her braids over one shoulder before she pulled his arm out of the way so she could get at the puffy bandages.

"I feel like I got run over by an automaton." His tongue was a mountain in his mouth.

"You didn't get run over by an automaton," she said in a gentle voice.

He tried to reconcile her overlapping images into one solid

form of the woman he knew. Miss Adams. Doctor Adams. It'd only been little over a year since he'd seen her, but she had more lines around her dark eyes, and her braids seemed thinner. Maybe longer. He squinted at them, trying to make his eyes focus. "Did you save me?"

Wren smiled as she examined his ribs. "You saved yourself, kiddo. And these won't scar."

"Wouldn't matter," he mumbled. He'd lost count of his scars. His body was a road map of near misses. "Where am I?"

"Epsilon. The medical center."

His brain tried and failed to do math. "How much longer?"

"Little less than twenty-six hours to dayside," she answered. She replaced the bandage and tucked the blanket around him like he was five and needed the cocoon.

"They're coming," he said. "The gargoyles. They're coming."

Wren made gentle shushing noises. "You're safe here."

"No, no one's safe. They're coming." Rumor's head swam, and he gasped for air over the sudden lightheadedness.

"You need to stay calm or I'll have to give you another sedative, understand?" she said firmly, but not unkindly.

Rumor nodded, trying to keep still. He glanced over his person, taking stock of the bandages and scratchy hospital shirt. "Where's my cuff?"

"It was damaged," Wren answered. "We had to pry it off you. We'll try to get you a new one, okay?"

He nodded, feeling oddly naked without his HUB2 cuff.

Wren watched him for a moment. "Dahlia's been waiting for you to wake up. Feel up to some familiar company?"

Dahlia. Right. Wren's daughter. His ex-girlfriend. He bobbed his head, hoping that conveyed an affirmative. Wren brushed his curls from his forehead and left the room. Rumor stared at the ceiling tiles. They formed patterns meant to keep his eyes busy and his brain distracted. Mazes and pictures and hidden puzzles carved into metal sheets and hung above soft beds and beeping machines.

He felt for his necklace. Still there. He closed his fist around the tiny copper coin strung on a black cord. Generations ago, back on Earth, someone in his family had collected coins. Earth currency from all different cultures. This coin was all that remained of that ancient collection.

And all he had left of his family.

The door hissed open.

"Hey," came a voice, familiar — but not.

Rumor blinked through blurry vision as he met silver eyes and freckles scattered like stars across midnight skin. The eyes were familiar, but the face around them was softer than his memory held. He smiled. "Wow."

Dahlia smiled, the line of her square shoulders relaxing a little as she approached the bed. Rumor held up one hand and made a sloppy *spin* motion. She ducked her head and twirled.

"You look incredible," he said.

She curled long fingers around the bed railing, rings clicking against the metal. "Hormones are magic."

"They are," he agreed. "How long have you…?" His brain lost the final words of his sentence in the haze of painkillers and pain.

She smiled, and it was as pretty as he remembered. "Eight months now? I started a little after we moved here from HUB2. I was waiting until I saw you again to tell you."

He shifted his head so he could see her better. Her hair rose in a natural cloud around her face. "You happy?"

Dahlia nodded. "I recognize myself in the mirror." She shrugged and picked at a nail. "That sounds weird."

"No, it doesn't." And he meant it. He remembered what it was like for Dahlia to hate reflections and hate the name listed for her in the colony databases. "You sucked at growing facial hair, anyway."

She grinned and flicked him on the shoulder. "Yeah, you grow enough for everyone." She scratched her nails across his stubble. "What is this, like, three minutes old?"

He pushed her hand away, the little laugh hurting his side. "I'm glad you settled on Dahlia. Fits you."

She licked her lips. "Other than being all banged up, how're you feeling?"

He knew this question. This question posed itself with concerned eyes and sympathetic smiles. This question presented itself in layers. After his mother's death, everyone had wanted to know how he felt. How he was coping. He was ten, and all he'd known were a lot of dirty words to explain how he felt. He'd never hesitated to yell them at anyone who asked. He hadn't wanted to be reminded that he'd never sit in her lap again while she told him stories of their ancestors. He hadn't wanted to be reminded that he'd never smell her hair when she held him because he was upset. He hadn't wanted to be reminded of that night when, no matter how many hellhounds he'd slaughtered, he hadn't saved her.

"Did anyone else make it out?" he asked instead.

"I don't know." Her words were apologetic, like it was her fault. "No one else came in after you. I think they sent a squad out to investigate."

He knew what they'd find. Burned-out hulls of buildings, and body parts. Blood. So much blood. The corpses of human and gargoyle—of *us* and *them* mingled together and reduced to little more than trash.

His dad was in one of those piles. Rumor blinked rapidly, shaking away the hellhounds circling his father.

He'd run away. When his father had needed him, he'd run.

Anger pushed through the drugs. Dahlia touched his hair, and he jerked away, the sudden movement sending a flare of pain up his side.

"Sorry," she mumbled.

He gritted his teeth against the raging heartbeat and rolling heat under his skin. His fingertips tingled. His cheekbones tingled.

He couldn't focus. "I can't breathe."

"Hey, yes, you can. Rumor, yes, you can. Breathe," Dahlia said in a calm voice, one she'd used with him many times in the past.

He nodded and pulled a breath in through his nose. Her fingers slid through his, and he gripped her hand. His other hand clutched the necklace tighter, the edges of the coin biting into his skin. He exhaled through his mouth, his breath catching on a sob. "What…what have you been doing here since you guys moved away?"

"I volunteer here at the medical center," she answered, her tone soothing. "Sort of like a nurse in training. I want to help with trauma and stuff. Like…mental things…after. A friend of mine, Nyx, volunteers here, too, but it's her night off."

"You like it?" he asked between breaths.

"Yeah." Her fingers combed through his hair, and he leaned into her touch. "There're two people who want to talk to you," she said. "They're outside. When you're ready. Breathe in, two, three, four. Out, two, three, four, five."

He obeyed. "Who are they?"

"Sara Tennant and her wife, Bailey. Sara's in charge of Epsilon. She's pretty nice. A little uptight sometimes. Okay, all the time, but Bailey's not as much, so I guess they balance?"

"Marines?"

"Sara is. Bailey's a science officer." Dahlia shaped his curls as she spoke. "I asked if maybe you could stay with them instead of a foster hostel. They have a son your age. He's cool. Pretty cute. You should meet him. Nyx is cool, too. She's Deaf. I've been studying sign language for when she and I hang out. Braeden knows sign already—that's their son. Anyway, Mama can tell Sara and Bailey to come back later. It's no big deal. Just, you know, tell me what you want."

He picked a spot in the tile maze above his head and traced it a few tiles over before he answered. There was a time when Dahlia's rambling grated his nerves, but now the familiar cadence of her run-on sentences grounded him.

"Okay, good," he said. "I need to tell them there's going to be another attack. Stay here while they talk to me?"

"Yeah. I'll tell them off if it gets too much, okay? You just tell me when to kick them out."

He managed a thin smile. "Does this bed sit up?"

"You sure? Your side—"

"Please."

Dahlia pressed her lips together and hit a button that raised his bed to a sitting position. He clenched his teeth as the pressure in his side increased with the movement. She smoothed the blankets around his legs. "Do you still carve? Whittle? Whatever you called it."

Rumor nodded. "I was making something before…" He waved his hand in a vague direction.

She squeezed his shoulder. "I'll find you some stuff. It'll help." She hesitated, then leaned over and kissed his temple before leaving as quietly as she'd entered. Rumor watched the door slide shut.

Silence slithered into the room in her absence.

Everything was too jumbled in his head for him to sort out right now. Was he happy to see Dahlia after all this time because of her, or because she was someone familiar? He blinked back the sudden burning in his eyes.

He wanted his clothes. His weapons. They were all he had left. He needed to get out of this bed. When the gargoyles were done picking the HUB2 buffet clean, they'd come for the colonies. It could already be too late. They could be on the road now, heading for Epsilon, the blood of HUB2 not even dry on their claws yet.

The door whispered open and Wren returned, a reassuring smile on her face. Dahlia trailed behind. Two women followed them. Rumor immediately knew which one the marine was. She was tall, with broad shoulders and a straight spine, white skin set off by brown hair pulled back. Bright red coated her lips and her nails. She examined Rumor with sharp hazel eyes. He'd seen that look in his father's eyes all too often. Assessing, calculating. He bristled at the sight of his sheathed blades in her hand.

"Rumor." Wren positioned herself next to his bed like a bodyguard. "This is Commander Sara Tennant." Dahlia sat on the other side of the bed and slid her hand into his, squeezing gently.

Sara offered a hand and a smile that was meant to be reassuring. "Glad to see you recovering, son." She spoke with a drawl, long vowels that took their time and letters dropped at the end of words.

"And this is Bailey Newell, one of our chief science officers and Sara's wife," Wren said.

Bailey smiled, hers more genuine as it crinkled the edges of her brilliant blue eyes. Light blonde hair pulled back into a messy bun blended into her white skin. Tendrils escaped the confines and framed her high cheekbones.

"Hello, Rumor," she said, her accent far more melodic, with a cadence that reminded him of the Shakespeare vids he watched in class. "How old are you, darling?"

"Seventeen."

"Our son, Braeden, is your age." She perched at the foot of Rumor's bed and folded her hands on her thigh.

He glanced between the two women. "Great."

"Your dad is Eric Mora?" Bailey asked.

Rumor nodded.

"I met him a few times in passing." Bailey's voice was gentle. "He was a good man."

"Tell us what happened," Sara said.

"Please," Bailey added.

Rumor met Sara's gaze, his growing irritation a stoked fire deep in his belly. Somewhere on the wall, beeping kicked up a notch. "Gargoyles attacked HUB2. I don't know how many. Broke through the wall and assaulted the city in waves, moving inward toward central command. It was a massacre." He licked his lips. "They had our weapons. They were using them without any problems…the ones with hands, anyway."

No one seemed surprised. The tales were true, then— stockpiles of weaponry had gone missing when the Crater Event happened twenty-eight years ago. When the ground opened up and swallowed HUB4 and its occupants. They'd never found bodies. Only a gaping hole where a city had once stood, and a maze of tunnels burrowing deep into the moon.

"There was a dragon, and a gargoyle riding it. Like a…leader. It spoke."

"Spoke how?" Bailey asked.

"It spoke our language," Rumor said.

Bailey and Sara exchanged a look.

"What did it say?" Sara asked.

Rumor shivered as the creature's voice scraped across his memory. "'Where is she? Find Vala.'"

"How did you escape?" Bailey wore rings on three fingers of each hand, and her nails were painted green. A tattoo of vines and flowers spiraled up the back of her hand and wrapped around her wrist.

"My dad…" Rumor cleared his throat and tried again. "My dad and I were going to escape on the sailboards. The wind riders. Hellhounds attacked. The ones that are like big dogs. He told me to run." His tone turned bitter, the words dripping from his lips. He could almost imagine if he looked down, he'd see stains across the pristine white blankets.

"It's still too early to definitively tell, but as far as we know, you're the only survivor," Sara said.

Rumor closed his eyes. He'd hoped someone further up the food chain had information Dahlia hadn't had.

"We saw your maneuvers with the blade when you arrived. Even injured, your skills are sharp." Sara held up his sheathed molten blades, the steel dark and cold. "You'll make a fine addition to the draft when you turn eighteen."

"I want those back," Rumor growled, possessiveness flaring in his chest. He ignored the second half of Sara's comment.

Sara tossed them on the bed. "They're older models than what the grunts usually train with. Where did you get them?"

"I repaired one. Then built the other using the first as a model." Rumor started to sit up to grab the blades but hissed in pain and fell back on the pillows. Wren picked the blades up and set them in his lap. Their familiar weight and smell grounded him, comforted him more than anything else in the world could.

"You built them?" Bailey's eyes widened for a fraction of a second.

"It wasn't hard," Rumor said.

"He'd be better in the sciences," Bailey said to Sara, as if Rumor wasn't lying right there.

"When are you launching a counter assault on HUB2?" Rumor demanded. "What are you doing to prepare for an assault here?"

Sara arched a perfect eyebrow. "What makes you think they're coming here?"

Goose bumps rose on his arms, and his stomach dropped. "Didn't you hear what I just said? They were organized. They had our weapons. They took down an entire HUB in less than an hour. They're looking for someone, and I don't think they found whoever it was there. Epsilon is the closest colony. You guys need to—"

"We sent a team to investigate and search for survivors. They should report back shortly," Sara answered in a tight voice. "I have a colony to keep safe. You're right. We're the nearest colony, which means *if* the gargoyles branch out tonight, we could be next. But the chances of them going after a colony so soon after demolishing HUB2 are low. We'll reassess after dayside, but I don't want to split our resources until we know more about what's happening."

Rumor gaped at them. "If you wait until dayside, you'll lose them. They'll go underground, and who knows where they'll pop up after thirty-seven hours."

"We know that," Bailey said.

"But—"

"This attack heightened the war, Rumor," Bailey said. "We've made this moon our home against all odds because of strategic planning, but the attack tonight is unlike anything we've seen since the Crater. If we don't de-escalate things, it could be the end of humanity on this moon."

Rumor rolled his eyes so violently his head followed the motion. "No way, Bailey. You know how many of those things I've killed over the years when they decide to get spiky and attack? Or whenever my dad…" He cleared his throat. "When my dad took me out hunting during the day, searching for nests? And that wasn't even a dent in their population."

Wren rested her hand on his arm and Dahlia squeezed his fingers, trying to calm him down. *No.* He'd watched everything he called home burn to the ground and get ripped apart, and they were asking him to ignore that. To move on and pretend he hadn't been dragged into a war he'd never wanted to be a part of. A war he'd been born into. A war that had torn his mother from him when he was ten, a boyfriend from him at sixteen, and now his father from him at seventeen.

Sara opened her mouth, but Bailey lifted a hand. She leveled an even look at Rumor, those crystalline eyes peeling back his layers and walls. "I'm forty years old. The gargoyles began their attacks in 2330, before I was even born. Back then there wasn't a choice between a gun or a lab coat. You fought. You fought your entire life. The Crater happened when I was twelve. The dragons woke up in the mountains right outside this colony in 2350 when I was fifteen. I saw what was supposed to be another generational ship fall from the skies in burning pieces in 2364, when Sara lost her husband and nearly lost their only son. At that time, it didn't matter who you were or what you did for the colony. You grabbed a gun and you fought. Now, ask me how many I've killed."

Rumor held her gaze, refusing to be intimidated.

Bailey lifted her chin. "Whenever you're done puffing up, I'll tell you that I admire your skills and think you'd be an asset. But this is bigger than you will ever understand, so do not pretend to school us on matters of gargoyle-human relations."

They existed in silence. Rumor curled his fingers around the worn leather handle of the blade in his lap. "I left my dad in HUB2 on his orders to come warn you. I could have saved him." His voice cracked. "But he wanted me to come warn *you*. Now he's dead and I've warned you, so when the gargoyles come, every death here is on your heads."

Bailey stood. "Rest. We'll talk later. We have a spare room for you for when you get out of here. It'll be better than the hostel." She glanced at Wren. "He can leave soon?"

Wren nodded. "I need to check his responses one last time before he leaves, but yes."

The talking past him was getting annoying. Dahlia squeezed his hand again, as if she knew he was about to pop off at them. He bit the inside of his cheek.

Sara and Bailey left, speaking in low tones to each other. Dahlia remained on the edge of his bed while Wren checked his vitals. He stared at some middle distance between his bed and the wall.

He saw only fire.

JUDE

Jude Welton had two dreams: a nightside without death, and for his strange abilities to vanish.

He wished those were his only dreams.

The colors were wrong in dreams. They lacked their usual breath, their fractured personalities. Their glaring vividness as they clung to people. In his dreams, colors *simply existed*, and that was how he knew this wasn't reality.

The chimera were there, too. They were always there, with their great wings and long fingers and mountainous crags of teeth connected to jaws that could crush stars and inhale comets. But he was never afraid, because, when they peered at him with too-wide eyes, there was nothing but curiosity in their gemstone gazes.

He felt safer in his dreams. Here there was no war. No destruction. Safer with creatures who spread their wings against the vastness of the cosmos and gave him shelter from how *big* it all was.

One of them lowered its great head to Jude's eye level. It wrapped long fingers around his shoulder, the points digging into his back below his shoulder blade.

Wake up.

Jude frowned, and the dream wavered, the colors bleeding as though someone had thrown sadness across them.

"Wake up."

Jude jolted awake. He lay there, frozen somewhere between the dream and the waking, blinking owlishly at the silhouette above him. He muttered a few choice curse words as he rolled over and pushed himself up.

He glared at his adoptive brother. "What in deep space, man?"

Patrick Solomon, called *Patrick* by no one and *Trick* by everyone, threw a T-shirt at him. "HUB2 was attacked."

Jude frowned at the shirt and then at his brother. "So? Why do we care about a forest group attacking the colonies?"

"It wasn't us. It was chimera."

Jude paused in the act of pulling the shirt over his shoulders. "Say again?"

Sounds from the rest of the forest colony of Azrou filtered in his open bedroom window. Unintelligible shouts drifted up from the ground level. Engines revving overlapped the anxious voices, sailboards peeling out of the community at top speeds.

Trick switched on a lamp, the amber glow casting long shadows across his deep copper skin. "HUB2 was destroyed. Chimera attacked an hour ago and demolished it."

"*What?* The entire city?" Jude lurched out of bed to search for his boots and his pistol. His heart thundered against his sternum, working its way up his throat. He stamped his feet into his boots. The war would never end at this rate. "What do you need me to do?"

Trick buckled on a pair of leather cuffs he'd swiped from Jude's dresser. "Kai and Yi-Min are organizing rescue parties. Yi-Min and I need you to come with us to HUB2." He took a deep breath. "We need to see if there are any survivors, and we have to move fast. George went on ahead to make sure the path is clear."

Jude nodded, nerves fluttering through his belly as he

watched his brother fill space in the room, his movements fluid and almost lazy in their ease and precision. Eight years ago, Trick and his much older brother, Kaipo, had agreed to take in a little blond ten-year-old orphan after a devastating cave-in had robbed Jude of his parents. Since then, Trick was the calm before the storm, the stable eye in the middle of fury. It was a quality Jude had learned to emulate, had forced his muscles to memorize. A groove he'd carved for himself to notch his emotions into.

Trick paused in front of Jude and peered at him. They were the same age but mere centimeters apart in height, which was enough to make Jude think of Trick as his older brother. "Are you okay?"

Jude swallowed sadness. "Fine."

Trick nodded once, his nebula-colored eyes calling Jude on his lie, and left the room.

Jude grabbed his gun and followed Trick through the house, ignoring video screens streaming hijacked channels from the main colonies, all of them united under the common theme of the deadly HUB2 assault — this one larger and far more devastating than eleven years ago when the dragons attacked the battleships sent to evacuate the humans. Voices pressed at him, knotting his neck and pulling his shoulders to his ears. He rolled his shoulders back and cracked his neck as he thumped down the spiral stairs that wrapped around the black tree trunk and onto the ground level of the house he lived in with Trick, Kaipo, and Kaipo's partner, Yi-Min Tsai.

The house twisted around him. Curving cream walls and silver support beams in straight lines and almost right angles. Windows of colored glass that let in light and warmth during the daylight hours. He ran his fingertips along the black bark, releasing a spicy scent into the air. They'd named it cinnamon, but according to the elders, it wasn't all that similar to Earth cinnamon. If it ever reached Earth, it would be labeled as *Saharan cinnamon* and sold for exorbitant prices.

Space cinnamon.

Jude and Trick headed out onto the drive. To their left, a gate hung open, exposing the entrance to a chimera tunnel. The gaping hole in the ground was ringed with colorful stones and flowers. This one—being so deep inside the community itself—had a simple metal fence around the edge and a gate to keep kids from toppling down the smooth tunnels. Jude latched it as he walked past. Not that the chimera here would do anything to them. Maybe bring them back a few toys.

Farther away from the populated areas of the forest, chimera tunnel entrances were more disguised with vines and plants, rocks and fallen trees. Some had sturdy trapdoors that people could rest a cart on to hide them from sight.

People milled about, their colors blending with each other and overlapping, creating a rainbow cacophony that assaulted Jude's senses.

Worry dripped from everything.

Trick paused in front of a waiting sailboard, glancing over his shoulder. His cosmic smear of a back tattoo peeked out the edges of his gray tank—a nebula on his back to match the one billowing above them. "What color is everyone?"

Jude shivered. "Gray and yellow," he whispered, rolling his shoulders and trying to move away from their indecision and fear.

Trick pressed his lips together and nodded, his eyes sympathetic. As useful as it was, Jude hated his gift most of the time. Hated that no one could ever lie to him about their emotions. He always knew when something was for show or when it was truth. He was a walking lie detector who often wished he saw the world in black and white.

And tonight, he was playing life detector.

He stepped to one side as a large automaton feline loped through, its metal plates clicking as it extended its long legs. Another automaton—this one a smaller canine version for disability services—sat next to young girl wearing blacked-out goggles. A faint smile touched Jude's lips as the dog grabbed a ball with its metal jaws and dropped it in the girl's lap. The forest communities used theirs for protection and farming and transportation.

The colonies used theirs for war.

"Trick!" Kaipo jogged over to them, his normal orange pessimism dripping off his brown skin in misty strands. Teal eyes identical to Trick's narrowed at them both. "You guys ready?"

Trick nodded. Jude shoved his hands in his pockets and waited.

Kaipo wiped his mouth, the light sliding over the mass of burn scarring on his hand, half his face, and throat. His long-sleeved shirt hid the rest. "Okay, find George first. Yi-Min will be right behind you. They're finishing up organizing search parties for survivors. Stay out of sight as best as you can. Come back here if anything happens."

Jude nodded. He stepped onto the back of Trick's sailboard, fitting his boot into the anchor slot. He grabbed the boom with his right hand and wrapped his left arm around Trick's waist. Trick revved the tiny engine, and they shot off into the vivid night.

Cold wind clawed at them. After a long while of gliding over the forest floor, Trick patted Jude's hand to get his attention and then pointed to their left.

Slightly ahead of them, a sleek black form slid through the trees, barely distinguishable through the foliage. Jude grinned, a knot easing in his chest. George was alive and okay.

The forest fell away just ahead, as if someone had drawn an invisible line in the dirt. Crunchy yellow grass blanketed the hills, becoming less lush quilt and more old, bug-eaten blanket the farther from the forest they flew. Piles of gravel from meteor impacts gave way to actual slices of meteor, their broken-open insides strewn about and glittering under the nebula light. The meteor remains gave way to foothills, which ringed the sleek, automaton-laden colonies and their man-made lake, which was, in fact, responsible for everything. Its birth seventy-five years ago was the beginning of it all.

Trick steered them down into the foothills, keeping to shadows as they wound their way closer to the burning horizon. They crested the hill with a view not blocked by the partially finished HUB2 dome and came to a stop.

"Red?" Trick asked, his voice tight.

Jude stepped off the sailboard and stood on the rocky soil, the smell of burned flesh and molten metal singeing his nostrils and burrowing into his bones. What was left of the once-gleaming city of HUB2 was bathed in the blood red of anger and death. The wall lay twisted and ripped apart in several sections. Wall cannons littered the landscape like tipped-over toys. The central spires cut eerie shadows as fires burned across the city. Gargoyles perched atop the mining equipment, clicking and roaring to one another.

He swallowed and nodded. "And black and yellow."

Secrets and fear. The horrible sort of bright, empty *goneness* to the entire cityscape. Roars echoed off the buildings, followed by screams quickly silenced with gunshots.

"How many survivors are left?" Trick asked. Yi-Min's board sailed out of the woods and came to a stop next to them.

"There aren't many." Jude forced words past the bile in his throat. Even as he spoke, red and black and yellow flickered or faded out all over the city as souls left one at a time.

A thud to his left had Jude shifting toward the massive black chimera almost instinctually. George resembled a gryphon with his sleek body and birdlike head. Huge, membranous wings folded to his sides, and he sat on his haunches, his long tail twitching through the rocks like an angry viper. Even sitting, his black eyes rested at level with Jude's.

"Who did this?" Jude asked.

"Reaper," George rumbled in his own language. The chimera language grated like the shifting of the moon and rolled like a rockslide, more feeling and impression than actual words or grammatical structure. "He's searching for Vala. Claims the humans have her in captivity, and many have joined him in his efforts. They're assaulting human cities until she's found."

Jude exchanged a look with Trick. Trick stared at the sky. "Angel's going to be upset when they hear it's Reaper."

"He'll keep going tonight, gathering more chimera to him," Yi-Min said, their dark eyes on the city. A mix of remorse and fury twisted around them in blue and red. They rubbed a palm over their jaw.

George nodded. "We must find Vala. Tonight. Or Reaper will go after every human he can before dayside."

Trick made a surprised noise. "He's not *that* powerful, is he?"

"He grows stronger by the moment," George answered. "And he fights for Vala's return."

Jude rested a hand on George's shoulder, his fingers digging into the smoothness of George's thick, rocklike hide. "Did anyone escape?"

"One," George answered.

"What?" Trick whispered in shock. "Only one? There aren't more down there?"

Yi-Min typed on their communication cuff immediately.

Jude stared at the ruined city. "Everyone there…they…they're all…" He couldn't bring himself to say it. *Dying* rolled up into a ball in the back of his throat. He grabbed at Trick's forearm. Trick slid his arm up until his hand met Jude's, and he wrapped his fingers around his brother's, grounding him. Grounding them.

Jude blinked back a sudden rush of tears. "Where?" He coughed and tried again. "Where is the survivor? Did you see them?"

"Young male of your years. He ran for the lake settlement."

"Epsilon," Yi-Min said. "Reaper will head there next if he knows about this." They moved away, tapping out a message on their cuff.

"Did he make it in one piece?" Jude was lightheaded with hope.

"With help." George shook his great head and flared his wings.

Yi-Min returned. "We head to Epsilon. Kai's orders. Reaper will cull survivors, and we need to get to the survivor first. Find out what he saw." They turned to Jude, pursed their lips, then spoke again. "And Vala's there."

Jude sucked in a breath. "How do you know?"

"We have a spy on the inside." They turned away.

Jude had never hated his ability more than at this moment, as the last flare of terrified yellow disappeared from HUB2.

NYX

HUB2 was gone. Destroyed by gargoyles two hours ago.
The city still burned on the horizon, as if hell itself had
opened and tried to swallow the nebula and everything under it.

Nyx sat on the roof of her house, her feet dangling over the
edge. Her messenger bag rested on her bed once more. There
was no way she was leaving Epsilon now. The entire colony was
already in lockdown because of the attack. No one in or out of
the gates unless they were marines or maybe survivors.

Tension crackled through her body that had more to do with
the moon under her feet than the anxiety climbing up her spine.
She blinked back a sudden burning of frustrated tears. So many
people had died so horrifically, and here she was, irritated that
an attack had prevented her from *finally* leaving to get answers
about the vibrations.

She brushed her hand through the latticework of vines
that covered her home like a carpet. Her street was a mix of
residential homes and squat, gleaming towers of burgeoning
industry, all covered in a rolling blanket of lush greenery that
regulated temperatures and scrubbed the air clean of pollutants.

The founders of the colonies had put practices in place

in an attempt to subvert the human tendency to be a parasite.

Use the moon and what she provides. Use the plants for air and temperature control. Use the water and wind for power. The results were buildings covered in blankets of ferns. Crops of massive wind turbines. Hydroponic gardens on everyone's balconies. Water houses dotting the shore like flung pebbles. Stained-glass solar panels that provided artistry for the eyes and power for the homes. The electrified web, which covered the entire colony like a giant net, stored energy and acted as a barrier against the gargoyles. Even the cuff Nyx wore around her left forearm could gather daylight and be used to power small devices like her tablet or recharge her hearing aids… whenever she wore them.

They were an agricultural colony that provided food and advancements in plant genetics to HUB2. But that wasn't the case anymore.

If it weren't for the gargoyles, Sahara would be a utopia.

Ironic, since they were at war with one of the indigenous species.

The Epsilon colony thrummed with life below her. Lockdown had sent most people inside where it was supposedly safer. If it escalated any further, everyone would go into assigned underground shelters and wait until dayside or death, whichever came first.

She chewed on her lower lip and picked at a leaf. Her fingers trembled.

Would they become a ghost colony?

Her gut tightened at the image of Epsilon in ruins, its plants and people dead or dying.

After HUB4 fell into the ground in 2347, her colonies slowly died, and the residents moved to the HUB3 or HUB2 colonies. Those former colonies were ghost towns now—stripped by humans and reclaimed by nature.

The thought of the four HUB2 colonies dying in the wake of

this attack, after they'd accomplished so much to make a home here, made her heart hurt. If the colonies failed, she'd have to pack up everything she knew and move two hundred and nine kilometers west to HUB and Alpha, Beta, Gamma, or Delta colonies. Either that, or move a hundred kilometers north across Lake Lyn to HUB3 and Iota, Kappa, Lambda, or Mu.

She couldn't bear it.

But she didn't have a say.

A vine to her right wriggled suddenly. Nyx twisted back, her heart leaping into her throat. But it was just Dahlia, picking her way through the rooftop greenery.

Nyx's fingertips prickled, and her mouth went dry. Gods, crushes sucked so much.

Especially ones on your best friend. Who had skin the color of deepest space and eyes like twin stars. Who preferred looser shirts that slipped off one shoulder and teased Nyx mercilessly with collarbone. Who wore a pair of green pants Nyx absolutely loved on her because they clung to her legs, her thighs, those hips. Hips made for grabbing.

"You okay?" Dahlia signed as she sat down next to Nyx.

Oh, how many ways could she answer that question? She settled on shrugging and nodding as she pulled a leaf off a vine and twirled the stem between her fingers.

"So the guy who escaped the attack?" Dahlia said when Nyx looked at her.

Nyx nodded.

"My ex."

"What?" Nyx's brain cycled back to everything Dahlia had ever mentioned about ex-boyfriends and girlfriends. "Which... um, who?"

"Rumor. The guy I dated before we moved here."

Nyx plucked a few of the palm-sized white flowers that grew from the vines and pushed them one by one into Dahlia's cloud of hair. "Is he okay?"

Dahlia shrugged. "Not really." She switched to sign as Nyx moved around to the other side of her with the flowers. "His dad died. He's the only survivor so far."

"Oh." Nyx chewed her cheek. "Is it weird seeing him again?" She stared at the curve of Dahlia's shoulder where it met her neck and was overcome by a nearly visceral need to press her lips...and maybe her teeth...in that very spot.

Horny in the middle of a crisis was not a good way to be.

"A little," Dahlia signed. Nyx sat down and swiveled around so they sat cross-legged facing each other, their knees touching. "He's all inside himself like a turtle. Real jumpy."

"You worried?" Nyx asked. She could have spoken aloud, but Dahlia liked to practice her sign, and Nyx liked giving her voice a rest. Besides, this way she could spend her time staring at Dahlia with her friend being none the wiser. Gods, she was beautiful. Her freckles, her silver eyes, her hair, her deep brown skin, her fingers when she shaped signs, her smile...

"A little. He's angry. Kept saying the monsters are coming here next. He's all..." Dahlia pursed her lips as she thought. "Worked up."

Nyx's leg muscles tightened, and her toes curled inside her boots. He was probably an ex for a reason. Besides, she had no claim over Dahlia's affections.

Oh, but how she wanted to.

Dahlia leaned forward a bit and started playing with a loose thread on Nyx's pant leg. She shook her head and shrugged. If she said something, it was lost to the chasm between their bodies. Mere centimeters separated them, and yet it felt like the entirety of Sahara. A few centimeters too close to be *just friends*, but a few centimeters too far to be *girlfriends*.

Nyx slid her hand over Dahlia's arm and squeezed gently. "You okay?"

After a moment, something dripped onto Nyx's pant leg. Dahlia was crying. "Dahl? What is it?"

Dahlia sat up, her eyes glassy. Swiped a thumb under one. "I can't believe HUB2 is gone."

And with that, Nyx felt like the worst friend ever. Dahlia had been born there. She'd lived there nearly her entire life, until a little over two years ago. HUB2 had been her home. And now, that home was gone, and the only survivor was her ex-boyfriend.

Life was bizarre sometimes.

"Did you keep in touch with people there?" Nyx rubbed her palms up and down Dahlia's arms in a soothing motion.

Dahlia nodded. She signed, "Friends," and nothing else. Tears rolled down her cheeks and dripped off the end of her square jaw. She smeared them away with the back of her hand. "And I broke up with Colt."

Nyx froze, certain she'd misread Dahlia's lips. "You did what? When?"

"Broke up with Colt earlier," she signed and offered Nyx a watery smile. "Right around start of nightside. Wasn't feeling it anymore. Great timing, right?"

"Are you…okay?" Nyx was asking that too much. How many ways could Dahlia tell her she was not exactly okay? And how traitorous was her own stomach for clenching when Dahlia said she'd dumped Colt? She wanted to curl up inside herself in shame.

Dahlia checked her communicator cuff. "Mom's calling. Rumor's awake. He's gonna stay with Braeden."

Nyx frowned, thrown off by the sudden subject shift. "Shouldn't a marine escort him?"

Dahlia hitched a shoulder. "Mom's worried about PTSD and thinks someone familiar to him will help, so she asked me to do it."

Nyx nodded even as jealousy twisted her insides. Did that mean Rumor would be hanging out with Dahlia from here on out? That sounded…so great.

Dahlia smiled crookedly. "Honestly, I want to see Rumor try

to flirt with him while it sails completely over Braeden's head."

A Dahlia deflecting was a Dahlia who was about to break down sobbing and didn't want to talk about it. Nyx managed a smile, pretending like it didn't sting a little bit that Dahlia wouldn't show her that side of herself.

"Really, Braeden's ace at fending off suitors." Dahlia grinned.

Nyx groaned and stood. "That was a horrible pun. You should be ashamed."

She offered her hand to help Dahlia up. Dahlia took it and stood, their hands staying linked for a heartbeat longer than necessary.

Nyx's insides were made of firecrackers. Every part of her palm that pressed against Dahlia's tingled, and she wished she could put this moment in a bubble forever…well, without the pain of Dahlia's loss. And the death.

And the attack.

And the fact that Nyx had been about to leave all of this behind.

How stupid had she been?

Another tear slipped from Dahlia's eye, tracing down her freckles. Nyx brushed it away, her fingers lingering on the soft curve of Dahlia's cheek. She wanted to kiss Dahlia there. One of many places, in fact. The words *I love you* rolled up her throat and waited, heavy on her tongue.

All she had to do was say it. Here was her chance.

Dahlia leaned forward and hugged Nyx tight, her voice vibrating against Nyx's shoulder. Nyx didn't even care what she'd said, just that Dahlia's body was pressed against hers and she never wanted to let go. She wanted to curl her fingers around Dahlia's hips and read every millimeter of her like a favorite book.

She stayed quiet and settled for the hug.

She was such a sap.

A cowardly sap.

Nyx swallowed the words. It wasn't the right time. Too many

big things with bigger consequences had happened tonight. Her heart would have to wait. Her lust would have to settle itself and take a backseat to more important things. "I need to tell you and Braeden something."

A line of wind riders sailed past the intersection as Nyx and Dahlia waited for the traffic signal to change. Nyx fidgeted, the secret whispers and thrumming of the moon louder the longer she stood still. She caught occasional sounds of the colony, far away and sporadic. The rumble of an engine. A shout. A bang that could've been a gunshot or an automaton starting up. There was a tightness in the air, as if the entire colony were perched on the edge of something vast. She didn't need to hear to know the air was filled with the distant roars of gargoyles. The furtive glances at the web or in the direction of the gates told her that.

Dahlia tapped something out on her cuff, her bottom lip trapped between her teeth. The flowers had stayed in her hair, the white wide-open blooms making her look like some sort of woodland sprite.

On the other side of the crosswalk, they were stopped by three marines sweeping the street. Dahlia had a quick, heated discussion with them that was too fast for Nyx to follow. The tension in the colony pushed at her from all sides. It was almost suffocating.

The marines moved away, and Dahlia rolled her shoulders back. "They wanted us to go inside," she signed with an irritated expression. "I told them we had to escort a survivor."

"Very professional of you," Nyx said.

Dahlia winked, and Nyx's stomach did a backflip.

The medical center was just like every other building in the colony save the manicured growth of red plants covering the side wall, forming a plus sign. Advertising and ecological living all in one.

The front doors whispered open automatically, and Nyx wrinkled her nose at the medicinal smells. No matter how often she volunteered here, she would never get used to the smell of death and survival.

She waved to several medics she worked with regularly. A few of them signed, "How are you?" and "Nice to see you."

Nyx spread her fingers and tapped her thumb to her breastbone. "Fine."

She even smiled to sell the story.

Several screens in the waiting area were showing drone footage of HUB2. Dahlia stopped and stared at one, her hand over her mouth.

Fires raged across the ground. Even from the zoomed-out aerial shot that masked details and avoided truly gruesome images, there was no mistaking the piles of bodies in the streets. Gargoyles swarmed over everything. No matter where the cameras filmed, they caught glimpses of death and destruction.

It was a massacre.

She followed Dahlia up to the second level and down a series of hallways until she stopped in front of a door. The glass walls were frosted for privacy, and a section to the right of the door glowed with the patient's public information.

> Name: Rumor Mora
> Age: 17
> Ht: 190.5 cm

She skipped the rest of the basic information and jumped down to the glowing codes corresponding to specific physical injuries. Nyx knew how to interpret most of them, and the more she read, the more she felt guilty for being in any way jealous of this guy when he'd obviously been through hell tonight.

Dahlia touched Nyx's arm to get her attention. "He's a little on edge."

Nyx wasn't surprised.

"Do you want me to sign, or do you want to try reading his lips?"

Nyx smiled, warmed that Dahlia always asked. "You can sign. I don't know him at all."

Dahlia nodded and opened the door.

Rumor stood the second they walked in, his mouth moving as his dark eyes landed on Dahlia. Lines furrowed between his brows, and his shoulders hunched upward like he was protecting himself. He held his side with one hand, the other gesturing as he spoke. His black hair spiraled in wayward curls away from his head and down to his shoulders, framing black eyes and brown skin.

Dahlia held up her hands in a placating gesture. "Rumor, this is Nyx."

Rumor paused, his attention flicking to Nyx as if he'd only just realized someone else had walked in with Dahlia. He spoke, but he didn't move his mouth enough for her to figure it out.

"He said he doesn't know sign language," Dahlia signed.

"That's okay," Nyx said with what she hoped was a friendly smile. He was way too cute for her comfort. "It isn't a requirement to be here."

Rumor nodded. He was nearly as brown as Nyx, but with more golden undertones instead of her rosy ones. What struck her the most was his height. He towered, nothing but long lines and sharp corners. The edge of his mouth could cut glass. He was elegant and beautiful in his own right, even cloaked in distrust and anger and grief. He glanced at the door, then back at them like a caged animal. "Time to go?"

Dahlia nodded, a gentle smile on her face, her body relaxed and comfortable.

He shook his head. "No, I need to talk to the commander

again. There's going to be another attack. It's already been two hours. We're wasting time."

The ground hummed beneath Nyx's boots almost in sync with Rumor's declaration as Dahlia translated. Nyx shuddered. Rumor reminded her of one of the black-barked trees that made up the sweeping forests outside the colonies where the rebel humans lived. Tall and intimidating. The twin blades buckled to his thighs added to the whole *don't touch me* vibe. Something about him put her on edge, and she had trouble believing her Dahlia had ever dated this guy.

A muscle on Rumor's jaw ticked, but he nodded and gestured to the door. They headed out, Nyx trailing behind as the thrumming rolled violently under her feet in a wave that could only be described as anger. It was even more tremulous outside and fought to drown out everything else in her awareness.

Nyx hurried after Dahlia and Rumor. She walked past them and took up the lead to Braeden's house. This route was familiar and unchanging. She needed to focus on something she *knew* so she wouldn't think about leaving or the whispers or whether she was going insane.

Maybe the humans back on Earth had been like this. Maybe they'd clung to normal in the face of impending destruction with the same nonchalance and acceptance. Or maybe they had possessed a healthy amount of fear. She often wondered about her ancestors back on Earth. Some knew details, but a lot had been lost in the two-hundred-year journey here on the generational ship. When the colonists first arrived, there had been a little more division. A little more clinging to humanity's roots.

I'm Palestinian.
I'm French.
I'm American.
I'm Moroccan.
I'm Cuban.
I'm Canadian.

I'm Japanese.

The accents and languages were more diverse.

Now, several generations down the line, people would discuss the First Generation of settlers as *from Earth,* and something about that made Nyx sad. As if, with each generation, they became more Saharan and less *Palestinian, French, American, Moroccan, Cuban, Canadian, Japanese.* All Nyx knew was her first name was Greek and her last name Cuban, which led her to wonder why the original colonists had picked the Greek alphabet as a naming convention. It made about as much sense as calling the colonies A, B, C, and D.

Braeden's family came from a little island called England and an even smaller country named Switzerland. She'd explored all the information she could find on all these countries, but it still seemed so intangible and far away. People she would never meet. Lovely old buildings weeping history she would never see. Traditions lost beyond the stars.

The goal of the generational ship had been to be the farthest reach of humanity into space, but that meant being cut off from everyone. An island out to sea. An uncharted land in the middle of nowhere. Even the constellations her ancestors told stories about weren't the same ones Nyx saw occasionally through the patches in the cloudy nebula.

Instead, the moon she walked upon spoke in a foreign language only she could sense, and the mountains wept gargoyles instead of history.

Nyx supposed that was the ultimate trade-off for exploring the cosmos. They'd gained the stars, but had lost the ground they came from.

BRAEDEN

Braeden Tennant wanted two things: to get out from his mother's shadow, and to unlearn Epsilon's darkest secret.

He'd never wanted *this*. He'd never wanted a life of scrutiny and secrets. Honestly, he just wanted to hang out with Nyx and Dahlia, maybe play some video games, eat food that was entirely too bad for him, and sleep. Not necessarily in that order.

Priorities shifted, after all.

He fiddled with the black ring on his middle finger and stared at the silver card on his desk. It was rectangular, roughly palm-sized, and had no markings on it save another slightly darker silver line that bisected the middle. The size and shape were similar to key cards used to access various buildings all around the colony. He had one. His moms each had one. High-ranking personnel had one. They were fairly common.

This one, however.

This one made his fingers tighten around the edges of his desk until his knuckles turned white. This one made his stomach lurch like he was going to throw up.

This one accessed two doors: one on the surface and one below the surface. And he hated that he knew this. Not so much because of *what* was down there, but because of how it made his conscience sit on his shoulder like a chirping cricket.

He shouldn't have this card. Then again, he shouldn't know half the things he did know, but thanks to the configuration of vents in his house, every conversation from his mom's downstairs office drifted into his room.

Braeden spun his ring around his finger and listened to the discussion in firm voices drifting through the vent.

"What about what Rumor said?" Bailey asked. "About another attack."

His chest tightened. Here? He chewed on his thumbnail, his knee bouncing. His attention strayed to the digital picture frame on his desk. It rotated through several images: him with friends, him with Mom, him with Bailcy, Bailey and his mom's wedding day, him with his dad.

Braeden turned the frame facedown, pretending he could protect his dad's memory from knowing what was going on.

"We're in lockdown," his mom answered, her tone sharp and almost exasperated. "Troops are sweeping the streets. Citizens are inside where it's safer."

"You know as well as I do it isn't safer." Bailey's tone went up like it did when her patience ended. "After what she told us, they could come through the ground."

"They haven't yet." Sara's voice grew thin.

"He called her by name," Bailey said quietly. "They're looking for her."

Sara didn't answer, but Braeden imagined her glaring at Bailey, her mouth a straight line and her eyes betraying none of the million thoughts churning through her military mind.

Braeden swiveled in his chair and faced the window. From the top floor of his house, he could see over the wall. While orderly lines of marines wound through Epsilon like trained bugs, the horizon glowed with fire. He'd seen the first explosions, watched in horror from the safety of his tornado of a bedroom while Epsilon's parent city burned.

At first he thought it was a repeat of '64, when the dragons had attacked the battleships as they'd tried to land. Then as the reports filtered in, he'd realized it was so much worse than that night. The death toll was in the thousands and still rising. The beasts had circled the city, blocked any escape, and closed the noose on every human who lived there.

Except one.

Braeden shuddered. He tapped the card with his fingernail as guilt gnawed his insides. As soon as the reports had come in that the gargoyles had swept through HUB2 in an organized wave, his mind went to this card and *that cage*.

They were looking for her.

Braeden pushed out of his chair, pausing as several marines walked by his house with their automaton cats prowling beside them. The sleek machines moved smoothly, their adamantine plates sliding and rotating almost effortlessly. They were a deep silver color that reflected the nebula like a mirror. Out in the open, when on the hunt, those plates shifted to camouflage, rendering the cats nearly invisible.

He pressed a palm to the glass, leaning against it until he couldn't see them any longer. He wanted to be an automaton handler so badly it twisted his stomach to even think of being mentally linked with one of those massive machines. The base of his skull tingled as if he could feel a real chip in his brain stem. Being linked to something with so much power and so much finesse . . . He bit his lip.

His palm fell away from the glass, leaving fingerprints behind. His moms didn't know. Bailey wanted him to be in the sciences, use his memory and smarts for research. His mom wanted him to lead, to head up a colony of his own one day. Maybe even a HUB.

Braeden dug his go-bag out of the closet. His moms had made him pack one for times like these. Times when the city had to go underground during threat of an assault. And if the gargoyle horde had taken down an entire HUB with minimal resistance, a colony wouldn't stand a chance. Even with their shiny new wall guns and orderly squads of highly trained marines.

It was just a matter of when.

He pocketed the card and headed downstairs, skipping the last three steps with a jump.

"Where do you need me?" he yelled. He dumped his bag on the couch and headed for the weapon safe in the corner of the living room. His mind spun with ideas and what-ifs.

"Northeast shelter," Bailey answered as she came out of Sara's office. "We may have to call an evac to shelters. I need you to help." Her lips were pursed and her eyes tight, a sure sign he'd get caught in the crossfire if he said the wrong thing.

He settled for giving her a two-fingered salute and punching the code on the safe. His favorite handgun, an older-model, high-powered revolver, went into a holster against his ribs, and his favorite blade, a very well-loved charged machete, went into a sheath that crossed his back diagonally.

"Button your jacket." Sara walked over to him and started straightening his coat on her own. "Remember, you're my face when I'm not around."

And you're your father's son, was what she had quit adding to that. Even though Braeden wore his dad's military jacket. Even though there was a rip in the right sleeve he refused to get fixed.

He stood still under her fussing, trying not to fidget as she fastened the shiny silver buttons and adjusted the seams across his shoulders. She ran her fingers over the embroidered last name above the left pocket. He was nearly taller than her now.

Say something about her. Tell them you know about her.

Braeden took a breath…

…and the front door whispered open.

Nyx, Dahlia, and a tall, dark-haired boy entered. The

boy glanced around the living room, his expression shuttered. Braeden raised his eyebrows in question at Nyx.

"Who's he?" he signed.

"This is Rumor. Survivor from HUB2 and your new roommate. His dad died in the attack. Let him be sad if he needs it." She lifted her chin and sent the signs off with sharp movements to emphasize her point.

Braeden scowled at her and didn't respond.

"I'm serious," she signed. "He's not a project."

Rumor straightened to his full height, which was maybe a few centimeters taller than Braeden, and stared at him, wary. Braeden smiled. "I'm Braeden Tennant, resident joker and the prettiest in all of Epsilon."

"Braeden," Sara admonished with a sigh.

Rumor frowned at him. "Rumor Mora."

"What's the plan?" Dahlia curled and uncurled her fingers over and over, her nervous tic. She kept stealing glances at Rumor, and Braeden wondered if she'd known him when she lived at HUB2. His name sounded so familiar.

"I'm at northeast," Braeden said, his hands also rolling out the signs quickly for Nyx. "I'm not sure about you guys."

"Nyx and Dahlia will go to the medical shelter to help. Rumor stays with Braeden." Sara moved through the room to the weapons safe. Dahlia quickly translated for Nyx.

"Me?" Braeden asked at the same time Rumor said, "Him?"

"Hey now," Braeden chided. "I might be scrawny, but I'm bendy."

"Which would be handy if you were in any way interested in sex." Dahlia's lips twitched against a smile.

Braeden shrugged lazily. "I don't understand the fascination, honestly, but hey, you do you. And others…I guess."

"Braeden," Sara said drily.

"Oh, hey, Mom, don't worry, that's the wonderful thing about me being ace." Braeden squeezed her shoulder and lowered his voice to a mock whisper. "I will never have The Sex. Like…ever."

That got him a few laughs. Even one side of Rumor's frown curved upward. It prodded at Braeden's guilt for a few moments, but the twisting sensation grew. His stomach returned to somersaults, and he could've sworn he felt every edge of the silver card burning against his thigh.

"Is northeast a battle station?" Rumor asked, an edge of impatience to his tone. Braeden couldn't figure out if he was angry or scared.

Maybe both.

"It's an underground shelter," Braeden answered carefully.

Rumor frowned. "You're hiding?"

Anger, then.

Bailey put her hand on his shoulder. "We don't know when an attack will happen—"

"Any moment now," Rumor interrupted, shaking off her hand.

"And not everyone who lives here is combat trained." She continued as if he hadn't spoken. "We have scientists, farmers, children, the elderly. We're preparing for any eventuality."

"They go underground," Braeden explained. "We make sure the people assigned to that shelter are actually in that shelter." This guy had to understand that. Surely they had a similar evac protocol in HUB2. He'd memorized the city layout the one time he'd visited, but hadn't actually read about their evacuation procedures.

"I'm not going to sit on my ass in some shelter." A warning note crept into Rumor's tone. "Those beasts took everything from me, and I ran away. There's a gargoyle out there responsible for all of this, and we have to find it. I'm not—" His voice cracked. He clamped his mouth shut, nostrils flaring. His gaze darted around the room, reminding Braeden of a cornered animal's. Before anyone could say anything, Rumor abruptly turned and left the house. The door whispered shut behind him.

Braeden stared at it. He rubbed his sternum, his fingertip

hitting one of the silver buttons on his dad's jacket.

"Give him a minute," Dahlia said quietly, avoiding everyone's eyes.

"You know, I read somewhere that doors used to be manual, so you could actually slam them when you made a huffy exit," Braeden said, his signs lazy. "I bet that was far more satisfying than upset! and *whishhhhhhhh* click."

Nyx snickered.

Her eyes on the door and her forehead getting those mom wrinkles between her eyebrows, Sara buckled a holster around her thigh. "I have to make the rounds and check squad readiness. Northeast."

Braeden nodded, wishing she'd just go already before she figured out he had a cloned card in his pocket. "Northeast, yes. Got it."

"If the alarm sounds, you help the squads get everyone in that shelter. Don't leave until it's over," she said, her voice a commander's tone but her gaze a mother's.

"I won't," he lied.

His moms left, their conversation from before picking up as they walked outside. His stomach lurched, the card heavy in his pocket. "I need to tell you guys something."

"Me, too," Nyx said.

"I don't," Dahlia said.

"Dammit, Dahl," Braeden said. "You always have to be contrary."

She flipped him off behind a smile, which was good to see.

Nyx fidgeted with her sweater, and Braeden straightened. She only did that when she was upset. Oh, and that was his sweater. He slipped his hand into hers and tugged gently, leading her to the couch. He sat forward a little, focusing entirely on her.

She squeezed his fingers. Dahlia sat on the other side of her, perched sideways, her expression concerned. Braeden warmed.

Their trio was a strong one, and one he'd do anything to protect. He and Nyx had grown up together, and she was the first one he'd come out to as asexual. Nyx had taught him sign language. When Dahlia arrived at Epsilon a couple years ago, she'd become a part of their circle as if she was family coming home. She'd had them both come with her when she started hormone replacement therapy. They were his home when he felt the most lost, like tonight.

Which was why he could tell them what he knew and trust they'd keep his secret.

"All right," Dahlia said. "We don't have much time. You both get one sentence."

"The moon speaks to me," Nyx said quietly.

"My moms are keeping a gargoyle in a cage underneath Epsilon," Braeden said quickly.

Dahlia stared at them. "Okay, you get more sentences."

They listened while Nyx told them about the moon's vibrations and how she felt it all the time. How it changed in strength and duration. And how she was absolutely convinced it was a language, and it was trying to tell her something.

"Wait, wait, wait." Braeden held up his hands. At the same time, Dahlia touched Nyx's elbow to get her attention and signed, "Are you saying the moon is alive?"

"I don't know." Nyx touched her fingertips to her forehead and swept them into the air to her right. "Maybe?"

Braeden touched her elbow. "Is it dangerous? How do you know it's…something in the moon and not the forest rebels or something? Someone else using it to send messages."

His mind tripped down the staircase of all the horrible things it could be. But if it were the rebels, then they'd all be able to feel it. Not just Nyx.

Nyx scraped her teeth over her lower lip. "I don't think it's human. It's not like it's Morse code. It's something else."

"Something alien?" Dahlia asked after she got Nyx's attention.

Nyx hitched her shoulders, stood, and pointed at her seat. "Scoot," she told Dahlia. "I'm tired of looking back and forth."

Dahlia slid over with a smile and leaned back against Braeden's arm, which he'd stretched across the back of the couch.

"Sure, Dahl, use me as a pillow," Braeden mumbled.

She patted his knee. "Thanks, B."

"It got really…angry just before the HUB2 attack—the moon, the vibrations—and it's been so angry since then." Nyx stared at her lap. "I was going to leave tonight before everything happened, and head to the rebels in the forests. They live out there with the gargoyles and might know what this is. Maybe they feel it, too. I can't get away from this awful feeling that HUB2 was just the beginning."

Braeden's stomach dropped, and a weird buzzing noise filled his ears. She'd been going to leave? How could she just…leave?

Dahlia folded her arms. "You were going to leave us?" Hurt bled through her voice.

Nyx's mouth worked like she was trying to figure out something to say.

"Were you even going to say good-bye?" Braeden asked quietly.

Her eyes glistened. "I didn't know how."

Silence filled the spaces between signs.

"I'm sorry," Nyx mumbled.

Nothing could make Braeden leave without saying good-bye. What would make him pack up and leave during nightside—the most dangerous time to be out? He couldn't think of anything. Not even a chance at automata.

"You said it felt like HUB2 was just the beginning. Rumor said there would be more attacks," Dahlia said, her voice distant. "He seems dead set on the idea the colonies are next."

"That would be a good way to wipe us out," Braeden said, taking her lead and signing as Nyx watched them carefully. "Take down our parent HUB and then fan out and chew up the colonies while we're scrambling to figure out what's going on. They stumbled on that with the Crater incident."

"So you guys believe me?" Nyx asked, her eyes wide.

"Well, I mean, it's bizarre, but you don't have a reason to lie about this. You know we'll always believe you, okay?" Braeden assured her. "You have nothing to worry about." He waited for her nod before continuing. "If you're right and if Rumor's right, I think I know why."

"The gargoyle in the basement?" Dahlia asked. "Yeah, let's talk about that. What the entire galaxy?"

Braeden winced. "My moms caught her—I don't know how—but I overheard them talking about her a few times." He leaned back and dug in his pocket for the card. "I cloned Mom's key card. I used it once."

"Wait, you went and saw it?" Nyx asked. "Is it in chains or a cage or something?"

"You went *alone*?" Dahlia's voice rose. "Does anyone else know about her other than you and your moms?"

Braeden's eyebrows went up. "Guys, I've fought gargoyles before, okay?"

Dahlia straightened, her expression sharp enough to make him flinch a little. "That doesn't matter. You went down there alone to…*what…exactly*?"

Braeden ran his hands through his hair and tugged. "To talk to her."

Both girls stared at him with identical frowns.

"Talk." Dahlia tilted her head to the side.

"To a gargoyle?" Nyx asked in a quieter tone.

Braeden suddenly knew how Nyx had felt, with both of them staring at him as if he'd lost his mind. He rubbed the back of his neck. "You guys should meet her. Mom thinks I'll be at northeast tonight."

Dahlia arched an eyebrow. "She did say go underground. Where's the gargoyle?"

"There's a maintenance shed along the western wall by the cornfields. It leads down to her cell."

"What about your ex?" Nyx asked Dahlia with a jerk of her head to the door.

"Wait, he's your ex? Oh, *that's* the HUB2 guy?" Braeden asked as it all clunked into place. He'd really been distracted if he'd missed that.

Dahlia tilted her head to one side. "Did the name *Rumor* not clue you in? Because it's not exactly common."

"Listen, I don't pay attention on the best of days," he said.

"Says the boy with the eidetic memory," Nyx said.

"It's only eidetic when he wants to show off," Dahlia signed with a smirk.

Nyx grinned. Braeden ignored them and rubbed a finger over his mouth. "Do you trust him?"

"To know about it, sure," Dahlia said with a shrug. "To not kill the thing immediately because he's pissed off and hurting right now? I make no promises."

"Good point." Braeden grimaced. "We need to hurry. If you guys are right about there being another attack, and this gargoyle is part of it…"

"Lemme go talk to Rumor." Dahlia climbed off the couch. "I won't tell about the monster in the basement. But lemme get a read on him and then see." She tugged on one of Nyx's blue spikes as she left.

If a human could actually be the definition of longing, Nyx as she watched Dahlia leave would qualify. Braeden waited until the door shut before signing, "When are you going to tell her you're in love with her?"

Nyx's wide-eyed surprise and subsequent blush was worth the pounce. She mock-punched him in the arm, and Braeden laughed. He stood, his smile faltering as he caught sight of Dahlia and Rumor talking outside the front window.

He had no proof the gargoyle wasn't violent. He'd met her

once. The four of them had spent their entire lives watching those creatures murder and maim.

But something…something about her. He had no explanation, just an almost visceral need to have his closest friends meet her, too. Maybe they'd feel the slice of hope he'd felt.

Or maybe they'd kill her.

The door swished open, and Dahlia leaned in. "He's game. Let's go."

JUDE

Gravel crunched and scattered under Jude's boots as he, Trick, and Yi-Min hurried along a narrow path winding down the mountain. The world was a wash of blues and greens made brighter by light from nearby moons, but his attention was on the foothills ahead. The rock formations separated his home in the black-barked forests from the military-run colonies that blemished Sahara's surface. Jude shuddered as fear crawled through his veins. Roars echoed off the rock, raising the hair on his arms. Tonight the world had tipped upside down.

"See something?" Trick asked in an undertone. When Jude didn't answer, Trick elbowed him. "Jude."

"No," Jude said without looking at him. He managed to keep his voice steady.

Yi-Min flipped a small blade over the back of their hand and back to their palm again and again as they passed the boys and took the lead, dark eyes narrowed on the surroundings and a small gun in their other hand. The three of them had stashed the sailboards in a tiny ravine at the beginning of the path. Approaching a colony on foot would be less threatening. Plus they couldn't let the colonies know the forest rebels had appropriated colonist technology for their own uses.

Jude followed the others, his insides a writhing mass of chimera tails.

A schism was breaking Sahara in two. On one side: the humans in their HUBs and colonies. On the other: the chimera, led by Reaper, who were convinced one of their own—a pack leader named Vala—was a political prisoner of the humans.

Jude and every human and chimera denizen of Azrou existed somewhere in the murky middle between the two extremes. The attacks had been escalating, and tonight's massacre at HUB2 put all sympathizers like them in a precarious position. *Forest rebels*. Those who believed everyone could live in harmony with the indigenous life. Those who refused to call the inhabitants of the moon *gargoyles* because of the mythos that word invoked and instead let the race choose a name humans could pronounce: *chimera*.

Another set of footsteps thunked on the ground next to Jude. A two-headed chimera matched him step for step. "Angel," said Jude, "you realize when we get to Epsilon, you can't go in."

The nebula light threw vivid color across their pyrite skin and reflected in their six too-wide black eyes. A set of horns twisted from their brows, curling up around their hairless heads before branching off in opposite directions. Jewels in every color imaginable dangled from various points across their horns like ornaments.

They draped their wings around bare shoulders and examined Jude. "I know," they said in a dual grating voice, thin lips forming the human syllables which were so foreign to the fanged mouth and two tongues of the chimera.

A word that bore with it the mystery and fantasy and imagination of the cosmos, instead of the demons and evil and darkness of the Earth-born stories of gargoyles. Beasts that came alive at night and tore into people's homes. Monsters that moved under cover of darkness and disappeared during the day.

Jude licked his lips. "Did you hear who it is?"

"I did," Angel replied. "I knew Reaper was passionate, but I never envisioned he'd incite so much death."

Pain pulsed in Jude's chest at the disappointed and almost sad expression on Angel's faces. Nestmates, chimera hatched from eggs in the same nest, were normally bonded. To hear their nestmate was responsible for death on such a scale had to be a blow to Angel.

"Do you know where he is?" Jude asked carefully.

"If I did, I'd go after him immediately," Angel said. They didn't sound angry with Jude for the questions, but frustration wrapped around every syllable, as if they were still wrestling with the idea of a sibling's betrayal.

"Should Jude go in?" Trick asked.

Jude rolled his eyes. "Not this again."

"It's dangerous if they find out—"

"He'll be fine," Yi-Min said over their shoulder.

"Okay, well, while you're playing emissary, he comes with me." Trick glanced at Jude, daring him to protest. Jude rolled his eyes.

Yi-Min pushed their partially shaved black hair over one shoulder, revealing the twisting scar running from the outside of their eye down to their collarbone. "The HUB2 attack puts everyone in danger. If Jude keeps his ability to himself, he shouldn't draw attention."

"I'm right here, you know," Jude muttered. "What are we doing about Vala? We need to stay until we find her, especially after what just happened."

Yi-Min shot him a sympathetic smile. "After we get the survivor to safety, we'll turn our attention to Vala."

"And if they have the survivor but won't give them up?" Trick asked.

The corner of Yi-Min's mouth ticked up. "Prison break."

"We're taking the survivor?" Jude asked. "Like kidnapping or...?"

Trick grinned and flexed a little. "I'll work a little magic, and he'll follow right after me."

Jude shoved Trick to one side. "Charm away, bro."

As they neared a rise, George appeared, having gone ahead to scout. He rumbled as he ran on four legs at Jude, a steady thrum from his chest that reminded Jude of purring. Jude smiled as he neared, bracing himself for the body slam of affection. The all-black chimera was a shadow sliding along the rock, his wings pulled tightly to his body and his long tail whipping back and forth. He lowered his head, his sharpened beak pointing to the ground, and bowled into Jude. Jude tumbled to the ground with a grunt as four onyx feet straddled him and large eyes blinked owlishly into his face.

"Hi, George," Jude managed, trying to get air back into his lungs.

"Did I hurt you?" George asked in a throaty grate. He could speak various human languages, but preferred the comfort of his native tongue. It made sense for Jude, and the others who were willing, to learn the chimera language even if the rumbling, simultaneous sounds couldn't be mimicked by humans. All chimera were born with two tongues, which could move independently. Their language layered sounds atop one another and made it nearly impossible for single-tongued beings to mimic it.

"If I say yes, will you stop?" Jude grunted. George moved when Jude shoved at his broad chest, fingers sliding across skin that felt more carved from solid stone than something organic and alive. He nudged Jude's shoulder with his beak, helping him sit up.

"We need to have a talk about this bowling-me-over thing." Jude stood gingerly and brushed the dust off his pants. A series of howls rose in the night—far too close to be from HUB2. "The rest of your pack?" he asked, even though the rock in his stomach knew the answer.

Angel shook one head while the second twisted around to scan the surrounding area. "Foe."

Trick cursed. "Reaper's squad?"

Angel nodded. "Fair guess."

George growled long and low.

"We have to reach Epsilon first," Yi-Min said. "Pick up the pace."

The group ran. Epsilon colony was at the base of the foothills. They only had a kilometer of hilly terrain to get through. Coming out at nightside was always such a bad idea.

They turned a corner and scrambled to a stop. Four chimera blocked the path, the largest one pushing at least two hundred and fifty centimeters tall and as wide as the front of a transport truck. Bony protrusions ringed his skulls like a crown, denoting him the alpha of the group. He stepped forward, massive horns polished and tipped in silvery adamantine. This one had four eyes—all red—and two heads. No wings, and massive arms that ended in multijointed fingers, tapering off to fine points and scraping the ground.

The towering, cloaked chimera who called himself Reaper wasn't in the group, but just the idea of seeing that scythe made the hair on Jude's neck stand on end.

The chimera growled, eyes snapping to Angel and George. A flurry of clicks and grunts and noises that sounded like boulders tumbling over each other spilled from their lips. Angel answered in kind, their expressions hard and unforgiving, and wings flared in front of Trick, Yi-Min, and Jude as protection. George added his rumbling and clicking to the conversation, and the argument escalated, judging from the red and orange clouds enveloping them. So much anger. It gave Jude a headache.

Jude could follow one-on-one, but he'd never gotten the hang of deciphering the overlapping responses of chimera conversation. Trick frowned, his head bent in concentration. He understood them better.

"We're trespassing," Trick murmured. "They're claiming this land for Reaper's army."

A shiver rolled over Jude. If Reaper claimed the mountain pass, that meant he actually was moving in on HUB2's satellite colonies: Epsilon, Zeta, Eta, and Theta. By felling an entire city, Reaper had positioned himself as *the* leader in the war against humans.

Anticipation shot down Jude's spine, muscles in his legs tensing and his fingers tingling. Trick slid his blade from the sheath on his thigh. Jude grabbed his wrist and shook his head. Even though they were blocked by Angel's wings, Jude didn't want them catching sight of the weapon. If Angel and George could talk them down or provide enough of a distraction for them to run, he'd rather that.

Trick arched an eyebrow at Jude and flicked the switch on the handle, the crimson light from the blade's inner core bathing the rock at their feet with its glow.

The chimera roared in anger, swinging to Trick. Angel snarled back, their speech rapid-fire and clipped as each head spoke over the other. They pulled their wings tight to their body.

"Reaper was never going to let us pass," Yi-Min whispered. "He doesn't let humans live. Especially tonight."

With a heavy exhale, Jude pulled his gun and leveled it at the leader, his sight line clear over George's shoulder.

"They invoke Mother," Angel said. "They claim She won't allow humans to trespass on Her land anymore, not after kidnapping one of Her favorite children. Reaper plans to exterminate one colony at a time until she's found. He's promised those who join him human blood."

So much red and yellow and black swirled around them. Even Trick's normal violet aura flared red around the edges. Yi-Min's colors blended red anger and blue sadness. It was as if the ground bled beneath Jude's feet. All he saw was red.

No matter how many times he faced this situation—standing up to chimera who would rather rip him apart than speak to him as an equal—fear remained a constant.

His fingers flexed around the smooth grip of the gun. The weight was comforting, familiar. He'd grown up with war. They were invaders in a land that wasn't theirs, but his entire generation was born on this moon. In the colonies. In the forest, like himself. It was their home now. What was he supposed to do with that?

He inhaled and closed his eyes for an eternity of one second. He wished he could float off into the deepest greens and blues of the butterfly nebula overhead. Leave the war and the red and the pull of both sides. The irreconcilable differences. The gun in his hand.

He opened his eyes and squeezed the trigger.

The gun kicked, the vibration rolling up Jude's arm as a bullet streaked from the muzzle in a trail of red. It punched the chimera who'd done all the threatening in the shoulder as he lunged at Angel with fangs bared and claws extended. He howled in fury but pushed forward, slamming into them. Jude dove out of the way, shoving Trick against the mountainside and firing. He hit one in the hip.

Jude gritted his teeth and released Trick. His brother's grin was nothing but glee as he charged, bathed in gold and red and his blade carving a path through the air. He slammed into another chimera. It roared at him, flashing its claws, but Trick was faster. He ducked out, bringing the blade up, and sliced deep into the chimera's side.

George roared and flew past Jude, tackling another chimera in a tumble of flailing limbs and claws and snapping teeth. Yi-Min was a flurry of hand-to-hand combat, landing precise cuts as they pulled one of the chimera away from the pack.

Jude spun around, looking for Angel and the big chimera. A trail of dark liquid spattered up the path and disappeared around the corner. *Angel, no, please, no.* He ran up the path and rounded the corner. Claws swiped at him from the corner of his vision. Jude slid to his knees. The claws missed the top of Jude's head and scraped the rock. Dust rained around his shoulders and into his hair. He raised the gun, but the creature swiped at him again, knocking his hand to the side as Jude pulled the trigger. The streak of crimson sailed into the blue-green night unhindered. Long fingers with extra joints wrapped around Jude's forearm twice and twisted. Jude spun with the motion to keep his arm from breaking, crying out as pain shot up to his shoulder. He landed on the ground hard, his arm bent at a weird angle and straining the socket. His fingers spasmed, and he dropped the gun, the metal clattering to the rocky ground with a horrible sense of finality.

I'm going to die here.

Jude's muscles tensed, bracing for the killing blow.

No, you're not, Jude. Get up and fight.

The ghost of his late boyfriend's voice whispered through his mind, seeping into his muscles and rolling under his skin like a warm fire. Jude kicked out, the heel of his boot driving into the chimera's knee. He brought his other leg up and kicked toward the chimera's lower abdomen, pushing him more off-balance. The chimera roared and swiped at Jude with his free hand. Jude dodged, his back scraping across the ground. Rocks bit through his shirt and ripped across his skin.

Angel's arm snaked around the chimera's neck and yanked. Jude scrambled to his feet, grabbing the gun with his uninjured hand and raising it, his breath sawing in and out of his lungs.

"No!" Angel yelled, twisting and contorting, ending up with the leader in a choke hold. They hissed words into the earholes along the sides of his head. Jude couldn't make out most of them over the pounding of his heart.

Trick's yell cut through the air. Jude held his throbbing arm across his body and ran. "Trick!"

One body lay on the ground—the curled and broken form of the chimera he'd already shot. Whether it had died from the gunshot or something Trick did, Jude didn't want to know. Another chimera had its arm wrapped around Trick's throat, its fangs bared at his scalp. Yi-Min was too far away still fighting their chimera to help. Jude drove his shoulder into the last one wrestling with Trick, knocking it to the side. Trick coughed and gasped for air as he fell to the ground. He pushed up to his hands and knees, blood flowing from his nose.

The chimera roared and charged again. Jude stood and fired, catching it in the thigh and making it angrier. He ducked away from a punch, firing again and trying to hit nonvital areas, but his brain blanked on where those were. He aimed for limbs. Last time he checked, there weren't any vital organs in the arms or legs.

"Kill it," Trick rasped.

"No," Jude snapped. Too much killing. Too much red.

"Jude!" Yi-Min yelled as they pulled their knife from the neck of another chimera.

"Dammit, Jude!" Trick lurched up and grabbed the gun. Before Jude could react, Trick squeezed the trigger twice and punched two glowing holes in the chimera's skull.

Silence slammed down around them, driving the breath from Jude's lungs and the warmth from his veins as the chimera toppled to the ground, lifeless. Yi-Min stood to one side, breathing hard, their knife dripping with black blood.

Trick shoved the gun into Jude's hand. "I know you want to do this without bloodshed, but we're at war. It's kill or be killed out here, and *you know that*." His voice shook in anger, but his eyes brightened with worry. "Especially tonight."

Jude stared at him, at the fear in his eyes and the fear swirling around him in flickering yellows. The blood on his face. His own mind and stomach churned. Mechanically, he put the gun back in its holster and pushed past Trick. "We need to get to Epsilon."

"Jude," Trick called after him.

Jude kept walking, not looking at the death, and knowing George and Angel would stay behind to clean up the bodies of their fallen. His hands shook. He swallowed back bile.

"Jude!" Yi-Min screamed.

A shadow blotted out the nebula light. Jude turned to the sky, instinctively ducking as the long serpentine body of a dragon soared overhead. Fat black drops spattered the ground as it passed by. Jude crouched and touched one of the puddles. Blood.

"It's hurt," he said as Yi-Min and Trick ran up.

"Is it flying off to die or for another attack?" Trick asked.

"Another attack would be my guess. We'll need the sailboards after all," Yi-Min said as they checked the remaining bullets in their gun. "It's headed toward Epsilon."

Jude rose slowly, his chest tight, unable to take his eyes off the dragon. "We have to save them," he whispered.

"You can't save everyone," Trick said.

Jude tore his attention away and met his brother's gaze. "I can try."

RUMOR

An alarm blared, lights flashed everywhere, and the staccato of gunfire peppered the night.

"What in deep space?" Rumor ran off the porch and skidded to a halt, then stumbled when Braeden clipped his shoulder. "Holy…" Rumor breathed as he stared straight up at the web.

"Guess you were right," Braeden said. "Oh. That…that's a lot of gargoyles."

Above them, gargoyles of various shapes and sizes scrabbled across the woven cables like monstrous spiders, swarming and pushing and roaring.

"I thought it was electrified," Rumor said, without looking away from the web. There were so many. "The colony webs are electrified."

"It was," Braeden said. "It's supposed to be."

There should have been sparks and the screeching of frying gargoyles. But the cables were dark and cold.

"They did this at HUB2," Rumor said. "Smashed lights and power housings. Anything to darken the city." He squinted past the glow of the overhead lights, trying to determine how many were up there.

"Can they get in now?" Dahlia's voice pitched up a degree. She moved closer to Nyx.

"They're pretty organized." Braeden checked his gun and signed something quickly to Nyx.

A shrieking howl set Rumor's teeth on edge. It was followed by a resounding crash that snapped his attention back to the web.

A dragon. Standing on top of the web. It rose on its two rear legs, then slammed down the front four. The web squealed in higher pitches with each crash. From somewhere in the distance came the sound of gunfire. Rumor's breathing picked up as he strained to see the dragon clearly. It turned and showed its flank, and Rumor's body went cold. Gaping wounds.

"Son of a bitch," Rumor whispered. "It's the same dragon that attacked HUB2."

"Are you sure?" Dahlia's voice shook.

He nodded, every nerve in his body going hot. "Very."

"I'm heading to the medical center." Dahlia clenched and unclenched her fists as she stared at the web. "I'll help evacuate the patients to the hospital shelter."

"I'm coming with you after I check on Abuela." Nyx's eyes darted to the web and back to Dahlia's eyes, every line of her face tight.

"I'll come with you in case she needs help," Dahlia said.

"You two should stick together as much as you can." Braeden hugged each girl tight. They headed away, and Braeden turned back to Rumor. "What's the plan?"

Rumor spun and looked northeast. "You should get to the shelter." He took off running before Braeden could respond.

"Rumor!" Braeden caught up. "Where are you going?"

Rumor pointed to an empty guard tower. "Up."

"Cool."

"And you are…?"

"Coming with you."

"I don't need your help."

"You aren't the only one with a vendetta, Rumor." Braeden's tone stayed even, casual, but his eyes spoke volumes.

Rumor didn't respond. He picked up his pace to a jog, weaving between residences and vaulting fences. He gritted his teeth through the pain radiating across his side. He couldn't stop. He had to keep going, keep moving, stay ahead of them.

Braeden matched him stride for stride and jump for jump. They kept to the outskirts of the crowd, blending into the shadows to not attract attention. The last thing Rumor wanted was an audience. He headed toward the guard tower, silently deferring to Braeden when he veered in a better direction or took them down a shorter path between two points.

So far, the webbing held fast. Rumor counted at least ten gargoyles swarming around, plus the dragon. More shadows swooped in and out of the already-dim lighting. The sounds of stony hide scraping against metal sent a waterfall of pinpricks down his neck and arms. "What happens if it breaks?"

"Don't get killed," Braeden deadpanned.

"Good idea."

Braeden flashed his crooked grin. "Best-laid plans and all that."

"Why aren't the tower cannons firing?" Rumor pointed to the massive turret guns mounted around the wall.

"If that thing dies on the web, it won't hold under the strain," Braeden answered. "They'll fire when it takes off again."

"If it takes off again," Rumor muttered.

They made their way through a series of streets, winding toward the northeast corner of the colony. There was another crash, and this time the shriek of stressed metal grew higher and higher, ending in a series of crackling snaps that stopped them cold.

"Oh, sh—"

The rest of Braeden's curse was drowned out by a chorus of gargoyle roars. Four cables had snapped; one was whipping toward them. Rumor hurled himself into Braeden. They tumbled to the ground. The cable whistled past, popping up debris. Rumor rolled over with a groan while Braeden lifted himself to his elbows, staring wide-eyed at the deep gouge in the pavement where they'd stood seconds before.

"Thanks for that," Braeden breathed.

"No problem." Rumor clenched his teeth against the pain, rolling to his good side and pushing up on adrenaline-shaky legs. Above, the beasts tore at an ever-widening hole. It was still too narrow for the dragon, but several of the smaller gargoyles slipped in and set to work on the cables from underneath. None of them were swooping down to attack.

Yet.

The organization of the attack was far too familiar. *Focus, Rumor.* He pulled both blades from their sheaths and switched them on. Braeden had an older-looking silver revolver in an expert grip.

Gunfire from the nearby guard towers sped up, bullets streaking through the air. One gargoyle fell with a screech. Another spread its wings and flew straight for the guard, who fired a killing shot.

Rumor and Braeden ran past straggling families who weren't in their shelters yet. Kids younger than him with shotguns and crossbows. Something ugly twisted in his stomach.

It wasn't like he hadn't seen kids with guns and knives. It wasn't like he hadn't fought alongside people his age before. Everyone was trained in some fashion. Just in case. But there was once a time and a place when children didn't carry weapons. So he'd heard in the stories from their home world.

But the children of the Saharan moon were born with guns in their hands.

Maybe he was tired of it. Tired down to his bones.

Halfway across a basketball court, a fleeting shadow was the only warning before something heavy bowled into Rumor and Braeden, sending them sprawling to the ground. Snarls and cold breath filled Rumor's senses. Sharp claws grabbed and ripped at his clothes. A cloven hoof stomped on his hand, and he yelled as two of his fingers made a sickening crunch. The blade slid out of his now-useless grip.

He rolled away as the hoof came down again, narrowly missing his skull. Rumor came up to a crouch, holding his broken hand to his chest for protection. The gargoyle was medium-sized, its skin brown as a cliff side, just like Rumor's. It matched Rumor's height and stared at him with an uncomfortably humanoid face.

"Go left!" Braeden yelled.

Rumor moved and swung the second blade in a wide arc. A series of muffled bangs came from somewhere behind him. The gargoyle jerked as holes exploded in its shoulder and neck. Rumor aimed for the nearest hole, driving the blade's heated edge into the stony flesh. The neck cracked, metal squealed against its bone, and the head rolled away.

Rumor turned, pulling in air to calm his heartbeat. He crouched next to Braeden, whose face was a little on the pale side. "What's hurt?"

"My leg. I don't think it's broken, but…" Braeden sucked in air through his teeth.

Rumor growled low in his throat. "Get back to your mom and Bailey."

"No way. I'm fine." Braeden's lips thinned, nostrils flaring as he breathed through the pain.

"You can't walk." Rumor yanked up Braeden's shredded pant leg, revealing a lot of blood. One long gash went up his shin.

"And you can't use your left hand. We're both down a limb." After a quick moment of patting around his person, Braeden shucked his jacket and ripped the sleeve off his long-sleeved T-shirt. He bound up the worst of his shin and pulled his pant leg back down. He relaced his boot, tucked his pant leg into it, and tightened the ties around his ankle with a grunt. Rumor helped him stand, and Braeden gestured to Rumor's injured hand. "Let me see."

Rumor hesitated. Braeden rolled his eyes and grabbed the hand, flipping it over to examine the broken fingers, then gave Rumor's ring finger a sudden yank. Rumor's yell was wordless, but angry. He barely kept from punching Braeden in the face.

Braeden grimaced but with a tinge of amusement. "Probably shoulda warned you, huh?"

"You think?" Rumor said through clenched teeth.

"They look like clean breaks. I need to pop the other one back and tie them so the swelling doesn't get any worse."

Rumor knew the drill. These weren't his first broken fingers. "Be quick about it."

"On it," Braeden said.

Rumor blinked back tears and let out a low groan as Braeden yanked and twisted his pinkie, snapping it back into place. Braeden grabbed his jacket from the ground, dug through his pockets, and produced a shoestring.

"Don't keep random stuff in your pockets, Braeden, you'll lose things," he muttered in a high-pitched mimicry, maybe of one of his moms. "This'll have to do." He bound Rumor's pinkie to his ring finger in a series of small loops, rendering both mostly straight and somewhat immobilized. "We'll get Wren to fix it later."

"Thanks," Rumor gasped, fighting the swimming sensation.

"No problem." Braeden picked up the cold, discarded blade and slid it into the sheath on Rumor's thigh. "Don't use your hand. I don't care what you think you have to prove." With a final look at Rumor, he turned and limped away toward the guard tower.

About a block before they reached it, they passed a shelter with its doors wide open. A burly man stood outside, an older Revenant shotgun in one hand and the other hand pointed into the shelter while he glared at a guy about Rumor's age. "Get in the shelter, Colt!"

The boy shook his head. He held an old revolver in one hand and a small dagger in the other. "I'm going to go fight, and there's nothing you can do about it."

The boy turned to leave, but the man grabbed him around the wrist and twisted his arm behind his back.

Rumor slowed. "Who is that?"

"The guy is Dahlia's ex. The dude is his uncle. I wouldn't get in the middle of it."

Something dark and slimy reared in Rumor's chest as he watched Dahlia's ex-boyfriend jerk out of his uncle's grip and stalk away anyway, gun in hand, cursing over his shoulder. "He's gonna get himself killed."

Braeden sighed. "We have a betting pool, actually. Don't tell him."

They reached the guard tower as three more main cables gave way, whipping out in great arcs. Several people screamed, and Rumor squinted up at the web, praying that it took the creatures longer to get through the secondary cables. "Have you ever had a dragon attack here?"

"Never." Braeden led Rumor around to a side door, which revealed a spiral staircase.

Rumor headed in, taking the steps two at a time, glancing over his shoulder every so often to make sure Braeden's damaged leg hadn't given out. Braeden climbed slow but steady, sending a tight smile and gesturing for Rumor to go ahead.

The top of the tower was like a covered balcony. Three of the four walls were chest height. Perfect for resting your elbows on and firing. From up here, Rumor had a great view of the colony, and he was so close to the web he heard the individual ticks of gargoyle claws and nails across the close-knit structure. Braeden slumped against the wall with a grimace and a soft curse.

"If you pass out on me, I'm rolling you down the stairs." Rumor zeroed in on a rifle on the floor.

Braeden laughed weakly. "If I pass out from some scratches, you have my permission."

Rumor checked the weapon. Fully loaded but not a guard in sight. "Where's the marine stationed here?"

Braeden pointed over Rumor's shoulder. Rumor turned. "Oh."

Still-glistening blood stained the floor.

A low groan vibrated the air overhead. The shallow eave of the roof blocked most of his view, but Rumor saw a giant, clawed foot, easily as big as his torso. He muttered a curse and aimed, firing at the arch and trying to hit the weakest point. Maybe cripple it.

He hit it.

Which was awesome.

And made it mad.

Which was not.

The dragon howled and moved to the side, bending its bulk to stare between the crisscrossed cabling. A giant eye the color of gold and darkness focused on Rumor. He stared back, looking for a hint of intelligence, something to explain the sudden organization. Something to explain why he felt like the gargoyles had been playing them all this time.

Its lip curled, a snarl rumbling from deep within its chest. Rumor fired again, aiming for the eye. It jerked out of the way, and he grazed its cheek instead. Great. He was pissing it off instead of doing any real damage.

"How's that going?" Braeden asked cheerfully.

"Nicked it twice. Made us a target." Rumor moved to another side of the guard tower.

"Excellent." Braeden limped to the opposite end of the tower and stuck his head out. He whistled low. "Big bastard, isn't it?"

"Has a hurt foot. You two can swap stories."

Braeden took careful aim and fired three quick shots. Another howl echoed through the night. He grinned. "Now he has a hurt hand. We can all be friends."

"One big, happy family." Rumor kept a careful eye on another gargoyle flying through the hole in the web, aiming as it turned and flew toward them. One blast, and its head snapped back. It fell and hit the ground with a hollow thud. "How long until dayside?"

Braeden checked his forearm cuff. "Twenty-five hours. No way we'll hold them off that long."

The dragon would be through the web in a little less than an hour at the rate they were ripping at it. It didn't matter how many of the little ones they took out. When the dragon hit the ground, Epsilon would go the way of HUB2 in minutes. How could Rumor get it down before the web broke?

"How close is the roof of the guard tower to the web?" he asked.

"About three meters. Why?"

"Scrap that idea," he said.

"Seriously? You'd get him to chase you?"

Rumor nodded. "Get it off the web and the wall cannons can take it out in the air. It dies over open ground instead of the colony."

Braeden pursed his lips and motioned him over. He pointed to the wall outside the tower. "If you can make the jump to it, that ladder will take you to the web. But your fingers…"

Rumor winced at the throbbing in his hand. "It's only two fingers. I've had worse. I don't need all ten fingers anyway, right?"

"Not any more than I'll need my leg."

"You aren't going."

Braeden's eyebrows shot up, and he rose to his full height. He was shorter than Rumor, but bulkier. "If you're jumping across, so am I. I'm a better shot than you."

Rumor gauged the distance between the tower and the wall. "Oh, this is such a bad idea." He dragged his good hand over his face.

"The worst. My mom's gonna kill me if I survive." Braeden

shook his head. "So when we get up there, there's a ledge we can walk on just fine. After we shimmy through the web, there's a lip on the wall above it we can run on. But it's pretty narrow. At some point closer to the front gates, there's a set of narrow maintenance stairs built into the wall that will take us to the ground." He shrugged one shoulder. "That is, if the gargoyles haven't destroyed them."

"Right."

"Anything else? Favorite color? Shoe size? What to bury me with?"

Rumor grinned. It felt good. Braeden climbed out of the window, balancing on the narrow lip outside the tower. When he leaped and missed the rung he'd aimed for, Rumor held his breath, only to let it out in a relieved *whoosh* when Braeden caught himself a few rungs down. Rumor leaned out the window. "Okay?"

Braeden shifted his weight to his good leg. "Yep. Let me get above you so you don't fall on me."

"Thanks for the vote of confidence."

"Being practical," he retorted.

Rumor spun back to the main view of the outpost and checked for nearby fliers. Getting picked off the ladder would suck.

"Hey!" Rumor called as Braeden got level with him. When he turned, Rumor motioned the rifle toward him once, then tossed it. Braeden caught it, slung the strap diagonally across his chest, and kept climbing. Rumor waited until Braeden's feet were higher than where he stood and climbed out.

The lip outside was about fifteen centimeters deep. His heels clung to it, toes out over thin air, and he stared down the ladder. His broken fingers burned, constant and deep. After a few steadying breaths, he pushed off and sailed through the air. The fingers on his good hand closed around one rung, while his broken hand banged against the rung below. He inhaled through his nose to get control over the pain.

"Okay?" Braeden called down.

"Yep."

He heard a screech and looked up as another cable snapped down, smacking the wall about four feet away. Braeden's whispered cussing pushed Rumor to climb faster. All the self-training and mental encouragement couldn't keep his back muscles from tensing against the thought of a cable snap.

As Rumor neared the top, Braeden leaned over and gripped his arm, helping him up the last few rungs. Standing, Braeden handed Rumor the rifle and pulled out his handgun. With a flick of his head, he limped toward the gaping hole.

Adamantine cables as thick as Rumor's wrist provided the main crisscross structure of the web, with smaller ones strung between in overlapping grids to keep the spacing tight and small. Right then, cables hung in tatters around the gap like cut marionette strings.

Rumor sighted down the rifle as two of the creatures noticed them. They bared their fangs and hissed guttural noises, but didn't move from their spot.

"You can pivot better, so stay behind and watch our backs," Braeden said over his shoulder. He leveled his gun at one of the gargoyles and fired, catching it right between the eyes. Its companion watched the body jerk and fall away. The gargoyle bared its teeth and scrabbled across the web toward them. Rumor fired.

Shouts floated up from the ground. Angry ones.

"We've been spotted." Braeden saluted the ground with two fingers and turned to the gap. "Now what?"

Good question. "We need to get outside the web."

The hole was at least ten feet away over empty air. Rumor curled his damaged fingers around a length of cable and pulled, biting the inside of his mouth as pain radiated outward. Pulling his fingers clean off would hurt less. What if he couldn't do this? Someone else's life depended on him surviving and making it.

Pain shot through his chest at the mere thought of failure because his fingers were broken.

Braeden fired at a gargoyle that darted at them. "You know, we could stay here and pick them off one by one. Maybe Big Daddy Dragon will get bored and leave."

"Or maybe it'll finish the job and grab us on its way down," Rumor said.

"Good point. All right, cover me." Before Rumor could protest, Braeden swung out into open air, gripping the one intact cable left. Hand over hand, he made his way closer to the hole. When he was about there, a gargoyle dove through the opening, aiming for him.

"Legs up!" Rumor yelled.

Braeden swung, wrapping his feet around the cable and pulling his body flush to the web. Rumor fired and hit the beast in its abdomen. It flipped backward and charged again, raining black blood from the wounds. Rumor growled, aimed, and fired, this time hitting it in the head.

Braeden shimmied closer to the hole. Before popping through it, he waved at the ground. He pointed to the web, pointed to the dragon, then pointed to the gates. With a cocky grin, he climbed out of the web and into unprotected space.

He motioned to Rumor and crouched on the loose structure, balancing while staying low, his attention fixed on the dragon's hind legs. A boom pulled Rumor's attention to the ground. Several people had set up launchers and were firing at the dragon's face, drawing its attention away from Rumor and Braeden.

Distraction.

Rumor slung the rifle across his chest, yanked the strap tight, and grabbed the thickest cable. He pulled his legs up and wrapped his ankles around the cable, supporting his body weight at three points instead of one. He looped his injured hand over the cable and held on with the crook of his elbow, the muscles in his arms straining.

"Nice," Braeden said. "You're good."

"Not like we have all the time in the world."

"Less talky. More shimmy." Braeden fired twice at an approaching gargoyle, setting off the familiar howl of pain followed by a crash.

Rumor slid along the cable. He was exposed and dependent on Braeden for protection. And he was oddly okay with it. Okay with having a partner in the chaos.

He managed to reach the hole in one piece and wriggled his way out, pulling the rifle off his back the second he was able. He nodded to Braeden, and they crawled across the ravaged cabling, moving as fast as they could to the outer edge of the wall.

"Will they trust that we're bringing the dragon to them?" Rumor moved to the side, keeping the back of the huge one in his line of sight.

"They'd better."

Rumor ducked as the dragon noticed them, swiping with one huge paw. Its accompanying roar threatened to blow out their eardrums.

"Move!" Braeden grabbed his arm and hauled Rumor after him. Another roar, and the whole web pitched as the dragon shifted. They stumbled, rolling down the web to the edge of the outside wall. Rumor hooked an arm around the lowest cable, halting himself with a sharp jerk that nearly pulled his arm out of its socket. He snagged Braeden's wrist as he tumbled past. Braeden planted his feet on the web to get his balance back, his face twisted in pain.

"Thanks for that," Braeden gasped. He helped Rumor up. "Big Daddy is after us. Time to run."

He leveled his gun at the dragon. Three shots later, they ran.

Blood sang in Rumor's ears, his heartbeat keeping time with his pounding feet. The dragon howled, the web shaking and rolling as it crawled after them. Braeden limped as he ran, his free hand in a tight fist.

They reached a bend in the wall, and Rumor paused long enough to spin and fire a couple of shots, not caring if he hit the dragon, just wanting it mad enough to keep following. As he spun, a human-sized gargoyle dove out of the sky, catching the side of his face with its foot and sending him stumbling to his knees on the roiling web. He fired square in its face as it banked for another pass.

The dragon was so close, the wall vibrated under his feet. About twenty meters ahead, Braeden skidded to a stop and then bobbed out of sight. The stairs. Rumor lowered his head and put on a burst of speed. He reached the stairs and jumped down three, then fired again. And again and again, heading down the stairs sideways.

The dragon appeared over the edge of the wall and took a flying leap. Cannons boomed and shells pounded into its side. It screeched and unfurled great, ragged wings that blotted out the sky. It flew high into the night, banking for another dive at the colony. The cannons fired again, most of the shots missing as it banked away in a roll.

Rumor grabbed Braeden, who sagged against the wall at the bottom of the stairs, his face pale, his breath coming out in stuttered gasps. As Rumor slung his arm around his shoulders, Braeden raised his gun and fired.

"Come on," Rumor urged. "The gate's around the corner."

They half ran, half stumbled down the length of the wall, achingly aware of the dragon behind them. Gunfire peppered the night from even farther outside the walls. The wall cannons boomed a third time. The beast roared and pulled away again, swooping up for another attack. A shell caught the dragon in the face and blew off one of its four jaws. It screamed and fell to the ground, landing in a messy heap. Bleeding and keening, it rose like a nightmare. It headed straight for Rumor and Braeden. Its eyes were wild, and blood poured from its ruined face.

The wall stretched forever. Braeden stumbled, sliding against it and toward the ground. Rumor tried to keep him upright, his own strength ebbing as pain crawled over his body. He sent a fleeting prayer out to the ether that Braeden hadn't lost too much blood or pushed himself too far. Losing the first friend Rumor had had in a long time would suck.

A flash of orange caught his attention as three sailboards flew toward them. The one in the lead pulled up next to him, a pale blond guy stretching out a hand. "Come on!"

The second rider with deep brown skin grabbed Braeden in one muscular arm and pulled him onto the board. Rumor slid his hand into the blond's and stepped behind him on the rider, wrapping his arm around the boy's waist.

The riders flew off down the wall, ahead of the dragon but not by much. The blond steered to the corner, rounding it and swerving out of the way of a marine unit assembled in front of the open gate. They sailed to safety, and the guy immediately spun the board around. "Trick!" he yelled. The lurch threw Rumor off, and he hit the ground hard on his hands and knees.

Cannon fire.

A howl.

A resounding crash that shook the ground.

Silence.

Rumor stared at the dirt between his fingers, willing his muscles to give him just a little more. A little more in case it wasn't dead yet. In case it charged through those gates—

"Target destroyed!" came the call.

The announcement gave Rumor's body permission to give out. He collapsed with a gasp of pain and relief. Braeden hit his knees next to Rumor and fell to his side, staring at the sky with a dirt-covered grin. "That was awesome."

Rumor huffed a laugh into the dust. "Yeah, it was."

Braeden tried to lift his head and gave up. "I'm in so much trouble."

"Of course you are." Sara's angry voice boomed above them.

"What in deep space were you thinking? You were supposed to be in the northeast shelter. We have trained marines for this."

They pulled themselves to sitting positions. Rumor met first Sara's face, then Bailey's. They looked angry, but maybe also proud. He couldn't tell.

Bailey exhaled and yanked her hair down, then immediately tied it up again with sharp, jerky motions. She opened and closed her mouth like she wanted to speak, then finally turned and walked away. She frowned hard at the three people who had appeared on sailboards, but said nothing to them.

Sara stared at Braeden, her expression softening from anger to confusion to resignation. "Don't…" Her voice caught, and she coughed. "Don't scare me like that again, Braeden."

She shook her head and followed her wife.

The strangers stood off to the side, cautious curiosity on their faces. Rumor locked gazes with the boy with green eyes for a heartbeat too long, something warm tugging in his chest. *Oh, he has freckles.*

Roars scraped the night, the angry cries of gargoyles billowing across the sky like the nebula overhead. Rumor finally closed his eyes and dropped back to the ground, throwing an arm over his face and letting the sounds wash over him.

"Now do you believe me?" he asked quietly.

"Yeah," Braeden murmured, his voice thoughtful and distracted. "I do."

NYX

Nyx pushed through the crowded waiting room, the muffled drone of conversation blending around her. She caught pieces of words, syllables floating in the air like seeds, snatched by updrafts and downdrafts.

The moon rumbled under her feet. It was anxious and anticipatory. As if everything was poised on a knife's edge.

She rubbed her temple, where a headache bloomed, as her brain tried to sort through the snatches of sound and overwhelming input of color and movement. The injured flooded in, fear on their faces along with blood and bruises. There were still people in the shelters, waiting for an all clear that had yet to come. Some of the staff had stayed in the medical center to take care of the newly injured, risking their own lives.

At least she didn't have to worry about seeing her abuela among the injured. When the lights flashed out their warnings, Reni had calmly gathered her crochet and was making her way downstairs when Nyx and Dahlia showed up. They'd helped her outside, where a marine transport idled at the end of the block, waiting for the elderly, small children, and disabled people. Reni had fussed at all the attention, but Nyx lingered until her abuela was settled and safe. It'd killed her to say good-bye again, and even now, tears blurred her vision as she thanked any deity who was listening that her abuela was safe.

A hand grabbed Nyx's arm. She tried to jerk away, but Dahlia cupped Nyx's jaw with her other hand, her silver eyes wide and concerned. Nyx sagged in relief and let Dahlia pull her out of the waiting room and into a side hallway. The hum of the moon followed her, but it was still at least some of a sensory break.

Dahlia wrapped her arms around Nyx and hugged her close, her voice vibrating in her chest and her throat, some words falling into Nyx's ears but not nearly enough. She was so warm and so soft and so *Dahlia*.

"I don't know what you're saying, babe." Nyx reluctantly disentangled herself from her friend.

Dahlia flapped her hands, her too-long sweater sleeves sliding over her fingers. "Sorry. You okay?"

She pushed her sleeves up her arms, her hands trembling. Nyx wanted to clasp their hands together, but would that be too far? Would that be a calming gesture, or would that send the wrong signals? Well, not the *wrong* ones, but not ones that maybe Dahlia wanted? Oh, gods, this was irritating.

Nyx smoothed a piece of Dahlia's afro back into place, which was legit and not an excuse to touch her hair. "I'm okay. You?"

"Is the moon talking to you?" Dahlia asked.

Nyx nodded. "It never stops."

Dahlia's silver eyes were metallic with a watery sheen. "That was close."

Nyx hugged her, and Dahlia held on tight, burying her face in Nyx's shoulder. They stood in the middle of the hallway, holding each other for an endless slide of seconds. A stolen moment Nyx never wanted to give back.

I love you. The words rolled around and around in her throat. Like she'd die if she didn't say them. She squeezed her eyes shut and held on tightly, part of her hoping Dahlia would just read her mind.

Eventually, Dahlia pulled away and swiped her fingers under her eyes, smudging her eyeliner. Nyx fixed that with her thumb. Dahlia leaned into her touch, or maybe Nyx imagined it. Either way, her hand curved around Dahlia's cheekbone, and Nyx just wanted to press her lips to that spot instead. Heat washed through her, and it was the most unbearable torture.

"Braeden and Rumor are here." Dahlia's hands still shook as she signed and spoke at the same time.

Nyx's stomach dropped to her toes. "Are…are they okay?"

Dahlia nodded. "Injured but alive. They…" She shook her head with a smile. "They went up on the web and lured the dragon off on their own."

"They what?" Nyx whispered.

"They saved the colony," Dahlia said. "It's completely ridiculous, but they did it."

"Wow," Nyx signed, unable to speak.

Dahlia nodded. "They're upstairs."

To be perfectly honest, Nyx wanted to stay in this quiet hallway with Dahlia until the end of time, but she nodded. Dahlia slipped her hand into Nyx's and tugged her back toward the waiting room. Nyx squeezed, and maybe Dahlia squeezed back, but she wasn't sure, and then they were back in the crowd.

The lifts were jammed with people, so they diverted to the stairs. Dahlia led her up to a room and stopped before the frosted door, her brow furrowed. She pulled her hand from Nyx's to sign, "Sounds like Bailey and Braeden are arguing."

Great. Nyx rolled her eyes and opened the door.

"…welcome for getting the big one off the web, Bailey…. gratitude is overwhelming." Braeden sat at a table, his leg resting on a chair. A bright orange bandage peeked out from the bottom of his bloody jeans.

"…was stupid…could have been killed." Bailey jerked her

hair down, and then messily tied it back up again, a sure sign she was stressed.

Nyx watched their lips, the syllables slurring together as her brain tried to process. Everyone in the room had deep vibrations, even Bailey when she was upset. They overlapped and tangled together and rattled her bones as she tried to separate them while Braeden and Bailey argued.

Braeden's eyes flicked to the door, and he brought his hands up to sign as he spoke to Bailey. Nyx shot him a smile of thanks.

"If I had a credit for every time you said that," Braeden shot back, his signs sharp and angry. Lines furrowed his brow, and a flush painted his otherwise pale cheeks. He pushed up from the table and limped to the sink, waving off help. Bailey glanced at the door, her shoulders dropping in either relief or surrender at the sight of them. Nyx wasn't sure.

Rumor watched from where he leaned against the wall, dark eyes narrowed and assessing. Two of his fingers were buddy-taped in bright blue. Cuts peppered half his face.

"Said...what?" Sara walked in, her syllables flying in and out as she brushed past Nyx and Dahlia.

"That I'm a hothead with a gun," Braeden said before Bailey could speak. His fingers flicked off the signs as if they were no big deal, but his eyes lost a shade of gold, becoming burnt and dark.

Pain flitted across Braeden's face before he turned his back on everyone, hiding his face from her. Hiding how he was the colony commander's son and more was expected from him. Hiding how he wondered if he was broken because he was seventeen and didn't care about sex when none of their friends would shut up about it. Hiding how he loved Nyx and loved Dahlia but didn't know how to translate that into a way that was comfortable for himself. Hiding so he could slip his mask back into place and smile.

She fought the urge to wrap her arms around him and bury her face between his shoulder blades. So she could inhale until he filled the spaces in her bones and she'd be the glue that held him together.

Bailey pinched the bridge of her nose and left the room. Sara watched her go with an almost sympathetic expression before turning to her son. She seemed to be weighing what she wanted to say. Sara's eyes flickered to Braeden's leg, and she sighed, tugging on his shoulder so he'd turn.

The mask was already back in place.

Sara rested one hand on his cheek. "I'm proud of what you did, but I hope you realize how lucky you are to still be alive."

Braeden nodded, a smirk pulling at one corner of his mouth. He rubbed his fist on his chest and looked appropriately apologetic.

Sara turned to Rumor. "Same goes for you, son."

Rumor's eyes widened in surprise, but he nodded and dropped his gaze to his folded arms. What little noise Nyx could hear faded to white as she watched him. His dark eyes grew glassy, but his face stayed dry. He hadn't even had a chance to grieve his father's death. His broken fingers drifted to the necklace resting over his sternum, and his blunt nails traced the coin's shape. Over and over. Around and around.

He said nothing, but his fingers said everything.

Sara glanced at her cuff, then at her son. Braeden nodded and wiggled his fingers good-bye. She left, and the room grew heavy with silence.

Nyx's brain spun. If that attack was because of what Braeden told them earlier, they needed to figure something out. The moon thrummed and rolled under her, tugging at her attention, almost begging for her to act.

"Are you going to tell him about the gargoyle?" she signed to Braeden.

Braeden hitched a shoulder, his fingers tracing an invisible pattern on the counter.

"What do we do now?" Nyx signed.

Braeden shook his head as he signed, "I don't know. I don't know what to do."

"Epsilon can't survive another attack like that." Nyx inhaled a shaky breath, her fingers trembling as she formed words.

"I know." Braeden tipped his head back and stared at the ceiling.

"Where'd those people go?" Rumor asked suddenly.

Dahlia frowned. "What people?"

"Two guys on riders grabbed us when we came off the wall," Braeden said. "I haven't seen them since we came here."

"I think they came from the forest," Rumor said. "They might be forest rebels."

Nyx's heart leaped with possibility. Forest rebels never came to the colonies. At least, not that she knew of. Tensions were so taut between the colonies and the forest that, even if they did, they wouldn't make their origins public. But if these people were? Maybe she didn't have to leave after all. She could talk to them. She needed to talk to them.

Rumor unpeeled himself from the wall. "I'm going to go find them since I have no idea what you're saying." He waved a hand between Nyx and Braeden.

Braeden held up both hands. "Wait, no, that wasn't—"

"It's cool," Rumor cut him off. "It's fine." A muscle on his jaw ticked. He looked like he wanted to say something else, but then he shook his head and grabbed his thigh sheaths from a nearby chair. He paused and stared at his bandaged fingers.

Dahlia moved over to him and held her hand out. The corner of his mouth curled up slightly, and something dark curled in the opposite direction in Nyx's stomach as Rumor handed over the sheaths. Dahlia squatted in front of him and buckled one around each of his thighs. Nyx's throat was made of dust.

She was just being friendly, right. She knew Rumor, and Rumor was having a bad day so Dahlia was just being friendly. Right. With her face *right there* as she snugged the buckles tight around his thighs, her slim fingers skimming his pants as she made sure everything was secure.

Nyx stared at the floor, chewing the inside of her cheek until it bled. Who was she fooling? Dahlia had just broken up with Colt. Here was her ex-boyfriend from before—someone she'd only broken up with because of distance, so who knew how she still felt about him. Plus, he was attractive.

Even though Dahlia was bi, maybe she preferred masculine people. Nyx was anything but. She was short and chubby and loved her makeup and nail polish and fun socks. Maybe Nyx was hoping for something that would never happen. Maybe this was the universe's way of showing her she was being selfish by wanting *more* than their friendship.

Dahlia stood, speaking to Rumor, but it was lost to the walls and the way Rumor's eyes softened in familiarity. He smiled thinly and left without a glance back. Braeden moved to go after Rumor, but Dahlia pressed a hand to his chest.

"He's fine," Dahlia said, but her eyes betrayed the lie, and Nyx's heart fluttered like a helpless bird trapped in a cage.

JUDE

"Hey!" The blond woman who'd eyeballed Jude and Trick at the gates strode up to them. She looked decidedly pissed. Jude opened his mouth to say something, but Yi-Min stepped in front of the boys, intercepting her.

"Ma'am?" Yi-Min said, lifting their chin.

The woman stopped short, her eyes narrowing. Every colony was different when it came to the forest communities. Some flat-out hated them. Some were indifferent. Some carried on secret trade. Jude had no idea how Epsilon felt about them.

"What's your business here?" the woman asked.

Yi-Min smiled—something they didn't do much—and offered a hand to shake. "Yi-Min Tsai. Perhaps we can talk? I have urgent business with your commander."

The woman relaxed and smiled, the angry red clouds fading. She accepted Yi-Min's hand and shook it. "Of course. If you'll follow me."

Gunshots echoed throughout the colony, and Jude flinched as clouds of yellow fear and red anger clashed. Trick rested his hand on Jude's shoulder, his warmth and proximity providing the anchor Jude needed when the crowds of emotions ran too intense.

Marines swept down the roadway, sleek automata following. Faces peeked from windows and doors, staring at the hole in the web, flinching away from the gunfire.

"Come on." Trick tugged Jude away and headed farther into the colony.

"Who was that?" Jude glanced back at the blonde talking to Yi-Min like an old friend—all smiles and relaxed posture.

"I don't know, but I'm taking a window of opportunity when I see it," Trick muttered.

Jude tried not to gape like an outsider, but it was hard not to stare at the fern-covered buildings and adamantine webbing that stretched far above his head. He'd never seen the inside of a colony; he'd been born in the forest. He'd been expecting stark precision and metal and combat fatigues. He'd imagined the colonists wore varying shades of gray to match their surroundings. He didn't expect the blanket of vivid plants and the bright colors of head scarves or patchwork coats or striped knee-high socks.

Trick shook his head, his expression hard. "We need to find out if Vala's really here before Reaper sends another attack."

Jude nodded. "And Yi-Min wants the survivor."

Trick stayed silent, teal eyes bright and jumping everywhere. "Where are those two dudes we helped? One of them was wearing a military jacket. We could start with them. See what they know."

Jude shrugged. "Medical center, probably? They were pretty banged up."

He pointed up the road to the big red plus sign decorating one entire wall of a building. As they walked closer, he realized the red was flowers surrounded by a blanket of white ivy. Clever.

He tried not to think about how the guy he'd helped had watched him as the dust settled, dark eyes mixed with curiosity and distrust.

The doors to the medical center opened, and the same guy walked out, flexing one hand into a fist and out again with a grimace.

Jude's breath caught, and he stopped walking. "Oh."

Beautiful. There was no other way to describe him. Even beat up and seeming like he wanted to cut the world to ribbons, he was elegant and fluid.

And he was the darkest red Jude had ever seen.

"Looks like your type showed up," Trick commented.

Jude elbowed him. "But not yours."

Trick snickered and then cleared his throat as the guy's attention swung to them. He crossed the street toward them, eyes pinned on Jude. Jude's heart bounced around his rib cage like a newborn chimera, unsteady and rambunctious.

"You're cheating, aren't you?" Trick murmured.

"Shut up," Jude said.

"Is he *I want to jump your bones* red?" Trick teased.

"I regret ever telling you what the colors mean." Jude's cheeks heated, and he shifted uncomfortably. Among other colors like anger and uncertainty, the guy was the particular vibrant shade of red that meant *oh hi*, and it made Jude's stomach free-fall to his toes. He swallowed hard, his breath stuttering.

"Remember, we need to find the survivor," Trick murmured. "No flirting with the locals."

"Take your own advice," Jude whispered without breaking his stare. Trick grunted.

"Hey," the guy said as he neared. The intensity with which he met Jude's eyes made Jude want to simultaneously hide and push the guy against a wall and kiss him.

"Hi," Jude said in what he hoped was a neutral voice.

Trick made an amused sound and stuck out his hand. "I'm Trick. This is my brother Jude. Usually he speaks more."

"Brother?" he asked as they shook hands, his glance flicking back and forth between them. It was a familiar confusion. Brown skin versus white skin. Blue eyes versus green eyes. Brown hair versus blond hair. The only physical feature Jude and Trick shared were freckles.

"I'm adopted," Jude said immediately. "We're the same age." Which was a pointless thing to say. *Get it to together.*

"I'm Rumor. Thanks for what you did back there. If you guys hadn't come along, things might've ended up differently."

Jude grinned. He shoved his hands in his pockets for lack of anything else to do with them. "Y'all were handling it okay."

"Until you were almost dragon food." Trick folded his arms, examining Rumor.

Rumor lifted his chin in silent challenge. Red flared brighter for a moment, then settled around him. Trick's violet darkened, reddening around the edges. Jude huffed at the alpha bird displays of anger and tapped his brother on the arm. "Go see if Yi-Min needs any help."

Yi-Min needed absolutely no help, and they both knew that. Trick nodded anyway and grinned at Rumor. "Nice to meet you. Glad you're okay."

He mock-punched Jude in the arm and tapped on the hidden cuff under his sleeve as he backed away.

Jude shifted his weight and put on his laziest smile for Rumor. He could use the colors wrapping around Rumor's long body to his advantage to find the survivor, and also to find out if this guy knew anything about a chimera in captivity. "Is your friend okay? The other guy you were with."

"His leg's a little messed up, but he'll be fine," Rumor answered.

Jude's attention darted to the swirl of black snaking through the red surrounding Rumor. Everyone had so many secrets tonight. "How about you?"

Rumor held up his hand. It trembled. His pinkie and ring finger on his left hand were swollen and purplish. "Broke these, but the doc repaired them okay. She said the swelling should go down in a few hours."

"Nice." Jude cleared his throat. Usually he was better at small talk, but the way Rumor stared at him glued his tongue to the roof of his mouth and made him forget every language he knew. "So all that at HUB2, huh?"

Rumor's eyes narrowed, and the red darkened to anger with tinges of indigo and yellow that weren't entirely clear to Jude. Loss and fear, maybe. "Yeah, it was a lot."

"Sorry, I didn't mean to…offend," Jude said quickly.

Rumor nodded, the movement jerky as he looked everywhere but Jude. "It's fine. I just…I just wanted to thank you for helping." He blinked a few times. "I need to go."

He walked away, his spine straight, his shoulders pulling upward. Jude's fingertips tingled as he watched. Should he go after him, or should he just leave it and find the survivor? Find Vala?

The blue swirling around Rumor in bands of sadness pulled Jude along the path after him. He caught up easily, matching those long legs stride for stride. Rumor glanced at him but said nothing, sniffing once.

"Did you know anyone at HUB2?" Jude asked in a quiet tone.

Rumor nodded, his lips pressed together in a thin line.

"I'm sorry," Jude said.

Rumor's throat bobbed as he swallowed, his eyes glassy. He veered off the path and into a garden inhabiting the space between two buildings. Ferns crawled up the walls to either side and curled over their heads, offering the illusion of privacy. Jude stopped just inside the entrance as Rumor sagged against one of the walls and rubbed his hands over his face. He took a shuddering breath, as if he couldn't get enough air.

Fist-sized flowers the colors of jealousy and fear drooped around him. Rumor plucked one from its stem and twirled it between his fingers. Golden nectar ran into his palm. He started to speak a number of times, but then shook his head. Eventually, he said, "My dad died tonight."

His voice caught at the end, a strangled sob finally breaking out of his chest.

Jude stood still. It was pain he understood well. The hard set of Rumor's shoulders reminded Jude of himself in the months after his boyfriend had died. So much loss and anger and confusion. Wanting to lash out at the creatures who'd killed the boy he'd given his heart to. If it hadn't been for Trick, Jude might've snapped and gone after them alone, sacrificing his life or doing something he couldn't take back.

"You don't have to talk about it," Jude said. *You don't have to tell me about your dad, because I know it's a punch to the gut anytime you think about him right now.* And what was Jude doing, trying to needle this guy for information, when his dad must've died in the dragon attack only minutes ago? How could Rumor even be this calm? Jude rubbed his forehead, prepared to leave Rumor alone with his grief.

"It happened so fast," Rumor said. A tear ran down his cheek and dripped off the edge of his chin, but he kept his gaze firmly on the flower in his hand as his fingers curled around the petals. "I couldn't…" He crushed the flower in his fist and threw it down. It fell—a mangled mass of green and yellow—and hit the mossy ground just as quietly as the tears that ran down Rumor's face. "I couldn't stop it. Couldn't stop them. And they…they…" Rumor slid down the wall to sit, his forearms on his bony knees and his head hanging, dark curly hair falling over his shoulders and around his face in a curtain, hiding his features from view.

Tears of sympathy tried to crawl up Jude's throat, but he swallowed them back. He picked his way across the garden, making just enough noise to signal he was there, and sat carefully next to Rumor. He had no idea why. He had a job to do, but he couldn't leave this guy to cry in an alleyway alone. Especially not tonight.

After a moment of sitting in silence, Jude curled a hand around Rumor's bicep. He forced himself to focus on helping and not on admiring the warmth under his touch or the way Rumor's muscles curved and shifted as Rumor raised his head.

"If you want, I can go." Jude offered a small smile. "But you looked like you could use a stranger."

A sad laugh broke out of Rumor's lips. "A stranger?"

Jude's grin grew, and he hitched a shoulder. "Sometimes strangers are easier to talk to than someone who knows you."

Rumor's dark eyes darted around Jude's face. Jude hesitated, then reached over and moved Rumor's hair out of the way, pushing it behind his ear.

"I'm sorry about your dad," Jude whispered. "I lost my boyfriend about a year ago to an attack."

Rumor stared at the ground. "The gargoyles that took down HUB2 and killed my dad are still there," he said in a flat tone. "The ones that attacked here were some of them. It was the same dragon."

Jude froze. The loss and rage swirling around Rumor made sense. "You're the survivor."

Rumor nodded, lines appearing between his eyebrows. He didn't seem to notice the shock coursing through Jude's body. Of course, the first guy to make Jude sit up and take notice since Adam was the sole survivor of one of the most horrific massacres in Saharan history.

How much of this attraction curling in Jude's gut was real, and how much was sympathy?

Damn his inability to see his own colors.

"Nice tattoo." Rumor cleared his throat, blue sadness creeping in around the red and black.

Of course he would notice the gryphon on Jude's forearm. Black like George with widespread wings that wrapped around his arm. The design was marred by bruising from earlier, which made it more sinister. "Thanks."

"Why a gryphon? Was that the first thing you killed?"

Jude swallowed his surprise and managed to keep his expression neutral. "First thing I killed?"

"Lots of folks get their first kill as a tattoo."

He'd honestly never heard that before. Maybe this was some sort of colonist custom Trick should've told him about. He kept his shrug lazy. "I just like gryphons."

"Okay?" Rumor ran his tongue over his lower lip and glanced away.

"Do you have a first kill tattoo?" Jude asked quickly even though the words tasted like blood coming out of his mouth.

Rumor exhaled slowly. "No. I...I have a solid band around my calf for every year since my mom died."

Jude's heart tightened. "How many bands?"

"Seven." The blue swirling around him flickered and darkened for a blink, and Jude wished he could sweep that cloud of sadness away from him. But oh, how he wanted to tease that *red* forward. The beautiful red that swirled with the anger. The red that showed passion and lust and attraction. It kept flaring brighter the longer Rumor stayed with Jude.

Rumor tipped his head back against the wall. "How many bands would you have?"

Rumor assumed Jude's parents were dead. He wasn't wrong. So many orphans on Sahara. "Since my parents died? Eight." Jude cleared his throat. "A cave-in got them both when I was ten."

What he didn't mention was the marines who were hunting chimera that night. What he didn't mention was the bombs thrown into chimera tunnel entrances to drive them to the surface, where they'd be met with guns and cages. What he didn't mention was his parents trying to get the youngest chimera to safety so they didn't grow up in colonist captivity like lab rats or zoo animals.

"You're a year older than me," Rumor said in quiet response.

Jude shrugged. He kept his mouth shut, even though all he wanted to do was ask Rumor a million questions. He'd found the survivor, and he was supposed to be convincing him to come back to Azrou with them. But all he wanted to do was sit with this boy, this broken boy, in this slice of frozen time under a bank of ferns hiding them from the rest of the cosmos.

"I know where you're from," Rumor murmured, so low Jude barely caught it.

Jude's heart hammered as Rumor rolled his head to the side to look at him. The slight puffiness of his eyes were the only indication to the outside world he'd been crying. Jude marveled at Rumor's ability to bottle up his emotions and lock them away. Even his colors were restrained. Almost as if he'd been able to physically pull them closer to his body.

"We have twenty-three hours to dayside," Rumor said before Jude could respond, his tone even but his red-rimmed eyes urgent. "You know as well as I do when the gargoyles go underground at suns rise, we'll lose them. They could come up *anywhere* next nightside."

Jude winced at the word *gargoyle*. Also, Rumor didn't know the biggest reason time was so urgent, and it was far more than just a countdown to dayside. They had twenty-three hours to stop Reaper from another massacre. He'd try Epsilon again or move on to another HUB2 colony in his rage. "And what do you think I can do?"

Rumor scratched the darkening scruff along his sharp jawline. "Why are you here? Why did you come to Epsilon?"

Vala, his mind said. "Need to find a friend," his mouth said.

"And me?" Rumor asked.

Jude broke eye contact, staring at the opposite wall and tracing the curling vines with his gaze. "I didn't know who you were when I said hi to you, or when I rescued you and your friend."

For all Jude knew, Rumor's friend with the military jacket was a marine and, at any moment, Jude would be arrested. But he found he didn't much care as he remembered the roll of Rumor's shoulders as he'd walked, and the way his long fingers twitched near the handle of his blade.

Jude took a deep breath, mentally tiptoeing onto a tightrope. "Maybe the—" He couldn't say it— "creatures have a specific goal in mind." He affected nonchalance as he still avoided eye contact. "Maybe…if someone were to try talking to them to find out what they want…"

He picked up the mangled flower Rumor had thrown, peeling its petals off one by one and smoothing them out on his thigh.

"Talking?" Rumor's tone fell flat.

Tiptoe. Tiptoe. Tiptoe. Jude's heart raced. One wrong word and Rumor could get mad and bolt. Or, worse, rat him out. He continued smoothing out petals. "Yeah, some of them are pretty intelligent, actually."

There it was. Ten minutes in the colony and Jude had already spilled the one secret that would get him killed if it fell on the wrong ears. Colony military was always on the hunt for dissidents. People like him who fought for the end of the war. Who existed in peace with the chimera.

Jude risked a glance. Rumor stared at him for an eternal moment, his eyes black and unreadable. They reminded him of Angel's eyes. Fathomless and constantly assessing. Betraying nothing and everything in the same breath.

Jude stood on his tightrope, on the verge of spilling everything. *Do you know Vala? Is she alive? Is she safe? By the way, I'm friends with a few chimera, and I also think you're really hot.*

Jude pulled a small rag from his pocket and wiped his palm. He reached for Rumor's wrist. Rumor froze but didn't fight or pull away. With careful, gentle motions, Jude cleaned the nectar off. "These flowers are bitter," he said. "Not that you were going to eat them, but the nectar can sting open wounds."

"Good to know." Rumor's voice tightened, softened. His pulse hammered under Jude's fingertips.

Jude released Rumor's wrist, his skin tingling and his heart climbing his windpipe. He expected Rumor to get up or move away, but he stayed. Up close, those nearly black eyes had flecks of brown and gold in them. Those eyes darted to Jude's mouth and back up again, his lips parting. A smile pulled one side of

Jude's mouth before he could stop it. In a world where every moment could be the last, people had to grab what they wanted now.

What Jude should want versus what he wanted pulled at him. He should want to get back to his mission, because Rumor stood on the other side of a wide gap in ideology. What he wanted was to close this space between them and follow that cautious interest in Rumor's eyes. But a bridge made solely of exploring lips and wandering hands would never be strong enough.

"Where did you come from?" Rumor's fingers curled around Jude's wrist, his thumb brushing across Jude's skin.

"Why does it matter?" Jude asked, his voice gentle. Their shoulders pressed together, and more of Rumor's sadness gave way to lust, but Jude didn't need the colors. Rumor's eyes and the feathering of his jaw said enough.

Heat rolled through his limbs while his brain beat out warning after warning after warning, all of which he ignored. Jude's fatal flaw was that he fell too fast, too hard. The fault lay in the colors. A vibrant red the precise shade of attraction coated Rumor's brown skin like paint. Jude's heart pounded, and nerves prickled down his body.

"I'm here looking for a friend," Jude repeated.

The statement hung in the blossom-scented air between them, its many meanings wrapped in layers of uncertainty.

"You're from the forest," Rumor whispered. He stated it. He didn't ask it. His fingers flexed around Jude's wrist, but he didn't let go.

Jude hesitated, then nodded. One secret was out. The other wouldn't screw him any further. Blood whooshed in his ears as he tried to read Rumor.

"Why did you help us?" Rumor's eyes dropped to Jude's lips. His eyelashes were like star-points.

"You were in trouble," Jude answered.

"I thought the forest rebels loved the beasts." Rumor leaned closer, his eyes full of challenge and knowledge. The barest of smiles pulled at his lips, knife-thin and razor sharp.

He was the most beautiful red Jude had ever seen.

Jude let out a tense breath, his lips wet and his heart pounding. "Not every beast."

A scream split the night.

RUMOR

Rumor jerked away from Jude like he'd been burned, his heart hammering, as the scream scraped across his skin like claws. While he wouldn't mind pushing Jude to the ground and kissing him, letting Jude poke around in his mind was a different matter. And he'd just *cried* in front of this guy. This guy from the forest.

Those people lived with the beasts. They were on *their side*. This boy, this…breathtaking boy thought they were something to be negotiated with. Respected. Treated as equals. But *gods*, that easy smile wrapped around Rumor like a warm blanket. He couldn't remember the last time he'd seen someone and his brain said, *That one. I want that one*.

He held Jude's brilliant green eyes for one more heartbeat, then scrambled up and took off at a run. People looked up at the web, around at the sky, down at the ground, searching for the source of the shouting and terror.

Gunfire.

Rumor's heart rammed his sternum as he cut through an alley, crushing plants as he ran, and paused at a corner. Jude caught up, his brow furrowed. He pointed down the street to nothing. "That way."

"How do you know?"

Jude licked his lips and glanced away. "I can see the fear."

"Rumor!" Braeden called.

Rumor spun around as Braeden and Nyx approached. Braeden jogged with a limp every other step, his lips in a thin line. His eyes darted between Jude and Rumor, then he grinned at Jude. "Braeden."

"Jude," Jude answered.

Nyx smiled when Braeden fingerspelled Jude's name. "Nyx."

"Gargoyles," Rumor insisted.

"Leftovers found in the colony, probably," Braeden said.

A small group of people had gathered around a shelter entrance. It was nothing more than metal doors in a frame on the ground. A set of steps descended into darkness.

Dahlia spun away from the group when she noticed Rumor, her eyes wide. She threw her arms around his neck, and he stumbled back in surprise, his arms sweeping around her waist on instinct. His heart lurched, emotions pinging around his insides. First, that whatever-it-was with Jude. Now this.

Dahlia spoke into his shoulder. "Gargoyles got into one of the shelters and grabbed some folks, then went back down into their tunnels."

"How did they break into a shelter?" Braeden asked in disbelief. "Those are dug into solid bedrock. It would take…a really long time to tunnel through that."

"What's going on?" Nyx asked.

"Colt went after them. To try to get people back." Dahlia pulled away, sniffing. "His uncle is trying to organize a party to go after him."

Rumor frowned and released Dahlia's waist, hands trembling. He didn't want to let go of her, and he didn't want to ask, but—"Who's Colt?"

"Colton Stewart. My ex. He saw you kill the dragon and he

knows who you are and we just broke up, so his ridiculous ass thought that…" She waved a hand in the air as she trailed off.

"You have got to be kidding me," Rumor said. "Where are the marines?"

"They won't go down. Gargoyle tunnels are a maze. They're considering him lost. All of them lost." Dahlia's eyes filled with tears again. "They said it's suicide to go down there."

"I can help navigate the tunnels," Jude said quietly.

Rumor shot him a look. Of course he could. "To deep space with everything tonight," he muttered and stalked toward the hole. Braeden grabbed at Rumor's arm, and Rumor pushed him away. "You're staying here. You can hardly walk, and it's pitch black down there."

Braeden's eyes narrowed. "Don't want me weighing you down? I only helped you kill a dragon."

"No." Rumor pulled out of his grasp and turned away.

Braeden latched onto his arm again. "Then what?"

"I don't want to watch any more friends die!"

Braeden's jaw slackened and his eyes widened. Rumor spun away, breathing hard, his hands shaking.

"What just happened?" Nyx asked.

"Rumor," Dahlia whispered. She followed him, holding a glowing wrist cuff and a black handgun with an extended barrel. It was sleek and lightweight. He examined it for a second, then raised his eyebrows in question.

"The tunnels will be too narrow to use your blade," she said quickly. "This is a new pistol with a built-in silencer. They're calling them chaos guns, and they've been testing them here and at Theta colony." Lines appeared between her brows, and she blew out a shaky breath. "You know gargoyles better than half the assholes here. Find him." She spoke firmly, but her eyes were bright and pleading.

Rumor grabbed the cuff and nodded. "I'll do what I can," he mumbled as he focused on snapping the cuff on his forearm. It was like the computer cuffs everyone wore, but this was a light and nothing more than that.

Going underground into danger to rescue his ex-girlfriend's ex-boyfriend. He almost laughed at the utter absurdity.

Braeden watched Rumor with an indefinable expression. Rumor wanted to say something, something to wipe away what he'd shouted, but words tumbled uselessly around his brain.

"Who are you?" a new voice shouted from the group around the shelter.

Rumor sighed. He didn't have time for this. Colt didn't have time for this.

If he was even still alive down there.

The guy in front of Rumor must have been Colt's uncle. He stared at Rumor with barely concealed rage.

"He's terrified," Jude murmured. He stood behind Rumor. "He's angry and scared."

Rumor didn't ask how he knew that—he didn't have time. "I'm Rumor."

Colt's uncle curled a lip. "You're the kid who put ridiculous ideas in my nephew's head."

"No, sir, but I am the kid who's going to save his ass if you'll move out of the way." Rumor sidestepped him, but a big hand landed on Rumor's shoulder. He jerked away, his glare on the uncle and his fingers flexing on the gun. "Don't. Touch. Me."

Braeden held his hand in the air over Rumor's wrist without touching him. He set his other hand on the uncle's shoulder. "Hey, Henry. Here's the thing." He angled himself toward Colt's uncle. "Rumor's going to go get Colt. You and I both know that Colt likes to do stupid things. If you want to go with Rumor and help"—Braeden leveled a *don't you dare protest* stare at Rumor—"you can, but you let him lead. He knows what he's doing. I've seen this guy in action, and he kicks ass."

"Why don't we wait for marines?" Henry sized Rumor up with a sneer.

Rumor shrugged. "They don't care. They're going to let him die."

"Rumor," Dahlia whispered, panicked.

Why in deep space was he even doing this? These people were no one to him. He stood to lose everything if he went down there.

Braeden offered a tight smile. His gaze flicked to Jude, who stood behind Rumor's shoulder.

"No need to send a big party down there," Jude said. "But the three of us should be able to get Colt back no problem."

"Four." Nyx rested a silver shotgun on her shoulders. It looked old, maybe an early Revenant model.

Rumor frowned at Braeden.

Braeden grinned. "Why are you looking at me? She's a badass. She doesn't need anyone's permission to go."

Rumor hitched a shoulder. "If you're coming, fine. But we're wasting time."

"Rumor." Dahlia grabbed his arm, tears tracing her cheeks. "Bring him back, please."

A thousand responses crawled up his throat. All he managed was a nod as he swallowed.

Rumor headed into the shelter. The metal steps led down to a wide-open room lined with shelves of supplies. He waited, surveying the space, as the others crept down after him. Panel lighting flickered on as they moved into the room, revealing the gaping hole on the far wall. He touched the edges with his good hand. They were perfectly smooth. No blast patterns or jagged corners. Just smooth, polished stone laced with the silvery adamantine the HUBs mined up from the depths of Sahara. The tunnel beyond the opening was dark. It was like stepping into a black hole. A gargoyle could be standing at the other end and they wouldn't be able to see it until it was too late.

"How did they do this?" he muttered to himself. He closed his eyes and listened. No growling, scraping, gunshots, or shouting. Just eerie silence. Tingles raised the hair on his arms.

Several years ago, he'd watched a gargoyle put its palm to the rock, and minutes later, several more appeared as though it had summoned them. What secrets traveled through the rock of this moon?

Rumor shook his head, an unsettled feeling twisting his gut as he climbed into the gargoyle tunnel. The walls were as smooth as the hole, as if they'd been carved and polished eons ago instead of now. "This doesn't make any sense."

Rumor glanced back and watched Jude climb through the hole. The guy didn't look surprised at the state of the tunnel, but he also avoided Rumor's eyes as he pointed. "They kept to the right."

Fresh gouges marred the surface of the right-hand wall of the tunnel, probably from claws or bullets. The wrist light bathed the walls in a blue glow, illuminating the path only a few meters ahead of them. Any imperfections in the tunnel's surface cast long shadows, like fingers pointing them deeper into the darkness.

"Colt!" Henry's voice echoed down the rock walls, bouncing away and pinging back to them in a distorted echo.

Rumor stopped and counted to five before he spoke, his voice low and hard. "If you would like to draw the gargoyles to us, please keep yelling for him. Otherwise, shut up."

"Excuse me?"

He spoke as quietly as he could, drawing patience from only the cosmos knew where. "They can hear through rock. Your voice echoes across the rock. That means every gargoyle within about a five-kilometer radius of this spot knows where you're standing right now. If you want a chance at finding Colt, then you be as quiet as you can. Otherwise, we're dead."

"I thought you killed thirty of the bastards when you were five years old."

Oh, for the love of… Rumor rolled his eyes as he turned back around, raising the gun again. "It was six of them, and I was ten. Now, be quiet. Please."

The tunnel sloped down, twisting around. At one point, it narrowed so much, they had to go through one at a time and Rumor had to duck after bumping his head on the ceiling. How did gargoyles get people through here? His shoulders scraped the walls on both sides, and the moon pressed in on him, reminding him of the meters of solid rock above his head, blocking the open sky and trapping him underground with monsters. Nyx kept stopping and pressing her hand to the rock, lines between her brows.

The tunnel took a sharp turn and opened into a small cavern. Maybe twenty people could fit in the space. Three tunnels branched off the cavern, all glimmering with the same metallic sheen. "Did Colt have a gun?"

"Maybe," Henry answered.

Rumor traced the gouges in the wall leading into the far-left tunnel. They were cold and jagged. "This way."

They were about ten meters into the narrow tunnel when shouts rang out.

"Colt!" Henry yelled and pushed past, his light swinging as he ran.

Rumor swallowed a curse and followed. Flashes of gunfire bounced off the walls ahead, the shots growing louder, echoing and overlapping each other as they got closer. They burst into another small cavern. Nyx pushed Rumor out of the way as a sleek, all-black gargoyle crashed into the wall where their heads had been. Its short wings fluttered, filling the cavern with rattling noises. More rattles answered it all around them. Shrieks bounced off the walls, echoing and sending shivers across his skin.

Claws clicked and slid across the rock. Outside of the halo glow of wrist lights, the gargoyles were impossible to see. Rumor collided with Nyx as he tried to move away from the rattling wings. His broken fingers hit her arm, and he hissed as pain flared into his hand.

Nyx raised her shotgun, tracking something through the air.

She fired twice, and a body crashed to the ground. The echoes of the shots reverberated through the tunnel, filling his ears with a high-pitched whine. He put a hand on the wall to steady himself, stretching the injury on his ribs. He held his side and tried to get his bearings.

"How many?" Jude's voice was far away and anxious.

"I count at least four more." Rumor fired at a gargoyle hurtling toward them. "Three."

"Rumor!" Jude shouted as another gargoyle leaped from Rumor's left, too close for Rumor to get off a shot in time.

A growl rolled out of an adjoining tunnel. A gryphon-like gargoyle, black and winged with a beaked face and a long body, slammed into the attacking gargoyle with the ferocity of a guard dog. Its wings flared and flapped as they rolled, and the same grating, rumbling noises came from its chest that he'd heard from the creatures on the web.

A gargoyle attacking another gargoyle.

A gargoyle had just saved him.

What in all of deep space was happening tonight?

It wasn't possible. Maybe it just wanted the kill for itself. Rumor raised his gun at the fighting creatures.

Jude grabbed Rumor's wrist, sending the shot wide. "Don't shoot him!"

"*Him?*" Rumor repeated in shock.

"Please don't shoot him," Jude pleaded, his fingers firm around Rumor's wrist. He held another hand up at Nyx, his eyes wide in the glow bouncing off the walls. Rumor glanced down at Jude's arm, the gryphon tattoo twisted by shadows and light and Jude's muscles.

"You just like gryphons," Rumor said in a flat tone.

The gryphon gargoyle wrapped one large paw around the other gargoyle's neck and shoved, breaking it with a sickening crunch. The gargoyle fell in a heap and the gryphon turned, its large eyes solid black and mere centimeters from Rumor's face.

It stared at him, a rumbling noise rolling out of its throat. Rumor tried to pull frce, but Jude tightened his hold.

"Thank you, George, now get out of here before you get shot," Jude said, over his shoulder.

Rumor couldn't breathe. This had to be a nightmare. Any moment Jude was going to peel off his skin and reveal he was a gargoyle, right? This couldn't be real.

The gryphon growled at them and clicked its beak, shifting in place as it swung its massive head from side to side as if listening for more gargoyles.

"I really don't care," Jude snapped at the gryphon.

Rumor stopped struggling, his body going cold. He'd heard a gargoyle speak human language earlier tonight, and now a human—someone he'd almost made out with in an alleyway—understanding a gargoyle. Ringing filled his ears. "You know their language?"

"What is he doing?" Nyx asked.

"Talking to it." The words fell out of Rumor's mouth, but he still couldn't believe what he was witnessing. His world had gone so far over the line, it was back on the other side.

Nyx didn't respond, but he was too stunned to check if she'd understood him or not.

Jude released Rumor and turned, facing the creature and keeping his body in front of Rumor and Nyx. "Please," he said. "Go find Angel. We're running out of time."

Rumor stepped back. Every muscle in his arm pulled taut with the desire to punch Jude square in the face. "What the...?"

Jude ignored him, his attention on the gargoyle he'd somehow understood. The gryphon, who apparently answered to 'George,' clicked its beak and ruffled its cowl, then backed away, its body dissolving into the darkness of the cavern.

"What was that?" Rumor grabbed Jude's arm. Anger and alarm rolled through him in waves.

"Accepting some help." Jude yanked his arm free.

"From *them*?"

Jude's eyes narrowed, and he stepped into Rumor's space. "My parents taught me never to kill unless absolutely necessary."

Rumor snorted. "Yeah well, mine taught me not to die, so I guess we both learned something valuable when we were little."

A very human scream echoed down the tunnel.

Rumor headed in the direction Henry had run. Could all forest rebels talk to the beasts? Did they have an alliance of sorts? Were the creatures even smart enough for that? Was that why Jude came down into the tunnels — to protect his friends?

This one helped you even though it knew you'd shoot it. His stomach cramped at the thought they'd been saved by a gargoyle.

"Where did that scream come from?" Nyx asked.

Another scream answered her and they headed to the right, into a branching tunnel wide enough for them to spread out a little. Rumor jogged ahead, gun up, eyes straining to see beyond the glow of the wrist cuff.

"Rumor!" Nyx yelled the warning right as claws dug into his shoulders and pulled him back with a sharp jerk. Cold, spindly arms wrapped around his neck, and hissing filled his entire world. All the heat in his body surged to his hands, the anger and betrayal he felt toward Jude condensing to a single point. He jammed the gun under his other arm and squeezed the trigger.

The arms dropped away. He spun and shot it in the head before it could get up again. Dark blood spattered the rock, and Rumor's lip curled at the slender, pebbled body perfectly adapted to narrow tunnels. Rumor glared at Jude, daring him to comment. Jude looked away.

"You okay?" Nyx called from farther back up the tunnel, shining a light at them.

Rumor gave her a thumbs-up and took off again, putting distance between himself and the others. Jude yelled for him to slow down. Rumor ignored him, skidding around a corner where two gargoyles had a guy about Rumor's age pinned against the wall. The light from Rumor's wrist cuff picked up a lot of blood dripping from the guy's face, arms, and midsection. "Colt?"

"Help." Colt's voice was raspy and thin, choked with fear.

He aimed and squeezed the trigger twice.

One

Two

Colt dropped to the ground between the gargoyle corpses.

"Over here!" Rumor yelled, not caring who or what heard him. After all, Jude was a gargoyle whisperer. He knelt next to Colt. "Come on, man, open your eyes."

"Who are you?"

"Name's Rumor. Can you walk?"

He coughed, and red stained his teeth. "The others are dead. The other colonists. I tried…"

Rumor closed his eyes for a moment, swallowing the helplessness in his throat. "Shut up. Dahlia's going to kick your ass for this, and I'm not gonna stop her." Rumor pulled him to his feet, slinging his arm around Rumor's shoulders. "Come on, you don't want to die down here, do you?"

"No."

"Good. Me neither. Now move." Rumor wrapped his arm around Colt's waist and gritted his teeth against the pain. "Jude! Nyx! I found him!"

"Dad," Colt gasped. He was pale and sickly, his eyes fluttering. "I saw my dad."

"Stop talking," Rumor gritted out.

"No. He was…" A wheezing cough that spat more blood from his lips. "He was here."

"Rumor!"

"Jude!"

Jude rounded the corner, his eyes wide. Blood spotted his face, but Rumor couldn't tell if it was his or someone else's. "Let me take him to the surface."

"I've—"

"Cut it out," Jude snapped. "And cover me."

"Don't want to kill your friends?" Rumor asked. "Prefer I do it?"

Jude didn't answer.

Rumor transferred Colt to Jude's arms and headed back through the tunnels to where he'd met 'George,' gun drawn. He nodded at Nyx. Her eyes widened. "Is he…"

"He's alive," Rumor said, holding his light up so she could see his lips. "Where's Henry?"

She pointed back down the tunnel. "He spotted three gargoyles and went after them."

"Deep space. Come on." He motioned for Nyx to come with him and met Jude's eyes. "Take him up. Make sure he gets to a medic. We'll meet you there."

Jude nodded and headed for the surface, his eyes dark and his hands bloody.

"Henry!" Rumor yelled as they headed deeper. Nyx dragged her hand along the rock, her brow furrowed in concentration. "Henry!" he yelled, his voice echoing down the tunnel and doubling back to them.

No answer.

Cold formed in the pit of Rumor's stomach. He held the light to his mouth and faced Nyx. "You sure he came this way?" She nodded. He closed his eyes and took a deep breath. "Stay behind me."

"Why?"

"Please." The tunnel was too quiet. Too empty. Scratches lined the walls and the floor in haphazard lines. Adamantine dust glittered in the light like a trail leading deeper into the moon's core. A metallic smell even laced the air, turning his stomach. HUB2 had smelled the same way.

Nyx made a surprised noise. She peeled her hand from the wall and backed away a step. The smear of blood across the iridescent tunnel wall was too red and too fresh. His heart plummeted to his toes. Nyx looked at him, eyes big. "That's not good."

"No." He swallowed, and they pushed forward. If they didn't find a body in the next twenty meters, they were turning back.

They found what was left of him in eighteen.

Rumor stared at the remains, the anger in his body morphing into cold detachment. Too often he'd stood at a scene like this.

"Come on." He pulled Nyx back the direction they came. She followed, her mouth pressed in a thin line.

Jude and Braeden were waiting when Rumor cleared the tunnel. Neither said a word when they saw his face. Braeden closed his eyes for a moment, then wrapped his arms around Nyx.

Rumor handed off the gun and the cuff and walked away. Unfamiliar eyes watched him go. Unfamiliar buildings loomed over him. This wasn't even his home, and he'd just defended it twice and why? So he could witness more death, more destruction, more chaos? Hadn't he seen enough tonight? When would it be enough, and when could he close his eyes?

It would never be enough.

His knees shook, and he stumbled to one side. He grabbed for the coin under his shirt, using its comforting shape to keep him from flying apart, scattering in pieces across the moon and into the stars.

Peace. What peace?

JUDE

"Rumor!"

"Go away, Jude."

"Rumor, please stop." Jude darted in front of him and grabbed his arm. Rumor stared at Jude's hand with a pointed expression. Red spun around him like a storm, angry and lost. Jude let go and held up his hands. "Please listen to me." He didn't care they were standing in the middle of the street. He didn't care he was pleading. He wanted to talk to Rumor about everything—about George, about Vala, about the chimera and the forest, about himself. "Please."

Maybe since he'd gone underground to help rescue Rumor's friend, Rumor would be more open to helping him. Despite the fury and confusion in Rumor's eyes when he'd seen George, the whispers of indigo curiosity that surrounded him didn't lie.

Colors never lied.

And maybe that's why Jude was so willing to risk it all. To tell this boy who craved the truth everything. To use stark reality to convince him to come with Jude to the forest. To prevent more catastrophe.

"Why?" Rumor's voice bit out hard. "Why did you go down there?"

"To help you."

"You mean save them." His hair fell in his face, curling around high cheekbones and lips twisted in anger.

"I want to save *everyone*," Jude said, exasperation leaking out of his tone. It sounded grand and foolish, but he didn't care. He was so close to pulling Rumor to him. So close to cracking open that cloud of anger. He had to believe the sacrifices in the tunnels were worth it. Blood had spattered his clothes from the boy they'd rescued and the chimera who'd died.

Rumor's eyes narrowed. "Everyone. Including monsters."

Jude dug deep for patience. "They aren't monsters. Not all of them. No more than the colonists and marines who hunt them."

"Says you. A forest rebel." At least Rumor had the decency to keep his voice down when he hurled the accusation.

Jude gestured to himself. "Yeah, okay, I live in a house built around a tree. You live inside walls and under a web. Sounds like a cage to me."

Rumor glared at him, his breath coming out in short pants. If he needed a punching bag, Jude would happily play that part. Maybe some of his reasoning would work through Rumor's walls.

"What was your plan in coming here?" Rumor asked.

Jude took a deep breath, keeping his voice as even and low as possible. "My *plan*" — he hooked his fingers in the air — "was to try to find my friend."

"You said that already. Is your friend even human?" Rumor asked.

Fear and foolhardy bravery lanced through Jude's chest, sending tingles up his arms as he met Rumor's eyes. Those dark eyes bored into him, slicing through his hesitancy. There was no use tiptoeing around this.

Jude made a frustrated sound and shoved Rumor into a lush space between two buildings so their conversation wasn't on the street for the entire colony to hear. "No, but you already know that."

Rumor pulled free and stalked away a few steps, deeper into

the alley, his hands curling into fists. "What in deep space is going on? You can speak their language. You're *friends* with them."

Jude rubbed his hands over his face, his stomach flipping with nerves. Tears crawled up his throat, but he swallowed them back. "Not all the chimera are bad."

"Chimera."

"What we call them. What they told us we could call them since we can't pronounce their language. Gargoyle is…" Jude trailed off, unsure how to describe the muddy feeling that encased his insides whenever he heard that word. "…not a great word. You know the old stories, right? Of the gargoyles on Earth? They were monsters and demons and wicked beasts that hunted humans and stole children."

"And?"

"It's…preconceptions. You hear gargoyle, and you think monster. What if…" Jude floundered for a comparison that was just as horrible and unconscionable. "Okay, what if we labeled certain people as monsters based on their skin color or hair color or gender or whatever? No matter what they did or had done or acted like. You'd have an issue with that, right?"

Rumor's shoulders relaxed a fraction, but it was enough for Jude to press. "You're painting an entire species with the same evil, and you don't bother to get to know them. You assume every single one you come across is trying to kill you—"

"Every single one I've come across *has* tried to kill me," Rumor snapped.

Jude tried to cling to his temper. "You don't know them like I do."

He held Rumor's glare past the point of anger, everything inside him pleading for a crack, a fissure, a break in the violent red coating Rumor like fine grit.

He rubbed his lower lip as his gaze shifted to the street. "Wouldn't it be nice if people didn't have to build giant cages to stay safe?" He looked at Rumor again. "What if, instead of fighting and surviving, we actually *lived*? I'm tired. I'm tired of hiding and fighting. I'm tired of chimera who bring down cities and kill thousands in retaliation. I'm tired of us versus them."

Rumor's expression softened. His dark eyes were sad. Exhaustion lined his face and his arms and his hands along with fresh and fading scars. The red flickered, the gray of uncertainty and the indigo of curiosity fighting their way through the angry clouds roiling around his beautiful body. "And you think being friends with them will make all that happen?"

Jude nodded. "I do. I really do."

"They killed my parents."

Jude closed his eyes. "They killed Trick's parents when the ships fell. Mine died when the marines invaded a chimera tunnel and caused a cave-in."

"Then how…"

Jude opened his eyes. "They're not all bad."

He took a shuddering breath and gathered every ounce of courage he possessed as he moved closer, stepping into Rumor's space again.

Rumor didn't answer, but the shift in his stance and the slight narrowing of his eyes was all the answer Jude needed. Make or break. He'd find another way if Rumor refused.

"What if we could…could take the steps toward peace?" Jude wrapped his fingers around Rumor's wrist. He might push Jude away if he went directly for his hand and those long fingers, but his wrist. His wrist was enough. His skin was warm, gritty with blood and dust from the tunnels, from surviving. Jude's fingertips were smudged and darkened with dried blood—human and chimera. He took a deep breath, his heart beating wildly, and met Rumor's gaze. "Help me."

"Help you what?" Rumor whispered, his eyes jumping around Jude's face.

Jude swallowed, heat rising up the back of his neck. He wanted…he didn't know what he wanted. Everything was too colorful, too bright, too precarious.

"I survived the worst attack we've seen since the Crater and the ships falling." Warning lined every one of Rumor's words. "My *dad* died. Of everyone here, I have the most reason to hate them."

Jude took in the colors surrounding Rumor in a shifting cloud. "But you didn't shoot George."

Rumor's uncertainty grew and braided with his underlying curiosity, battling back the anger.

"You could have killed him despite what I said." Jude licked his lips, and Rumor's eyes followed the movement.

"I could change my mind."

A shudder ran through Jude's body. "You could."

They stared at each other, bodies mere centimeters apart. Rumor's cloud of anger and uncertainty filled the space between them, pulling Jude in deeper. Jude's breath grew short as scenario after scenario ran laps in his brain. His thumb brushed across Rumor's warm skin, and he could've sworn the red flickered toward the passion end of the spectrum. Everything in him wanted to push through those last couple centimeters, pull Rumor to him physically and mentally. If only he'd see—

"I still might." Rumor pulled his arm free and backed away with a shake of his head, shattering their private moment and Jude's hope into a million tiny pieces. "Something's not right here, and I'm going to find out what it is." He walked away, leaving Jude standing in the alley alone, his heart in his throat and dread in his belly.

BRAEDEN

The look Nyx had worn on her face when she'd finally come out of the tunnels would haunt Braeden for the rest of his days. They'd all seen death. It was impossible not to when you were born into war. Some people grew calloused to it, covered themselves in thick skin and emotional armor. Others lost themselves in work, like his mom. Or dreamed of leaving this moon entirely.

Like him.

He sat on the front steps of his house, unable to go inside, where pictures of his moms stared at him. Unable to head to the shelter where he was supposed to be because all he could see was Nyx's face and Dahlia's tears. A spindly black-barked sapling stood in his tiny front yard, its yellow leaves tiny and undamaged. Out of everything ruined tonight, that baby tree was fine. His leg hurt, but he didn't care.

Maybe he deserved it. If he'd confronted his moms about the gargoyle they held captive, demanded its release or something. If he'd broken it out himself and set it free. If…

If

If

If

Nyx had gone with Dahlia to the medical center. To be with her while they awaited news of Colt's injuries. That left Braeden alone with his thoughts and no one to joke with to keep him from thinking about tonight. Or his mistake.

A pair of automaton cats lumbered by. Three marines accompanied them, patches on their arms designating them as handlers. A wistful feeling lodged in his throat as he watched them patrol. The cats moved fluidly, their great heads swinging from side to side as they walked. They seemed so real, so alive. One of the cats paused, its tail flicking back and forth as it sensed the surroundings. One of the handlers stopped and pressed their hand to its flank, murmuring softly like a trainer speaking to a real animal. The automaton nudged the marine with its nose and started walking again.

Even though it was man and machine, there seemed to be a bond there. A bond Braeden didn't have with anyone. The closest he came was with Nyx, which was special and he wouldn't trade that for anything, but it didn't fill that hole in his chest. That hole that wanted a connection. Not a boyfriend or a girlfriend or even another best friend. He had friends. He had close friends.

He didn't have a bond.

He tore his attention away from them and stared up, searching for the web repairs but losing himself in the vast beauty of the nebula. What would it be like to take a ship and an automaton and explore the cosmos? Surely travel had evolved since the original settlers came to Sahara. He twisted his ring around his finger. If only he could just hop a cruiser and…vanish.

You got mad when Nyx almost left without you, dumbass. Braeden wrinkled his nose. She would be just as crushed if he left, but at least he'd say good-bye first. There was more to this existence than war, than surviving, than a rocky moon and a shadowy planet. There were universes and stars and life out there he wanted to see.

Maybe Nyx and Dahlia would come with him. He rubbed his chest, everything in him wanting to run away. Far away from all of this and everything he knew and hated.

He tugged on his hair, wishing he could pull the knowledge of that gargoyle out of his brain by the roots. He wished he'd never found out about it, because now he had no idea what to do. Who could even help him? Who would understand?

"Hey, you okay?"

Braeden shook his head automatically, quippy answers and sarcastic comments falling by the wayside, as he looked up at Rumor. The guy still had blood smeared across his shirt from rescuing Colt.

"I should find you a new shirt," Braeden said.

Rumor glanced down and plucked at the stained clothing. He hitched a shoulder. "Probably ruin that one, too."

Braeden managed a small smile.

Rumor sat down next to him, his forearms on his knees and his hands clasped. His necklace dangled in the air, the coin catching the amber colony lights.

"What's the coin?" Braeden asked.

Rumor tucked it back in his shirt. "It was my mom's."

"Got it."

"What's the scar?" Rumor pointed to the long roping scar that wound up Braeden's arm.

"A little over a year back, gargoyle grabbed me one night while we were outside the gates helping a transport get into safety. Colt shot it out of the air. Saved my life." Braeden rubbed his fingers over the shiny, pink skin. It was the closest he'd ever come to dying. His nightmares were of that night. Of the gargoyle grabbing him and Colt not being there.

"I'm sorry I didn't get to him sooner," Rumor said quietly.

"Dude, you went down there when not even trained marines would. You're the last person who should be apologizing." Braeden's stomach churned. He exhaled shakily. He didn't want to talk about Colt. Or the dragon. "So that blond guy that went down in the tunnels with you, he's the same one that was on the sailboard, yeah? The guys who grabbed us."

Rumor nodded, a faraway look in his eyes.

"Are they from the forest like we thought?" Braeden asked that queasy, unsettled feeling in his gut growing. His good leg bounced.

Rumor's expression tightened. "He is. He and his brother both are."

"Why are they here?" Braeden asked, already knowing the answer.

"Searching for 'a friend.'" He hooked his fingers in the air, then dragged them through his curls with a heavy sigh. "He can speak to them. The gargoyles."

He had to have heard wrong. "He can do what now?"

Rumor told him about what happened in the tunnels. About the gargoyle attack. About a gargoyle named George who saved his life. About Jude talking to it. About Jude's impassioned plea afterward for him to talk to the gargoyles, creatures the forest people called chimera.

Braeden closed his eyes, the overwhelming urge to either punch something or cry welling up in his chest. If he'd just…

"I know—I know why we were attacked. Why HUB2 was attacked," he whispered.

Rumor made a disgusted noise. "The gargoyles want us wiped out. That's why. They're going to keep coming until we're all dead."

Braeden was already shaking his head. "That's not the reason." He took a steadying breath and stood, his heart climbing into his throat and making it hard to breathe. "I need to show you something."

NYX

Nyx sat on a hard plastic chair in the medical center waiting room, the chrome frame distorting the surroundings and warping them like broken mirrors. Vibrations crawled up her legs and into her belly, pulling her into the ground with the weight of panic and frenzy and fear. She kept one hand on Dahlia's arm, the anguish of her friend crawling up her skin like bugs. Dahlia needed her, but she didn't know what to do.

Dahlia swiped her palms across her cheeks, smearing tears across her freckles, and gave Nyx a shaky smile. Her hand wrapped around Nyx's and held on tight. Nyx swept her thumb back and forth over Dahlia's skin.

"He'll be okay," Dahlia said.

I love you, the words echoed in her mind. Nyx pressed her lips together and nodded, squeezing her hand. She blinked back the horrifying imagery dancing around her head. The tunnels had rolled with vibrations. Angry vibrations that seemed to come from hell itself. The entire moon focusing its energy on that one instance and rumbling its vitriol under her fingertips. She didn't know how to respond to it or *if* she could, but if she ever figured out a way, she'd tell the planet they meant no harm.

The humans mean no harm. Was that even true?

Before HUB2, before all this death, she'd nearly grabbed her bag and left Epsilon in search of answers. In search of *why* she could feel the moon vibrate under her boots when no one else seemed to notice. What in deep space was it trying to tell her? As much as it scared her, she desperately wanted to know in case it was a way for her to help.

Hey, guys, the moon says maybe you should cut it out.

Now, she wondered if the answers lay here. Maybe with Rumor's new friend, Jude, who maybe came from the forest with the answers she needed to stop this. But that also meant he was probably friends with the beasts and… Her heart stuttered.

They showed up right after Braeden told her and Dahlia about the gargoyle under Epsilon. *Oh gods.* If Jude and the others were here because of that… She ground her molars so hard her jaws ached. If this Jude guy hurt Braeden or even Rumor because he chose the monsters over people, he'd have a very short, angry brown girl to contend with.

Wren strode toward them down the hall. Blood spotted her cuffed sleeve. Sadness seeped from her dark eyes. Dahlia bolted out of her chair, rushing at her.

All Nyx saw was the expression on Wren's face. Her words were swallowed up by the background noise, and her lips were blocked by waving hands, her face turning, or Dahlia's cloud of hair. Nyx sat in auditory darkness, tinnitus buzzing and whining, and a headache crawled behind her temples.

Her ears always gave up trying to decipher sound and meaning the more stressed out she became. All they wanted to do was go to sleep and try again tomorrow when everything was quieter and no one was dying.

Dahlia went rigid. Her head shook back and forth, the constant movement of denial, and she clutched at her mom's hands. Wren looked sad, her nostrils flaring and her brown eyes glassy. Nyx's heart shattered. She pushed off the chair and slid her arms around Dahlia's waist from behind, pressing against her and resting her cheek on Dahlia's shoulder blade. She could dimly make out the frantic thumping of Dahlia's heart.

Dahlia trembled, turned, and wrapped her arms around Nyx, her body shaking with sobs as her tears dampened Nyx's shirt. If she was speaking, Nyx couldn't hear it, but it didn't matter. No combination of twenty-six letters could ever adequately unlock the right words for this moment.

I love you weren't the right words.

Dahlia pulled away, her eyes bloodshot and red-rimmed. She wiped her nose with the back of her hand and signed, "I'm going to go see him."

Nyx nodded.

Dahlia inhaled, her shoulders shaking as her eyes filled up with tears again. "Alone. Okay? I want to be alone with him. Say good-bye."

Nyx nodded again, this time slower. She tried to pretend it didn't hurt. She watched Dahlia head down the hall to say good-bye to someone she may have loved, or at least cared about and given her heart to for a few precious moments.

You have her friendship. Stop being selfish. The admonishment pounded through her headache and she tipped her head back, blinking rapidly to keep from crying. Why was this all so messed up? Why had they settled on a moon inhabited by monsters? Why were they even still here? Why had no one else come to rescue them? Why did Colt have to die? Why did Rumor have to show up *now*? Why couldn't Nyx just be happy with Dahlia's friendship and not want…need…*crave*…more?

Why?

Nyx sank down into a chair, curling her fingers around the edge. The vibrations of the medical center tickled her palms. Heels on polished floors. The rattle of medical carts. Something hitting a wall somewhere to her right. Blood permeated the air she breathed, its metallic tang sitting on her tongue and gluing it down. The anger of the moon seeped through the metal and plastic of human structures, the vibrations scraping up her arms. All she could interpret was pain and anger and... fear. Her vision blurred with tears.

She couldn't just sit here while her best friend—someone she loved with everything inside her—ached and lost. She had to try to stop this. She couldn't think of anything the humans hadn't tried. They'd tried to leave. They'd surrounded themselves in walls and webs. They'd armed and trained anyone who would pick up a weapon.

Nyx wanted to speak with the moon, instead of being spoken to.

Think, Nyx. Don't just sit here doing nothing.

She stared at her hand, white-knuckled around the chair. The vibrations ebbed and flowed, lapping at her like crashing waves and splashing their humming farther up her arms until they tickled her neck.

Wren squatted in front of her to get her attention.

Nyx raised her eyebrows in question.

Wren signed "hurt" and pointed at her in question.

Nyx shook her head. "It's not my blood."

Wren nodded and squeezed her knee. She signed "grandmother," her lips moving, but Nyx shook her head. "She's at home where it's safe."

Lines appeared between Wren's brows, and her eyes softened. She squeezed Nyx's knee as a nurse rushed up to her in a flurry of words and gestures. Wren held up her finger in a wait-a-minute gesture and pulled out her tablet. **Do you need to talk to someone?**

Nyx shook her head.

Wren gave her a dubious eyebrow and a head tilt.

Nyx managed a tight, hopefully reassuring, smile. "I'm okay."

It was the biggest lie she'd ever told.

The nurse pulled Wren's attention again, her body language

on the verge of panic. Nyx nodded to back up her statement. "I'll go find Abuela. Make some tea."

Lie number two.

Wren gave Nyx one last concerned look and followed the nurse down the hall.

Nyx peeled herself from the chair, her left hand leaving a red smudge. She curled her shaking fingers into a fist and walked out of the medical center, the vibrations of the moon wrapping around the bones in her legs and burrowing into the marrow with each step she took.

She crouched and placed a bare palm against the bare ground. *What do you want?*

Her fingertips curled into the dirt, the red clay sticking under her nails and smearing across her hand. Her heart ached for Dahlia, for the friend she'd lost. Her heart ached even for Rumor and all he'd been through since HUB2 fell. She gritted her teeth and squeezed her eyes shut as her mind screamed at the moon.

We don't mean you any harm.

The vibration ebbed, then pushed back at her like a pulse, like a thump. Her heartbeat sped for a fraction of a moment, and her eyes flew open in shock. She stood and ran down the walkway, heading for Braeden's.

RUMOR

It had only been seven hours since HUB2 fell, but Rumor felt as though he'd spent days clawing and fighting. A part of him had died tonight at HUB2 along with his father. Even standing next to Braeden, he felt utterly alone.

"Rumor," Braeden said as they walked down the street. "Is the story true? The one from when you were ten years old."

Rumor cleared his throat. "Where did you hear that?"

"Mom left your file open on her tablet earlier. It said that—"

"I'm pretty sure I can guess what it said." Rumor closed his eyes against flickering images of hellhounds and blood and screams. A shotgun out of shells. A high-powered revolver out of bullets. A charged machete covered in blood. Six hellhounds dead at his feet.

His hands shook, and tingles ran across his cheekbones. He inhaled shakily and grabbed for his necklace, tracing the familiar circle through the thin fabric of his shirt.

"I'm sorry about your mom," Braeden said quietly. He watched a marine squad patrol by.

"Did you have a dad?" Rumor asked.

Braeden nodded. "He died when the ships fell. I was six."

Too many kids told these same stories. Braeden. Dahlia. Rumor. Even Jude.

He didn't know what to do with that.

Braeden nodded toward the western side of the colony. "Anyone asks, we're headed to check on the western shelters."

Rumor nodded, the sudden absence of Braeden's dry wit and sarcasm sending pins over his nerves. He glanced down side streets as they passed them, telling himself he was learning more about Epsilon, since it was probably his home now. Telling himself he was memorizing patrol patterns. Telling himself, with a twist in his chest, that he wasn't looking for Jude.

His stomach fluttered. Freckles and bright eyes had always drawn him in. But there was no way in all of deep space he could reconcile with Jude's affinity for the monsters. How a human could even stand to be in the same proximity as one and not kill it was beyond him.

One saved your life in the tunnels. George.

Why had Jude name a gargoyle George? What in the actual… Rumor snorted softly before his brain reminded him he was supposed to be angry at Jude. Not…amused.

Braeden raised an eyebrow. "Care to share with the class?"

"Not really."

"I really like this bond we share, Rumor," Braeden said, deadpan. "Gets me right here." He rapped his knuckles against his sternum.

"Where are we going?"

"Agriculture fields." Braeden pointed at the end of the road where it seemed to dead-end into a wall of head-height green plants. "Corn."

The plant-covered buildings of the residential colony blocks gave way to a small field filled with crops and towering water sprayers that reminded him of enormous teapots. Giant water pipes connected each sprayer to a reservoir along the western edge of the field. Rumor mentally oriented himself. Lake Llyn was right on the other side of the wall.

"What is this place?" Rumor asked. HUB2 was military and mining only. They imported agriculture from other colonies. His insides constricted. Past tense. He had to think of HUB2 in past tense now.

Another building sat on the far side of the field, next to the wall. Braeden cleared his throat. "That's the agriculture center. Mostly hydroponics and study. Growing more in small spaces. And this is one of ten areas for rotating crops or letting animals graze. There's three on this side, two north, two south, and three east, kind of like an outer ring to the colony between us and the wall." He pitched his voice lower. "Anyway, so I followed Mom a few days ago when she and Bailey got into an argument about something."

Rumor ran his fingers over a veiny leaf. "What was it about?"

Braeden grimaced. "I missed the beginning and they shut up pretty fast when they noticed me, but I caught enough to realize they'd done something. And that no one knew about it." He led Rumor around the field, closer to the wall and away from prying eyes. "I started listening to as many conversations as I could."

"Creepy."

"Valid." Braeden pointed to a maintenance shed in the middle of a clearing. "Seem out of place to you?"

Rumor shook his head. "I've never been here before."

Braeden ran a hand through his hair and tugged on it. "If you stay here long enough, you'll notice no one goes in it. Ever. Except my mom and Bailey."

"So what's inside?" Rumor asked, a tiny nugget of suspicion germinating in his brain. That same roiling anxiousness he'd felt when listening to Jude confess about his *friend* sloshed around his stomach.

Braeden headed around the back, deeper into the shadows of the wall. "They can't put a guard on it or it would draw attention, so they hid it in plain sight."

"Hid what?" Rumor asked slowly as he followed. His fingers twitched toward the handle of his blade.

Braeden paused at the door. "They caught one."

Rumor raised an eyebrow. "Caught…one? One what?"

"A gargoyle," Braeden said.

The moon stopped. Rumor stared at him as chunks of tonight clunked into place, snapping together like pieces of a blood-stained puzzle. The attack, Jude and his brother showing up, the same dragon from HUB2, all of it spiraling together in Rumor's brain like some terrifying tornado.

Rumor's body went cold and still. "A what?" His voice came out thin and whispery.

Braeden produced a silver card from his pocket. "I cloned my mom's key card, and I went down there. Mom never said anything to me, but she had to have been alerted by the access, right? So I'm thinking"—he pressed the card to a panel next to the door—"she can't bring it up because bringing it up would be admitting to it, but it could also mean that I could broadcast it if she tried to take the key away or ground me or something."

The door opened with a soft thunk of metal releasing.

Rumor's heart pounded against his sternum so hard he thought his chest would crack open. Everything spun around him, connecting into something that had nothing to do with him, but had dragged him into the center and ripped away everything.

"You have a gargoyle." He didn't know if he was directing that statement at Braeden or the air or if he'd even spoken loud enough for Braeden to hear.

Braeden took a deep breath. "Trust me, you want to see this."

The door opened—not to the interior of a shed—but to a set of metal stairs leading underground. A light flickered on, bathing a smooth tunnel in a white glow. Braeden headed down the steps, and Rumor grabbed his arm.

"Your mom probably has sensors to let her know this door is open." He didn't want to believe what Braeden was implying.

He didn't want to think about the fact that an actual monster was in the colony on purpose. He didn't want to think about the implications of this. He didn't want to think about every single horrible scenario racing through his mind at top speed. There was still blood on his clothes. He could smell it.

Braeden nodded, either oblivious to Rumor's internal spiral or pushing on in spite of it. "Mom still hasn't done anything."

Rumor chewed on the inside of his cheek as he followed Braeden down the steps. The hallway was narrow, white, and lined with stripes of adamantine. It stretched for an infinity, narrowing to a dark point at the far end. He blinked and could almost imagine himself back in those tunnels, waiting for gargoyles to rush around the corner and rip his stomach open. His hand trembled as he brushed his fingers along the adamantine stripe. His side pulsed with remembered pain.

At the end of the hall, Braeden stopped in front of a large door. "Okay, when I was down here before, she didn't try anything. But, to be safe, stay near me and no sudden movements. Got it?"

Rumor rubbed his hands over his face, grimacing at the spike of pain in his damaged fingers. "Wait, *she*?"

Braeden hitched a shoulder. "She calls herself Vala and—" Braeden frowned. "She requested female pronouns."

"Vala," Rumor echoed.

"She's not like the others I've fought. She's…smart and like us." Confusion ghosted through his eyes, as if he couldn't believe what he was saying. "I don't know. It's—" He licked his lips and tugged a hand through his hair. "It's not adding up. All the news coming from the military says they're monsters, right? Look up *gargoyle* in any of our databases, and it shows a ton of pictures of dead bodies and the flying ones and the dragons and the ones that look like humans and the ones that run on four legs. Some basic description, but they're all called *gargoyle*. There's no information."

Rumor couldn't say anything. He didn't know what to say. His heartbeat increased and his breaths grew short. Part of him was curious, sure. The part of him that wondered why some colonists split off fifty-four years ago and went to live in the forest despite all the warnings and fear.

Find her.

Find Vala.

She was here.

"You sound like Jude." He wanted to throw up.

Braeden waved his hands like he was brushing aside a smoke cloud. "The marines and the scientists, right? They tell us the gargoyles are monsters. I mean, have you read the old Earth stories about gargoyles? Statues that came to life at night and ate kids? Those things were terrifying. They give us the bare amount of facts that support that claim. We nickname a few. Hellhound. Demon. *And the scientists let us.* They don't differentiate anything about them. But we name everything else to minute detail. The raptor birds, carrion bugs, soft crabs, not to mention all those plants up there. Thousands of names. But the gargoyles?" His shoulders slumped. "Just monsters. Just *gargoyles*. Seventy-five years and that's all we've ever called them. Why? There's…there's more here. More than anyone's telling us."

He inhaled like he'd just run a marathon and watched Rumor with hesitant eyes.

"So if they aren't monsters, what are they?" Rumor asked, his voice sounding like it came from somewhere else. Somewhere very far away. The floor under his feet gleamed like a highly polished mirror, showing his warped reflection. He didn't recognize himself.

Braeden gave a prolonged shrug. "I don't know, but this war we're in? It's a lot more complicated than most people know. And I'm not—I'm not sure how I feel about that."

Rumor tried to focus. "You attacked a dragon with me."

"I know, and I'd do it again to protect other humans, especially my family. But why are we constantly being told 'kill them' with no more information?"

"They aren't human," Rumor said in a low voice. He curled his fingers into fists to stop the shaking.

"Technically, no. But…they were here first." He dragged his teeth over his lower lip and sighed. "Talk to her and decide for yourself."

"How do you know I'm not going to kill it?"

Braeden grabbed the door handle. "I don't."

Rumor's insides twisted into a billion tiny knots as Braeden heaved open the door. Cold air whooshed out of a dark room. His hand hovered near the handle of his heritage blade. Shivers rolled down his spine that had nothing to do with the temperature. Braeden stepped inside. "It's Braeden. I brought a friend this time."

Silence.

The only light came from the hallway. Rumor couldn't tell the size of the room. He grabbed the handles of his blades and held tight.

"Afraid." The voice came from in front of them, beyond the reach of the hall light. It was grating and growling, a clattering rush of stones, each syllable chaotic and distinct.

The same grating syllables from HUB2. *Find her.* Sweat broke out on Rumor's upper lip and between his shoulder blades. They could speak human language. Jude could understand their language.

"I'm not afraid." Rumor's voice scraped out of his throat. He swallowed hard. "I don't trust you."

"Mutual."

He gripped the handles tighter. "Is there another light in here?"

He needed to see it. He needed to see its eyes.

"A dim one," Braeden answered from somewhere else in the darkness. "Non-UV so she won't crystallize."

A few of the colonies had constructed UV spotlights to chase off the gargoyles at night, but the beasts basically sacrificed their own bodies to destroy the lights. The prevailing theory was that it cost too much to keep making them, which is why the military never sent more to the outlying colonies. Something in Rumor's gut curled uncomfortably.

We have marines!

Do we?

A bluish-green glow filled the room, mimicking the nebula. It illuminated a massive cage in the center of a large space. Thick bars shone with the familiar iridescence of the adamantine that was mined from under the HUBs. But the cage wasn't what held his attention.

It… *She* was definitely one of them, with stonelike flesh the color of white marble and silvery veins tracing over her entire body. There was a monstrous beauty to her. Horns curled up from her brow and wrapped around her bare skull like a crown before twisting upward and branching off in various directions. Blue crystals dangled from various points. Wings were pulled tight to her body, jointed along the top and clawed at the end. She was long and lean and bare without anything to indicate any sort of sex. Her long legs bent at the knee like a human's, but then backward like a bird at the next joint, and ended in massive clawed feet.

The only gargoyles he'd ever seen up close were corpses. Mangled and bloodied and broken. Jaws open wide, revealing sharp teeth and sharp tongues. Torn wings and broken fingers. Lifeless eyes and pools of black blood.

Not this.

Not alive and calm and standing perfectly still, watching him with something that bordered on curiosity. Rumor's jaw ached and he realized he'd been grinding his molars.

She crouched and tilted her head, too-wide sapphire eyes peering through the bars. "Name."

Braeden folded his arms. "Vala, this is Rumor."

Vala turned her head to Braeden, then back to Rumor.

She wrapped her wings around her shoulders like a cloak, her unblinking gaze never leaving Rumor's. "You seem lost."

Lost? "I arrived after the attack on HUB2."

"Alone?"

"Yep."

"Impressive."

"Apparently," he gritted out.

The corner of her mouth curled up slightly.

The whine in his skull grew louder. His lips tingled. "You aren't surprised about the attack."

She shook her head once.

He squeezed the handles of his blades to keep his hands from shaking. "Where do you come from?"

"This land."

"Why do you kill us?"

If he even believed the creatures had emotions, he would have sworn sadness flitted over her face. "You trespass, and you kill."

"Trespass," Rumor echoed.

"Our land," she said, as if it was difficult to wrap her lips around the words. He caught a glimpse of sharpened teeth and two tongues moving in her mouth like snakes. "You trespass."

"You weren't here when we landed." He knew that much. The gargoyles hadn't appeared until nearly twenty-five years after the colonists were settled. After the first generation of humans were born on a new world.

"Yes, we were. We slept. Every cycle we sleep." She frowned as though she couldn't find the words. "We awoke, and many died. Your water killed them."

Braeden licked his lips. "The lake we built when we first arrived here seventy-five years ago. When we dammed up the rivers to create the lake, we flooded several of their tunnels."

"You started a war because of an accident?" Rumor asked incredulously. "Thousands died tonight!" His voice cracked.

"They were looking for you. They attacked HUB2 looking for you. They attacked *here* looking for *you*."

"Rumor," Braeden said. "Put the blade away."

Rumor glanced down at the blade he'd pulled in his rant. It gleamed black under the lights. One flick of a switch. One swift movement. Not even Braeden could stop him.

She pointed a long, clawed finger at his blades. "You cut our heads off."

He bared his teeth at her. "You pick us up and drop us from the air to watch us splatter. You chase us and tear our limbs off. You stalk us in the darkness and wait for our guard to fall before you see how much blood you can spill." He panted for breath, his vision dotting around the outside. The muscles in his arms burned with the force to stay still. His knuckles ached from clenching his blade so hard. "And now?"

He just wanted a reason. He just wanted one reason to drive this into her chest.

She lifted her chin. "You are weak. We are strong."

"Oh yeah? How's that going for you?" Every muscle in his body sang with anger.

"Your race clings to our land."

"I was born here. It's my land now, too."

"Is it?" She leaned against the bars, her eyes boring into his, stripping back layer after layer after layer. "Did you ask?"

"Ask what?"

"Permission."

"No. I wasn't born yet."

She made a noise that could have been a growl or a hum. "You're hurt."

He leaned close to the bars, smiling at her through the rage clouding his vision. "Don't worry, I took a lot of them with me." He was too close now to inflict any real damage if she decided to attack. But Rumor didn't see hatred in her face. He wasn't sure what it was, but it wasn't the hate or bloodlust he'd seen so many nights. "Who even are you?"

"Leader."

A political prisoner. Rumor wanted to punch something. Humans had taken a political prisoner. Gargoyles retaliated by wiping out an entire city. How would the humans escalate now? Executing her? Bombing the tunnels again?

"None of this makes sense," he whispered.

After a long moment, she turned to Braeden. "I like him."

That was the last thing he'd expected to come out of her mouth.

Braeden nodded. "I figured you would." He tapped Rumor's arm. "We should go. Find the others and figure this out."

Rumor stared at her. This was the second gargoyle tonight who not only spoke, but hadn't attacked him. Hadn't threatened him. *She's a monster. She's a gargoyle. Her kind ripped your parents apart.* He pulled in a deep breath, willing everything to calm, and turned away to follow Braeden out the door before he flew apart into a billion tiny pieces. He shoved his blade back in its sheath.

"Who did you lose?" Vala's voice stopped him.

"What?"

"Everyone has lost someone in our war. Who did you lose?"

"My parents. Everyone." Rumor swallowed around the hoarseness of his voice.

"This night?"

"My dad tonight. My mom…" Rumor cleared his throat and tried again. "My mom when I was ten. I tried to save her."

"From us?"

"Hellhounds. The dogs. I killed so many, and it didn't matter. She died, and all that happened after that was everyone wanted to know how I killed that many and lived, but the point was I wasn't focused on me living, I just wanted *her* to live and she didn't." He gasped for breath at the end of his run-on confession, shocked it'd burst out of him in the first place. Shivers ran from his fingertips to his face. A rubber band tightened around his chest.

She inclined her head. "I am sorry."

Rumor frowned at her, tamping down curiosity and revulsion. "You're awfully human."

She peered at him. "Meaning?"

Rumor waved a hand at her, focusing on her and not how the room felt smaller. Darker. "The way you're acting. How you move and respond. It's very human."

"Does that upset you?" she asked.

He needed her to be a monster. It was easier.

"Why don't you break out of here?" he asked instead. Something about the situation nagged, poked him with an increasing sense of wrongness. She was too calm. Too composed. Too…friendly. The memory of the too-smooth hole in the side of the shelter flickered. "Why are you still here?"

She examined him for a long moment, her expression unreadable. "Knowledge."

Rumor backed away a few steps, the world feeling too small and too open all at once. "I need to find Jude."

He turned and raced out of the room, up the stairs, and into the nebula-light. The noise of the colony punched him as he emerged, and he barely registered Nyx running up to him. She spoke, but her words flew away as he ran past her.

He had to find Jude. He had to stop this.

Run, Rumor. Warn Epsilon. Tell them to warn the others.

NYX

"Rumor?" Nyx asked in bewilderment as he ran past her. He'd looked frightened and upset.

Braeden stood in the doorway of the maintenance shed, his smile gone, concern in every line of his face as he watched Rumor run away.

"What's going on?" she asked.

Braeden shook his head as he signed. "He went to find Jude."

"Is the gargoyle down there?" Nyx asked.

Braeden shifted his attention to her, his eyes widening at her tear-stained face and dirt-stained palms. "You okay?"

Nyx pulled in a breath. "No. I need to talk to her."

"Colt?" Braeden fingerspelled the name slower than usual.

Nyx flipped her palms over. "Dead."

He closed his eyes and sagged against the doorframe.

"This isn't your fault," she said. "Even if you broke her out of her cage—"

Braeden's eyes flew open, and he straightened. "That's exactly what we're going to do."

"What?"

He hugged her tightly instead of answering. She squeezed her eyes shut and wrapped her arms around his waist. The pulse of the moon couldn't compete with the pulse of his heart under her cheek.

He pulled away, his hazel eyes alight with ideas she was sure would get her into trouble. "Her name is Vala," he signed. "Do you want me to go down with you? I can stand right outside the door if you want privacy."

She glanced at the stairwell and chewed on her lower lip. "Will she hurt me?"

"She's in a cage. If you stand out of reach…" His signs paused and he shrugged.

"Do you trust her?" Nyx asked.

Braeden hesitated, raising his hands to sign several times. Lines appeared between his brows. Finally, he shook his head and signed, "I don't know."

Nyx wanted to ask him why he might trust a gargoyle. Wanted to ask him why he hadn't killed the monster yet. Wanted to ask him why he was so conflicted over this when his mother was the commander. Wanted to ask him what was going on in that genius mind of his.

But the moon pulsed and thrummed under her feet, almost rolling toward the shed like a breadcrumb path.

Nyx took a deep breath. "Stand outside the door?"

Braeden squeezed her shoulder and followed her inside.

Through the door. Down the hallway. To the second door. It shuddered as she pulled it open. It probably squealed, but she couldn't even hear that at this point, the buzzing too loud. Braeden pulled his old revolver and checked it. He smiled gently at her, but his eyes glowed with nerves. She stood up on her tiptoes and kissed his cheek. He nudged his forehead against hers, then motioned to the doorway.

She stepped into the room alone, and the vibrations rolled up her legs, clawing and pulling at her to listen. She sucked in a breath at the massive cage in the center of the room.

Vala watched, her mouth closed and her eyes wide. Her

wings hung to the side, exposing her lean form and the mass of spiderwebbed veining that covered her moonlight skin in silvery metallic lines. She was a topography of rivers and mountainous desert as the binary stars of her eyes watched Nyx walk closer.

"Can you read?" Nyx asked.

Vala shook her head, jewels swinging from her fractal horns and catching the light. She spoke, but Nyx waved her fingers at her own ears. "I can't hear."

Vala tilted her head and crouched to the floor of the cage, extending her arm through the bars, multi-jointed fingers splayed wide and beckoning. Nyx stood rooted to the spot, her throat dry as she stared at those too-long fingers and stoneskin palm. She'd never touched one on purpose. Fear skittered across her arms and legs, raising all her tiny hairs, and pushing her to the very edge of indecision. Was this the next step? Was the moon trying to lure her into a trap, or was it trying to get her to understand this creature behind shining cage bars?

"Are you going to pull me to you and kill me?" Nyx asked, her voice more breath than sound.

Vala shook her head and placed her other hand over her mouth as if to put a barrier between the world and her teeth.

Nyx held out her hand and took a step, hesitated, then took another step. She reached forward, her heart thundering in her head, then slid her hand into Vala's.

Vala's hand was cool and smooth. Vala curled one finger at a time over the back of Nyx's hand, her eyes never leaving Nyx's face. The same thrumming power of the moon flowed up Nyx's arm and the back of her neck. Not words or sentences or structure, but meaning that she couldn't sort through. "I feel this vibration all the time. In the ground. Is this how you talk to the others of your kind?"

Vala nodded.

"How come I can feel it? Can all humans feel it?"

Vala shook her head, the jewels swinging and clicking against each other. She kept her other hand over her mouth.

Nyx's insides were swarming insects as she sucked in air, trying to follow. "I don't understand. I feel this every day. I have for years—since I was little and before I even lost my hearing—and I don't know what it is, and it scares me."

Vala tightened her grip. The thrumming shifted, becoming softer and slower. Nyx took another step closer to the cage, so close she could reach through the bars and touch Vala's face.

Vala slowly removed her other hand and touched a fingertip to Nyx's cheek. A single teardrop beaded on her thick skin. Nyx pulled in a shaky breath, wanting to sob and scream and curl up in a ball all at the same time.

"Some of you...of them...got in tonight. They came up through the ground. They killed people. They hurt my...my best friend's... He died, too. And when I left the medical center I tried I tried I tried to tell the moon we don't mean any harm and...and it pulsed back like...like I don't know, like it disagreed." She rambled on, the words spilling from her mouth, humming over her lips and up her closing throat, but she couldn't hear them over the buzzing in her ears. It was all muffled and so far away, even as the hollow sounds filled her head and tried to fight through the buzzing. She forced the words back down her throat and clamped her lips shut, focusing on the sensations from Vala.

Listen, Vala's gemstone eyes seemed to say.

Nyx took a shaky breath and closed her eyes. Fear pushed at her, but she tightened her grip on Vala's hand and tried to ignore it. She didn't know how, but the thrumming—the vibrations of the moon—it was language. Language she could feel even though she didn't completely understand the meaning. The emotion pushed at her seams—feeling and reason and pleading and so so *so* much anger.

She jerked her hand out of Vala's and stumbled back, falling to the floor with a thud that bruised her tailbone and stung her palms.

Nyx pulled her knees to her chest and, in front of one of the creatures her species swore to eradicate, she cried.

RUMOR

Okay, if I were a hot guy from the forest hunting for a missing gargoyle or whatever I call them, where would I be? Rumor ran through the colony. He slowed to a purposeful walk when two separate sets of patrolling marines gave him the suspicious side-eye. Epsilon was still in lockdown, and most citizens were still in shelters, at least until the web was repaired. The citizens who were out moved with purpose, glancing up at the gaping hole in the web every so often.

Two gargoyles in the past few hours had existed in the same space as him—shared the same air—and not attacked him. Not tried to take his head off. Not tried to carve his body open. He didn't know how to fit that in line with everything he'd been raised to believe, everything he'd experienced tonight.

To say it was messing with him was a hilarious understatement.

He reached a central plaza, which looked so similar to HUB2's that a pang of homesickness sliced through his chest. Smooth adamantine-laced stonework on the ground, five twisted columns arranged around the outside. He drew in a shuddering breath and stopped in the center. The tingling once again crept across his cheekbones and pricked his fingertips. This was all wrong. His home, his family, nearly everyone he'd known, wiped off the map because of one captured gargoyle.

Rumor curled his tingling fingers into fists, fighting back the panic pushing at his insides. He grabbed the necklace, focusing on the tiny disk of metal in his palm, the warmth and realness of it. He tried to pull in a full breath but couldn't. His lungs seized, and he pressed a hand to his chest. He could kill every gargoyle he saw, but he was powerless against the panic attacks. Everything sped past him in a smear of color and bad decisions that left a sour taste in the back of his throat. He heaved, his muscles clenching and his ribs aching, but nothing came up.

A hand touched his shoulder, and he flinched away, curling in on himself. His knees hit the hard stone, the coldness of the ground seeping through his pants and chilling his bones. He squeezed his eyes shut until spots danced behind his lids, fighting the encroaching emotions, but all it did was make him dizzy.

There was a voice, but it all seemed far away, inaudible over his breathing and thundering heartbeat. Claws grabbing. Gnashing teeth aiming for his legs. He smelled smoke. He opened his eyes and saw twisted metal clawing for the sky. Rubble lay cracked and split and broken around him. A bloodied hand held a tablet, still playing that party song. Blood splashed across the ground, staining everything a deep and permanent red.

"Rumor."

"Dad?" he gasped. He twisted around and saw his father kneeling next to him.

His dad frowned, his dark eyes shifting to bright green like the clearing of a storm cloud. "Rumor. Hey, come on, breathe." The black hair faded to blond, the brown skin to a suns-kissed tawny scattered with freckles. "Rumor."

That wasn't his dad's voice.

The plaza columns towered above him, intact and unharmed. The smell of smoke dissipated.

Jude crouched in front of him, watching him with concerned

eyes. He stayed out of arm's reach, his expression wary.

"You back with me?" he asked, his voice soft and nonthreatening.

Rumor nodded, shame burning the back of his neck. Two panic attacks tonight already. He hadn't had one in over a year.

"You need me to find someone for you?" Jude asked.

"No, you're enough," Rumor said before he could stop himself. The corner of Jude's mouth quirked and he stood, offering a hand. Rumor slid his fingers into Jude's, letting him help him to his feet. Rumor didn't let go.

And neither did Jude.

He told himself it was because he was still a little light-headed.

Jude's gaze darted around Rumor. "What's going on?"

Rumor stepped closer, their hands still clasped between their bodies. Jude's eyes widened a fraction, and his throat bobbed as he swallowed.

Rumor dragged his teeth over his bottom lip. "Why did the gargoyles—"

"Chimera."

"Why did they attack HUB2?" Rumor's throat ached.

Jude moved one of Rumor's wayward curls out of his eyes. "They're hunting for one of their own."

"The same one you're looking for," Rumor said. "Your friend."

Jude glanced around before speaking in a low tone. "She's one of their leaders. She leads a pack who claimed this territory, one of the largest chimera territories on Sahara. Right now her pack is in upheaval while they try to find her, and several smaller groups have splintered off and joined another pack leader who's trying to find her." He took a deep breath. "His name is Reaper, and he's the one who assaulted HUB2."

Rumor licked his lips, pushing back the frustrated, angry words. Right now, all he wanted to do was keep holding Jude's hand, and most of those responses would crack the chasm between them even wider. "So all this tonight...HUB2, my dad, the dragon, the tunnels…"

Understanding dawned in Jude's eyes. "Rumor, I—"

Rumor shook his head. "Don't try to make it better with some excuse. You want me to help you."

Jude nodded, the understanding shifting to confusion. His eyes darted to the left, and Rumor glanced back over his own shoulder. Two marines walked across the plaza, talking to each other but eyeing the boys. Rumor slid his other hand around Jude's waist and pulled him closer. Their hips bumped. "Laugh at something I just said."

Without hesitation, Jude grinned, his smile overtaking his face and stealing every bit of breath Rumor had in his lungs. Rumor returned it without thinking, without remembering it was just a ruse, and for one stolen moment, the world wasn't on fire.

Jude leaned in as if he were telling Rumor a secret. His lips brushed the corner of Rumor's lips and hovered there, his breath warm on Rumor's cheek. Goose bumps prickled across Rumor's scalp and down his neck. His fingers curled into Jude's shirt at the small of his back as his body reacted. There was no way he could hide his erection. Not with Jude pressed to him knees to chest. Everything in him wanted to turn his head and make it a real kiss.

But this was make-believe. In no reality did a boy raised to love monsters fall for a boy raised to kill them.

The marines passed them without a word. Jude turned his head, his jaw brushing Rumor's lips, and watched them stop on the far side of the plaza to speak with two other officers.

"Good plan," he murmured, not making any move to let Rumor go. His free hand slid over Rumor's hip, his thumb finding bare skin and grazing over it. Rumor inhaled, and his skin burned.

"Yeah," Rumor said, his voice as shaky as his resolve. And Jude pressed against him wasn't helping, either.

Especially since it was more than obvious Jude wanted this just as badly.

Rumor bowed his head, his temple pressing to Jude's jaw,

wanting nothing more than to kiss the pulse point on Jude's throat and shift his hips a few centimeters to the right to see how far down his body Jude's flush went. Jude's breath hitched as if he'd just read Rumor's thoughts.

It was almost painfully obvious the physical attraction bound them together, but what more could ever happen?

Time was running out, and he couldn't waste any more precious minutes. At the end of this, they'd still be on opposite sides of a war. Jude wanted peace. Rumor wanted revenge.

Rumor couldn't give Jude stolen moments, but he could give him something just as important.

"I know where Vala is," he whispered.

Jude's fingers tightened. "What?"

"If she's free, does this all stop?" Rumor asked instead. His fingers traced the faint bumps of Jude's spine and pressed into the lean muscle on either side. He peered over Jude's shoulder at the officers. Their conversation continued, one of the women watching them with interest.

"Yes," Jude murmured, the tip of his nose touching Rumor's ear. His breath was warm, his breathing a little shallow. "Reaper just wants her released."

"So if we break her out and give her back, the colonies can be saved. They won't survive the night at this rate."

Jude exhaled shakily. "We?"

"I just want to save the colonies." Rumor smiled for the marine's benefit and nuzzled Jude's neck. He smelled like cinnamon, and his skin pinked everywhere Rumor's stubble scratched it. "I haven't changed my mind."

Liar.

Jude didn't answer. His fingers dug into the curve of bone peeking above Rumor's waistband. He stepped back, pushing his hands through his hair and rolling his shoulders. "I got a… um…message from Trick. He went to meet Yi-Min—the other person we came here with—and a forest spy here in the colony."

Jude kept his back to the marines while he pushed his sleeve up, revealing a bronze forearm cuff.

"Where'd you get that?" Rumor asked.

"I know a girl who knows a girl," Jude said absently as he tapped off a quick message.

"Did you tell them about me?"

Jude paused, his fingers hovering over the keypad. "Sort of. I said I'd found the survivor but didn't give them any details. Said I was still working on it."

"Why?" Rumor asked, not sure he wanted to hear the answer.

Jude sighed and rolled his sleeve back down. Green eyes met Rumor's, full of sadness and uncertainty. "Because if you come with me, I want it to be your choice. Not something I talk you into. Either way, I'm leaving here with Vala."

Rumor chewed on the inside of his cheek, his nerves pricking. Jude wanted to take Vala home, but Rumor needed her to track down the one who led the HUB2 assault. This gargoyle named Reaper.

"We can stop this." Rumor's gut churned. If they managed to free Vala, that might give him his chance. His shot. His revenge.

Jude's gaze darted around Rumor's right side. "What aren't you telling me?"

"Sorry to interrupt." Braeden approached them, his eyes bright and his expression serious. "If you two are planning what I think you're planning, we need to talk first."

Rumor shook his head. "You can't be a part of this. You're the commander's son."

Braeden smiled a troublemaker's smile. "Exactly."

BRAEDEN

"You were *born* in the forest?" Braeden's voice pitched up in surprise, sounding almost too loud in Nyx's small kitchen. "I didn't think anyone was born in the forest."

Jude stared at him as if he was trying to figure out whether Braeden was serious or joking. In hindsight, that had probably been a rude thing to say. Of course, there'd be kids born in the forest. He cleared his throat and set the plate of sandwiches on the table, the back of his neck warm.

Rumor's eyebrows went up. "You said you wanted a snack."

Braeden limped to the counter for a separate plate of cut fruit. "Nyx's abuela likes to feed people, and I would love to see you try to refuse her. I haven't eaten in a while, and I want to get to know your rebel friend here before we make more plans."

Rumor huffed and slumped in his chair. "You don't need to be a part of this."

"Really? How are you getting into that maintenance shed, exactly?" Braeden asked, his tone light. Rumor glared at him. Braeden winked. "Down, boy."

"Vala's been missing for two weeks, and her pack is worried." Jude's tone reminded Braeden of Bailey when she'd had to explain something to his mom for the fifth time.

"Her pack." Braeden slid into his chair and grabbed a sandwich. "Are these gargoyles or Earth wolves?"

Jude leaned back in his chair, an easy smile on his face. "The chimera travel in packs, have a social order, economy, religion, leaders, take care of their young. But what do I know," he drawled, the smile falling. "I'm just a dumb forest kid who lives in a tree."

Braeden made a derisive sound.

Jude's eyes sharpened when no one responded. "They're a peaceful society."

Peaceful. Right. "Tell that to the families of those who've lost loved ones to gargoyles."

"The chimera are reacting out of defense. They see humans as a threat. We attacked them first by flooding their tunnels when the original explorers made the lake," Jude countered.

"Well, since that was seventy-five years ago…"

"War doesn't care about birthdays."

"Hey, how many are there?" Rumor plucked a purple apple off the tray and picked at the soft skin with jabs of his index finger.

Jude raised an eyebrow at the fruit decimation. "You do realize that not every creature on this moon is one species, right? It would be like calling every mammal back on Earth a buffalo or something. I mean, there are dragons in the mountains."

"Which are gargoyles," Braeden said.

"No…that's not… No. They're a distant relative of the chimera," Jude said. "Like really distant. The chimera have culture and language and pack structure and communal child-rearing and jobs. They answer to a leader and group in smaller communities to conserve resources and make sure the children are well cared for. The dragons are…dragons."

"Then how do you explain HUB2?" Rumor asked without looking up from killing his fruit. "There were hundreds of them. Plus a dragon."

After a beat, Jude hitched a shoulder, focusing on the stained-glass solar window behind Braeden. "One really angry chimera leading a whole bunch of other angry chimera because the humans took a political prisoner. They want her back, and the entire chimera nation isn't going to agree on the best way to do that."

Braeden shifted, wincing at the soreness in his leg. A joke about not understanding wanting anyone bubbled to the surface, but what came out of his mouth instead was, "They won't stop coming, will they? Until they find Vala."

Jude shook his head. "They'll tear apart everything the humans have built."

"Why is she so important?" Rumor shifted, and his chair squeaked.

Jude frowned. "She's one of their own. Isn't that important enough?"

Nyx's abuela shuffled into the kitchen and puttered about, pulling out supplies for tea and paying them little attention other than to smile at Braeden when she caught him watching. His dad's family had been long dead when he was born. His mom's family lived in Beta colony, and he only saw them for special occasions. He had no idea about Bailey's family. She never talked about them. Reni Llorca had been the grandmother he'd never had—teaching him sign and how to make tea. She'd tried to teach him crochet, but he could never get the hang of it. He was content to let her make him things instead.

Nyx hurried in after her, fingers flying in rapid signs. "Not the time" was all he caught before her back turned. Her abuela ignored her until she'd put on a kettle of water, then wrinkled fingers flicked a few signs back.

"Always time for tea."

Braeden snickered.

Nyx sighed and rolled her eyes. She headed to the table and slid into a vacant chair across from Rumor. Braeden touched two fingers to her forearm and signed when she looked at him. "Okay?"

Her brown eyes were red-rimmed, and traces of mascara or liner smudged the corners like she hadn't gotten it all when she cleaned up. Bracelets slid down her forearm when she signed back. "Vala helped me understand the vibrations a little. Something bad is coming."

Braeden frowned harder as his hands moved. "Another attack?"

Nyx glanced over her shoulder, but her abuela had her back to them as she prepped spices for tea. She shook her head along with her sign. "I don't know."

"You want me to sign for you?"

Her smile was tired. "Please, yes. You don't have to ask."

"Yeah, I do."

She smiled at Jude, but it didn't reach her eyes. "You're from the forest."

Jude nodded, his eyes flickering to Nyx's abuela.

"She's Deaf like me," Nyx assured him. She leaned forward. "You were born there?"

Jude's eyebrows jumped.

Braeden shrugged.

"She loves origin stories. History. Where people come from. Ancestry. Especially if you know where your family came from back on Earth." He signed as he spoke.

"Oh, my dad's family was from New Zealand. My mom was, um, Dutch," Jude said. "That's all I know."

Nyx grabbed a piece of paper from the counter and a stubby pencil. She wrote down the places and then smiled at Rumor. "What about you?"

Braeden hid his grin behind a hand as Rumor frowned at her. She smiled expectantly at him, undeterred. "It's okay if you don't know. A lot of people don't."

Rumor slouched in his chair and folded his arms, silent for

so long, Braeden was sure he was refusing to answer. Rumor licked his lips, staring at the shiny tabletop as he spoke. "My mom was Indian. Like India. My dad is…was…" He sniffed and blinked rapidly. "He was Portuguese and Nigerian." He wore a sad smile. "I only know because we had a school project to see what, if anything, we'd kept from our Earth ancestors."

Nyx's smile softened, and she wrote down the countries. Behind them, the kettle whistled. It was an old ceramic thing that had been passed down since it'd made the journey on the generational ship. Braeden turned sideways in his chair and watched Reni add hot water to the teapot, put a crocheted cozy on top, and then shuffle out of the kitchen again. Some of the tension in the room left with her.

"Where are you keeping Vala?" Jude straightened and put both hands on the table.

Braeden rubbed a hand over his mouth before answering. Oh, this wasn't going to go over well. "Underground. There's a room."

"With a cage," Rumor added in a distracted tone. Braeden nearly kicked him under the table.

Jude made an angry sound and stood. "You locked her up in a cage?"

Braeden stood slowly, using every centimeter of his height and the broadness of his shoulders to stare down Jude. He might be to blame for a lot of things tonight, but. "I didn't lock her up. My mom did. She doesn't even technically know that I know. As far as anyone in this colony is concerned, only she and Bailey know about her. So *back off.*"

Nyx pulled on Braeden's shirt to get his attention. "What's going on, guys?"

"Sorry," he signed and quickly filled her in. She rolled her eyes when he was finished.

"What kind of a cage did you build that actually holds her?" Jude asked. He sat slowly.

"Adamantine," Braeden answered as he sat again.

Confusion passed through Jude's eyes, but he said nothing. Rumor watched him carefully for a long moment, then shifted his attention to Braeden. "Look, if you just give us the card, we can get her out. Jude's not a colonist, and I'm an angry kid who watched his dad die tonight." The ease with which those words fell out of Rumor's mouth sent a chill down Braeden's spine. "If we get caught, it's no big deal. Not like if you do."

Braeden wasn't about to acknowledge Rumor's logic. "No, then it incites a war against the forest people because my moms will think Jude was sent here specifically for that purpose. But if I go with you, my moms will keep my involvement quiet. The colony doesn't know about Vala. Plus, Mom is big on appearances. She wouldn't want people knowing her own son broke a gargoyle out from under her nose and sided with the rebels."

"You're siding with us?" Jude asked in surprise.

Braeden shook his head and held up a hand. He didn't know if he could explain the thoughts that'd been rolling around his head since the attack. "I didn't say that. But a lot of people died tonight. If I'd said something earlier or done something about it, maybe they'd still be alive."

Rumor leaned forward. "You realize what you're talking about is treason. If you do this, you can't come back. It's not like you can drop Vala off and return home before your mom realizes you've snuck out your bedroom window."

"Whoever comes with us can't return home," Jude said. "Maybe not ever."

"Why are you okay with it?" Braeden asked Rumor.

Rumor glanced at Jude, something unspoken passing between them. "I'm not going to figure out what happened at HUB2 by sitting here waiting for the next attack to happen. And I have nothing left to lose."

Braeden stared at his fingers. Spun his ring around and around. Unless he managed to end the war or something equally as momentous, he'd be a fugitive from the colonies. Exiled. He was a commander's son. If anyone found out about what he'd done, that would reflect on his mother.

But she'd kept an actual gargoyle in a cage below the city, quite possibly triggering the attack on HUB2. Maybe by removing Vala, he'd keep them out of trouble. Maybe he could come back when this was all over and explain.

Then again, away from his moms, he'd have a chance to leave. Or at least get outfitted for an automaton command. They wouldn't forcefully pry a chip out of his brain stem, would they?

Reni entered the kitchen again, paying them no mind as she headed for the teapot. He watched her go through the motions of straining the tea into the individual mugs she'd lined up on the counter.

"Braeden," Nyx said in a quiet undertone, bringing him out of his thoughts.

"You have a lot to lose," Rumor said. "I get it. Believe me."

"What are you protecting me from?" Braeden leaned forward and rested his elbows on the table, his heart pounding. "Ever since the dragon, you've been trying to shelter me or something. What's the deal?"

"What?" Confusion clouded Rumor's face. "You're hurt."

"So are you." Braeden pointed to Rumor's taped fingers. He hadn't put it together until this moment. The tunnels. Now leaving. At every turn since the dragon, since meeting Vala, Rumor had been pushing Braeden away. "You barely know me, man, and you keep saying you're protecting me. You're lying."

A muscle in Rumor's temple ticked. He pushed away from the table. "There's no one to miss me if I die tonight."

Jude's eyes closed. Braeden's lips parted. He stared, words emptying out of his brain. "You can't make that decision for us, man."

"I'm not." Rumor shook his head. "I'm just reminding you what you're leaving."

Braeden stood. "You think I don't know that?"

"Guys," Jude said quietly without looking up.

Braeden turned to Nyx and raised his hands to sign.

"Don't you dare tell me not to go," Nyx said, her eyebrow arched and her back to her abuela. "I was already going to leave tonight. My bag's already packed and everything. Just gotta get it from upstairs."

"Are you sure?" Braeden signed.

She gave him a look that was best interpreted as, *Ask me again. I dare you.*

"I'm going to ask you again because you're in love with Dahlia and she'll be crushed if you go," he snapped back, his lips tight and his signs sharp.

"I'm going to ask her to come with me," Nyx signed, a determination he'd never seen on her before filling her expression. "I'm going to tell her I'm leaving and that she should come with me because you're going out to risk your life and we'd be bad friends to not come help you."

"What about Abuela?"

Nyx glanced over her shoulder as Reni turned her back to them to set more water to boil. "She'll be fine," she said out loud. "I'd already thought of that. She's smart, she has her wits, she can take care of herself."

"That's not what I asked," he said out loud before he could stop himself then switched back to sign. "What about her losing you to this? She already lost your parents."

Nyx's nod lost a little of its force. She glanced at Jude, who looked mildly confused, but Braeden had no desire to catch the guy up right now. "I need to know what the vibrations are. I'm not going to find that out here. And staying here doesn't bring my family back."

Braeden didn't know what to do with that. His stomach rolled over the food he'd just eaten. He felt like crying, but he didn't know who or what for. "I'm going," he said, meeting Rumor's eyes. "I'm not just a commander's son, but this is my home, and if leaving saves it, then I'm gone."

Rumor lifted his chin, silent as his gaze raked over Braeden's face. After a moment, he nodded slowly. "Okay."

"If we don't do this tonight, another assault on Epsilon will happen," Jude said, mostly to the table.

"Okay," Nyx said. "Then we get her out tonight."

Jude nodded, the tiniest of smiles pulling at his lips. He seemed somewhere between relieved and high-strung.

"One more thing: we free Vala, then you take me to Reaper," Rumor said, turning to Jude.

"Rumor," Jude said, looking pained.

"That's the deal." Rumor pointed at him. "You want me to free your gargoyle, then you help me find the one who killed my dad and destroyed my city." He walked out of the room before anyone could respond, ignoring the cup of tea Nyx's abuela held out to him.

"Rumor. Stop." Braeden took the tea from Reni with a quick kiss to her powdered cheek and bolted after Rumor. Now was not the time for Mr. Grumpy to be stalking off all huffy.

Rumor smacked the button to open the front door and nearly bowled Dahlia over.

"Sorry." He grabbed the doorframe and her shoulder to stop himself.

Rumor's dramatic exit all but forgotten, Braeden paused halfway through the living room, his heart sinking at the devastation on Dahlia's face. "Dahl?"

"It's okay," she said in a muted voice. She gave Braeden a hesitant smile, which he returned.

"I didn't thank you before," she said to Rumor, her fingers fidgeting with the hem of her shirt. "You didn't have to go down there."

"How is he?" Rumor asked.

Dahlia opened her mouth to speak, then closed it, silver eyes welling as she shook her head once. Rumor pulled her into a fierce hug, holding her tight to his body and burying his face in her neck.

Braeden's chest physically ached at the loss spilling out of them. He heard a soft noise. Nyx stood in the doorway, her face a mess of emotion he couldn't completely decipher. She may have been upset at Dahlia being upset. Or upset that Rumor was hugging her. Or both. He wasn't good with others' emotions sometimes. Attraction was weird.

"I'm sorry I wasn't fast enough," Rumor said, just barely loud enough for Braeden to hear. He didn't know if he should sign it, so he stayed still. He was already intruding on a private moment.

"Stop," Dahlia said with a sniff. She pushed away. "Don't blame yourself. You tried, which is more than anyone else in this stupid colony did."

Rumor moved so she could slip in the doorway. He stared at the street. Braeden didn't know whether to stop him from leaving or let it play out. His muscles twitched, wanting to move, but Dahlia shook her head. Braeden handed her the tea, but it felt so inadequate. She took it and headed for Nyx.

The door whispered shut with Rumor still in the house. He turned and faced them, his expression determined. Jude appeared in the kitchen doorway and leaned against the frame, his gaze darting over all of them.

"You went down in the tunnels, too," Dahlia said. "I didn't get a chance to thank you. I'm Dahlia."

"Jude." He held out a hand, which she took.

"What's with the party?" Dahlia asked Braeden.

"We're going to break Vala out and head to the forest," Braeden said, his heart leaping at the words spoken aloud. No sense in sugar-coating it. This was it. He was leaving. Goose bumps rolled up his arms, and the hair on the back of his neck stood up.

Dahlia scowled at Rumor. "This your idea?"

"Why would it be my idea?" Rumor asked in alarm.

"Seems like one of the dumbass ideas you had when we were dating," she said.

"Yeah, let a gargoyle loose so we can go have a chat with more gargoyles. Completely sounds like me."

"Guys." Braeden huffed and scrubbed a hand through his hair.

Rumor blew out a breath. "Not my idea."

"Fine," she said and looked away.

"Girls?" Jude asked Rumor, his expression a little too stiff suddenly.

"I'm bi," Rumor answered, his shoulders tight but his expression easy.

Jude nodded, as if that was the end of it.

"Moving on." Braeden rolled his eyes, glad he didn't have to deal with any of that. It was all far too stressful.

Jude cleared his throat. "I need to find my brother and Yi-Min. My cuff isn't working here anymore. If you're serious about helping, you need to figure out how to get Vala out of whatever your moms are keeping her in. The longer she goes without direct contact to the moon, the weaker she'll get."

"Yes, because a pure white creature with horns will be easy to sneak out of the gates," Braeden said with a grin, his hands flicking off the signs as sarcastically as his voice. "Piece of cake."

"It's nightside," Jude countered.

Braeden pointed out the window. "Dude, we have a nebula. It doesn't get that dark, in case you haven't noticed."

Jude frowned. "You guys need more trees."

"I'll put it in the comment box," Braeden muttered.

"I'm only repeating this once now that everyone is here," Rumor said in a calm voice that sent shivers down Braeden's spine. "If you do this, if you come with us, you can't go home. You'll be listed as rebels, as fugitives. If they catch you, you'll be tried for treason. Most likely put to death as an example. I've seen it happen."

Braeden looked at Dahlia. She'd be leaving her medical

studies, her mom, everything she'd known. She looked at Braeden and Nyx. "You two going?"

They nodded.

"Everyone in this room is leaving?"

More nods.

She folded her arms. "Without me? Again?"

Nyx grimaced and signed quickly, "I want you to come with me. Please."

"Why?" Dahlia smacked the sign off her forehead and curled her fingers into a Y. Her chest hitched as she set the mug on the table with a thunk. "You two are all I have left and you're leaving?"

"That's not what's happening. I'm not going without you," Nyx signed in a rush.

Dahlia's shoulders dropped a fraction as the silence grew thin and tense. "Everything here hurts too much now." She glanced at Rumor. "I know all of you. You're my family. Except you, but we'll fix that," she said to Jude. "I go where my family goes."

"What about your mom?" Braeden asked. "Your studies?"

"You guys got medical facilities in the forest?" she asked Jude.

"Stocked with plenty of leaves for bandages," he said with a wide grin.

"He's joking," Rumor said.

"I am," Jude said, his tone serious. "We stopped using leaves last week."

Dahlia waved a hand. "Okay."

Nyx's abuela shuffled through the room with a tray of mismatched teacups. She set it on the coffee table and smiled at each of them pleasantly before selecting a delicate cup with flower patterns and heading upstairs. They all watched her go, tension curling around them like snakes. Nyx wore guilt all over her face.

Braeden stared at his colony-issued cuff for a long moment before unlocking it and tossing it on the table. It bounced and fell to the floor, facedown. "Okay, well, I have an idea."

NYX

Nyx, Dahlia, and Braeden headed for the sailboard lot to get Jude, Trick, and Yi-Min's boards. Rumor took Braeden's card and headed underground to get Vala and escape through the secondary water intake tunnels. If they were caught, the story was Rumor stole the card while Braeden was showering after the last attack. Braeden clearly hated that part of the plan, as evidenced by the constant tightening of his jaw muscles as he walked, but there was no other way around it. If he was going to go down as a rebellious commander's son, they wanted it to mean something.

Nyx's stomach swooped at the thought of Braeden risking everything for this. For a gargoyle...*a chimera*...she corrected herself. And maybe for her, too. To help her figure out what these rumblings were. What they were trying to tell her.

Meanwhile, Jude had tried to contact Trick, but his cuff wasn't working properly anymore. He'd left to find his brother and Yi-Min so they could get out of the colony and warn Jude's oldest brother, Kaipo, and any other chimera who were willing to help in case they needed it.

The major worry now was Rumor and how he'd treat

Vala when he was alone, but Jude seemed to naively think he wouldn't harm her.

Nyx paid more attention to the vibrations as they walked than Braeden's brooding. Ever since she'd met Vala, a new sense of realization had crept through her consciousness like rains washing the grime away. New details emerged, new sensations were apparent. The vibrations were less words and phrases and more sense and emotion. The fear still wrapped around her middle and made it harder to breathe and concentrate when she was on the bare ground, but Vala had somehow translated. Acted as a conduit to funnel the vibrations and make her stronger by giving her support to understand. Maybe that was all she needed—direction.

Foundation.

The fact that it came from a gargoyle split her insides in separate directions. On the one hand, the gargoyles were intelligent creatures with language and reasoning. And wasn't that the basest and easiest way to sum up humanity? Other than external appearance, what differentiated humans from the gargoyles?

Braeden elbowed her and held up a K with his eyebrows up in question.

She nodded, not sure how to speak her thoughts or if she even wanted to give them a voice. It all felt spectacularly treasonous.

"We do this, we can't come back," she signed.

Braeden nodded, his face grim. "I'm not going to find answers here."

She hesitated before signing, "Have you considered asking your mom or Bailey?"

He shook his head. "They won't tell me anything. They've hidden Vala this whole time." His signs stabbed the air.

Nyx rolled her eyes. "You think she'd confide military secrets in you?"

Braeden stuck his tongue out at her.

She swallowed a smile and looked past him at Dahlia. She seemed far away, her eyes distant and her lips thin. She twisted a lock of hair around her fingers as they walked. Nyx stopped at a covered walkway and plucked several bright purple flowers from the overhang. She pulled on Dahlia's arm to stop her and pushed the large flowers into her afro like before, turning her into a freckled fairy princess with sad silver eyes.

Dahlia smiled ever so slightly. It wasn't much, but Nyx would take it and hold it close.

"They'll fall out when we use the sailboards," she signed.

"We'll find more," Nyx said.

Dahlia's smile was a touch bigger that time, and Nyx's insides fluttered. She turned away and caught Braeden's gaze. His smile was encouraging.

Nyx glanced back at Dahlia. Dahlia was frowning at the entrance to the sailboard lot, where an automaton cat waited with its marine handler.

Braeden touched Nyx to get her attention. "You guys hold back. I got this."

Nyx arched an eyebrow.

He kept his signs close to his chest. "If the commander's son is going rebel, then I need to use my pull now, right?"

Nyx stood by Dahlia, her heart in her throat. Braeden walked up to the marine, his hand out in greeting. The vibrations of the moon rolled up Nyx's legs. Dahlia's arm brushed hers, and goose bumps erupted across her skin.

Dahlia squeezed her arm. "You okay?"

Nyx nodded, then shrugged, then shook her head. "I need to tell you something."

Dahlia raised her eyebrows in question, then looked away suddenly. Braeden was waving them over, wearing an especially pleased expression. Dahlia held up a wait-a-moment finger.

"What is it?" she signed to Nyx.

"Later. We need to get out of here." Nyx darted across the

street before Dahlia could answer, her eyes burning as emotion translated to tears she didn't want or need at the moment. Braeden shot her an odd look as she walked past him and into the sailboard lot.

She was such a coward. Why was it so hard to say *I love you*?

She'd said yes to treason, but she couldn't tell her best friend she was in love with her.

Silly girl.

They split up and ran down the rows, searching for the markings Jude had described. Sailboards came in all sizes: from the tiny one-man riders that bore messengers around the outpost to larger two-man boards with glowing sails, more suited for longer distances. There were also boards that switched from air travel to water travel with the flick of a button, pulling the engine into a waterproof compartment. Boards that required fingerprints to activate. Older models that only needed a code punched into a weathered keypad.

Nyx found two of the boards Jude had described. One had a stylized gryphon on the board, its tail wrapping around the engine and its wings flaring up into the sails themselves. A smile pulled at her lips. The design was beautiful, even if the memories it evoked weren't.

The rider next to it had a blue sail and a smaller red sail. The board was solid black with silver insets for feet. It was sleeker and newer than the gryphon one.

She didn't see the third one Jude had described anywhere.

She pulled her tablet out and sent off a quick message to the other two, then tapped the five-digit code into each keypad near the engine compartment. The engines hummed under her fingertips, a gentle thrumming that tingled her skin and made her smile. Her heart gave a little lurch at the thought of riding one. She'd only ridden one a few times, and she'd even asked Abuela for one many times.

Brown fingers with silver rings slid over her arm and

squeezed. Nyx smiled weakly at Dahlia, then pointed to the two boards. "I don't see the third one."

Braeden hopped onto the gryphon one, one hand adjusting the sail as he locked his feet to the board. Dahlia climbed onto the black board, the beginnings of a grin pulling at her mouth. Dahlia loved speed, and it was so good to see something distracting her right now.

Dahlia gestured to Nyx, pointing to the space behind her on the board.

Nyx hesitated. "Will it hold both of us?"

Dahlia nodded.

Nyx gestured to her body. "Are you sure?"

Dahlia rolled her eyes and pointed at the board with an emphatic fingertip before grabbing the boom with both hands as she adjusted the sail. She spoke over Nyx's head, but Nyx lost the words as they flew past her in a snatch of syllables.

Braeden grinned and signed as he headed toward the other sailboard. "She says you'd better stop worrying about your fine ass and get it on her board or she's gonna kick it."

"I hate both of you," Nyx muttered even as she blushed fiercely. She stepped onto the board. Dahlia helped her fit one foot into the imprint and showed her where to grab the boom. She grabbed Nyx's other arm and pulled it around her own waist, snugging them close together. Dahlia had to be able to feel Nyx's heart pounding against her spine.

Dahlia patted her arm and eased the board out of the space. Nyx gasped at the sudden bobbing movement and held on tighter. Braeden watched for a moment. He frowned, turned his attention up at the web repair work, then across the colony at some unseen point in the distance.

"If we get separated, you two keep going," he signed.

Dahlia's back stiffened. Nyx frowned at him. He rolled his eyes.

"I'm not sacrificing myself. The plan is to head through the reservoir gate and make for the forest. Don't stop until you're in the trees, then find a place to wait for the others." He smiled, and it was beautiful. "Just in case."

Nyx nodded and squeezed Dahlia's waist. Dahlia leaned against the boom to steer the rider away. Once the way to the lot exit was clear, she gunned it.

Kids on boards zipping through the colony wasn't anything abnormal. Messengers were usually teens anyway, making parcel runs for a few credits in tips. The tense silence of lockdown permeated the entire colony, however. Sailboards were sparse at best. Dahlia kept their board to the messenger lanes, cutting through narrow alleys coated in ferns and flowers. Nyx risked a glance over her shoulder every so often to make sure Braeden was still close behind them. He was hunched low, his dark hair flying back from his face.

Dahlia tapped Nyx on the arm twice and pointed straight ahead. They were nearing the reservoir. The gate at the far end of the man-made river opened up to Lake Llyn. Nyx wasn't even sure "lake" was the proper designation. How big could a body of water get before it was called "small ocean" instead?

A marine squad milled about just outside the gate, guns in hand and eyes sharp. In the wake of the attacks, the normally empty guard towers on either side of the gate held two guards apiece.

Nyx tightened her hold as Dahlia shifted her weight and gunned the engine, aiming straight for the walkway that snaked along the river and outside the walls. The sailboard thrummed under her boots. Nyx buried her face in Dahlia's back, breathing in her scent. She didn't want to see guards taking aim at them. She didn't want to see marines trying to stop them. She didn't want to see the inevitable death awaiting them on the other side of the wall, where gargoyles lay in wait for stupid prey to fly out dressed in *eat me* colors.

The board banked one direction, then another. Dahlia's voice rumbled through her back, but Nyx squeezed her eyes shut and held on as the board sped faster. The wind whipped at her, clawing at her clothes and skin, whistling in her buzzing ears. She thought maybe she heard yelling or gunshots, but it could've been her imagination. Fear-induced sounds echoing deep in her ears where sound never hit its target.

Dahlia tapped her arm. Nyx looked up, expecting to see blood and bullet holes. Guards with rifles. Gargoyles with outstretched claws and bared fangs.

All she saw was the lake whipping past on their left and the foothills growing larger on their right. The nebula sprawled above them, brilliant and beautiful. Stars peeked out from the clouds of color, pinpricks of light against the void.

She forgot how to breathe. The lights of the colony always blotted out the stars, turning the sky into a smear of nebula. She'd never known how brilliant the sky was beyond the nebula. Their host planet darkened a third of the view, its outer edge a wash of reds and pinks as gaseous storms raged on its poisonous surface. In seventeen hours, the binary suns would break the planet's edge and light up their moon's atmosphere in blues and greens, nearly washing the nebula from existence with their brightness.

"We made it?" she yelled.

Dahlia nodded and grinned over her shoulder. Nyx risked a glance behind them. Oh thank gods, Braeden was still behind them. He gave her a thumbs-up. She was about to respond in kind when several dark figures exited the walls after them. They were huge.

They were riding automata.

"We're being followed!" she yelled, hoping she was yelling loud enough for Dahlia to hear over the engines. She pointed for Braeden's benefit.

He crouched lower over his board, banking away to the right and into the foothills. Dahlia pulled up and turned, following him into a narrow valley that snaked away from the colony and brought them closer to the forest of black trees. Their golden leaves picked up the light from the nebula, glowing with a strange ethereal beauty. Nyx had no idea what lurked in the forests of Sahara. The colonies were self-sufficient and self-contained. You could go your entire life without leaving the security of the walls.

The wind barreled down the valley, pulling at the sails and pushing at the board under their feet, trying to upend them. The ground blurred as they flew over it—scrubby plants and bright flowers blending into a washed-out cacophony of color.

A rock to her left broke and little pieces exploded outward. A white line appeared across the gray stone to her left. A skid from a bullet as it missed its mark.

Her heart tripled its beat. "They're firing at us!"

Dahlia pointed straight ahead. Nyx peered over her shoulder, spotting Jude's shock of blond hair through the trees. A scaring pain cut across her arm. Heat flooded her body.

RUMOR

Rumor shoved the silver key card in his pocket as he jogged down the long hallway leading to Vala's cell. He pulled open the heavy door and froze at white light slicing across the room from another door open at the opposite end of the room. Two figures by Vala's cage whirled around, one with a gun aimed. Rumor's hands went up. "It's Rumor."

Trick cocked his head to the side but didn't lower the weapon. "You alone?"

Rumor nodded.

"Why are you here?" the other person asked, their voice suspicious.

"Yi-Min," Vala said in a gentle tone. "Rumor is helping us."

"I watched this kid kill a dragon and a handful of chimera a few hours ago," Trick said without taking his eyes off Rumor. "Forgive my distrust."

Rumor nodded without hesitation. "They attacked us. If you're waiting for me to apologize, it won't happen."

Trick made a disgusted noise. "Why are you here?"

"To set her free. Your brother's been looking for you. I guess both of you." His fingers itched to grab his blades, but he didn't dare. "Opening these doors set off alarms. We need to go."

Trick's eyes flicked behind Rumor and back to his face again. After a moment in which Rumor was nearly positive Trick was going to shoot him anyway, Trick lowered the weapon and pointed over his shoulder at the other door standing open. "We're taking her out that door. There's a tunnel that goes under the colony wall and lets out near the lake."

Rumor pulled the door shut behind him and hustled to the cage. "How do you know that?"

"They have friends in high places." Trick pointed to Yi-Min as they pressed a key card to the cage door then handed the card to Trick, who pocketed it. A light flashed white, and a beep filled the room. The door let loose with a clunk and swung open. Trick held a hand out. "My lady."

Vala's palm dwarfed his, her fingers draping most of the way down his forearm. She stepped out of the cage and straightened, her wings flaring to their full width with relish passing over her face. She opened her mouth wide in almost a yawn, showing off double rows of sharpened teeth lining a jaw that opened far wider than Rumor was comfortable with. Her dual tongues curled like twin snakes, and her sapphire eyes glittered.

Rumor's heart pounded. Could he do it? Could he kill her before the others stopped him? One fewer monster in the world. A monster he was *helping*.

Vala's head snapped to the door Rumor had come through. "They're coming."

"Come on," Trick urged. "Can you run?"

Vala nodded. "Get me to the rock."

They rushed toward the other opening.

"Do you have a gun?" Yi-Min asked Rumor. They wound their hair up in a bun and wrapped a cord around it. They pulled a silver chaos pistol from a holster under their arm.

Rumor shook his head. "Heritage blades."

Trick rolled his eyes. "Always carry a gun, man. Go with

Vala. We'll cover."

Rumor swallowed a biting retort and headed after Vala. He let her go through first. Shouts for them to stop followed them as they ran down the narrow hallway, its faint white glow dimming the farther they went. Vala pulled her wings tight to her body and hunched. Her clawed toes screeched across the metal floor with every step and set Rumor's teeth on edge. Gunshots rang down the tunnel, the sound distorting and throwing off his senses. Bullets punched the wall by his head and he ducked.

They reached a T-junction and dove behind the corner. Trick held his shoulder, blood seeping between his fingers, and sagged against the wall. He held out a tsunami pistol with a trembling hand. "Take it. I can't shoot righty."

Rumor took the gun, the grip slick with Trick's blood.

"Get him to safety," he said to Vala.

"The key card," Trick gasped.

Rumor dug Braeden's card out of his own pocket and held it out to Vala. "Press it to the pad like you've seen them do."

She nodded and wrapped a muscled arm around Trick. Rumor checked the ammunition quickly and peered around the corner. Two bodies lay in the corridor. Three more guards swept down the hall, guns raised.

"Freeze!" one shouted.

Yi-Min checked their ammunition and snapped the magazine home. They cracked their neck, winked at Rumor, then fired around the corner. "Go!"

Rumor blew out a quick breath and fired three warning shots at the floor by the guards' feet then took off running.

His back muscles tightened, and the shiny walls of the tunnel seemed to peel away with every blink, darkening and curling back like paper on fire. He smelled smoke and saw flashes of HUB2 crumbling and burning. He heard an echoing roar and flinched away from a flash of light to his left. When he blinked again, the hallway was back and a bullet hole smoldered in the wall.

Not now, he begged his brain.

Yi-Min grabbed his arm and tugged. "Don't stop or I'll leave your ass behind."

"You forest people are so nice." Rumor pounded down the dim hallway, snaking around a gentle curve, the air cooling around him the farther he went. More shouts followed him, and he fired twice over his shoulder in warning. He didn't want to kill the guards; they were just doing their job. Yi-Min seemed to have a different idea as they fired and someone screamed.

He spotted Vala and Trick ahead at a metal door. Why was it still closed?

"Go!" he shouted, his voice echoing off the cold walls.

"It isn't working," Trick said in a tight voice.

Rumor cursed.

Trick turned to him. "Try this key card. Left pocket. I can't reach it."

Rumor slipped his fingers into Trick's front pocket. Trick smirked at him, his eyes still full of pain. Rumor shook his head. "Don't get any ideas, dude."

"You're not really my type," Trick said.

"Trick, stop it," Yi-Min said as they took up a ready stance a few feet away, gun aimed the direction they'd come.

Rumor pulled a key card from Trick's pocket, his eyes on Trick's. He flashed a cocky grin as he moved away.

Rumor slapped the key card to the panel, holding his breath as it felt like forever until it flashed white. "Whose is this?"

Trick shouldered past him without an answer. Rumor briefly entertained the image of throttling him before following. Yi-Min brought up the rear, gun aimed until the door whooshed shut.

They'd entered a ten-by-ten room with a bright yellow door on the opposite wall and a digital panel covering half of one wall to their left.

"What is this?" Rumor asked.

"This is how they brought you in?" Trick asked Vala.

Vala nodded as she crouched and put her hand to the floor. "Water." She extended one long finger to the digital panel. "Behind that wall."

Rumor crossed to the panel. "You're saying the lake is on the other side of this wall? Like if I open this, a zillion gallons of water will flood this place?"

Vala nodded. Trick raised his eyebrows. "Do it."

Rumor threw Yi-Min the key card, and they opened the yellow door. Night air rushed in. Yi-Min tossed the card back to Rumor and headed out into the night, eyes sharp and gun ready. "It's clear," they called over their shoulder.

"A storm is coming," Vala said as she wrapped an arm around Trick again.

Trick accepted her help with a grimace. "We'll worry about that later."

Rumor's stomach dipped, and he jumped with surprise at the sudden bang on the first door. Trick motioned to him. "Hurry up. Set that to open, then get out here."

Rumor pressed the card to the panel, sending up a prayer to any deity that might exist. Trick shouted in alarm as the screen filled with scrolling commands. Rumor glanced over his shoulder.

The door to freedom slid shut. He growled in frustration. The banging increased on the other door. Muffled shouts and cursing bled through the cracks. He sucked his teeth, did some mental math, and made a quick—and probably very foolish—decision.

Rumor pulled out one of his blades and slashed at the controls leading outdoors before he could second-guess himself. It melted in a shower of sparks and oozing plastics. That would trap the guards in here long enough for the others to escape. Trouble was, it also trapped him.

Not even a day ago, he'd wanted to kill every gargoyle he saw.

Now he'd just sacrificed himself for a gargoyle and some forest kids.

But he was one step closer to his revenge.

He slashed the controls on the first door, rendering it stuck unless the guards could open it manually. Even an override couldn't get through the melted connections.

He had three bullets left and both his blades. The commands finally stopped scrolling, and a prompt blinked at the bottom, waiting for instructions. He typed in the command he'd spotted: the one to open the lake doors.

It asked for confirmation.

He pushed his hair out of his eyes and typed yes.

It asked for the key card.

The banging grew louder, and the tunnel doors opened a centimeter.

He pressed the key card to the plate.

A ten-second countdown began.

Rumor headed to the other side of the room, pressed himself in the corner with the gun aimed at the ever-widening doors, and counted off in his head.

5...

4...

3...

2...

Rumor took a deep breath and held it.

1

The doors opened, and the lake exploded into the tiny space.

JUDE

Jude hadn't been able to find Trick and Yi-Min. Worry knotted his insides as he crouched in the forest with George, who he'd met up with in the tunnels under Epsilon. He'd been forced to leave Epsilon alone and on foot when he ran out of time. He'd snuck out the same tunnels he'd followed Rumor down into earlier, his stomach turning over at the smell of death that infused the stale air.

They'll be fine. They can take care of themselves. I need to be here to help the others get out. He kept telling himself this over and over to ease the guilt in his chest. He glanced at George, who crouched in the shadows next him. "They'll be fine. They can take care of themselves."

George clicked his beak once, his black eyes fixed on the open water gate.

"They'll be fine," Jude repeated, mostly to himself. He cleared his throat. "Okay, you're going to have to head back and warn Azrou about the prison break."

George turned his head slowly to stare at Jude.

"Just warn the outer ring of security. They'll ferry it to Kai, but they have to be ready in case we're chased."

George grumbled a few harsh words in chimera and shot off into the darkness. Jude took a shaky breath as he watched the chimera disappear. George was fast and could hide in shadows. The woods were crawling with chimera both for and against humans.

Jude stood and crept along the tree line, staying out of sight as best as he could, his revolver in his hand. They had to rescue Vala before Reaper could circle back for another assault on Epsilon or any of the other colonies. Too many people's lives were at stake. He prayed to Mother that Angel would get the news in time and could work on relaying it to Reaper's troops. At least delay Reaper until he could see Vala for himself. Freeing Vala had to stop the assaults. Returning her had to be enough.

It had to be.

Seventeen hours left to dayside. If this didn't stop Reaper, they might not have enough time for whatever came next.

He curled his hands into fists until his nails bit into his palms. Was he so desperate for Vala's safe return that he'd agreed to killing Reaper?

Or was he simply foolish for continuing to hope that any sort of peace without bloodshed was possible?

Was he a fool for Rumor, or a fool in general?

It was ridiculous to think that something between a colonist and a forest rebel could amount to anything more than a few stolen kisses and exploring fingers on a warm body. The attraction was there, plain as dayside, but he hadn't seen anything deeper than that in Rumor's colors.

Jude flexed his sore wrist as he watched the ridge that separated the forest edge from Epsilon's walls, his heart pounding. What was taking so long? He took two steps forward, intent on heading in after them, then changed his mind and crouched, one hand on the black bark.

He strained his hearing against the chirps of insects and the rustling of nocturnal birds for boot stomps or gunshots.

For motors or shouting. For Vala. For Rumor. For chimera or automata.

A branch snapped behind him. Jude rose and spun, revolver aimed at the face of a hooded figure standing a few meters away, partly hidden in shadow. The style of the hood wasn't familiar. It was worn around the edges with braided stitching along the shoulders.

"Who are you?" Jude asked. His back brushed a tree, and he planted his feet.

The figure didn't answer. They carried a crossbow in one gloved hand. A larger recurve bow was strung diagonally on their back. A quiver of black arrows peeked over their left shoulder.

No cloud of emotions swirled around them. A tremble rolled down his arms and he tried to see through the shadows in case their emotions were black and blending in with the surroundings.

Nothing.

Not a single color.

His heart pounded. "You're not from Azrou."

No answer.

"One of the other forest communities?" he asked.

No colors.

Shivers rolled up Jude's spine as the figure tilted their head in a mirror of Jude's. He could have sworn the nebula-light caught their eyes in a bluish-silvery sheen, but it was gone in a breath. Jude licked his lips. "Look, I'm really busy right now, so either tell me what you need or keep going to where you're headed."

The figure flexed their fingers around the crossbow.

Jude arched an eyebrow, his muscles tensing. "Don't even think about it."

The staccato of gunfire broke the standoff. Jude's heart leaped into his throat as he glanced over his shoulder toward Epsilon. A flash of color caught his attention. A sailboard with one passenger appeared over the edge of the ridge. Braeden. Another rider followed close behind, carrying Nyx and Dahlia.

He sighed with relief and turned back around.

The hooded figure was gone.

Jude swallowed a curse and turned, heading out of the tree line to flag the sailboards down.

Gunfire behind them pulled him up short. As the riders zipped around a curve, several automata bounded after them, each carrying a figure dressed in black who was holding a rifle. Epsilon guards. Jude darted to the left, along the line of the ridge out of sight but parallel to the riders. He skidded to a halt by a boulder and aimed, wincing against the stiffness in his sprained wrist. He fired toward the cats, wanting to deter them, not kill anyone.

The bullets struck rocks, pinging debris at the guards, who turned and fired in Jude's direction. Tiny shards splintered from the boulder as he ducked behind it, slicing across his arm. That was way too close.

"What in deep space?" he muttered. Apparently killing the commander's son didn't faze them at all.

He veered left back toward the trees then cut diagonally toward another bend in the valley. He turned a corner and skidded down a short embankment to a line of small scrub brush. Their limbs twisted up toward the nebula like slender fingers, gnarled and an ashy gray color with tufts of crimson leaves. He stopped and listened for the sailboards, waiting until they were near enough before stepping out of the brush.

Braeden spotted him in time and held out an arm. Jude grabbed it and stepped onto the board in front of Braeden, who scooted back, placing a hand on Jude's hip for balance. Jude slid his feet into the grooves on the board and grabbed the boom, using his back heel to tap the switch twice to increase the speed. He crouched, streamlining his body, zipping through the air. Nyx and Dahlia followed as they climbed higher. He glanced down at their pursuers. The three guards raised their guns and fired, the muzzle flashes pops of crimson color in the greenlit night.

Pain seared across his thigh and he gritted his teeth. Braeden yelled something, but it was lost in the speed and wind and guns. A bullet ripped through the sail by Jude's shoulder. He zigzagged out of the way of their fire.

"Jude!" Braeden called, pointing at the ground.

The roar reached his ears before he followed the point.

George.

The black chimera slid through the foothills, wings unfurled and beak clicking as he tumbled into the lead automaton like a rockslide. Jude yanked on the bar, executing a perfect flip. Braeden held on tight, whooping at the sudden movement. One of the guards crawled away from their ruined automaton and George's flashing talons, raising their gun at Nyx and Dahlia, who were still several yards back. Jude and Braeden shouted warnings.

A flash of white streaked past them and crashed into the guard, sending their shot wide into the night. Jude pulled the rider up short, eyes wide and heart in his throat, all his attention on the one chimera he'd relentlessly searched for.

Vala rose to her full height in front of the guard, wings wide and fangs bared, her silver-veined skin practically glowing in the nebula light. She snarled, reaching for his neck with her long fingers.

Jude opened his mouth to scream.

"Vala! No!" Yi-Min jumped in between her and the guard. They looked over their shoulder at the marine. "Get back to the colony! Go!"

The guard didn't need to be told twice. He scrambled to his feet and ran, leaving the gun lying at Yi-Min's feet. Yi-Min held their hands up, panting and eyes wide as they stared down Vala. "You kill them, and it makes all of this so much harder. You know that."

Vala growled something in her own language that Jude didn't catch, but she pulled back. Jude landed the board, jumping off before it was on the ground and running to her, not bothering to slow as he slammed into her. Strong arms wrapped around Jude, and he pressed his face to her sternum.

"Little one," she rumbled in her language.

Her hearts thumped gently under his cheek.

"I thought they'd killed you," he said, his voice somewhere between a relieved laugh and a sob.

"Jude."

Jude jerked in surprise and pulled away from Vala's chest, meeting Trick's wide eyes. Trick gave Jude a relieved grin that didn't reach his eyes. "You okay?"

Jude nodded. "Y'all?"

Trick's normal violet was tinged with clouds of gray and orange. He was holding his arm to his chest, blood covering his shoulder. "Have you seen Rumor yet?"

Jude swiped his palms across his eyes. "What do you mean?"

Nyx and Dahlia landed their board, Nyx holding onto her own bicep with her other hand. Dahlia was signing quickly, her eyes wide. "Braeden!" she shouted over her shoulder. "Nyx was shot!"

Braeden shoved Jude out of the way as he ran for Nyx.

Jude held Trick's gaze. "Trick, what happened? Where's Rumor?"

"What do you mean, 'Where's Rumor?'" Dahlia interrupted. "Why isn't he with you?"

"He was going to flood the tunnels to stop the guards," Trick said quickly. "But then the doors shut before he could get out to us."

"There's a sealed tunnel leading from the lake to…where they kept Vala," Braeden said, not looking away from Nyx's arm. "It was for ancillary water storage if we ever needed it. Does anyone have anything I can use as a bandage?"

Yi-Min handed a handkerchief out of their pocket and the leather tie out of their hair to Braeden, and then started examining Trick's shoulder.

Jude's stomach plummeted to his feet as his brain latched onto water storage and lake access. *Rumor's okay. He can take care of himself.* "Could he have gotten out that way?"

"Depends on if he was able to get the lake doors open before the guards got to him," Trick answered, his words cutting off with a sharp yelp of pain as Yi-Min pulled his shirt collar to one side.

"We can't leave him here," Dahlia said, her eyes wide as she rubbed Nyx's back.

"We have to go back in for him," Braeden said as he wrapped up Nyx's arm. She had her face buried in Dahlia's chest. "I can get back in since I'm the commander's son. The guards won't—"

"You mean the guards who just tried to shoot you out of the sky?" Yi-Min asked as they glanced around, every muscle strung tight. "Are you changing your mind, colonist?"

Braeden set his jaw and met their gaze. "It was just an idea. Nyx needs medical attention."

"So does Jude." Yi-Min pointed to Jude's bleeding thigh.

Jude looked down in surprise. He hadn't even noticed how bad it was. Pain flared through his leg as soon as he acknowledged the wound. "Oh."

George sniffed it then whined low and long.

"So do I," Trick ventured, his face tight with pain. Sweat dotted his forehead.

Jude stared at George, indecision pulling him in two directions. He had to get them to safety. Especially Trick and Nyx, who were losing blood. Rumor would be fine. He would take care of himself.

"Jude," Yi-Min said in a quiet tone as they pulled Trick's arm around their shoulders and held him up. "If he opened the lake doors but wasn't able to get out…"

"No," Jude and Dahlia said at the same time.

"Don't." Jude sucked in a shaky breath. "Okay, I'll sneak back in with Braeden and find him. The rest of you—"

Vala rose suddenly and pointed toward the lake. "There."

Jude didn't hesitate. He bolted down the narrow valley and over rocks, running as fast as he could for the shoreline. Yi-Min called after him, and pain lapped through his thigh in waves, but he didn't care. He skidded to a stop on the rocky beach and spun in a full circle, looking up and down the water's edge, his heart hammering. George growled and nudged Jude's hip with his beak, gesturing down the beach.

Rumor crawled out of the water and collapsed on his side. Water streamed off him, plastering his clothes and his hair to his skin. As Jude neared, Rumor rolled to his back, gasping for air and staring at the sprawling sky. Jude collapsed to his knees beside him. "Are you okay?"

Rumor slung his forearm over his eyes and nodded, coughing. Water ran off him in rivulets, staining the rocky shore under him. His lips were an alarming shade of blue, and as he lay there, he shivered.

Jude reached for him, but then pulled back. "Are you hurt?"

His hands shook as he reached for Rumor again and examined his torso for injuries, checked his pant legs for blood. There were a few small cuts around one eye. His bandage had come off his broken fingers, which were swollen and as blue as his lips.

"I think one of the guards maybe got me, but I can't feel my legs right now so I don't know. That lake is really cold, did you guys know that?"

Jude snorted. "You're fine."

"Is Vala safe?" Rumor asked without moving his arm.

"I am," Vala answered. "I am in your debt."

Rumor didn't answer.

"Vala, can you fly?" Jude asked as he watched Rumor's chest rise and fall with every breath. *He's fine. He's fine. They're all alive for now.*

Vala nodded once and spread her great wings. "The destroyed city?"

Jude shook his head, emotion splintering every bone in his body. For once, he was glad he couldn't see his own colors, because he had to be a veritable rainbow of confusion. He shook his head again, his voice lodged in his throat in a mass of questions with no answers and plans with no logic. He watched the others make their way toward them. His eyes burned in the corners.

"How much time is left?" Rumor pushed himself up on one elbow.

"A little over sixteen hours," Dahlia answered, her face tight with concern.

"Home," Jude managed hoarsely. "Let's get everyone home."

RUMOR

Rumor's skin prickled as gargoyles slid through the underbrush around him. Several leaped from branch to branch above, clicking and rumbling to each other as the group slowed to a stop. Rumor flinched away the first few times, his heartbeat thundering against his ribs and his hands going for his blades every time.

"I don't like this," he muttered while Trick spoke to two people standing in front of the base of a cliff.

"You'll be fine." Dahlia squeezed his arm and turned her attention back to Nyx, who was apparently too busy gaping at everything to worry about her injury.

He'd stayed next to Dahlia during the walk through the forest. There were twisted paths through the trees and checkpoints with people who gave them narrow-eyed looks as they checked the group's weapons and—sometimes grudgingly—handed them back.

Jude stood by Trick, answering questions. He glanced back at Rumor every so often, his eyes dark. Rumor shivered, unsure if it was his wet clothes or Jude's piercing stare. Blood stained Jude's pant leg, spreading outward from a long rip in the thigh.

He'd limped the whole way through the forest, more focused on his brother's injury than his own.

"Here," Braeden said, grabbing his jacket.

Rumor shook his head, curling his fingers around the heavy fabric and pulling it back up Braeden's arms. "This was your dad's, wasn't it?"

Braeden nodded. "How'd you know?"

Rumor pointed to the cuffs. "They changed the emblem here about five years ago."

A half smile curled the corner of Braeden's lips. He blinked rapidly as he stared at his sleeve.

"You four will be subject to a check by our doctors," one of the guards said to Rumor, Braeden, Nyx, and Dahlia. Braeden signed for Nyx in the dim glow of one of the guard's lights. Nyx's mouth pressed knife-thin as she held her arm.

"Well, seeing as how she's shot, let's get right on that instead of standing here sucking our thumbs," Dahlia said.

The guard's eyes snapped around the group as if someone would take responsibility for her. When no one spoke, he cleared his throat. "We've called medical already. They'll meet you inside."

Security stepped aside. Jude let Trick go first, resting his hand on the cliff face. His fingers seemed to disappear into the rock itself, and Rumor wondered if he'd been deprived of too much oxygen in the lake.

"Ohhhh, that's nice," Braeden breathed in awe as they neared Jude. The passage entrance was an optical illusion, only visible from a precise angle. What looked like a solid cliff wall was actually the narrow opening to a mountain pass, which sloped downward in a zigzag fashion.

Braeden caught up with the others, glee across his face, as Rumor paused by Jude.

"Where does it go?" Rumor nodded toward the path.

"Home," Jude said in a tired voice. He limped in and glanced back. "Coming?"

The exhaustion in Jude's eyes and relaxation of his broad shoulders put approximately twenty-three images in Rumor's brain of the two of them curling up together. The moment on the plaza jumped to the forefront of his mind, flushing his body with heat. He wanted that again. He wanted it to be real and for there to be no one around to interrupt them. He had sixteen hours to kill Reaper. As his eyes swept up and down Jude's body, sixteen hours suddenly felt like enough time. His insides knotted as he fell into step with Jude and they followed the others down the zigzag path. "How's your leg?"

"I'll make it," Jude said.

"That's not what I asked," Rumor said.

"Careful, Rumor." Jude's voice quieted. "Someone might think you care."

Rumor caught the teasing undercurrent in Jude's voice, but the quip hit him just the same. Care. Sure, he cared about Jude. Just like he cared about the others…well, about Dahlia. Just because his heart did a little lurch when Jude's eyes landed on him, or his stomach fluttered when Jude ran his fingers over his bottom lip, that didn't mean anything.

Care.

There'd been missed moments and *almosts* between them several times so far tonight, but was it even worthwhile to entertain anything beyond a stranger to make out with in an alleyway for a few precious minutes?

They'd won, right? Part of him said yes. The other part, the part still bent on revenge, said no. Said he still had a job to do. But what if he could satisfy that part with everything they'd done tonight? How much further could he push himself tonight before he took one too many risks?

Reaper killed your dad.

You're also exhausted.

Couldn't he rest for a moment? Wasn't Rumor finally free to push Jude against this very mountain and kiss that curve of his neck right where it joined his shoulder?

Rumor shoved his hands in his pockets so he wouldn't grab Jude's slender fingers and hunched his shoulders, trying to pay attention to the surroundings instead of the constant warmth of the blond boy limping next to him. A breeze swirled out of the path ahead, and Rumor shuddered when it hit his damp shirt.

"Should get you out of those clothes," Jude murmured.

"What?"

Jude raised his eyebrows, his face overly passive. "Because they're wet."

Rumor's cheeks went hot. "Right. Wet."

"Drenched," Jude said.

Ahead of them, George clicked his beak once, and Jude grinned but said nothing. Rumor didn't want to know.

But oh man, Jude was beautiful when he smiled.

They left the mountain pass and entered the forest, reaching more checkpoints and collecting more narrowed eyes and expressions of distrust. Sometimes, Jude would move almost as if shielding Rumor, his green eyes hard at whoever stared at them malevolently. Even gargoyles growled at them, causing Rumor to tense and his breathing to quicken. Jude rested his hand on Rumor's arm more than a few times, calming him down or holding him back.

"They don't trust colonists," Jude murmured as they neared Azrou.

"Really? Couldn't tell," Rumor muttered.

"No one will do anything," Jude said.

Rumor raised an eyebrow. "Why, because you brought me here, so I belong to you now?"

Jude's lips twitched in a smile. "Sure, if you want to call it that."

Rumor ignored the pang in his chest at the brush-off. Just a colony boy and a forest boy. Never more.

He focused on the growing signs of civilization as they

walked. The mountain pass widened into a road which split off into various branches leading to clusters of either domes along the ground or multistory buildings soaring high in the treetops. Even though the tree buildings were constructed and painted to blend in with the surrounding foliage, there was no hiding the signs of life. Washing hung on a line to dry. An overturned trash bin lay to one side, dented. A scrap heap of automaton parts gleamed in the nebula light. Staircases spiraled up trees to lofted homes. Bridges connected trees high in the canopy, swooping from building to building and creating a whole other level above them. Repurposed transport trucks dotted an outdoor market, panels removed to create open-air shops. Amber lights spaced along the pathways provided more than enough light.

Jude leaned closer to Rumor, pride and comfort in every line of his body. "Welcome to Azrou, the capital settlement of the Saharan forest."

Word had spread fast of their impending arrival. Children swarmed Vala, laughing as they ducked under her great wings and hugged her legs. Even though many adults shot worried glances in the direction of HUB2, Vala's safety brought tight smiles to their faces. Gargoyles greeted her with bows or forehead touches. A two-headed gargoyle named Angel embraced her the longest, both faces awash with joy. It was as if she was a conquering hero returning home after battle, or a revered queen or high priestess returning to her people. She greeted each of them as if they were an old friend.

Rumor frowned as he watched the displays of affection. His hands shook. He curled them into fists then stretched his fingers out to quell the instinctual reaction. *They aren't the ones who attacked HUB2. They aren't the ones who killed Dad.*

He peeled off from the group, standing to one side while Vala embraced a tall, brown-skinned man with the same piercing blue eyes as Trick. Yi-Min kissed the man briefly then escorted Nyx to the medical clinic. Braeden went with her, his face concerned.

Gargoyle babies tumbled past, squawking and flapping tiny wings as they played with human children.

Jude joined Trick, speaking to him in low tones. Rumor started to move in that direction, but several strangers gathered around him. They tried to shake his hand, but Dahlia intercepted them in time, smiling warmly. Rumor's fingers twitched. Too many people. The trees closed in on him. Tingling spread across his cheekbones.

Slim fingers slid into his, pulling them away from his weapon and curling around his palm. He clutched at Dahlia, her calming presence seeping into his skin and pushing at the roiling anxiety rushing through his veins.

"I saw you drowning." She offered him a cheeky grin.

In a world of black bark and red dirt and yellow leaves and creatures the color of stone, Dahlia was the only thing from his past who was familiar. Who knew him as much as anyone could. He'd been moving nonstop since HUB2 fell. He'd killed and clawed and sliced and broken himself open, and for what?

To walk alongside the creatures who'd taken everything from him?

Now, standing here, it hit him—he'd done it. He'd done what his father asked. With Vala's return, the assaults would stop. He could breathe.

He could stand still. He could have a memorial for his dad.

He should be happy and relieved. He should be looking for a bed—preferably one containing Jude. But all he could think about was his city in ruins and the bloody trail left by the hellhounds taking his father's body. He stood in the middle of a rebel community deep in the forest, where the trees were as wide as buildings and towered above them taller than any colonist structure. The dense foliage blocked so much of the nebula that the area outside the glowing amber lamps was actually dark.

"Needs more trees," Rumor murmured.

"What?" Dahlia asked.

He shook his head.

"What's wrong?" she asked.

He cut her a sideways glance and raised an eyebrow.

"Well, I could ask you if you're okay, but you'd say you were fine, which is a lie. And I'd call you on it and you'd sigh at me and then I'd ask what's wrong," she explained. "So I figured I'd skip all that and ask you what's wrong."

"This feels off. I've never seen anything like this, and I can't stop wanting a weapon in my hands." He scraped his teeth across his bottom lip, catching a bit of loose skin and pulling at it until it peeled off. His lip stung, but the pain centered him and gave him something to focus on. "What about you?"

"It feels like something we're supposed to be doing," she said. "You're bleeding."

Rumor wiped at his lip. "Supposed to be doing?"

Dahlia huffed and grabbed his chin with one hand while she dabbed at his lip with the hem of his T-shirt. He took a moment to examine her. She'd always carried herself with her chin up, silver eyes daring the world to pass judgment on her. Even when she was figuring out who she was and sliding into different gender identities trying to find the right fit, she still walked with her chin up, and that was something he'd always loved about her.

He rubbed his thumb under her left eye. "Your eyeliner smudged."

She smiled at him and dropped his shirt. "I probably look like I haven't slept in days."

"Normal, then."

She pushed at his shoulder. Her eyes met his, and his heart lurched. Was he falling for her again, or was he clinging to something familiar?

"Why are you here?" he blurted.

Dahlia frowned. "I got my reasons."

"Dahl," he said.

"My dad might be alive," Dahlia said quietly. "I think he

might've been at HUB2 or here."

Rumor's heart twisted. "I thought your mom said he died when the ships fell."

Dahlia swiped her fingers under one eye. "It was a guess on her part based on transfer rotations and stuff she knew but never told me. I was going to apply for an internship at the medical center in HUB2 when my classes were done next year so I could find him."

"I didn't know," he finally managed.

"I only know my mom's Latina. I got no idea where my dad's from. Where I get my silver eyes."

Rumor shifted. "I hope you find him."

Dahlia gave him a smile. "Me, too." She backed away a few steps and flung her arms out to the side. "We did it, Rumor. We freed Vala and escaped and no one died. Reaper will stop attacking the colonies. Smile, man. We won. You can take five minutes."

As she jogged toward the medical center where the others had disappeared, Rumor dug for the happy relief Dahlia had displayed. Some of the tentative elation that wrapped around this community at the return of their own.

Jude limped out of the medical clinic and sat down on a nearby bench, staring at the ground.

We won. You can take five minutes.

JUDE

Jude sat on a carved bench, his elbows on his thighs and his head hanging. The last ten hours had caught up to him as soon as they'd stepped foot within the safety of the community. He'd held still long enough for Yi-Min and then one of the docs to check his leg. The bullet had grazed him, ripping his pants and skimming the skin enough to leave a burn and shallow cut. They'd sponged it off, smeared some medical gel across it, and pressed a bandage to it. He'd left as soon as he could. Away from the walls and medicine and simple uniforms that never ceased to remind him of the night his parents were crushed to death.

Now, he sat well away from everyone and stared at the forest floor. The grayish-red dirt was covered in patches of yellow grass and fallen golden leaves, which turned deep crimson and then brown as they died.

He chewed on one of his fingernails, not paying attention to anyone or anything. His body ached. He'd gotten enough sleep before the HUB2 attack, but exhaustion whispered at him. His mind felt loose and slow, almost fogged in the wake of the last few hours and what he'd seen. He had no idea where to go after this. What to do.

Reaper would stop as soon as he heard Vala was free. He had to. They could rest easy for now.

He should be celebrating with the others. Sneaking the moonshine a few of his neighbors made. Grasping the tiny victories as they came. Instead, introversion reared its head, cloaking him in weariness and solitude. The colors were almost too much—bright and constricting. Vivid color mixed with the foggier wisps of distrust as the citizens of Azrou took in the new colonists. It made him itchy.

Who was the hooded person in the forest? They were probably someone from another forest community. It wasn't like he knew every single soul who lived in these woods. But he did know many of them, and something about the figure poked at him. The fact he couldn't read their emotions raised the hair on his neck. He'd never met anyone whose colors he couldn't see.

Something gritty crossed his teeth, and he tasted metal. He pulled his hand away to check. There was dried blood under his nails. Vestiges of his foray into the underground tunnels with Rumor and Nyx. His gut lurched at the hard expression on Rumor's face when he'd killed the attacking chimera. Jude pulled in a shaky breath. His left hand trembled, and he curled it into a fist before anyone noticed. His jagged, bitten nail scraped his palm. He filed it against the seam of his pants as he looked around.

George sat nearby, his wings folded and his eyes sharp, growling at any celebratory person who drifted too close to Jude. Vala stood across the glade with Angel. One of Angel's heads watched the surrounding area while the other head bent toward Vala in conversation. Kaipo spoke with Yi-Min and Trick, frowns on their faces. Secrets and worry swirled around all three of them, muddying their colors.

Vala was safe. She was *safe*. Jude could breathe again.

"You okay?"

Jude's heart fluttered as nerves sang at the sound of Rumor's voice. He managed a smile. "Tired."

They both knew he was lying.

"How's…George?" Rumor asked.

"Lazy," he said, loud enough for George to hear him.

George clicked his beak in response.

"Why the name George?" Rumor asked.

Jude huffed. "It's the name he liked."

"You named a big, badass, scary gar…uh, chimera…George."

"Shut up." Jude's ears heated while his heart warmed at the conscious effort to not say *gargoyle*.

Rumor grinned, and it was like the twin suns breaking over the horizon. Jude's stomach lurched. It was almost that same smile as at the plaza back in Epsilon, but this wasn't for show. This smile was real, and it dove deep into Jude's body and made a home in his core.

Rumor hesitated for a beat, then sat on the bench next to him, straddling the end so he could look at Jude. His hair fell in his face, and Jude resisted the impulse to move it. There was something about Rumor's near-black eyes that tugged at Jude's insides. Their depth and wealth of secrets called to him.

He couldn't stand it any longer. That curl was blocking his view of Rumor's eyes. He reached up and used two fingers to push it out of his face and tuck it behind his ear.

"I should get it cut," Rumor said.

Jude quelled the knee-jerk *no please don't* reaction and shrugged. "Up to you."

Rumor's lips quirked as if he could read Jude's mind anyway. He leaned forward and rested his forehead on Jude's shoulder. Jude swallowed and fidgeted with the end of his shirt.

"Thank you," he said.

"For what?" Rumor asked without moving.

"Rescuing Vala. Bringing her home."

Rumor sat still for a long moment. Maybe he'd fallen asleep.

"I almost didn't," he murmured to the ground.

Jude bowed his head, closing his eyes against the wave of sadness and confusion that rolled off Rumor and hit all of Jude's senses. He fought to stay still, as if by moving, he might scare Rumor off like a skittish animal into the underbrush. Rumor held everything so close that letting those words fall to the ground had to mean something. Admission of guilt? Trust in Jude?

He didn't know.

"I wanted to leave her there," Rumor whispered. "I wanted to kill her." He rubbed his forehead against Jude's shirt and shifted until his cheek pressed to the back of Jude's shoulder. The bruised and scraped knuckles of his folded hands brushed Jude's hip.

Rumor might be able to feel his heart hammering.

"Why didn't you?" Jude turned his head, staring at Rumor's drying curls that spilled forward. He twirled one between two fingers. It was dry at the very end, soft and looping upward.

Rumor lifted his head and rested his chin on Jude's shoulder, his eyes confused and thoughtful. "I don't know."

Jude nodded. "Fair."

The corner of Rumor's mouth quirked. "I'm angry at them."

"I know."

"But I don't want you pissed at me."

"Okay."

"I don't know what to do with that."

Jude rolled his lips inward since he had no solution to give, and Rumor's bluntness jarred him. *Don't hate them and I won't be pissed at you* wasn't a great response. Rumor had to find his peace with the chimera for himself. Not for Jude.

Rumor pulled back, and Jude missed his warmth. "So, um, tell me about the *I can see their fear* thing from before we went into the tunnels."

Jude blew out a breath. "I see emotions as colors and feel their energy."

"Like auras?"

Jude scrunched his face up. "Sort of? But not something constant."

"Synesthesia?" Rumor guessed.

Jude shook his head, awkwardness eating his insides. "Not exactly. Well…" He made a frustrated noise. "Like everyone has a color that's their normal color which, I guess, represents them and their basic personality. I guess that's your typical aura. Then, depending on what emotion you're feeling, you can get shifts in color or…stripes or something. But…I can see the remnants of emotions or group emotions. Earlier when I said I could see their fear, all I saw was a smear of yellow in the distance, which could be happiness or fear. Every color has a positive and negative meaning, and that's the part that I"—he tapped his chest and shrugged—"that I feel."

Rumor watched him with an unreadable expression, even though his colors spoke to his curiosity and caution. "Have you always been able to do that?"

"As long as I can remember. I thought it was something everyone could do, until my brothers told me it was just me."

"What color am I?"

Jude grimaced. Colors had associations for everyone — good and bad. "Red."

"I'm guessing that's not good." Rumor's smile was thin and carved out of glass like the rest of him.

"Red is determination, action, energy," he said.

"And?" Rumor coaxed.

He moved his hand toward Rumor's face, hesitated as Rumor's hair brushed the ends of his fingers. Rumor leaned forward almost imperceptibly, his colors softening as Jude's fingertips slid through Rumor's curls, letting them wrap around his skin and spring back into place. "It's also anger, violence… passion."

Warmth crept up his face, and he forced himself to hold Rumor's gaze.

Rumor's throat bobbed as he swallowed. "Interesting. So it's magic?"

"If there's such a thing, sure."

"We live on the other side of the cosmos from our ancestors," Rumor said.

Jude tilted his head, curiosity piquing. "That's science."

Rumor didn't answer, spine straightening and eyes narrowing at something on the other side of them. Jude followed his gaze. Vala stood at a respectful distance, watching them. George leaned against her leg in a show of affection, his large eyes fixed on Jude.

"It is good to see you love another," Vala said, her dual tongues rolling out the melody of her native language.

Rumor stiffened. "What did she say?"

Warmth crept into his cheeks. "Nothing bad." To Vala he said, "It's not like that."

"Like what?" Rumor asked, his voice wary. Jude sort of wanted to glare at Vala for ruining their moment.

"If you say so," she said. She'd learned that phrase from Trick, and used it way too much for Jude's comfort.

"It's complicated," he said.

Rumor made a low sound in his throat. Jude faced him, fighting the urge to wince away from the angry crimson growing around Rumor. "She commented on—" He waved a hand between them. "Us, okay? It wasn't anything…" He gestured off in the general distance of the colonies. "Warlike."

Rumor's frown swung from Vala to Jude, wariness in his eyes. "What about us?"

Jude swallowed an inappropriate and somewhat frustrated laugh. "Just that she's happy to see me, um, smile at someone again."

Something on Jude's face or in his voice must have given him away, because the red anger softened and pulled back, only to be highlighted with curious tinges of turquoise.

Jude dragged his teeth over his bottom lip and blew out a

breath. This was not what he wanted to talk about. Not now. Not with the happiness around him and the *need* simmering low in his gut. "The full story would take too long, but my boyfriend was killed a year ago."

"By gargoyles?" Rumor winced. "Chimera."

"Not by chimera, no." Jude ran both his hands through his hair, his fingers catching a snarl. He worked it free as he spoke, focusing on the pain of pulling on his hair rather than the pain lodged in his chest. "By demons. Those little poisonous bastards." He stopped there before he spilled the entire tale.

"I'm sorry," Rumor murmured.

Jude met his eyes. "I'm sorry about your dad."

They sat in silence, holding each other's gaze, for nine heartbeats.

Rumor cleared his throat and looked away, shivering slightly. "I need dry clothes, if that's okay. And I need to figure out how to get to Reaper."

And he was back to revenge. Jude's insides deflated, and a tiny pang hit his heart. He wanted five more minutes. To see that smile one more time.

Jude rubbed a hand over his lips and stood. "Let's get you some dry clothes."

BRAEDEN

"It's fine, stop hovering." Nyx shot Braeden an exasperated look. "It's just a cut."

Braeden's signs were sharp and emphatic. "Yeah, from a *bullet*."

His stomach turned at the horrible gash across her upper arm. It wasn't terribly deep, but it bled enough to make his imagination go haywire with *what if* and *almost*. He was overreacting, sure, but it gave him something to focus on besides the consequences of what he'd just done.

The medic (whose name Braeden had missed in all his hand-wringing) smiled. "It'll scar and be sore for a bit, but she's fine. Nothing major hit. No infection. Keep the bandage on it," he said to Nyx. "Try not to get it wet for a few hours. Let the medical gel do its thing."

Braeden translated, and Nyx gave him an *I told you so* smile. He huffed, annoyed that his concern wasn't being taken seriously. "Fine, but when your arm falls off, don't come crying to me."

"I'll just get a badass cyborg one with a gun built into the wrist compartment," Nyx retorted.

"Smart ass," he signed.

She stuck her tongue out at him. He grinned, unable to resist her buoyancy and light. Part of him refused to believe what they'd accomplished. They'd broken a political prisoner out of captivity and returned her to her people, hopefully stopping tonight's assaults on the colonies. Maybe even turning the tide of the war. His mind spun with new ideas. If they could just get word back to the colonies—to the nonmilitary folk—explaining what many of the gargoyles...chimera...were like, maybe that would be enough to stop all of this. Push back against the military's insistence that all chimera were a race of monsters and evil creatures in need of eradication. Yeah, there were bad ones—really bad ones—but humans had been so wrong about them.

The creatures that went bump in the night were misinterpreted shadows. Braeden had no idea how to turn on the lights, but he needed to.

As a commander's son, he had a duty to his people, his colony. He didn't want to abandon them. Maybe he could be the one to shine a light on tired ideology and twisted truths.

If he wasn't shot for treason first.

The door opened, and Dahlia walked in, silver eyes bright.

"Hail the conquering heroes?" She smiled as she stepped out of the way of the departing medic.

Braeden rolled his eyes. Dahlia peered at Nyx's arm. "How's this?"

"I'm fine," Nyx said again, her tone softer toward Dahlia than it'd been to Braeden. Dahlia arched an eyebrow. Nyx gave her a charming smile. "Don't worry about me."

"Too late," Dahlia signed. They stared at each other in silence until Nyx's cheeks flushed, and she looked down.

He took it as his cue to leave. "I'm going to go explore." Braeden headed out of the medical center. It killed him to see those two pine after each other for so long.

He took the spiral staircase down to the ground level,

dragging his fingers along the black bark as he descended. A spicy scent filled the cool night air.

Braeden reached ground level, a smile tugging free at the muted celebration around him. He smelled meat roasting. He smelled alcohol. He smelled pipe grass. People moved around him, laughing and talking and stealing this brief moment in time. Two girls wandered past him, giggling as they caught his eye. They hurried away, and he shook his head. He didn't entirely get it, but okay.

"Welcome to Azrou," an unfamiliar rumbling voice said.

Braeden jumped and flushed in embarrassment at the short, stocky chimera standing nearby. It (he? she? they?) was mottled red, with large, powerful legs and a narrow torso tapering up even further to slim shoulders and long, gangling arms. It had a long whiplike tail with spikes running up the spine from tail to head, ending in massive horns which curled up and back.

"Gideon." The chimera pointed to himself. "Male."

Braeden grinned. "Braeden. Also male."

He wondered if that was the standard greeting. Name. Gender. It felt weird to define it like that, but whatever. He could roll with it.

The chimera smiled, showing off pointed teeth and twin tongues. "You come from the colonies."

Braeden nodded. "We helped bring Vala back earlier. Me and my friends."

"Are they your pack?" Gideon asked, his eyes like huge spheres of polished amber set in the very center of his narrow face.

Braeden frowned. "I suppose so?"

"And you're their leader?"

"Oh, um." Braeden hesitated. "We're all sort of equal, I guess."

Gideon pursed his lips and hummed. "Interesting. You have no hierarchy in this pack? No leading authority? Who are the breeders, then?"

Braeden sputtered. "Well, we don't have any. I mean, we don't have any straight…people in the pack…group… Not that we can't breed."

He pressed his lips together, trying to order his thoughts.

"Gideon, stop confusing the new people," Trick said as he walked up, saving Braeden from further awkwardness.

"I merely asked questions," Gideon protested.

"Did he ask which of you is the breeder?" Trick winked at Braeden.

He nodded, sensing he'd missed an inside joke.

"Chimera don't have the whole 'two people go off and make a baby thing' that humans do, so some, like Gideon here, are endlessly fascinated with human reproduction," Trick explained.

Gideon huffed. "I was trying to be nice."

"And I've told you not everyone is okay talking about sex," Trick replied in an overly patient tone.

Gideon waved his hands dismissively and lumbered away, his powerful legs reminding Braeden of a creature called a faun in a book he'd read once.

"Thanks for that," Braeden said.

Trick nodded. "We didn't get a chance to talk earlier. Trick Solomon. Jude's brother."

"Right. I went to the medical center right after the, ah, dragon thing. Never actually thanked you." He held out his hand. "Braeden Tennant, colony commander's son. Wanted for treason."

Trick laughed and shook his hand in a firm grip. "Well, rebel, welcome home then."

Home. Braeden smiled back as he looked around the forest community, but his insides writhed around that simple word. What was home, anymore? The colony he'd betrayed, or the forest he had no business being in. He'd never felt more alien than he did right now. Everyone else moved past him, connected and where they were supposed to be, while he stood by trees older than he was, on a moon that was trying its hardest to spit him out into the stars.

"Kaipo is your older brother?" Braeden asked.

Trick nodded.

"Must be way older to adopt a kid," he said.

Trick relaxed and laughed a little. "Right, I haven't been around anyone not used to it. I'm what you'd call an 'oops baby' in that I wasn't planned. Kai was eighteen when I was born."

Braeden rubbed the back of his neck. "Got it. That was cool of him to take in Jude." He cleared his throat. "This place is bigger than I thought it'd be."

The houses built around existing trees were stunning. Even he—someone who'd grown up in the lap of technological advancement—could appreciate the exquisite artistry of an entire community built with the forest.

"This is just one district. There are a bunch scattered across the forest and connected by a network of chimera caves and aboveground trails." A little bit of pride snuck into Trick's voice. "A lot of our dwellings go underground, too. Chimera helped us form the spaces, and we built our homes there as well. Those connect directly to chimera nests. Forest dwellers number about three-quarters of the colonist population."

Braeden's eyebrows slid up. "Tens of thousands of people live in the forest?"

"Military hates us, but they can't really do anything. Forest doesn't fall under colonist jurisdiction, so we're not beholden to their laws or taxes."

Braeden snorted. "Bet that makes them angry."

He met Trick's teal eyes, which were filled with understanding. "Kai and I used to live in the colonies. When the ships fell, Kai grabbed me and got us out of the house in time. Our parents didn't make it. He decided then that the colonies were no place for us, so in all the chaos, he took me to the forests. Yi-Min found us stumbling around after a few hours and brought us here." Trick rubbed a hand over his shaved head. "Felt really out of place for a long time. Angel helped, but..." He shrugged. "I get it."

Braeden nodded, unsure of what to say. His gut knotted with guilt. He was a traitor. Him, the son of a commander, had betrayed his people for *the enemy*. He could never return home, never watch the jagged horizon from his room, never see the suns light up their kitchen window during dayside. He exhaled shakily.

"But you have your friends with you," Trick said as they watched an automaton canine walk by. "The guy my brother's fawning over. And your girlfriend."

Braeden gaped at him. "My what?"

Trick raised his eyebrows, confusion ghosting through his eyes. "The girl with the blue hair?"

"Nyx?"

"Yeah, aren't you and Nyx...?"

"What? Oh. No, not at all. *Best* friend, not *girl*friend." Braeden laughed and fiddled with the black ring on his finger. "Like, childhood best friend."

"Ah, sorry." Trick shifted his weight, his eyes darting away.

This was flirting, right? Trick was flirting. No, he was being friendly. Friendly was good. Friendly could still be flirting though. Ugh. "No, it's just kind of hilarious. Nyx is pansexual, and I'm asexual. I mean both of us can appreciate a pretty person and seriously enjoy some cuddling, but hers goes further with 'what would they look like naked' while I'm over here, just 'I wonder what kind of pizza they like.' I'm just generally excited about food. Dahlia calls us 'all or nothing.'"

Trick laughed. "Clever."

"Isn't it? I want to get shirts made." Braeden shoved his hands in his pockets.

Trick shook his head, smiling. "Sorry for the assumption. You just seemed really fixated on her when you guys got here. I mean, like beyond the obvious her being hurt thing."

"Well, I love her. I mean, I love both Nyx and Dahlia, but…
you can love someone without wanting to sleep with them.
There's a difference."

Trick nodded, his lips quirking. "Never said you couldn't.
Sorry to pry."

Braeden patted him on the shoulder. "Nah, it's fine. Some
days I think I know exactly how I feel, and then others it's all…"
He wiggled his fingers at his head and grimaced. Why was he
spilling all this? How had Trick managed to get him babbling
uselessly in a few minutes? "You ever get that?"

Trick hitched a shoulder. "Not really? I've always known I
was gay, I guess. When I started liking people, I never checked
out girls, always guys. Jude was the same way. Is that weird?"

Braeden shook his head. "Nyx always knew, too. Equal
opportunity, she says. Anyway, I'm rambling, so…"

Trick laughed. "It's fine. I was actually coming to tell you my
brother wants to talk to you."

Braeden's stomach lurched. Of course, one of the forest
leaders would want to talk to him. He was a commander's son.
Probably an excellent piece of leverage or bargaining token if
they needed one. He hadn't even considered that possibility
when planning the prison break. He'd been so focused on what
his moms would think of him, what their bosses would make
them do should he be caught, what the colony would do to him
or Nyx or Dahlia if they ever found out.

Trick peered at him. "Whatever horrible thing you're thinking,
I can tell you you're wrong. He needs to tell you something, not
ask you questions or throw you in a cage or anything."

"Ohh-kay," Braeden said.

Trick nodded toward a path snaking away from the medical
center. "Onward."

Braeden fell into step with Trick, unable to hold back gaping
at the community as they headed deeper into it.

"What are those?" He pointed to one of the brightly painted gates.

"Chimera tunnel entrances," Trick answered. "They live underground and only come to the surface during nightside. But we don't want little kids tumbling down the holes and getting hurt, so we gated them."

"The gar—uh, chimera let you do that?" Braeden asked.

"It was their idea, actually. Their babies are just as fragile as ours, so they understood the importance."

"What's with the bowls of fruit and candles?"

Trick grimaced. "There are some people who think the chimera are…not quite gods but somewhere around there? People who were raised by super religious ancestors, so they're searching for faith out here. The chimera seem to provide that for them."

That sounded weird, but okay. He'd never been especially religious, even though he'd listened to Nyx tell him all about her research into human history, which included some pretty horrific things done in the name of religion. Something ugly twisted in his gut at the mere thought of human zealots pushing the war even further in the name of some chimera god.

"This is so different from what we've been told."

"That we're backward and feral?" Trick asked with a knowing smile. "Or that we eat our young?"

Braeden nodded, his cheeks warming. "Sorry."

"Not your fault. You didn't write the database entry on us." Trick headed down another path, this one ending in front of a staircase which wrapped around a tree wider than Braeden could reach. "Propaganda and hearsay are elegant weapons for killing questions."

Braeden climbed the steps, wincing at the soreness in his leg. His brain spun at light speed, turning over everything he was learning and ripping apart everything he'd been taught. When the colonists first set out into the stars, they'd been given a massive database which held all of Earth's history plus room for new history to be added. The plan was to send it back across the stars one day. That generational ship was going out farther than any known ship at the time. Sahara was, in a sense, its own leap of faith. They were the farthest human outpost.

As grand as it sounded, it really meant one thing.

They were alone.

He'd been lied to about the forest people; that much was obvious.

What other lies had he been told?

Trick knocked on the door. A muffled voice on the other side told him to come in. The door opened as Braeden turned around, rubbing the back of his neck against building tension. He froze in shock. Not at the two chimera standing in the room, but at the person standing next to Kaipo at a table covered in maps.

"Bailey?"

NYX

"Why did you come?" Nyx asked as Dahlia poked around the room they'd been shown to by someone whose name Nyx missed. She leaned against the wall by the window so she could see Dahlia's face and pointedly ignore the one large bed in the middle of the room. It wasn't like she hadn't been alone in a room with Dahlia before. Or even slept in the same bed together with her. They'd done that numerous times.

This all felt different.

Dahlia pulled the window sash back, revealing a stained-glass photovoltaic window. She ran her fingers along the individual solar panes, her eyes going distant.

"Can I say that I…" The rest of her words were lost as she moved her face.

Nyx touched her arm. "I can't read your lips if you turn away from me."

Dahlia rubbed her fist on her sternum. "Sorry." She chewed her bottom lip. "I didn't want you to leave without me."

Nyx's belly fluttered, but as much as she wanted that to be true, Dahlia's silver eyes said that wasn't the whole of it. "What else?"

Dahlia smiled. "You know me too well."

Nyx winked at her and folded her arms, hoping she didn't come across too cocky. They were alone, they'd won, everyone was safe now, and she was free to finally tell Dahlia how she felt. The same fear wiggled in her chest, though—that Dahlia would reject her and she'd lose so much more than hope. She'd lose her friend.

But she'd been hovering in this *what if* for too long. Suspended between the reality of their friendship and the unknown of a romance. She needed to dive into this headfirst, no matter the consequences. If anything, the events of tonight had shown her the tragedy of running out of time. Any one of them could die, and while it was an exceptionally morbid way see things, at its core, it was the only truth of their lives.

Grab what you can carry and hold it safe, they said.

All she wanted was Dahlia's heart.

"I'm looking for my dad." Dahlia broke the silence and Nyx's internal pep talk. Her signs were as hesitant as her voice.

"What?" Nyx asked in surprise. "I thought he was dead." Dahlia hardly mentioned her father—a man she'd never known. The only thing Wren had told her was that it was a whirlwind romance with a marine who eventually was transferred to a colony far away. She couldn't follow him with her own medical placement and didn't want to jeopardize her own career to do so. After he left, she discovered the pregnancy and made the decision to keep it to herself. It wasn't fair to him, she'd said, especially since he couldn't have done anything about it. Then the ships fell in '64, and according to Wren, he'd died when the colony where he'd been transferred was struck by falling debris, killing over half of the colony's population.

Dahlia shook her head, turning to face Nyx. "I pawed through all of Mama's stuff one day when she was at work. She's got nothing from him—no letters, no pictures, no presents that I could tell." She frowned, and her signs sped up. "But I was going through the databases at the lists of the deceased and it hit me, what if he was taken by forest people? There was this little note on a report saying some rebels came out of the forests to help find survivors, but it didn't add up. Like the number of survivors versus the bodies never recovered and the deaths recorded. It was weird, so I started thinking that maybe he'd ended up here and was either listed as dead or missing in the database."

"How are you going to find him? The settlements here stretch through the entire forest." The topographical map hanging in her abuela's living room showed the forests of Sahara, covering a good third of the moon's surface. In theory, it could shelter millions of people as the population of Sahara grew. If the chimera didn't wipe them out first.

Dahlia shrugged. "No idea, but I'm here now, so that's a big part done. I've just got this feeling in my bones that he's alive. Does that sound weird?"

"Well, the moon talks to me, so…"

Dahlia laughed, and the joyous expression on her beautiful face made Nyx feel warm all over.

"So," Nyx said with a smile. "I'll help you. Maybe the chimera know something."

Dahlia shook her head. "You don't need to do that. I don't even know where to start." She rubbed her hand across her forehead and winced.

"I know, but I want to," Nyx said, her heart doing somersaults in her chest. "Because I love you." She closed her eyes right after the words fell from her mouth, drowning herself in darkness and embarrassment.

That was not how she'd imagined that going. *Lemme help you find your long-lost dad, oh by the way I'm in love with you.* Maybe if she kept her eyes closed long enough, she could disappear, and then it would be like it never happened. If she kept her eyes closed, she didn't have to see the surprise or rejection on Dahlia's face. She could forever preserve Dahlia's laughing face in her mind and wouldn't have to see the pity. Her heart pounded up her throat and nausea burned in her belly. It was laughable, really. She'd fought monsters tonight and broken a chimera out of jail and escaped in the midst of gunfire, and *this right here* was what she was most terrified of.

Warm hands slid over her cheeks and cupped her jaw. Nyx's eyes fluttered open, and Dahlia was *right there*, silver eyes wide and bright and…hopeful.

"Do you really?" she asked carefully, since her hands held Nyx's face instead of signing.

Nyx swallowed, her fingers itching to grab Dahlia's hips and pull her closer. She nodded. Oh god oh god oh god oh god oh god oh god. She was going to faint. She was going to admit she loved Dahlia, then faint at her feet like some swooning damsel.

"I love you, too," Dahlia said.

Nyx stared at her. "What?"

Dahlia took one hand off Nyx's cheek and extended her index, pinkie, and thumb. She started talking then, her voice a faraway thrum of syllables and intonation, but Nyx heard none of it through her shock. All she could do was stare at Dahlia's eyes and her full lips and the lines of her cheekbones and her beautiful, beautiful cloud of hair, which still had three flower petals stuck in its strands. She plucked one out and held it up. "She loves me."

Dahlia stopped talking, a question in her expression.

She pulled the second down. "She loves me not."

Dahlia wrinkled her nose, her eyes dancing.

Nyx pulled the last one down. "She loves me."

"That better be the last one," Dahlia said, her signs emphatic and playful. "Because I'm gonna kiss you now, if that's all right with you."

"It's more than all right, because I'm gonna kiss you back." Nyx closed the petal in her fist and slid her arms around Dahlia's soft waist as their lips finally finally *finally* met. And oh god oh god oh god it was everything. It was everything and more. It wasn't like those first kisses Nyx had read in her abuela's old, tattered romance novels she kept in a box beneath the bed. There was no blood singing or angels singing or heart singing or any other implausible choir song creation.

There was just Nyx kissing Dahlia, and Dahlia kissing Nyx. It was a little messy. It was a little unpracticed. It was a whole lot fervent.

Dahlia pressed against her, the long lines of her body molding to Nyx's, pushing her back against the wall as they kissed harder. Nyx had been so hungry for this for so long. She'd been starving for this moment, and now that it was here, she was going to inhale and inhale and inhale until every empty space in her bones was filled with Dahlia's everything.

Nyx scraped her teeth across Dahlia's lower lip and kissed down her jaw, smiling at the faintest tickle of stubble under her lips. Dahlia's fingers slid around the back of Nyx's neck and squeezed gently as Nyx kissed down her throat, pressing her lips to the dip in her collarbone.

"So beautiful," Nyx said against Dahlia's skin. She was the color of the cosmos, of the wide reaches of deep space, with stars for eyes and a constellation of freckles scattered across her skin. She wanted to connect those constellations with her fingertips, with the tip of her nose, with her tongue.

Dahlia's voice vibrated in her chest as Nyx kissed her collarbone. Nyx pulled back to check, to make sure she was okay. She wasn't prepared for the brightness of Dahlia's eyes or the flare of her nostrils or the way her chest hitched as she pulled in air. The corner of Dahlia's mouth ticked up, and she squeezed Nyx's neck again, furrowing her fingers up the back of Nyx's head as she leaned over and kissed Nyx's ear, her jaw, her pulse point.

Nyx closed her eyes, her world condensing to the flare of heat everywhere Dahlia's lips touched. Her heart thumped wildly against Dahlia's, beating out alternating celebration and anxiety. Their breasts pressed together, all softness and want. Dahlia dragged her teeth down Nyx's neck and kissed the juncture of her shoulder while her other hand slid up Nyx's ribs but stopped just under her breast.

Nyx's stomach flipped, and she tingled all over. Oh gods, she wanted...she didn't know what she wanted. She wanted Dahlia to touch her everywhere. She wanted, oh how she wanted, but what if what she wanted wasn't what Dahlia wanted? Oh, what if Dahlia wanted more than this? Wanted less? How was she supposed to know?

Was she supposed to be touching Dahlia like this, too? Nyx curled her fingers into Dahlia's hips—*those hips*—and didn't know what else to do.

Dahlia lifted her head, her eyebrows up in silent question, concern in her eyes.

"I'm okay," Nyx said quickly. Maybe too fast? Yeah, too fast based on Dahlia's eyes widening.

"Do we need to stop?" Dahlia asked.

Nyx shook her head. "No. Please. Never. I mean, unless you want to? We can if you want to. Do you want to?"

Dahlia rolled her lips inward, the corners twitching against a laugh.

Nyx blew out a breath. "I don't know what to do. Well, not like 'don't know what to do' do, I do know what...to do. I just, not with you. I mean, I don't know what you want? Do you just want to kiss? Do you want to do more?"

Dahlia pressed a finger to Nyx's lips, her smile soft.

"What do you want?" she signed.

Nyx swallowed. Hard. Her toes curled inside her boots as she slid her hand over Dahlia's and hesitantly moved it from her own ribs to her breast.

Dahlia's lips parted. Her thumb slid over the outline of Nyx's nipple, and Nyx inhaled sharply. Lightning gathered in her belly, and Nyx pulled Dahlia to her. She kissed Dahlia again as if they'd never get another chance. Dahlia massaged Nyx's breast, and Nyx *burned.*

She was a comet. She was a meteor. She was a supernova. Her hips rocked against Dahlia's. She was a star on the verge of collapse. She worked her fingers under Dahlia's shirt to the warm skin of her back, her ribs, her stomach. Dahlia's thigh slid between Nyx's thighs, and Nyx was a sky on fire.

This was everything she'd ever wanted.

But what if after this moment, after this heated moment, their friendship crumbled? Oh, but this was exactly what she'd been dreaming of for so so long. Her fingers tightened on Dahlia's hips, pulling her impossibly closer.

Dahlia moved Nyx off the wall, her lips on Nyx's lips again, holding her in her strong arms as they stumbled to the bed and crashed onto it, giggling and kissing each other's smiles as they tangled together. Dahlia's smile was bright and full of heat. She rolled off Nyx and onto the bed, stretched her long frame out, and opened her arms. Nyx's cheeks started to tingle from smiling so much as she crawled into Dahlia's arms and settled against her body, their faces centimeters apart as they stared at each other.

Dahlia held up her hand. "I love you."

Nyx held her hand in the same shape and pressed it to Dahlia's sign. "I love you."

Dahlia touched Nyx's cheek with her fingertips, tracing her cheekbone and up to her forehead and down her nose to her lips and across her lips to her jawline. Nyx remained perfectly still as Dahlia mapped her face with such open intent that Nyx believed Dahlia could shape the universe with those fingers.

Dahlia pressed a kiss to Nyx's forehead, resting her lips against Nyx's skin, as she reached for Nyx's hand and laced their fingers together with a deliberateness that brought tears to Nyx's throat. She closed her eyes.

She'd done it. She'd conquered it all. She'd been a hero and gotten the girl.

RUMOR

After being waylaid by several citizens who wanted to ask him a million questions, Rumor finally followed Jude up a staircase that wound around the black trunk of an enormous tree. Where a lot of homes went underground into the chimera tunnels, some went up into the treetops. He dragged his fingers along the bark, inhaling the cinnamon that tangled around him. His brain listed everything he needed to do to get back on the hunt for Reaper. He needed clothes, he needed dry shoes, he needed a way to HUB2, he needed—he needed the others to come with him.

He didn't know if he could do this on his own.

Jude led him to a door at the end of the hall, which slid open with a quiet brushing noise when he pulled on the handle.

"Manual doors?" Rumor asked.

Jude shrugged. "It's not that big a deal for me to open a door."

He moved out of the way for Rumor to walk past him and slid the door shut behind them.

The quiet *snick* of the door settling into place made Rumor's heart jump. Suddenly, he wasn't so exhausted anymore. His mental list fluttered as he stared at Jude, who stared back, his eyes darting around Rumor's face and then to the air around his body.

"What color am I?" Rumor asked, his fingers tingling, his body aching with every possible *want* imaginable. He wanted revenge.

He wanted Jude.

They were alone.

They had fourteen hours.

You can take five minutes.

Jude licked his lips. "Red," he said softly. He blinked fast blew out a breath. "Lemme find you some clothes. You can put your wet ones, um…" He spun in a circle, and then pointed to the corner of the room. "There."

His cheeks pinked as he turned away, either to look for clothes or give Rumor privacy.

Despite being nearly dizzy with the need to throw Jude on the bed, Rumor forced his attention back to his soaking clothes, which were itchy and uncomfortable as they dried unevenly. He grabbed his shirt around the back collar and pulled it over his head, turning his back to Jude. Water from his hair rolled down his back, two cold lines that made him hiss in surprise.

"You okay?" Jude asked.

"Wet." Rumor balled up the shirt and threw it in the corner. He toed off his boots and peeled out of his socks. He thumbed open the button on his pants and stared at them, trying to figure out the best way to get out of wet, plastered-to-skin pants.

A fingertip touched his back between his shoulder blades. Ice went through Rumor's insides as he froze, inhaling deeply through his nose. He forced himself to remain still and not react *don't react* as Jude's fingers traced the silver scar running the length of his spine from the nape of his neck to the small of his back.

"What's this from?" Jude asked in an almost reverent tone.

Training exercise gone wrong. Rescued colonists from hellhounds. Saved some orphans. The truth choked him, forcing its way into his mouth. "Night my mom died."

Jude didn't ask him to explain, and Rumor closed his eyes,

dropping his chin to his chest as Jude's fingers reached his lower back. His palm spread and pressed to Rumor's skin above his waistband. Rumor thought his heart would burst out of his chest when Jude's lips pressed to the top of his spine, right at the start of his scar.

"Rumor," Jude whispered.

Rumor raised his head and turned, his skin on fire as Jude's fingers dragged around his waist. He met Jude's eyes, the deep green hesitant and needy. The very real truth was that they might never get this moment again. Rumor might walk out that door and into the same fate as his father. As much as Rumor craved revenge like water, Jude was air.

He needed both to survive tonight.

"Can I kiss you?" Jude asked in that same reverent tone, and it sent shivers to the bones of Rumor's legs.

Five minutes.

Rumor slid his hands to either side of Jude's neck, his thumbs on that elegant curve of jaw.

"Yes," he whispered as their lips met. A tiny sound escaped Jude as they kissed, their bodies pressing together. Jude's hands curved around Rumor's ribs. Rumor's hands pushed up into Jude's hair. They held each other in place and together.

This he understood. *This* he could do. He could turn his brain off and his body on and just lose himself in Jude's mouth, Jude's fingers, Jude's body. He could figure out what made Jude kiss him harder, what made him gasp, what made him pull at Rumor even though there was no more space between them.

He could forget about everything else tonight except the boy in his arms.

Jude pulled away long enough to yank his shirt off, then he pounced on Rumor again, kissing him like he'd been set loose. Desperation rose in Rumor's throat, impatient and hungry. This was a language they both spoke fluently. Something bridging the gap between two worlds.

"Pants," Jude mumbled between kisses. His warm chest pressed to Rumor's with every inhale. His muscles were long and lean, his chest scar-free and mostly smooth. He only had the tiniest blond curls on his sternum. Rumor rested his hand over that spot, feeling Jude's heart pounding against his palm. *He* did that to Jude. *He* made Jude's heart race.

"Yes, I'm wearing pants," Rumor said, smiling against Jude's mouth. Maybe Jude didn't mind the scars across Rumor's stomach and up his back. Maybe he did and wasn't saying anything?

"Yeah, that's a problem." Jude slipped his fingers under Rumor's waistband and tugged.

"Says the guy also wearing pants." Rumor bit at Jude's lower lip, pushing all thoughts of scars out of his head. "Or is this a *do as I say, not as I do* situation?"

Jude pulled back, his eyebrow arching and a smirk curling one side of his mouth. A delighted shiver rolled down Rumor's arms. He stepped out of Jude's embrace and frowned at his pants. "They're glued to me."

Jude laughed softly and stepped toward Rumor again. Rumor reached for him, but was rewarded with a hard shove. He stumbled backward with a yelp and landed partly on the bed. Jude's laughter increased in volume as he grabbed one of Rumor's feet and yanked on his pant leg. "Help me out here, man."

Rumor lifted his hips off the bed and shoved at his waistband, practically peeling himself out of his pants a centimeter at a time, which was extra challenging while hard. Jude's laughing seeped into Rumor's skin, wrapping his bones in warmth and his heart in comfort. Rumor laughed as they wrestled with his clothes. When Rumor's pants finally came free, it caught Jude off guard, and he tumbled to the floor.

Rumor sat up. "You okay?"

Jude grinned up at him, his hair wild and his eyes shining. "Fine."

He tossed Rumor's pants to the corner.

Rumor dropped off the bed to the floor, crawled over to Jude and kissed him. He swung a leg over Jude's hips and straddled him. Jude's hands sank into Rumor's hair, holding him in place as they kissed. Hovering above Jude like this was so awkward, but Jude murmuring Rumor's name and other things against Rumor's lips did a great job of erasing that. He swallowed every sound, every whisper of his own name, everything Jude gave him as his own hips moved and Jude rocked up to meet him in the same rhythm.

"We might want to get on the bed," Jude gasped.

"Floor too hard?" Rumor teased.

Jude laughed, the sound breathy. He grabbed Rumor's hips and pulled them flush. "That was an awful pun."

"It got a rise out of you," Rumor said against Jude's neck. He dragged his lips up Jude's jaw to his mouth and kissed him again. He rested his weight on his knees and traced the curve of Jude's shoulders, marveling at the leaner definition. Jude was muscled, but his muscles were long. The more Rumor worked out, the more he'd bulk up. Did Jude like big muscles?

"Please don't tell me your entire sense of humor is puns," Jude groaned into his mouth.

"Okay, I won't tell you my entire sense of humor is puns." Rumor bit at Jude's lips as his fingers traced Jude's chest. He sat up, resting his weight on Jude's hips, and stared down at him.

Jude's skin flushed pink at Rumor's stare. "What?"

Rumor shook his head. "Just looking at you." He cleared his throat, his entire body one heartbeat. He was no stranger to being with someone else, but the fact that Jude knew every emotion Rumor felt—maybe even before Rumor knew what it was himself—added a whole new weight to the moment.

"What color am I?" he blurted. His face went hot because that was the most ridiculous thing to say. What in deep space...

Jude rested his palms on Rumor's thighs and squeezed. "Why?"

"I just…" Rumor trailed off, distracted as he dragged his fingers down Jude's stomach and stopped above his waistband. Goose bumps rose across Jude's pale skin, and he squirmed a little, the muscles in his stomach tensing. Jude was gorgeous. "I'm curious. I mean, you don't have to tell me. This is fine. I mean good. This is…this is good. This here." He spread his hands out across Jude's stomach and leaned over to kiss him again. His knees were beginning to ache, and he probably looked awkward straddling Jude on the floor, but he didn't care. He had the most perfect boy in the cosmos under him. The only way he'd move now was if an actual gargoyle—chimera—crashed through the window.

Rumor kissed the column of his throat, resting his lips on Jude's collarbone. Jude was so warm, so strong under Rumor's body. He closed his eyes and breathed in cinnamon and sweat.

"Still red," Jude murmured. "Always red. But brighter."

"Brighter is good?" Rumor asked.

Jude slid his fingers through Rumor's curls and tugged on his hair until Rumor lifted his head. Jude smiled. "Yeah."

Rumor kissed him, pawing at him as if they could somehow get closer than they already were. Jude pushed at Rumor's shoulder and rose while they kissed, rolling them until Rumor lay on the ground with his legs wrapped around Jude's hips.

Oh gods, that felt good.

"Jude," Rumor whispered as Jude rolled his hips once.

Jude lowered himself and kissed Rumor softly while Rumor planted his feet on the floor. They stared at each other for a long moment, and anxiety crept in around the edges of Rumor's contentment. What did Jude see when he saw Rumor? A scarred orphan? A tragedy?

"What's this?" Jude hooked a finger under Rumor's necklace and lifted it to get a better look.

Rumor swallowed and wrapped his fist around the coin. "Nothing."

Jude pressed his lips together and nodded. Was that flash in his eyes disappointment or understanding? They'd only known each other a few hours, and here they were, practically naked on the floor together. Sometimes sex was the easiest form of communication.

Rumor closed his eyes and tried to focus on Jude's weight above him. He clung to Jude's body, suddenly wildly fearful if he opened his eyes this would all be a dream and he'd still be in the middle of a burning HUB2, right at the start of it all.

"I'm not going anywhere," Jude murmured. His lips pressed to Rumor's forehead.

Relief and fear shot through Rumor. No one could promise that. But he wanted that. Oh, deep space, he wanted that. He wanted *Jude*. He wanted Jude for longer than a distraction. For longer than a stolen moment on his bedroom floor. He wanted Jude's fingerprints on his skin and his words etched into his bones.

"Jude," he managed, his voice hoarse. "I—"

An explosion just outside the treehouse painted their world in startling orange, yellow, and red, blowing the windows inward. Jude threw his arms up to shield Rumor's face from the raining glass. Tiny stings peppered Rumor's arm, but all he cared about was Jude's safety. "Are you okay?"

Jude nodded and pushed off Rumor. Rumor scrambled to his feet and stumbled to the blown-out window frame.

"What is it?" Jude asked.

Rumor's high crashed around him like the glass at his feet. "Marines. They're attacking Azrou."

JUDE

Jude dug through the shirts in his drawer and threw Rumor a thin long-sleeved one. "That should fit you. Let me find you some pants."

Rumor snatched it out of the air and pulled it on, the muscles of his torso stretching as he moved. Jude swallowed the immense annoyance at the colony marines who'd picked *this precise moment* to attack his home. He should be more upset with the attack itself, but he couldn't shake the large part of his brain dancing at *finally* kissing Rumor.

And…more.

Jude's cheeks heated, and he pulled a clean shirt over his head. He grabbed a pair of pants that he hoped would fit Rumor and turned, surprised to find Rumor standing beside him, staring at him intently. "What?"

He handed Rumor the pants.

Rumor's tongue darted across his bottom lip, resting in the corner of his mouth for a minute before he spoke. "We'll continue this—" He gestured between them and then pulled the pants on. "After we go kick some marine ass, right?"

Jude's heart lurched at the almost hopeful tone in Rumor's

voice. For all his bravado… Jude pulled Rumor to him for a harsh, but brief, kiss. Rumor clutched at him, exhaling like they'd both jumped underwater.

"Yes, we'll continue this." Jude turned, grabbed his gun from the table, and headed out of the room. "But we're not kicking marine ass."

"Wait…we're not?" Rumor hurried after him. "Where are we going?"

"Down," Jude answered as he paused halfway down the stairs, straining his hearing. He held up a hand for Rumor to stop.

Outside, the sounds of gunfire and shouts and another explosion all muddled together. Jude motioned for Rumor to follow him and headed to the first floor. He sent up a quick prayer of thanks that Yi-Min always closed their shades during nightside and hurried through the main room toward the kitchen at the back of the house.

"What do you mean down?" Rumor asked.

"Opposite of up." Jude opened the pantry door. Which shelf was it again? Fourth? No, fifth. He moved some jars to one side and felt for the loose panel in the back.

"Jude," Rumor said in a tight voice.

"Rumor." Jude didn't even need to see him to know irritation swirled around him like an angry swarm. There it was. He pressed the panel and the entire shelf jolted forward a centimeter. He pulled on it, swinging the whole thing forward like a door. Behind it was a stash of weapons in a hidden closet, but Jude ignored all of it. He pushed aside a crate of ammo and grabbed another loose board. It popped out easily, revealing a hole just large enough for Jude's hand. He reached in, feeling around for the handle, muttering about Kai and his elaborate escape systems the entire time.

There it was. Cold and metal and gritty with what Jude hoped was dirt. He yanked on it, and a square section of the floor swung upward, revealing a ladder descending into darkness. "Go."

"Where does that go?" Rumor eyed the dark opening with doubt.

"Do you trust me?" He was almost afraid of the answer.

"Yeah," Rumor said without hesitation. He pressed his lips together and looked at Jude. "Yes," he said in a quieter tone.

"Good." Damn every single marine out there for ruining all of this for him. "Go down the ladder. We're not hiding. We're meeting others."

Rumor stared at him a heartbeat longer and headed into the hole. Jude pulled the pantry door shut, then the hidden panel behind the shelf. He waited for Rumor to clear the ladder before he swung himself in, replaced the loose board, and descended, pulling the trap door shut behind him.

"Will they find that?" Rumor asked when Jude hit the bottom.

"Hopefully not unless someone tells them. Come on."

"Are there any lights?" Rumor whispered. "I can use my blades."

Jude smiled in the darkness as his eyes adjusted. "Give it a second."

"But—"

"Rumor."

Rumor quieted. Jude reached for his hand and pulled him forward. He'd planned on bringing Rumor down into the caves later for a full tour. Wow him a little. Introduce him to chimera babies and show him the truly peaceful side to the race.

Maybe a little romance. Taking their time.

Not this.

"Whoa," Rumor breathed, his eyes going wide.

"Told you," Jude murmured as they walked, Rumor gaping at the softly glowing walls. "It's some sort of algae or moss native to here. It latches onto the veins of adamantine in the rock and glows blue."

"Does it damage the metal?" Rumor dragged a finger along the wall just above a vein, careful not to disturb the plants.

"Not that anyone can tell. The chimera use it as a natural light source. They shape the adamantine into various large shapes and wait for the algae to grow. Ta-da, lamp." Jude turned a corner, hurrying as he dragged Rumor along behind him. They were so far underground, they couldn't hear anything from above, but who knew what the marines might be doing to the ones who didn't escape down their hidden ladders or shut the safety doors on buried homes.

The ground vibrated, and dust fell from the ceiling.

"We need to run." Jude's heart climbed into his throat.

"Jude, it's okay. The marines don't carry anything large enough to blast down into a tunnel like this. They'd need—"

"An entrance," Jude snapped. "Yeah, I know. I was there."

Rumor didn't say anything, and Jude didn't look back to see his colors or his expression or anything. Memories flooded Jude's brain, memories he'd squashed and locked away. An explosion. A rush of sound and air. A horrible cracking sound. Screams.

Jude shook his head and ran faster through the tunnels. Rumor followed him. They twisted and turned and wound their way down down down to the more protected areas of the nest.

Chimera heard him coming and poked their heads out of various dwelling areas, relaxing when they saw him and pushing babies back to safety.

"Stay in your homes," Jude yelled as he ran by, hoping at least a few understood human language.

A large chimera with broad shoulders and a barrel chest stepped out of the next cavern, blocking their entrance. It peered hard at Rumor, then at Jude.

"He smells of colonist," the chimera growled in its language.

Jude replied in human. "I'm Jude Welton of the nation of Azrou, and I vouch for him."

The chimera straightened, stared at them for a long while, then moved out of the way.

"What happens if I do something they don't like?" Rumor asked in an undertone as they headed inside.

"It's an honor system. They trust me, and I tell them to trust you. If you break that trust, then they can no longer trust me, which is akin to me lying. I would basically be in trouble for a long time."

Rumor blew out a breath. "Got it."

"So, don't do anything offensive."

"I don't know all the rules."

"Which is why you shut up and pay attention," Jude replied. "You're a guest in their home. This is their space. When in doubt, don't touch and don't talk."

Rumor pressed his lips together, nodding. Jude hated this was the way Rumor was thrust into the chimera social structure and tradition. It should've been slower, with more explanation, but they had no time for that. All Jude could do was pray Rumor's assumptions didn't overwhelm his curiosity and that tiny bit of doubt swirling around him. Jude needed that doubt.

He needed Rumor to realize everything he'd been taught about the chimera was wrong.

But how could anyone undo seventeen years of ingrained hate in a few hours?

They entered another large cavern, but this was cleared of all but one stalagmite, their stumps ground down to the floor. A large adamantine square sat on the remaining stalagmite, the algae glowing a fierce blue and lighting up the entirety of the space. Ramps and stairs spiraled down the walls from higher tunnel levels. The small hole at the very top of the cavern—the top of a mountain—let in fresh air circulated by enormous leaf weavings that moved constantly. Chimera children splashed in a shallow wading pool. The walls bore the painted history of the chimera race, from the seed planted by Mother to their time now.

Jude watched Rumor's colors shift from curiosity to guilt to sadness when he saw the recordings of the war—the pictures of children drowning, the dragons who lay dying after the ships fell.

"Jude!" Kai called. "Oh, thank Mother, you're okay." Kaipo wrapped his arms around Jude, holding the back of his head and patting his shoulder like he couldn't believe Jude was real. "When I didn't see you down here and heard the explosions, I thought…" His voice choked.

"I'm okay." Jude managed to extract himself. "And I have Rumor with me. Did any of the others make it down? What about George and Angel and Vala?"

"Your two female friends did," Kai answered. "They're over there with Vala." He pointed to the other side of the cavern where Dahlia and Nyx sat, talking with Vala, who seemed to be mimicking sign language as the girls spoke. "George and Angel are helping move the hatchery eggs to safety. They're unharmed."

Jude closed his eyes as relief poured over him.

"What about Braeden?" Rumor asked.

"Where's Trick?" Jude asked at the same time.

Kai held up his hands. "Trick and Yi-Min went to get everyone out of the main command center. Trick was there with Braeden and Bailey."

"Wait. Bailey?" Rumor asked in a shocked tone. "Why is she here? Are those Epsilon marines up there?" His colors flared bright and angry red as his expression hardened into something close to terrifying.

"Those are Epsilon marines, but Bailey didn't bring them. She's here because she's one of us." Kai's eyes narrowed.

Jude put a hand on Kai's arm. "Rumor's the survivor from HUB2. Rumor, this is my older brother, Kaipo."

Rumor straightened, glaring at Kai and seemingly not even registering Jude's words. "Bailey's a forest spy? For how long?"

"Most of her life." Kai met Rumor's gaze evenly.

Rumor turned on Jude, his lips pulling back into a snarl. "Did you know this?"

Jude raised his hands and backed away a step. "No, I swear. I had no idea. I'm not part of strategic planning. At all."

Rumor stared at him, anger and distrust rolling around him. A muscle in his neck—the same place Jude had kissed so recently—jumped with his pounding pulse. Out of the corner of his eye, Jude saw Dahlia, Nyx, and Vala get up and hurry over to them. In fact, they were drawing quite a bit of attention.

"Are you sure Bailey didn't bring the marines?" Rumor asked.

Kai shook his head. "She wouldn't betray us like that. There had to be a way they found us. We searched all of you when you arrived, and no trackers were present."

Dahlia made a face. "Sara wouldn't put a tracer in her own son."

Rumor tilted his head at Vala. "They would put one in you."

Vala met his gaze, not speaking. Jude's stomach flipped.

"Did they give you a shot?" Rumor's voice trembled. "Or press a black gun to your arm, and you felt a sting?"

Vala nodded once. "They said they were scanning me for diseases."

Jude's insides fell to his toes. He stared at Vala, horror and shock and confusion roiling through him as he dimly registered the cavern echoing with various noises of anger and alarm. The chimera language scraped across his nerves. The shouts of humans pounded against his skull.

Vala wouldn't betray us. She found me. She wouldn't betray me. Jude's world wavered slightly, and he squeezed his eyes shut to right it. When he opened them, he shuddered at the expression on Rumor's face.

"Did you know?" Rumor whispered.

"I suspected," Vala said.

Tingles rolled across Jude's face as he stared at Vala. "You thought they might be tracking you?"

Rumor lifted his chin. "You knew."

"How quickly the colonist changes sides?" Vala asked instead.

"We're not discussing me," Rumor growled. "Why did you let them track you? Why did you lie?"

"Hey!" Jude made a grab for Rumor's arm. "She said she didn't know for sure."

Rumor jerked his arm away. "She knew. She's lying."

"Rumor." Jude's chest tightened as Rumor turned his glare on Jude.

"Really? You told me yourself they're intelligent. You think she had no idea what they did to her?"

"You wish to kill me?" Vala's voice was devoid of fear or apprehension, even anger.

Rumor rounded on her. "Can you stop them? The ones killing the cities. The marines capturing people up there."

"My brethren? No. Your brethren? No."

Rumor's red flared bloody. "Can't or won't?"

"Either."

Before anyone could stop Rumor, his arm was up and the gleaming blade pressed to her neck, the edge making a faint scraping sound against the thick flesh of her throat. The glow from the depths of the weapon slid across her skin like a burn. Someone shouted in alarm. The cavern around him reverberated with the chambering of guns.

Vala held up her hands to stop them and flared her wings protectively around Rumor, her eyes never leaving his.

"Rumor," Jude said, but stopped. He had no idea what to say. Words failed him as he watched the boy he was falling for pressing a blade to the throat of the chimera he considered family. The chimera who'd found him in the collapsed tunnel and provided a way out. The chimera who saved his life when he was a child. The chimera who'd been there for every day afterward, patiently teaching him, protecting him.

"People are dying. Innocent people. Everyone's dying tonight because you want to play a game." Rumor's voice hardened into ice.

She didn't flinch. Didn't attack. Didn't move except to tilt her head, exposing more of her throat.

"Will you feel better? About your kindred who die? Will my life be enough payment for your family's?" Her words stretched and curled, her voice curving around every syllable, as if she were handling delicate glass.

"Maybe."

"By all means." She tilted her head back farther, her stare fixed on Rumor.

"Vala!" Jude shouted. No, no, no, nonononono this wasn't happening. Not to Vala. Not Rumor.

She didn't move.

Neither did Rumor.

"Rumor," Jude said, urgency lacing his tone. His voice cracked when he tried again, the corners of his eyes burning.

With a growl, Rumor jerked away from Vala, his blade clattering to the ground. Vala's wings flared wide and carried her off the ground. She soared straight up, her form growing smaller and smaller until she disappeared out the hole in the cavern roof.

"What in deep space just happened?" Kai breathed.

BRAEDEN

When the first explosion hit, Braeden was in mid-sentence yelling at Bailey about family and loyalty and any other word ending in -y he could think of. How *dare* she marry his mom and be another parent for him, raising him and helping him through the loss of his father when she was a forest spy the entire time.

His blood boiled, and the back of his neck ran hot and, when the boom filled the air, for a split second, he wondered if either he or Bailey had shot each other.

"Get down!" Bailey yelled, running for him and pushing him to the ground with her body as the stained-glass photovoltaic windows lining one whole side of the command building shattered. Braeden landed hard on his shoulder and bad leg. Pain twisted up to his hips, and something in his shoulder popped.

Glass tinkled around them. A high-pitched whine filled Braeden's ears and he shook his head trying to clear it.

"I can't hear," he said, hopefully loud enough for Bailey to hear him.

Bailey patted him on the back and squeezed his shoulder as she came up to a crouch, gun in hand and her blue eyes sharp.

Braeden pushed himself up, holding his shoulder and wincing against the whine.

"My ears are whining," he signed, forgetting no one but Bailey was in the room. Bailey seemed to understand, because she patted him on the knee to get his attention and pointed to the opposite wall.

Braeden glanced at the wall of monitors and then back at Bailey with his eyebrows up in question.

Another explosion made the ground under them roll, and the tree where command was located shuddered.

"They're trying to fell the tree," Braeden yelled.

Bailey nodded patiently as she pushed stray blonde hair out of her eyes. She pointed to the wall and then signed *G* and *O*.

Braeden frowned and limped to the wall, staring at the individual monitors. Nothing was on them that would help here now. These were images of the HUB2 attack.

Bailey nudged Braeden and handed him his revolver. He took it gratefully, wrapping his fingers around the worn grooves created from years of use by his father. Braeden's fingers fit perfectly in them. He checked the bullets and nodded at Bailey.

She placed her palm flat against one of the monitors. Then she moved to another seemingly random one and pressed her palm to that one. She repeated the action with three more monitors.

"It's a code," Braeden whispered.

Bailey tugged his arm while she glanced over her shoulder.

The tree shuddered again. The floor shifted, and Braeden stumbled. The monitor wall swung open to reveal a hidden weapons cache.

"We're making a stand?" Braeden asked. "I don't know that rifles are a great idea when we're falling out of a giant tree."

She ignored him and hurried into the room. She grabbed another tsunami gun, a knife, and several clips of ammunition. She pointed to the ammunition while she crouched on the floor, feeling along the seams of the black panels.

Braeden grabbed a brand-new heritage blade as a backup weapon and strapped it to his thigh. He also grabbed two more for Nyx and Dahlia in case they didn't have anything. He peered around hopefully for a sniper rifle for Nyx, but saw nothing. He stuffed his pockets with extra gun clips.

Bailey tugged on the hem of his pant leg. He looked down in surprise. "Where'd that hole come from? Wait, are we going down the middle of the trunk?"

She nodded and beckoned for him. Her eyes went wide at something behind him, and she climbed down quickly. Braeden looked over his shoulder while moving toward the hole. The monitor wall door was swinging shut, cutting off the command room.

But just before it closed, the main doors opened and Sara Tennant stood in the doorway, gun in hand. Braeden's world condensed to a single moment in time as he caught the shock and betrayal on his mother's face before the panel clicked shut.

"Well dammit," he muttered as he headed down the ladder. They descended into near darkness. Tiny discs of blue light lined the inside of the massive tree trunk, giving them just enough light to see the ladder.

It descended forever. As Braeden's hearing slowly returned to normal, the explosions faded, replaced by a creepy stillness broken only by his and Bailey's breathing. His palms sweated. His legs shook. Pain radiated from his shoulder and his leg. One entire side of his body felt run through an adamantine refinery.

He stopped, scrubbing the heel of his palm against his sternum.

"You okay?" Bailey called.

"A little pain. No big deal," he said through gritted teeth. "Also I'm sort of tired of ladders tonight. It's been very life-or-death each time."

"We're nearly there," she said.

"Great. Wherever that is."

"Chimera nest underneath Azrou." Bailey's voice faded as she kept descending.

"Oh, that makes it all better." Braeden rolled his eyes and climbed down, focusing on the descent and not the hard ground below somewhere in the darkness. "Hey, can Mom get through that panel?"

"With explosives, yes. Hurry up," Bailey said, her voice thin. "We'll seal the tunnel at the bottom."

When he was about to groan with impatience again, they reached the bottom. Braeden stepped off the ladder onto—not dirt, as he expected—but a smooth, stone floor. The blue discs had disappeared. Splintering, vein-like patterns of blue light etched across the walls like cracks.

"It's algae. I'll explain later. We need to go." Bailey pulled on his arm. "I need to find a builder."

Braeden followed her at a limping jog, the shocked face of his mother permanently seared on his brain. "Why was Mom there?"

Bailey shook her head. "I don't know. She wouldn't lead an attack on civilians."

"Well, she just did. Last time I checked, Azrou isn't a military stronghold."

"I know," Bailey snapped. She blew out a breath and stopped running. "I get it, you don't trust me right now, and you're angry. I don't know why Sara's here, but she wouldn't be unless it was a direct order."

Disgust and anger gnawed his empty stomach, turning his hunger into nausea. "So orders trump morals. Got it."

Braeden moved away, but Bailey grabbed his arm.

"Reaper's planning a rally," Bailey said, her voice hushed and her eyes wide. "HUB2 wasn't the end. He's gathering every pack across Sahara to HUB2 tonight. He's going to demand their pledges and their loyalty. With a united army that size, he'll wipe out humanity on this moon."

Braeden wanted to feel fear at her words. He wanted to feel something beyond the betrayal and rage at his mothers right now. "So fly over and bomb him. There aren't any humans left in HUB2 anyway." He yanked his arm from her grasp.

"You know we can't do flyovers at night."

"Oh do I?" Braeden tilted his head. "Seems there are a few things you can do I don't know about." He turned away as hurt flashed over her face. He ignored how it stabbed him in the heart and made him want to apologize.

He sort of understood why it was so hard for Rumor to let go of his anger.

"Bailey!" Yi-Min appeared out of an adjoining tunnel with a shoulder-height chimera following them. "Thank Mother you're both safe." They hugged Bailey tightly. "Did you find anyone else besides your son?"

Your son. The words prickled over his brain.

"He was the only one with me." Bailey turned to the chimera. "Are you a builder?"

The chimera nodded.

"I need you to seal the access to the ladder. Hurry."

The chimera took off at a loping run. Braeden stared after it in confusion, but no one seemed to feel the need to explain it to him.

"Braeden, are you okay?" Yi-Min rested a hand on his shoulder.

Braeden nodded. "Fine."

Neither of them pushed.

"What about the others?" Bailey asked as the two fell into step together. Braeden followed.

"Kai made it down to the cavern with the two girls who came with Braeden."

Oh, thank every deity in deep space. Braeden let out a heavy breath. "Thank you."

Yi-Min inclined their head and returned to Bailey. "Jude and the boy he's with, Rumor, just arrived."

"What about Trick?" Braeden asked. "He was with me when I first got to command but left with Kaipo."

"Trick was there but came with me to get you two. He veered off when we heard cries for help. Several citizens were trying to escape. He stayed behind to help them while I went ahead for you," Yi-Min said.

Braeden stopped walking, alarms going off in his head. "Where is he?"

"Braeden, come on," Bailey said over her shoulder.

"No, where is he? He might need help," Braeden insisted.

"Trick knows these tunnels," Yi-Min assured him.

"But I know Epsilon marines." Braeden glared at Bailey. "And so do you." He stood still, waiting, fidgeting through the dull pain in his body. All he needed was one walk through the chimera tunnels and he'd know them by heart.

And he needed to help Trick. He couldn't explain why, but the thought of the boy who'd welcomed him to Azrou without judgement or reservation getting captured or killed sent a shiver down Braeden's spine. He knew he was an outsider asking a veritable stranger to change their plans for him, but he couldn't stand the thought of leaving Trick to fend off trained Epsilon fighters alone. Not after he helped Vala escape.

And there was this odd sense of debt. Like he owed the people of this forest for having Vala in the first place. If he'd said something, a lot of tonight might have been avoided.

He shifted his weight from one foot to the other and raised his eyebrows at them. "We should help him."

Bailey finally nodded. "Okay, let's go find him."

"This way." Yi-Min pointed back to the tunnel they'd come out of. "Weapons out. We don't know what we'll find." They pulled a knife and took the lead.

Braeden pulled the knife from the sheath over his shoulder

and the blade from the sheath on his thigh. Bailey followed, holding her military-issued tsunami pistol in both hands.

The tunnel twisted and headed steadily upward. Braeden bowed his head, unsure if his hearing was one hundred percent. Something echoed down the tunnel. "Is that gunfire?"

Yi-Min nodded and broke into a run. Braeden followed as fast as he could, pain shooting up his side with every step. His stomach growled with hunger. He chewed on the inside of his cheek as Yi-Min slowed. The gunfire was much louder here, but still suppressed. Or perhaps Braeden's hearing wasn't all the way back yet. His head felt fluffy around the edges.

The tunnel narrowed at a natural T-junction. The gunfire cracked around the corner to the right. To the left was a partial collapse with several large chunks of rock strewn across the ground.

Yi-Min's eyes narrowed as they pointed to the right. "There's an entrance to the caves that direction. How did they find it?"

Bailey crept to the other side, hiding behind the rubble. Her expression was grim, her blonde hair falling out of its ponytail around her face. Braeden noticed blood from a split lip and several rips in her shirt.

He hadn't even asked her if she was okay after the explosion.

He and Yi-Min crouched at the corner.

"Trick! You there?" Braeden yelled.

"About time, man!" Trick yelled back. "How are things with your stepmom?"

Braeden glanced at her. "Fantastic!"

"She's right there, isn't she?" Trick called.

"I am!" Bailey shouted.

"Hi, Bailey! If you guys could please come out and maybe fire some bullets, that would be helpful." Trick's voice drifted nearer until he peeked around the corner. His face was covered in dust, and blood trickled from a long cut above his eye. "Hey, Yi-Min."

Yi-Min nodded and darted around the corner, two high-powered revolvers drawn. Trick slid into their place, his back against the wall. "Tell me one of you has a spare clip. Tsunami's empty."

"I do," Braeden said.

"I'll help Yi-Min," Bailey said. "Where are the Azrous?"

Trick nodded to the partially destroyed tunnel branch. "Hidden down there in some old housing."

Braeden blinked at him. "Housing?"

Bailey stood from behind the rubble and opened fire. Braeden winced away from the sound, his hearing still fragile. Trick watched him in concern. "Were you up top?"

Braeden nodded. "My ears are ringing."

"Lemme make sure they aren't bleeding." Trick grabbed both sides of Braeden's head and turned him one way then the other, peering in his ears. "No blood, but I can see through to the other side, so you might want to get that checked."

"I just met you, and you're already insulting me." Braeden stood so he could get to his pockets. He dug out a clip and handed it over. He put the blade back in the sheath and pulled out his revolver instead. "How many are left?"

"Not sure." Trick wiped at the cut with the back of his hand. "I got a few of them, and two of the Azrou guys had guns. They stayed while the others hid." Trick's nebula-colored eyes darkened. "But…"

"Marines got them," Braeden said.

"Head shots," Trick said with a nod. "Right before y'all got here."

Braeden's stomach twisted, and the next gunshot made him flinch. He flexed his fingers around the grip and took a deep breath, tracing his father's imprint. Fighting his own people—his own marines. Epsilon colonists he probably knew. He never thought it'd be this way. He moved away from the wall, his insides churning. He felt as though he was falling and didn't know where or how he'd land.

Trick's hand closed around Braeden's arm. Braeden looked at him. Trick chewed the inside of his cheek, seeming at a loss. His eyes darted down to Braeden's jacket and back up again, and Braeden understood. Trick's older brother had been one of those very marines, years ago. If Trick had stayed in the colonies, would he be one of the ones out there right now? Would Kaipo?

Finally, he met Braeden's eyes. "I'm glad you're okay."

Braeden swallowed. "I'm glad you're okay, too."

Trick's hand dropped, but he held Braeden's attention. "We only need to keep them out of the tunnel."

Braeden nodded. "How did that collapse?"

"No idea. It was like that when I got here."

Bailey dropped behind the rubble again, checking her gun. "It's recent. Whatever you're doing, do it fast. They'll have sent for backup."

She came up to a crouch, then darted out to join Yi-Min in the other tunnel.

Braeden took a step after her before he realized what he was doing. That need to protect his moms rose in him like a wave, strong and unrelenting. He forced himself to examine the broken ceiling. He mapped the jagged crack, narrowing his eyes at the origin—right above his head. "Oh, that's fantastic."

"What?" Trick looked up. "Oh." He sucked through his teeth. "Okay, we need to move the Azrous to this tunnel."

"Without being shot," Braeden added.

Trick grinned and rotated his shoulder. "Aww, come on. It's fun. Med center has this cool pink gel they squirt in it afterward."

Braeden snorted and pressed his back to the wall. "Bailey!"

"Yeah!"

"Getting the kids!" he yelled. His voice echoed around them, mixing with the uneven bursts of gunfire. He had no idea what the marines heard on their end.

"Copy!" she called. The gunfire from her end quickened and moved away from him.

He grinned over his shoulder at Trick. "She's pushing them back."

"We don't have much time." Trick brushed past Braeden and darted into the other tunnel.

Braeden huffed and followed. He deepened his voice. "That was really clever, Braeden. With the half-assed code on the fly." He spoke normally. "Aw, thanks, man. It was nothing."

Trick snorted. He ran through the tunnel, which curved gradually downward. A few darkened and crumbling alcoves dotted the walls. "I need y'all to come with me now!"

Soot-covered and dirty faces peered out of various entrances. Braeden counted nearly twelve, almost half of them kids. He didn't know if he was going to be sick or angry or trapped somewhere between the two.

He couldn't find it in himself to believe his mom would order open fire on civilians. There had to be more to this.

Trick headed back toward Braeden, a little girl on his back. Her head was tucked behind his neck. Another man took point as Trick paused next to Braeden. "I'll help lead them back. You bring up the rear and make sure everyone follows."

Braeden nodded. He waited until everyone passed him, then he started back up the tunnel, pausing every so often to hurry a distracted kid along. As he reached the rubble, he heard a yell that sounded like Bailey, followed by several shots in rapid succession, then silence.

His heart dove to his toes, and he was running before he'd even decided to. Trick yelled after him, but Braeden kept running, heading down the branch Bailey and Yi-Min had disappeared down. He strained to pick up any sound. Anything.

Please don't let her be dead. He couldn't handle one of his moms being dead on top of everything else tonight. *I take it back. I don't want answers anymore. I just want Bailey to be okay.*

He skidded to a stop when he reached the end of the tunnel. "Whoa," he breathed.

Several bodies lay on the ground, all wearing similar uniforms. Bailey held her side with one hand and leaned against the wall.

"Azrous get out okay?" she asked. She was breathing hard, her hair sticking to her pale face with sweat.

"They did. Are you hurt?" Braeden moved toward her. He barely noted bodies on the ground, the part of him who would have recoiled at death squashed by the driving need to make sure Bailey was okay.

"We need to get Yi-Min help," Bailey said, instead of answering.

Braeden stopped. Yi-Min was lying on the ground, their hand over a wound on their hip. Blood stained up their side and down their thigh. He knelt next to them, looking back at Bailey.

"Are you hurt?" he asked again, his voice sharper, his heart pounding.

"It's just a graze." Bailey moved her hand, revealing the bloodstain on her side. "Braeden," she said in a firm voice. "I'm okay. We've got to get Yi-Min back to the others."

Braeden swallowed and nodded. "Trick!" he yelled.

A moment later, Trick yelled back, his voice impatient.

"Yi-Min's been hurt!" Braeden listened for breathing and a heartbeat. He gingerly lifted their shirt up enough to expose their hip. "Knife wound?"

"I think so." Bailey winced as she moved. "Can we move them?"

Braeden nodded. "Do we have anything to put pressure on this?"

Bailey pulled her shirt off, leaving herself in only a sports bra. She handed it to Braeden as Trick ran up to them. "Theirs is worse than mine. It was a tsunami bullet. It's mostly cauterized already."

Braeden frowned at her but snatched it anyway and pressed the shirt against the wound. Yi-Min groaned, their eyelids fluttering. Braeden leaned over them. "Yi-Min, can you hear me? We need to pick you up, okay?"

No answer.

Braeden glanced at Trick, who was staring at Yi-Min with a mixture of anguish and rage on his face. "Trick, you need to get your brother."

Trick didn't answer. Braeden motioned to Bailey to take over for him and keep pressure on Yi-Min's wound. He stood and planted himself between Yi-Min and Trick, capturing his attention. "I need you to get the others to safety and get Kai. We'll be right behind you."

Trick's chest hitched with short breaths. He nodded, a muscle on his jaw ticking. Without another word, he took off at a run, his footsteps echoing down the tunnel.

The back of Braeden's neck grew hot. He knelt next to Yi-Min again and slipped his arm under Yi-Min's shoulders. He pulled their arm over his shoulders.

Bailey mimicked the motion on the other side, helping him pull them up. Yi-Min's body weight sagged between them, their head lolling like a doll's. Braeden cursed under his breath as they started walking.

He carefully stepped around the body of a man, frowning at the jacket cuffs.

"They aren't green," he muttered.

"What?" Bailey asked, her voice strained.

"Epsilon jackets have green cuffs. Those were red. Alpha colony is red."

"Why would Alpha colony marines be all the way out here?" Bailey asked.

Braeden shook his head. "Did any of them have green cuffs?"

"I was too busy trying not to die to notice their fashion."

The corner of Braeden's lips quirked upward, but fell a moment later. Why red cuffs?

When they reached the junction, Braeden used his free hand to pull his revolver from the holster. When they were far enough down the tunnel, he paused and shot at the crack in the ceiling until the tunnel started to rumble and groan.

As they limped away, the ceiling fell, blocking the tunnel from any access to the outdoors. Braeden adjusted Yi-Min's weight and set his jaw. Hopefully he hadn't just blown their only escape to pieces.

NYX

Nyx chewed on her fingernail and watched everyone milling around her in the enormous blue chimera cavern. Being down this far inside the moon itself was like cranking the volume on the vibrations to one hundred. The hum rattled her bones, jangled her insides, raised goose bumps on her flesh. Dahlia had tried to speak to her when they first arrived, but Nyx was so distracted by the thrumming, she couldn't read lips. Every time she stood, she lost her equilibrium for a moment.

"Still loud?" Dahlia signed, her expression soft and concerned. Nyx still couldn't believe this stunning, sexy girl had said she loved her. Said. *Said.*

Nyx swallowed, unwanted doubt creeping in again. How much of this was reaction to tonight and all the mayhem they'd been through? How much of this was a feeling of the last time ever for everything? That they might very well die tonight, and that meant throw everything to the wind.

Was that why Nyx had admitted her feelings?

Was that why Dahlia had claimed to return them?

What if she was mistaken? What if Dahlia just *thought* she loved her because she needed someone to distract her? What if

Dahlia was so upset by Colt's death that she hadn't been thinking clearly and later, after all this was done, she changed her mind?

Dahlia tapped her on the arm, her eyebrows up.

Nyx swallowed all her doubts and signed, "Worried about Braeden."

Dahlia gave her a sympathetic smile and slid her arms around Nyx's shoulders. Nyx nestled against her chest, trying to find Dahlia's heartbeat amidst the moon's vibrations, but she couldn't feel it over the shaking of the moon. She frowned and tried not to associate that with the thoughts rolling around her brain, but she couldn't. Nyx glanced down at her hands, half expecting to see them shaking, too.

She kept an eye on the tunnel exits she could see, hoping Braeden would come through one at any moment.

Rumor and Jude sat with Kaipo a few meters away, but Nyx could only see Rumor's face. He seemed upset—more so than earlier with Vala, if that was possible. He spoke, his lips moving fast and the lines of his face all angles and corners. He kept shaking his head at whatever Kaipo said to him.

Nyx straightened. "Do you know what's happening over there?"

Dahlia shook her head, her brows knitted as she watched them. She signed as she stood, "Okay, I'm done sitting here. Let's go find out."

"What's going on?" Dahlia asked and signed at the same time.

Jude immediately turned to make room for them. He smiled at Nyx, a little shy but not unkind. She knew that smile, though. That was the "I don't know how to talk to you" smile.

She smiled back and touched Dahlia's elbow to get her attention before signing quickly. "Jude's weirded out by me."

Dahlia arched an eyebrow. "I'll kick him in the junk."

"Rumor might get mad."

Dahlia's smile turned evil, and she flicked off the signs. "Baby, I can handle Rumor."

Nyx's body tingled at the pet name, and suddenly she wanted nothing more than to be very, very alone with Dahlia right at this moment. Dahlia winked at her and turned back to the conversation.

Nyx warmed at the attention, crushing all the doubts into a little box in her head. *She wouldn't lie to me about that. Not even if tonight were our last night.*

One doubt wriggled free. *But what happens when this is over and the suns rise?*

A flurry of movement by one of the tunnel exits caught her eye. Several bloodied and frightened people entered the cavern and made the long descent to the floor. Nyx stepped away from the group and stared at the blackened archway, folded out of the cavern walls. *Please.*

Her heart was going to explode if Braeden didn't walk through that exit right now.

Please.

Another person limped through, but it wasn't Braeden. It was Trick. He scanned the crowd from his vantage point. Nyx's heart slid to her toes when his eyes landed on their group and he pressed his lips together.

No.

She shook her head as Trick jogged down the ramp, waving off anyone who stepped forward to help him.

No. No. No. Nyx clutched her sweater. Braeden's sweater. Her eyes burned and her stomach flipped over. She reached for Dahlia's arm, digging her nails in. Dahlia jerked but immediately stepped in front of her. "What's going on?"

"Trick's back. Alone." Nyx gestured behind Dahlia, who turned right as Trick approached them. Nyx's chest felt like someone was standing on it. Dahlia stepped back, her fingers twitching to sign as everyone looked at Trick.

The moon trembled and rolled under Nyx's feet, and she tightened her hold on Dahlia for balance even as her eyes blurred with tears. Dahlia's eyes were wide, darting all over Trick as if she could read his mind or his expression or something. Anything.

"Kai," Trick said. "Yi-Min's been hurt."

Kai reached out as if to anchor himself on Trick's shoulder and stared at him. "How bad?"

"Bad." Trick glanced over his shoulder again. "They were right behind me, but they fell back. Bailey told me to keep going and get the other Azrous to safety first."

Kai lips parted like he couldn't get enough air. He tried to speak several times, and Trick grabbed his arm, steadying his brother. Nyx looked from Kaipo to Trick and back again.

Tears flooded her throat and burned her nose. She couldn't stand this. "What about Br—"

Dahlia smacked her arm four times and pointed.

Bailey and Braeden walked slowly out of the cavern, holding Yi-Min upright between them. Braeden said something, his voice echoing, but Nyx couldn't make it out. Kaipo ran, other people following, to the ramp to help them.

Braeden and Bailey carefully transferred Yi-Min to Kai, who swept them up in a cradle carry on his own. Another person slid Bailey's arm around their shoulders and walked away with her.

Braeden waved off help with a tired, thin smile and headed down the long ramp to the main level.

Nyx was already running.

She crashed into him at full speed, her arms wrapping around his waist and her face buried in his chest as the tears she'd been holding in all night broke free in a rush of emotion. "I thought I lost you."

The mere thought of never seeing him again filled her with fear and anxiety and so much sadness she thought she'd split open. She felt like Alice from *Alice in Wonderland* when she'd cried so much, she'd filled a room with her tears.

Braeden held her tight, his nose pressed to the top of her head. He shifted so his cheek rested on her and rubbed her back.

He said nothing.

She couldn't speak anymore. Nyx closed her eyes, trying to rein in her crying. People were suffering far worse than her right now. Braeden was alive.

Nyx wiggled, and his arms loosened. She disentangled herself and smiled up at him. He swiped away her tears with his thumbs, then signed, "You can't get rid of me, girl. You love me too much."

She rolled her eyes and nodded, sniffling

"You okay?" He made no move to join the others, his attention focused squarely on her.

"A little better now," she signed. "Dahlia and I—" She stopped, not sure how to phrase it.

Braeden's eyebrows shot up. "Whoa wait what? You two finally…you know what? I don't need details."

He shook his head and waved his hands, making a face the whole time.

She swatted his chest. "We didn't have sex." Yet? Although now that image slid around her brain, and her insides grew hot. "We just kissed."

Braeden's smile grew wide. "Congratulations!" His smile slipped when she only shrugged. "Or no? What's wrong?"

Nyx took a deep breath. This was the wrong time for this, what with everything going on, but if she didn't get this out to someone, she was going to explode. "I'm afraid that we moved too fast and now if anything goes wrong then our friendship will die and I can't lose her like that she's my best friend and I love her so much and I don't know what to do now."

Braeden watched her run-on signing, his expression softening. "I don't pretend to know the first thing about romance, but I know you and Dahlia. And I'm sure it's scary and I'm sure it won't be easy but you two are…" He trailed off as he thought, his lower lip caught between his teeth. He smiled and signed, "Perfect." He tilted his head, his eyes wide and reassuring. "Try not to worry. I believe it's a good thing, and Dahlia wouldn't risk your friendship for something like this unless she meant it."

Nyx nodded, letting Braeden's words seep into her doubts and fears and calm them. He was right. Dahlia wouldn't do this unless she was sure. Their friendship was too strong and too important.

"She's probably just as worried as you are, so you should try to talk to her about all this when you can." Braeden wiped his thumbs under Nyx's eyes. "Okay?"

She nodded again and touched her fingertips to her chin. "Thank you."

She'd just needed someone else—someone not her own brain—to tell her it wasn't a mistake. That it wasn't wrong. That she hadn't lost Dahlia in her urgency to kiss the girl.

Braeden quickly signed what had happened up top with him and Bailey and the fight in the tunnels with Trick. "I had picked up two heritage blades for you and Dahlia, but I dropped them in the tunnel to help. Then we had to bring Yi-Min back here and I forgot them. I'm sorry."

"It's okay," she signed. "We'll find something else."

He rubbed his eyes with the heels of his hands then signed, "Where's Rumor and the others?"

Nyx led Braeden back to Rumor and Jude and Trick, who were already talking about something that had Jude sitting with his head in his hands and Rumor standing over him like a guard.

Nyx glanced at Dahlia while she signed the conversation. She had no idea how much of that conversation Dahlia had been able to read from over here. Did she know about Nyx's fears now? Did it matter? Would Dahlia get upset that Nyx hadn't told *her* about them before Braeden?

Great, doubts and fears accounted for once again.

"Reaper's not stopping tonight," Braeden said without any preamble.

Everyone looked at him.

"What?" Rumor asked.

Braeden ran his hands through his hair. "Apparently, going after Vala was his way of whipping the chimera into a united frenzy. Now that the ball is rolling and they've had a big taste of victory, he's pressing forward. He's going to pick off all of HUB2's colonies, then move to another HUB and its colonies and keep going."

"Until everything is gone," Nyx said quietly. Her scalp prickled, and her heart thudded. It was all a ruse. A pretense of rescue when, in reality, it was extermination.

Braeden nodded. Dahlia wrapped her arms around herself and stared at some middle distance across the room. Trick wiped a hand over his mouth and tipped his head back. Jude moved closer to Rumor and pressed his nose to Rumor's shoulder, his eyes closed.

"Where is he?" Rumor asked, his expression tight.

"HUB2," Braeden answered. "Some of the chimeras split off when Vala returned, but he still has a sizable army. He's gathering leaders of several packs in the next few hours to rally them together. Using HUB2 as evidence of what they can do together might convince them to keep going tonight."

"That would basically, what, double his army?" Nyx asked. The moon growled under her feet, and she swayed.

"Maybe even triple," Jude said, his eyes dark and his mouth in a thin line. "If he unites the packs, then it's over."

Rumor watched Jude with an unreadable expression, his fingers twitching.

"Where did you hear all this?" Dahlia asked.

"Bailey," Braeden said with a frown. "Before the explosion. We also saved Bailey the trouble by releasing Vala on our own. Apparently, Vala was bait to lure Reaper to Epsilon."

"Did she know she was bait?" Rumor frowned. His shoulders squared, drawing his height up and slicing his face in long shadows.

Braeden hesitated. "Bailey 'caught her' and revealed it to my mom, intending to let Mom talk to her. I guess Vala thought she could convince my mom that chimera weren't all bad. But Mom insisted on putting Vala in a cage as bait to lure Reaper."

"Why Reaper?" Nyx asked. She hadn't heard of him before tonight.

Braeden smiled thinly. "He's a revolutionary. One of the foremost voices against the colonies. General wants him pretty badly."

Nyx's arms tingled with the desire to hug Braeden as he tried to hide how much his mother's ambition bothered him. "Your mom wanted to be the one to bring him in."

Braeden hung a hand on the back of his neck and nodded. "Bailey didn't want to break cover, so she went along with it, but she was planning on freeing Vala as soon as she could. Then HUB2 was hit." He turned to Rumor, his eyes wide. "Mom told Bailey he'd come straight for Epsilon, that he didn't have the force to go after HUB2. She didn't intend for any—"

"Intent and reality are two different things," Rumor snapped. "I don't care what she *intended*. My home is gone. My dad is dead." He turned away and bowed his head, his shoulders shaking.

The moon rolled and thrummed under Nyx's feet, tugging tugging tugging at her to follow. "We need to go," she said. "We need—" She cut off as the moon pulsed at her so sharply she gasped. "To HUB2. To stop the rally."

Trick shook his head. "Too many marines up top. They'd see us and come after us."

Braeden rubbed his fingers over his lips. "Not if they're looking for me."

Nyx knew that expression. "No. Braeden, no. Don't you dare."

Braeden grinned at her. "She saw me escape with Bailey, so she's definitely looking for me. Right now, I'm probably the only one who can get near her without being shot."

"Are you serious?" Dahlia asked.

Braeden tilted his head. "Extremely. I have a few questions for her. Starting with why she let her squads open fire on civilians."

"Why?" Rumor asked.

"Well, I mean, personally, I think it's horrible to shoot civilians—"

"No," Trick interrupted. "Why do you want to go to your mom?"

"To convince her to help us stop this rally." Braeden frowned like that should be obvious. "Even if she only brought half Epsilon's manpower, that's still a decent number of people to help track down Reaper, plus it gets them out of Azrou. You can't honestly think we can find and kill Reaper just the six of us."

Trick and Rumor exchanged a glance Nyx couldn't read. Jude scratched his neck as he studied Braeden.

"If he's gathering all the packs, how many gargoyles—I'm sorry, chimera—is that?" Nyx asked, afraid to know the answer.

Jude turned his attention to her. "Thousands. More."

A fist-sized stone sank in her stomach.

"This is such a bad idea," Dahlia muttered.

"Braeden, please don't," Nyx said. Her throat grew tight. "Something awful is going to happen. I can feel it here"—she pressed a hand to her belly—"and here." She pointed to her feet where the vibrations scratched and yowled at her. Tears blurred her vision, and she pulled in a stuttering breath.

"Mom will have sent a picture of me to every person she has up there to make sure I'm captured alive." Braeden leaned over and kissed her forehead. "I'll be okay," he signed.

Tears balled up in Nyx's throat again. She couldn't lose him again. Not tonight. "You have a death wish."

He gave her a tiny shrug. "Maybe a tiny one."

"How do you know she'll help?" Dahlia asked.

Braeden shook his head. "I don't. But I have to try." All amusement faded from his eyes, and real hurt flashed through them, darkening the gold. "She's my mom. I have to try."

"I'm going, too," Trick said. He held up a hand when Braeden opened his mouth to protest. "You don't know your way around Azrou. I do. I can get you close to your mom without getting caught. Then I'm going to see how many people I can round up to come with us. Everyone has some level of fight training. The more bodies—even just to sit on top of a building with a rifle— the better. When you get away from your mom, I'll help get you out." He gestured to the other four. "Then we come back here and get these guys and go."

"No, I'm going now," Rumor said.

The moon thrummed at her, tugging like a hook around her ankle. She tried to listen to the thrumming and follow Dahlia's signing at the same time, but it all howled in her head, making her lose words and entire meanings of sentences. She barely processed Trick and Rumor arguing and strangers pausing to watch. Vala was gone and couldn't mute the hum and it kept building and building and building and—

A hand pressed to her back, long-fingered and strong. The thrumming sank to the background like a stone falling in the lake. Angel towered over her. One face watched her with concern. The other face watched the argument with a different type of concern.

Nyx leaned against their hand and breathed out, finally able to sort through the tangle in her head. She glanced at Dahlia, who was still signing for her.

Jude rubbed his face. "This is the worst plan."

"Do you have a better one?" Rumor asked.

Jude shook his head and stared at his hands. The sadness and resignation drifting off him was nearly palpable.

Angel squatted so they were at eye level with everyone. Both faces examined Rumor for a long moment. "Do you still plan to kill Reaper?"

Rumor stared back. "He killed my dad."

Nyx stiffened. Was Angel angry? Would they stop Rumor? "Maybe we should wait. Like Trick said."

Dahlia and Jude looked at her. Rumor barely acknowledged that she'd spoken. He tilted his head a little, waiting for Angel's response.

"Do you feel killing him is the only way to stop this?" Angel asked.

"Do you have another option?" Rumor straightened.

"Angel," Trick said. "If we capture Reaper, his followers will come for him, which puts a lot of people in danger. And we can't let him keep going at this rate. He's created an uprising."

"Then, even if you take his life, it may not stop those who follow him," Angel said.

"But they might not unite, which might buy us time. They may refuse to unite for anyone else." Trick shook his head. "If he wasn't planning on attacking more colonies tonight, then we'd hold off, but we can't afford that. People's lives are in danger, and we only have a few hours."

Jude stared at the ground again, his mouth in a thin line.

"I would like the opportunity to speak to him," Angel said. "One last time."

Trick closed his eyes. Nyx's heart twisted.

Rumor pressed his lips together. "Are you going to stop me from killing him?"

One of Angel's heads looked away while the other maintained eye contact. "No," they said.

Maybe Angel saw it as a necessary sacrifice or maybe they truly believed the only way to stop Reaper was to kill him, but either way, it bruised her soul. She'd be the first to admit she didn't understand how *family* worked within the chimera pack system, but there had to be a connection shared between nestmates.

There had to be.

And if Reaper and Angel came from the same nest, maybe there was a chance—a sliver of hope—that the same openness inside Angel hid somewhere inside Reaper, too.

"Listen," Trick said. "There aren't many options right now. We only have a little over eleven hours until dayside. Less than that until Reaper attacks another colony. Kai's with Yi-Min and in no shape to plan an assault strategy right now. We get this done—we get Reaper and drive the marines out of our forest—that'll be a huge win for us."

Jude stared at his brother with a funny look on his face. "Or we all die."

Trick tilted his head. "We're gonna die anyway, little brother. You want to go out waiting down here or up there fighting?" The lines of his face softened with each word.

Jude didn't answer. No one needed to.

Rumor shifted his weight a few times, nodding, his fingers twitching for his blades. "Okay. Eleven hours isn't that much. I'm going to find Reaper. If you guys are coming, we leave now." He glanced at Braeden. "If you can get your mom to send backup, that would probably help."

His eyes slid away before Braeden could respond.

Jude's attention shifted to look up at Rumor, and Nyx would've bet all the credits to her name that the boy was infinitely sad.

BRAEDEN

"Commander, we found him." The marine tightened his grip on Braeden's upper arm like he'd bolt at any moment. Braeden rolled his eyes and flexed his fingers as tingling numbness rolled down his arm. He tried to see if he could spot Trick, but the marine jerked him forward again. Trick had detoured to lead a patrol away so Braeden could get closer to the colony and find his mom. But Braeden only managed to make it within about twenty meters of the fallen command center tree when he was ambushed by a squad hunting for him.

The air smelled like smoke. It stung his eyes and made them water. A tear slipped out and ran down his cheek. His insides spun as he took in all the damage. All the death. He nearly threw up at the branches of someone's home in a twisted heap on the ground. Still-burning fires threw orange light across the glossy blood on the bark.

This didn't make any sense. This wasn't what his mom did. This wasn't her.

Was it?

Three lines of forest people knelt, hands behind their heads. A few of them stole glances at Braeden. Guilt flushed his neck.

His mom turned around, surprise and sadness and something else he couldn't decipher flitting through her eyes before her carefully composed mask of disappointment covered it. Braeden met her gaze evenly, refusing to feel guilty for what they'd done. "Hey, Mom."

"What are you doing here? Tell me they forced you."

Braeden hummed. "Would that make it easier for you? If I was forced at gunpoint to free a chimera? Then I wouldn't be guilty of treason, Mom, right?"

Fire crackled out of his peripheral vision, eating another home that'd done nothing more than provide shelter. The air smelled of blood. Several chimera corpses littered the ground, cut down and kicked aside like nothing more than trash in the way. His stomach churned, and bile crawled up his throat. So much needless death. Why hadn't he seen this before?

"You chose to betray the colony?" Sara asked. "We've known for a while there was a spy in Epsilon. Too many of our supply trucks went missing for it to be coincidence. Forest rebels knew things they shouldn't have known. Who are you working with?"

"You think I'm the spy?" Braeden gaped. He would've rather one of these marines punch him in the chest than hear that accusation from his mother. "Your own son?"

She raised her eyebrows. "Tell me it isn't true then."

"Why are you doing this?" Braeden's voice cracked. "These are peaceful people. These are peaceful chimera."

Her face blanched. "How dare you."

"Me?" He straightened as much as he could while being held. His entire body trembled. "I'm not the one who mowed through innocent families." His voice caught on a sob. "What is going on? Why are you here with Alpha colony squads?" He gestured with his free hand to the people around them, their jacket cuffs as red as the blood soaking into the dirt. Several marines swung their weapons at him at the sudden movement. He glared at them and bared his teeth in a snarl. "Really? I'm her son. That would be the worst career move ever."

Sara remained expressionless, but a slight tremor in the side of her neck caught Braeden's attention. "Where are the others? Where is Vala?"

"I am here." Vala stepped out of the trees, her wings fastened around her shoulders and her palms visible.

"Vala—" Braeden tried, but the marine twisted his arm. The rest of his words morphed into a cry he couldn't control as pain shot down his arm. Tears sprung to his eyes, and he forced himself to get under control. He was a commander's son. He couldn't cry in front of these marines. He couldn't cry in front of Vala. "I'm sorry," he whispered.

"Now isn't the time for that," Sara said.

Braeden met her furious gaze. "I was talking to Vala."

"How could you betray us?" Sara asked. "How could you spy and turn against your own for these..."

"These what, Mom? The people who lived here? The humans who lived here away from your rules? Oh, not them. You didn't care about them. You meant what? Monsters? Creatures? Not-humans? How about chimera? How about intelligent, loyal, and curious? How about a race that lives and loves and fights and dies just like we do?" His voice rose with every question until he was shouting. "*Look at her* and tell me she's a lumbering, savage monster. She is just. Like. You. A leader. Protective of her kind. Trying to keep everyone safe."

"How long, Braeden?" Sara asked in a controlled voice. "How long have you been—"

"He's not the spy, Sara." Bailey stepped out of the trees where Vala had been moments before. She'd found a new shirt, but it was already streaked with soot and torn in places. She raised her hands in surrender. "Braeden wasn't the spy. He didn't know anything until a few hours ago."

Sara's carefully composed mask cracked at the sight of her wife standing in surrender. "Bailey? You?"

Bailey's sad smile broke Braeden's heart. "We need to talk, love. Bring a few marines if you want."

Without asking permission, she turned and walked toward another building.

"Commander!" Another marine appeared, pushing Trick into the clearing. Trick stumbled and fell to the ground. Braeden jerked instinctively to go make sure he was okay, but the marine tightened his grip in warning. Blood poured from a cut on Trick's forehead and broken nose. "We found this one in the woods. He fought back."

"Of course I did." Trick spat blood on the ground and slowly got to his feet. He held his side as he straightened. "You're invading our home without cause. I was keeping my people safe."

Sara stared at Trick, her eyes narrowed and assessing. Braeden's heart pounded, and his breath quickened. Before tonight, he never would've imagined he'd be afraid for someone else's life in front of his mother. But now he had no idea what she'd do.

He needed to keep his mom occupied and, while Bailey's revelation could do that, he knew what would get his mom's gears turning. "Mom, we have information about the HUB2 attack."

Sara frowned at him. "What do you mean?"

Braeden licked his lips. "Bailey can tell you more, but we were planning to go to HUB2 and get Reaper. We can tell you about it." He pulled a little on the marine's grip. "If you can get Asshole here to let me have blood flow back to my fingers."

"Let him go," Sara said. He couldn't tell if she was angry at him, the situation, or Bailey. Maybe all three.

The marine released Braeden's arm and he rubbed his biceps, wincing at the soreness. He flexed his fingers as pins rolled down the side of his hand. "Dude, do you do like those hand clamp exercises, or are you compensating for something?"

The marine's nostrils flared, and Braeden backed up a step,

grinning. No one stopped him from standing next to Trick and pulling Trick's arm around his shoulders for support. Trick shot him a grateful look, his eyes tight with pain. The blood from his forehead dripped into one slowly swelling eye. He leaned on Braeden, and it took everything in him to not go off on everyone for this. For Trick. For the bodies on the ground. For Azrou.

Sara watched silently, her eyes betraying how conflicted she was. Braeden had always been able to read his mother's eyes. They were so like his own.

"Come on," Sara said to him, her voice flat.

"He needs a doctor," Braeden said, in one last bid for any of the humanity he knew his mother contained. "Bailey can tell you—"

"We'll send for one," she said over her shoulder as she turned away and headed toward Bailey.

"Go." The same marine who'd grabbed Braeden pushed his shoulder.

Trick tensed, but Braeden patted his chest to calm him. "Come on, bud," Braeden urged, then lowered his voice. "Were you able to get anyone before they got you?"

Trick nodded as if Braeden had asked if he was all right. "Found Gideon. He's rounding up chimera, too." He winced as they walked. "You're on edge."

Braeden swallowed. "Something's off."

Trick spat more blood on the ground as he nodded. "We're a sight."

Braeden huffed. "Look, I realize you want to be my best friend, but you didn't have to get a matching limp."

Trick snorted, then sucked a harsh breath through his teeth. "Oh, don't make me laugh."

"Ribs broken?"

He shook his head. "Bruised, I think." His expression sobered as they passed two chimera corpses, their limbs bloodied and tangled as if they'd been holding onto each other when they fell.

"Why would they do this?"

Braeden had no real answers. None of this made sense to him. Even with the animosity between the colonies and the chimera, and the colonies and the forest. He had the excuses he'd been taught, but they shriveled under the truth of what he'd learned tonight.

"It's not your fault," Trick murmured as they neared the building where Sara and Bailey waited. It didn't have a sign, and Braeden didn't care. "We'll figure this out. Stay with me."

"I'm with you." Braeden forced a bright smile at his moms. "Family reunions. So great."

RUMOR

The ragged remains of HUB2 jutted out of the landscape like teeth biting at the stormy nebula. A yawning mouth inhaling the dust of space into the bones of the moon. In the flickering greens and blues of the nebula, the wreckage looked like an abandoned underwater city. It grew darker by degrees as storm clouds roiled inward like the closing of a drawstring bag.

Rumor swallowed sadness and guilt and revulsion as he, Nyx, Dahlia, Jude, and Angel followed George around a wide perimeter that kept them in the shadows of the foothills. The muscles in the back of his neck tightened with every howl or roar that came from HUB2. He exchanged a look with Dahlia. Her brows lowered as she watched dark shapes fly above the wall and dive again.

No one knew of any chimera tunnels that connected directly to HUB2, so the plan was to find the new tunnels around the wall and use them to enter the city undetected. Rumor had wanted to go straight for Reaper, but Dahlia had convinced him to at least find a sniper rifle for Nyx. If something happened when Angel spoke to Reaper or when Rumor confronted him, Nyx would be backup.

He'd refused to let her be the one to take him out initially, but Jude had talked him into letting her be there just in case. They were stalling Reaper, holding him back until help arrived. The logical part of Rumor's brain berated him, telling him they were right. That he should wait.

His hands trembled, the tremor working its way up his forearms. He needed this. He was so close.

I should've come back sooner. Come back immediately. Five minutes was too long. Rumor hated himself for wasting time. Hated himself for seeing it as wasting time. He glanced at Jude, wondering if the colors Jude saw betrayed every thought in Rumor's head.

Rumor rubbed his eyes and clenched his jaw until his teeth protested. He didn't know what he was.

Red.

With every tick of the clock, Rumor felt more despair. He'd believed, like the others, that rescuing Vala would stop it for now. Would stop it long enough for rest and careful revenge planning. That Vala could speak to Reaper directly and convince him to back down so Rumor could go after him later.

They finally stopped near a stretch of broken boulders and twisted frames of wind turbines, their blades torn off and thrown into the ground like spears. Rumor pressed a palm to the cold metal. It shimmered under the darkness of his skin. Or that could be the tears gathering in his eyes. He turned away, staring at the remains of his home as Dahlia paused next to him, her arms folded as if she were cold. She trembled as she stared at the decimated city. A tear dripped off the edge of her chin.

"Everything's so...dark," he whispered.

"Look up," she said softly.

He frowned at her. She tilted her head and raised an eyebrow in challenge. He sighed and did as she said, turning his attention to the night sky.

"What do you see?"

"The nebula. Our host planet. The moons. Some stars," he listed off dutifully.

"Beautiful, isn't it?" Her shoulder pressed to his arm as she stared up at the sky with him.

"Yeah." He looked at her.

She met his gaze. "You can't see the nebula or the stars without darkness. That beauty? Invisible in the light." She squeezed his arm and moved away before he could respond.

Rumor closed his eyes for three heartbeats. Tears rolled up his throat, and he swallowed them back. His hands shook as he curled them into fists. She was right. This was something much, much bigger and far darker than his tiny little quest for vengeance. Not all chimera were evil. He could—and should—work *with* them to cut out the disease of Reaper and anyone else like him.

He never believed those thoughts would roll through his brain with such conviction, but there they were, tattooed across his mind and his heart as he opened his eyes and met Jude's gaze.

The silence wrapped around them, tying them up in awkwardness. Finally, Jude held up a black hair tie. He gestured to Rumor with his eyebrows raised in question. Rumor held a hand out for it, but Jude made a spin motion instead. Rumor's heart climbed into his throat as Jude stepped up behind him and combed his fingers back through Rumor's hair, gathering it at the back of his skull. After a few tugs that made Rumor's scalp prickle, Jude cleared his throat and stepped away. Rumor patted the messy bun in the back of his head and raised an eyebrow as he turned around.

Jude shrugged. "Out of your face, right?"

"Where'd you learn to do that?"

"Yi-Min. Don't tell me you never pulled your hair back. It's long enough."

"Well, yeah," Rumor answered. "Just wondering."

Angel landed with a thud and rose to their full height. One of their heads tilted and peered at the city, the other head speaking to Jude in chimera language.

"Yeah, I know," Jude said over his shoulder as he took off down the hill toward the city.

"What in deep space?" Nyx's voice stopped them as they rounded a corner.

The ravaged main gate of HUB2 was only a few kilometers ahead at the base of the foothills, but the street was blocked by a row of hellhounds. Five. Rumor's stomach tumbled, and cold washed through his body as he stared at them.

Had one of them killed his father? Maybe the leader; the one standing point, while the other four fanned out behind it. Rage burned through his body.

Jude's fingers closed around Rumor's arm, gentle but firm. If he felt the tremor, he didn't say anything.

"Are those considered chimera?" Nyx asked.

"Distant kin," Angel said. "More feral than anything. Some chimera use them as trained guard pets."

"Actual monsters." Rumor stared at them, only seeing a trail of blood. "If anyone wants to go back—"

Dahlia shook her head before signing as she spoke. "Do not lone hero us. We're here to get Reaper and get answers."

"Come," Angel said. "We will take another path."

They followed the shadows for as long as they could, winding their way closer to the outermost edge of the ruined city.

"Are those military transports?" Dahlia pointed at three large boxlike vehicles parked in a row.

Rumor stopped walking. Transports? Why would they be out here?

Jude followed Dahlia's gesture. "Abandoned in the attack?"

"No one came," Rumor said, ignoring the way the others saw him.

"They have Alpha colony insignias." Dahlia scowled at them.

"So does that mean there are marines here?" Nyx asked.

Rumor's heart twisted. If there were marines here, then either they were dead or they'd already taken out Reaper. Disappointment spiked through him, sharp and cold.

"We'll scout the transports." Jude motioned to Angel.

Rumor started to protest but snapped his mouth shut. This caution made him itchy. He didn't care about abandoned transports unless one of them housed Reaper. But he wasn't going to find Reaper without George or Angel, and they deferred to Jude. *Speaking of…* He felt a presence on his left and glanced at Jude, his traitorous heart fluttering.

Rumor opened his mouth to speak, to apologize for what he'd done to Vala, to say something that would put that easy smile back on Jude's face, but paused as a rushing sound filled the air. Like the flutter and flurry of hundreds of tiny wings. "What's that?"

Jude paled, and his eyes widened.

"Jude?" Rumor hesitated then grabbed his arm. "Jude, what is it?"

"We need to find cover," he said in a shaky voice.

"What are we hiding from?" Dahlia took Nyx's hand.

"Demons." Jude's hands shook as he pulled out his gun.

The storm clouds billowed closer, casting HUB2 in long, broken shadows from pummeled buildings. The fluttering grew louder and more pronounced. Shadows flitted across the ground, swirling and swooping. Nyx turned around, her eyes going wide. "Holy…"

"Go!" Jude broke into a flat-out sprint, aiming for the abandoned transport vehicles at the bottom of the hill. Angel took off, their great wings buffeting the group with air as they headed up to meet the demons head-on and buy a little time. George fell to the back of the group, his incessant growling following them down the slope.

Thunder boomed, lightning streaking across the sky. The flare of light threw everything into stark lines and long shadows, followed by immediate darkness. The rustling and shrieking grew closer.

The sudden tug on Rumor's shirt was the only signal the creatures had caught up. Rumor spun with a yell, swinging his blade. It sliced through a tiny, thin body about the length of his forearm. Jude pulled ahead, darting through rubble and gouged sections of ground, pausing only briefly to sight and fire at swooping demons.

The demons chittered and squawked, their screeching filling the air. The sky broke open and released a torrent of rain. The world went black.

A scream, then gunfire. In the flashing lightning, Rumor made out several of the tiny demons grabbing at Nyx. One was on her back, long arms twined around her neck. Two more swooped down and grabbed her arms. Their wings pounded the rain-soaked air, hauling her up. Her scream made his blood run cold.

Dahlia tackled Nyx around the waist, pulling her to the ground. The demon on her back howled as it was pinned. Dahlia plunged her knife into its skull. The two demons on Nyx's arms leaped over to Dahlia, catching her in the face and chest. Surprise and momentum carried her to her back. Rumor swung his blade, slicing the lower one in two. Nyx reached out of the darkness, wrenching the other one off Dahlia's face.

They ran.

Mud squelched up around Rumor's boots, pulling and sucking at his feet. Through the gloom, he spotted Jude wrenching open one of the massive side doors of the Alpha colony transports. Dahlia pushed Nyx aboard and climbed in after her. Rumor flung himself into the compartment and turned, holding his hand out for Jude.

Jude grabbed his arm just as a demon landed on the back of his neck. Rumor snarled, grabbed the demon before it could bite, and ripped it off. He hurled it into the storm as he yanked Jude into the vehicle. The door slammed with a resounding bang and threw them into muffled silence.

They collapsed in the cargo hold, gasping and soaking wet. The roaring of the storm did little to drown out the screeching wail of the demons as they swirled around the transport.

Rumor wasn't sure if his shaking was from cold or fear or some combination of both. He was still holding Jude's arm. Jude hadn't moved it out of his grip.

"You sure they can't come in here?" Dahlia's voice was pinched with pain.

"Nope," Jude said.

Someone sighed.

"I didn't build these transports, dude," Jude snapped.

Rumor squeezed gently, almost on reflex, then uncurled his fingers from Jude's arm. Jude's hand closed over his, stopping him for a breath, then let go and moved his arm out of Rumor's grasp. Rumor closed his eyes and inhaled slowly. He didn't need this right now, not when he should be focused on the mission at hand.

But he wanted *this*.

Minutes passed, the only noise their breathing and the storm. Rumor held up a blade, the molten core throwing light and heat around the tiny compartment.

"You said they were venomous," Dahlia said.

"Yeah." Jude sounded distracted.

"They didn't bite us." Dahlia pulled her knees to her chest. "They just tried to carry Nyx away."

"And me," Rumor said as unobtrusively as he could.

Jude was silent so long, Rumor wondered if he hadn't heard Dahlia. "We don't know what they do with the ones they carry off. Mostly they kill, but sometimes they carry people off and we never see them again."

Dahlia nodded at Rumor. "Reaper sent them for you."

Rumor met her eyes, willing himself to feel scared of Reaper, but all he felt was a deep cold in his chest like he'd swallowed ice.

"Probably," Jude murmured. "You're the one who escaped.

He wants you to himself."

Rumor ignored the guess and risked a glance at Jude. "Are you hurt?"

"Yeah," Jude said, his voice flat and his eyes staring through his lap and into the past. Blood ran down the back of his neck.

Rumor fought to keep his voice from shaking. "Bad?"

"No."

"Your neck?" Rumor brushed Jude's hairline and trailed lower. Jude hissed and yanked away from him when he brushed the cuts. "Hold still. All I'm doing is looking," Rumor said, his heart pounding. He watched Jude's eyes slide to him then away again, and Rumor could only guess what colors he'd seen.

He guessed still red. Knowing precisely how someone saw him was something he couldn't shake.

A bang on the side of the vehicle made them jump. Rumor snatched his hand away from Jude.

"Demons are gone," came Angel's voice. "Need to go before Reaper is alerted to our presence."

Rumor and Dahlia heaved open the door, cold wind and rain whipping into the compartment. Lightning cracked across the sky, illuminating the chaotic blanket of clouds roiling above.

They clambered out of the vehicle, eyes wide. Angel watched in silence, black blood streaming down their arms and dripping from their fingers. Rumor knew even before he saw the bodies strewn across the ground that the blood wasn't Angel's.

"Are you immune to their poison?" he asked. Water rolled down his face, dripping into his eyes and rolling along the seam of his lips. It tasted metallic and old.

Angel nodded.

Four fingers of lightning arced across the sky, illuminating three spires in the center of the HUB2. Two red lights blinked from one tower. "Did you see that?"

"See what?" Dahlia peered in the direction Rumor indicated.

"Light," Rumor said.

"Military?" Dahlia raised her eyebrows.

He scraped his teeth over his lower lip. "Might explain why these transports are pristine."

"But not why they're so far away." Dahlia frowned at the towers.

Jude pushed wet hair out of his eyes. "There could be a reason."

"What do you mean?" Rumor asked slowly.

"What's happening? I can't follow," Nyx interrupted. "Slow down."

Dahlia spun around, rubbing her fist on her chest in a sign Rumor didn't know and started signing quickly.

"This could've been an inside job. The entire attack." Jude kept his eyes on Rumor.

"It wasn't an inside job." Rumor took a step closer. "My dad worked for the military."

"So? My older brother was a marine before the ships fell and burned half his body. Means nothing." Jude folded his arms, his stance wide and challenging.

Anger burned hot and heavy through Rumor's veins. "Those chimera destroyed *everything*. Killed my dad. There's no way humans were involved in an attack that large."

"Really? If the military was so wonderful and great and just, then why did colonists break off from them twenty-six years ago to live in the forest?" Jude snapped. "Why don't they trust General Stewart?"

Get out of here, Rumor. Find help. Don't stop. Don't look back.

Rumor went cold at the echo of his father's voice. Jude couldn't be right. "This wasn't an inside job. This was Reaper."

"Not just Reaper." Jude's voice softened.

"Rumor." Dahlia tugged gently on his arm, pulling him out of Jude's space.

"You're fixated on only one monster." Jude didn't look away from Rumor. "You run in there gunning for Reaper and only

Reaper, then you're cutting off only one head, and you're risking all our lives to do it."

Find help.

Jude shook his head, turning away, his expression pained and angry. Water tracked down his face, blurring his freckles and dripping onto his downturned lips and off the edges of his jaw, disappearing into the sopping mess of his shirt.

Rumor turned away before he did something stupid. "Let's go see who left a light on."

JUDE

Jude honestly believed the attack on Azrou had pushed away any remaining anger toward Rumor, but Rumor's adamant loyalty to all things military brought it all boiling to the surface again. How could he fall for someone so rigidly devoted to a lie? How could he let someone in who was so single-mindedly fixed on revenge?

It didn't help that his traitorous body wanted to mold itself to every hard line and deep shadow of Rumor's. He didn't know what to do about this almost forbidden attraction. He couldn't erase the image of Rumor with his blade to Vala's throat. So much rage and hopelessness in his dark eyes.

"We should go," Rumor said. "Use the storm as cover to find the rally."

"I think it'll be in the central plaza," Dahlia said. "Big space, access to the avenue through the center. It's almost like a stadium."

Rumor nodded, and his willingness to defer to her when he fought Jude on so much twisted something ugly in Jude's chest. It didn't matter that he never saw either of them with shades of lust directed at each other.

Jealousy existed outside of magic gifts or logic.

Nyx scowled at the storm. "Are you sure about this?" Her words were almost carried away on the wind.

Jude didn't answer. His heart pounded, pulsing in his ears even louder than the storm as he took a breath of wet air tinged with smoke and blood. Even the torrential rain couldn't wash away the taste of death. He watched Rumor's expression grow hard and unfeeling as he stared at the mutilated city. If what Jude had experienced watching Azrou burn was anything to go by, the pain and loss and frustration that wrapped around Rumor was permanently embedded in his bones.

For a moment, Jude understood the anger. He wasn't so sure what he'd do if faced with the marines who'd destroyed his home.

Not having heard from Trick yet jangled his nerves even more. Jude checked his cuff again. Still nothing. He and Trick were the only ones with computer cuffs, since the others had left theirs back at Epsilon to prevent tracking.

Not that any of that had ultimately mattered.

Jude rested his hand on George's shoulder, and the chimera leaned against him, his gentle rumbling soothing something raw under Jude's skin.

"You haven't ventured an opinion on any of this," Jude said quietly.

George clicked his beak twice. "Opinions are like tongues. Everyone has two—a safe one and a risky one. How you speak defines your legacy."

"That doesn't really work for humans, but okay." And that wasn't helpful in terms of how George felt about any of this. "Thank you for coming."

"You are my friend," he rumbled in the chimera tongue. "I protect you."

Nyx frowned at the pooling water at her feet. Curiosity and fear swam around her in teal and yellow stripes.

"The moon's angry," she said. Jude straightened, prickles

running over his scalp.

"Very," Angel agreed. They curled their long fingers over Nyx's shoulder, and she glanced up, blinking as rain fell into her face. After a moment, she nodded and set her attention on the city.

"Most of it is that way." Nyx pointed to the spires where Rumor had spotted the lights.

Angel nodded again. "And south."

Nyx took a shaky breath and wiped water out of her face. "If we approach from the north, we might not run into many."

"How do you know that?" Jude asked. His heart pounded while Dahlia translated.

Nyx swallowed, her eyes darting around to each of them. "I…I can feel the moon. The vibrations."

Jude's lips parted in surprise. Numbness stole through him as shock filtered through his nerves. A colonist. He looked at Angel. "She can interpret them?"

Angel nodded.

"You can feel them?" Nyx asked, her eyes wide and almost hopeful.

Jude shook his head. He'd trade his emotional gift for being able to hear the moon language any day. "Trick can, but he doesn't know what they mean."

Trick had never understood what it meant, no matter how many times he tried or how patiently Angel explained things to him.

Nyx smiled despite the storm lashing at them. "I thought I was the only one."

Jude smiled back even though it felt weird given everything happening. "When we get back, you guys can talk about it."

His heart lurched as the full impact of what he said hit him. *If* they got back.

"We should go," Rumor broke in, his voice clipped and harsh. He walked away without another word.

Lightning arced across the sky, illuminating the dense clouds rolling like someone snapped a giant blanket over the sky. The wind howled, rain lashing the ground and pricking exposed skin like a thousand tiny needles. All conversation ceased, since they'd have to shout to be heard over the storm. Rumor kept glancing at Jude, like he wanted to say something. Jude didn't know if he should just wait Rumor out or break the tension between them himself. Of course, he had the advantage. Jude read the guilt smearing through Rumor's anger like pages in a book.

He didn't know if he was ready to forgive Rumor just yet. No matter how much his heart tripped every time those dark eyes met his.

"The rain is too much!" Dahlia shouted over the wind. She held a hand up to shield her eyes. "They could be on us and we'd never hear them coming!" Fear wrapped around her in streaks of yellow.

George paced around the group, keeping tabs on everyone like an anxious parent. The wind pushed at him, trying to pry his wings from his body and tear him away.

"The tunnels!" Jude yelled over the wind at Angel. "The entrance to the tunnels leading into the city has to be close!"

Angel pointed to a hole in the side of a small hill about a kilometer from HUB2's decimated wall. They ran for it, sliding over slippery ground. Jude fell, ripping his pants at the knee as wet gravel grated over his exposed skin. Rumor grabbed his arm and pulled him up. He let go and hurried to the tunnel, then ducked inside.

They stopped a little way in, safe from the storm but soaked to the bone and freezing. Jude's teeth chattered and his knee throbbed. The back of his neck stung from the demon attack.

"We must keep moving," Angel said. "You will warm as you dry."

Rumor drew his blades, but Jude put a hand over his before he could turn them on. "Algae, remember?"

The mere memory of Rumor's lips on his and his hands mapping nearly every centimeter of his skin made Jude's blood pool in his hips. He turned away before he pushed Rumor against the nearest wall and kissed him. Rumor's tiny sigh stabbed him right between the shoulder blades.

Angel took the lead, and George brought up the rear, his tail snapping back and forth with tension. Angel watched the tunnels with both heads, focused and strung tight. Everyone stopped in the entrance to a large cavern off the main tunnel.

Rumor took two steps into the massive cavern, his shaking hand resting on a stalagmite as he stared open-mouthed at the rows and rows of military transport trucks. Orderly stacks of crates all bore the Alpha colony insignia—the primary colony for weapon production. Several strategically placed lamps used the curve of the cavern ceiling to ricochet light everywhere, illuminating the entire space in a soft white glow.

"What is this?" Nyx's whisper crawled along the walls.

Rumor's breathing grew harsh. "Was all this here when they attacked? Why did they abandon us?"

Jude moved behind Rumor, his heart thudding to his stomach at the swirl of blue despair. It nearly edged the anger completely out. He didn't want that. As much as he wanted Rumor to stop being so angry, he never wanted this.

He pressed his palm to Rumor's lower back, fully expecting him to jerk away. Rumor leaned into his touch, turning his head to look over his shoulder. Jude's insides lurched at the wetness in Rumor's eyes.

"You were right," Rumor whispered.

"I wish I wasn't." Some of the deep blue sadness lightened—trust. Jude nearly kissed him.

"Let's get this done," he said instead.

Surprise flitted through Rumor's dark eyes, but he nodded.

Jude moved past them and toward the crates. He pulled a knife from his boot and pried the lid of a crate open.

Ammunition. Stacks of different-colored boxes holding various sizes and types. He hesitated, then grabbed a box of bullets for his pistol. He slid the clip out, reloaded it quickly, and stuffed the remainder in his pocket.

He pried open the next crate. Blades. Like Rumor's, but sleeker and newer in design. Requiem prototypes, if Jude had to guess.

"What did you find?" Rumor asked over Jude's shoulder.

Jude turned, his traitorous heart fluttering at the sight of Rumor's dark eyes, red-rimmed as they were. "Things to poke people with."

The corner of Rumor's mouth quirked. "I'll show you something to poke people with," he said as he reached for one of the blades.

Jude's neck warmed, and he bit his lip against a grin.

Rumor handed a blade to Dahlia, then grabbed another for Nyx. "That rally is going to start soon, if they want enough time to launch another attack and get back underground before dayside. We're running out of time."

Jude put the lids back on the crates, and Angel pushed them into place. They looked around curiously at all the vehicles. "They brought these down here somehow."

Jude spun in a slow circle. "They'd need a huge opening to get these transport trucks in. Are these from HUB2?"

Rumor wandered toward the trucks. "The crates are from the weapons plant at Alpha colony, but..." He headed down a row of transports. Jude jogged after him.

Rumor squatted down by the fender of one of the trucks, running his fingers along the identification plate. "It's one of ours." He bowed his head. "I don't understand this. When did they put all this down here? HUB2 was destroyed. I watched them swarm vehicles and tip them over or rip them apart. These are untouched."

"They would've had to have been moved down before the attack," Nyx said after Dahlia signed.

Jude swallowed hard as Rumor's shoulders tensed. "Rumor."

Rumor shook his head. "Let's find that tunnel."

He rose swiftly and walked away, spine straight.

Dahlia laid a hand on Jude's arm. "Don't push him. He may have admitted you're right, but he'll still fight the idea. This was his home. This?" She waved a hand around at the trucks. "Was his life."

She held a hand out to Nyx, and they walked after Rumor.

Jude nodded, his insides twisting as he stared at the rows of trucks. Why take down an entire HUB? Why orchestrate this? *Who* orchestrated this? Was it just Reaper, or was he working with humans?

He scrubbed his palm over his jaw and followed.

They found the large tunnel on the far side of the cavern. Even from down here, they smelled death coating the air. The tunnel headed straight as far as their lights would shine with what looked like several branches veering off the main artery at various points. Without a word, the group headed into the darkness. Jude's neck prickled, and George rumbled faintly as he took up the rear again, his tail twitching. Nyx walked in front with Angel, her hand trailing along the wall.

Rumor's curse brought Jude hurrying to the front of the group. "What is it?"

No one answered him. No one needed to.

"They did this on purpose," Rumor said quietly.

A mountain of rubble blocked the only path to the surface. Slabs of rock bigger than Jude, some bigger than George, were piled on top of each other.

They had no way into the city.

BRAEDEN

B raeden rubbed his forehead. His ability to see the humor in any situation had atrophied as Sara and Vala went around in circles. They'd taken Trick away an hour ago. Bailey sat on the other side of the command room, two Alpha colony marines on either side of her.

He hadn't seen Kaipo or Yi-Min. He prayed to every deity he knew of that the squads hadn't found the secret tunnels.

Braeden leaned against a console, shifting his weight off his bad leg and trying to look as bored as possible even though his insides were jelly. He had no way of knowing if the others had made it to HUB2 safely. He had no way of knowing if they were alive or if they'd been captured by Reaper already.

He chewed on his lower lip, listening for another opening in the conversation so he could wedge his way in and basically beg his mother to send squads.

"What?" Sara turned on him suddenly.

He arched an eyebrow. "What?"

"That's the fifth time you've sighed in the last two minutes. What is it?"

"Are you asking as my mom or my commander?" he asked

in a pleasant voice.

Sara flinched, as quick as a breath, but he caught it and he found himself somewhere between guilty and pleased that it'd cut her.

"How did you find this place, anyway?" he asked. "Did you tag me?"

"I wouldn't tag my own son." Sara's eyes slid to the marines in the room and then back to Braeden. "Or my wife. Do you really think I would?"

"Well, no, but I also didn't think you'd bust into a peaceful community with guns and bombs and marines in riot gear."

"These are rebels, Braeden. They broke from the colonies—"

"To live our own lives away from military intervention," Bailey interjected.

"And steal supplies from our transport trucks on a regular basis," Sara finished.

Bailey didn't protest that one.

"Cool excuses, Mom. Still senseless slaughter."

Something cold and sad passed through her eyes. "Braeden, you're seventeen. You cannot possibly understand everything that's going on."

"Okay, let's see." Braeden counted on each finger. "We killed a metric ton of them when we arrived because we wanted a lake. Chimera retaliated because, hey, murder. Military told us the chimera were monsters and needed to be destroyed. War. More war. Yet even more war. Some folks weren't down with it anymore so they headed to the forest to live in peace. You," he pointed at Bailey, "screwed my mom in more ways than one. And you," he pointed to Vala, "came up with this awesome scheme to talk to humans, but didn't tell anyone, which in a shocking turn of events, resulted in *death*. And now," he held up all ten fingers, "we're all standing here jerking off while Reaper's out there planning a rally that will result in, surprise, *more death*." He folded his arms. "Did I miss anything, Commander Mom?"

Sara sighed.

Braeden pushed off the console. "Okay, whatever. I'd hoped to be able to talk to my mom alone, instead of a bunch of military, because I needed—" He shook his head as he turned away, hoping his mom would call for him to stay. Would excuse everyone else so he could talk to her. Talk some sense into her. Ask her for help.

If nothing else, appeal to her need to get Reaper for her bosses. Appeal to her pride.

He exaggerated his limping to the door and glared at the marine blocking the way. "I'm assuming you have marines strategically placed around the perimeter. My leg is messed up. Do you really think I'm going anywhere?"

The marine glanced over Braeden's shoulder. Braeden didn't bother turning around but smirked as the marine stepped to one side. He mock saluted with two fingers and left.

Sara didn't call for him.

When the doors shut behind him, he grabbed the nearby railing as his knees weakened. He'd never spoken that way to his parents. He'd always joked and been the sarcastic, but obedient, son. Maybe he'd never truly understood what it was his mom actually did as Epsilon's commander.

Maybe he'd never wanted to understand. Didn't want to destroy his mental image of a loving mom who'd been there for him no matter how busy things were. He couldn't reconcile that image with a cold military commander who would order a troop to open fire on families and burn homes. Braeden rubbed his hands over his face and blew out a long breath. He didn't know what to do now. They were rapidly running out of hours, and even if Braeden managed to convince his mom to send help, would they even get there in time?

His heart thumped along with the ticking in his brain.

Think, asshole. He tugged on his hair. *Trick. Find Trick.*

He straightened his clothes, shifted his weight off his bad leg, and limped away.

The bodies were gone. He didn't want to know where, but he'd wager any amount of credits they weren't buried or burned. He surveyed the damage now that the dust had settled. Several treehomes smoldered, their fires extinguished and the smoke white. Three trees lay across the main road into Azrou's community center. They'd been felled on purpose. Five automaton animals lay on their sides, their bellies pried open and their robotic innards pillaged and strewn around the ground One of them bled viscous oil onto the red dirt. Everywhere he looked, all he saw was destruction. Silence permeated the entire community. The area lay still and dead, its life sucked from the air by bullets and camouflage.

He didn't know how many marines hid in the foliage, so he kept up the exaggerated limp and shoved his hands in his pockets as he walked. He scanned every tree, every doorway, every shadow, for signs of life.

"Braeden," whispered a familiar voice.

Braeden stopped next to an overturned cart and righted it while he snuck a peek at the shadows. Gideon stared at him from the shadows.

With a furtive look both ways, the little chimera beckoned. "Quickly!"

Braeden hurried to the space between two large trees where Gideon waited. His heart sank at the pattern of bullet holes across the smooth bark. Without another word, Gideon turned and disappeared through some hanging ivy. Braeden pushed through and was immediately grabbed by Trick, who clapped a hand over Braeden's mouth to muffle his surprised shout. Trick put a finger to his lips and raised his eyebrows. Braeden nodded and waited until Trick removed his hand.

"Your hand tastes like dirt, dude," he whispered.

"Don't lick my hand next time. It's weird," Trick shot back as he led the way through the trees at a crouched jog.

Braeden followed, ignoring the burning in his leg, relief

flooding him that Trick was free and safe. "How did you get free?"

"Gideon's a builder," Trick answered.

Braeden waited for more explanation. None came. "That's great. What's a builder?"

Trick held up a hand and dropped to a crouch. Braeden crouched next to him, holding his breath as a patrol passed a few meters away. Trick watched them walk away, waiting for them to disappear entirely before he spoke. "All chimera can manipulate the rock and create tunnels. But only certain ones can create tunnels safely. They can hear or feel the pathways in the rock that run parallel to fault lines, avoid weaknesses." He waved a hand. "Those are builders. Gideon's a builder in Vala's pack. He tunneled up into my cell and closed it behind him after we left."

Braeden blinked. "That…that would take hours. Days. Cycles. What?"

Trick grinned. "I'll have him show you sometime. It's cool. I told him to go round up chimera who were willing to come to HUB2 with us while I came to find you." He massaged his three-fingered hand as he spoke.

Braeden nodded to it. "You okay?"

Trick nodded. "Marines thought it would be fun to step on the crippled hand for a bit." He curled his fingers into a fist and flexed them. "I made them think they broke it so they'd stop."

He spread his fingers wide and popped his index finger out of joint backward.

"Okay, that's disgusting and awesome." Braeden cleared his throat as Trick righted his fingers. "Did you lose them in…You know what? Never mind. None of my business."

Trick hitched a shoulder. "I don't mind, if you don't stare or treat me like I can't do anything. I was born with it. Two fingers just…didn't grow. No one knows why." He wiggled his thumb, index, and middle finger. "When we were still in the colonies, I used to watch old videos of the ninja turtles. They all had three-fingered hands, too." He looked around. "All right, come on."

"Cowabunga, dude," Braeden whispered.

Trick led him in a seemingly random zigzag pattern through the forest. The trees grew denser, the trunks bigger, the foliage more layered. Soon, Braeden could barely see his hand in front of his face. "Hold up, I can't see."

"It's okay, we're here," Trick said from somewhere to Braeden's left.

A faint glow spilled onto the ground as a layer of brush moved and Kaipo stepped out. "About time. Did you find Vala?"

"She's with my mom," Braeden answered. "How's Yi-Min?"

"They'll be okay. Bullet missed anything vital. Lost a lot of blood, but you guys got them back in time." Kaipo squeezed Braeden's shoulder. "Thank you." He moved to one side so they could duck into the tunnel. "Don't go outside."

Braeden nodded. Kaipo patted Trick on the shoulder and walked away. Trick watched him go with an unreadable expression.

"Family trouble?" Braeden asked.

"You have siblings?" Trick asked in return.

"Nope."

"Be glad." Trick ran a hand over his shaved head. "I mean, he's great and an awesome leader. They normally don't let colonists or former colonists take on leadership roles, but Yi-Min recommended him. Their family has been Azrou leaders since the beginning." He waved his hand dismissively.

"You want to lead, too," Braeden guessed.

Trick squinted. "That obvious?"

"You seem to jump into the role easily. He won't let you?" Braeden ran his fingers over the smooth walls, careful not to disturb the algae.

"He doesn't think I'm ready," Trick said. "Just wish I knew how to prove him wrong."

Braeden snorted. "Well, you might have your pick of opportunities, with the way tonight's going." He sobered abruptly. "Any word on the others yet?"

Trick shook his head and led the way down the tunnel.

They reached a junction, and Trick put his hand on Braeden's arm to stop him. "So these are hideout tunnels. They were specifically created to shelter children, older chimera, and so on. They're not connected to the main nests in any way. But there are more people and chimera down here. Those Kai and Yi-Min could get out before it got too dangerous."

Braeden put it together quickly. "And I'm a colony commander's son."

Trick nodded. "I couldn't warn you before because of everything that happened with Yi-Min. Stick with me, okay? They know you helped rescue Vala so you've got that going for you for now. But several of them believe you're how the marines found this place."

Braeden let out a breath. "I searched all my clothes, my weapons, and couldn't find a tracker."

"I believe you." Trick patted his arm and turned away.

"Why?" Braeden asked. "Why do you trust me? We just met. I could be lying."

Trick was quiet for a long moment. Finally, he held up his three fingers. "I've learned not to judge people by appearance. So if you're lying to me, that'll bite me in the ass later. Until then…" He shrugged and headed down the tunnel.

Braeden didn't know what he was walking into, but Trick had his back for now.

He just hoped the others were still alive.

NYX

The thrum of the moon and the others' tension wrapped around Nyx, squeezing. Being underground wasn't helping either. She reached out for Angel, her fingers brushing across their arm. One of Angel's heads turned to her, and they wrapped their fingers around Nyx's arm, muting the thrum to something she could actually think through.

George rumbled something at Angel and swung his head toward Nyx. Angel nodded and spoke, but Nyx couldn't read their lips with all the blood and shadows.

"Might be able to what?" Dahlia signed while she spoke.

"She hears the moon much like our builders do. She might be able to find a stable spot," Angel answered.

Nyx closed one eye, then the other as the moon vibrated. "A stable spot for what?"

Dahlia signed quickly, "Apparently, neither Angel or George are builders, whatever that means, so they need you to find something in the wall so they can get us out of here."

In some strange way, that made sense to her. She turned to Angel. "Tell me what I'm looking for."

Angel moved out of the way and pointed at a large fissure

in the wall. Dahlia stood off to one side, signing everything Angel said.

"Place your hands on either side of the rend and listen," Angel said.

Nyx bit her lip but did as instructed. The rock was cold and smooth. It shone in the red light in such a way that she almost expected it to be wet when she pressed her palms to it. She closed her eyes, cutting off the world in its entirety except for the humming.

Angel's hand moved from her arm to her back, their fingers curling over her shoulder. The vibrations quieted in their ferocity as Angel helped her channel and focus. She took a deep breath and tried to listen. "I don't know what I'm supposed to hear."

She slid her hands to the right and tilted her head as the thrumming felt more faraway, like something was blocking it. She frowned and slid them to the left—to the other side of the fissure. The thrumming increased. She followed it, skimming her hands up and to the left, chasing the twisting vibration like following a string to a prize.

She stopped when the thrumming dulled and slid back to the right. The string seemed tethered to her insides. She visualized it running straight through the wall to freedom. Her heart leaped as the moon hummed under her feet in confirmation.

"Here," Nyx said as she opened her eyes, excitement bubbling up her throat. "Right here."

"Straight through?" Angel asked.

Nyx nodded. "I…think so."

"I trust you." Angel removed their hand and stepped up to the wall.

Nyx's heart fluttered at the declaration. Her head swam, but in a good way. She'd done something no one else in this group could do. She grinned at Dahlia, who smiled back, pride in her eyes. *That's my girl.* She pressed herself to Nyx's back and slid her arm around Nyx's shoulders. Nyx leaned against her, pride spiraling through her veins. Her nerves were sparklers. She wanted to spend hours with her hands pressed to these walls and listening to what the moon had to say.

She wasn't afraid of it anymore.

Rumor moved aside as Angel placed their hands where Nyx had indicated. "What are you doing?"

Jude folded his arms. "Watch. This isn't something many humans ever see."

The rock under Angel's hands shimmered like sunlight over water.

"Oh," Nyx said in shock. Dahlia stepped out from behind Nyx, and her eyes went wide.

Rumor stepped back as the wall started to melt. "What the...?"

"It's how they build tunnels," Jude explained while Dahlia signed. "They talk to the moon, and she opens the ground for them."

"Oh my god," Nyx breathed.

"Not god," Angel said as one head spoke directly at her. "Mother."

Goose bumps rose up Nyx's arms. Power thrummed through this place, radiating outward from where Angel pressed their palms to the melting stone and adamantine.

"Come." Angel headed into the tunnel. Nyx followed, her hand firmly in Dahlia's. Rumor and Jude came next, while George brought up the rear.

"There is a tunnel on the other side of this wall," Angel said. One head swiveled to look at Jude. "Be ready."

Jude nodded and pulled up his gun.

Angel placed their palms on the wall and concentrated. The wall shimmered and bled adamantine and algae before rippling apart like the surface of a lake. The hair on Nyx's neck rose as she watched.

This was tremendous power, and somehow she was connected

to it. She didn't know what that meant, but after all this time, the pieces were snapping into place. Why was she like this? Why did she have this gift?

"If you can do this, why don't the ones who hate us sink the cities? All of them?" Rumor asked. Dahlia translated with a deep frown as she watched him.

Angel turned and hunched down so they were level. Six black eyes peered into Rumor's two. "The moon gives if we respect her. Plunging your cities into her flesh would be like stabbing her with a weapon. The moon did not eat your city. She was run through with an iron spike." Without another word, they turned away to resume their task, leaving Rumor staring.

The way Angel spoke about the moon. It was almost as if it were a living thing. Far more living than any other rock floating through the cosmos. It made her think of a giant beast with cities built on its back.

"It's not black and white, Rumor. Hate and like. There's more to this than us versus them." Jude looked tired, as if he'd resigned himself to something unknowable.

Nyx clenched her teeth and focused on the moon instead of people. She pressed her hand to the wall as Angel opened the last of the tunnel. *Thank you.*

The moon hummed.

NIGHTSIDE **2900**
HOURS TO DAYSIDE: **8**

RUMOR

The tunnels deposited them aboveground into the main
storage facility near the center of the city. Rumor headed
for the mangled set of silver doors on the other side of the
storage room, his mental map of HUB2 unfurling in his head.
The central spires had a big plaza out front. All of it was only a
block from the main avenue.

Dahlia spun in a slow circle. "This should be…full, though."

Jude nudged an overturned box with his boot and frowned
at the empty shelves. "Well, it's very much not."

She squatted next to a shelf and peered at the few remaining
bottles. "Question."

"Answer," Rumor said. "Let's see if they match."

She rolled her eyes. "If your city is under attack by the largest
army of chimera you've ever seen in your life, do you stop to
raid educational storage?" She stood and gestured to the shelf.
"This held school supplies."

"Maybe people holed up here to escape?" Jude suggested
as George prowled the perimeter of the room, tail flipping and
a low growl humming out of his throat.

"Cool story, bro. And then what? They ate glue?" Dahlia

arched a perfect eyebrow. "Where's the blood from when they were found out?"

She was right. If a chimera had destroyed the doors, there would be blood and body remnants everywhere. Antihuman chimera never left survivors. Rumor looked around, trying to make sense of the senseless.

"Maybe Reaper's chimera took them prisoner." Jude's voice was heavy and hesitant.

Nyx and Dahlia exchanged glances.

"Why would he do that?" Nyx asked.

Rumor licked his lips and tasted blood. He couldn't meet anyone's eyes. "Demonstration."

No one answered. The room grew hot.

"Let me see that, okay?" Jude reached for Rumor's face. Rumor flinched away, and Jude huffed. "Let me see your cheek. It was too dark down there, but you're bleeding."

Rumor's eyes fluttered shut as Jude's fingertips brushed over his skin. He winced when Jude hit the edges of the open cut bisecting the length of his cheekbone.

"This might hurt a little," Jude murmured. "I need to check if it's broken."

"Not like we can do anything about that," Rumor mumbled as Jude pressed around the swelling and felt for shifting.

"You'd just have to refrain from talking," Jude said in a flat tone.

Rumor opened one eye to glare at him and Jude was *right there*. He could trace the freckles splattered across Jude's nose and under his eyes. His heart climbed into his throat, and *I'm sorry I threatened Vala* tried to squeeze around the pounding, but he couldn't get the words out again. That would be begging for forgiveness. Would he ever act that foolish?

For Jude?

Maybe.

"I don't think it's broken," Jude said finally. His fingers slid down Rumor's cheek, his eyes tracking the progress as if he was lost in it.

Rumor held perfectly still, held his breath, held everything so this fragile moment wouldn't shatter.

Jude's eyes flicked to his, and he dropped his hand, looking away as he took a step back. "Should be okay once you can get to a med center."

"Thanks," Rumor managed. "We should go. We're running out of time."

They paused at a hole in the wall just shy of the main entrance to the storage facilities, looking out over the rain-soaked remnants of HUB2.

"Oh." Dahlia's voice was small, shocked, pained.

Rumor stepped out of the relative dryness of the facility and into HUB2 itself. Into the storm. Water streamed into his eyes, blurring his vision and chilling him to the bone. The storm howled with the same anger building in Rumor's chest at the ruin that used to be his home.

The city was a corpse—twisted and still. The remains of human and chimera littered the stone walkways and paved streets, piled atop each other as if some great beast had gone through with a broom and pushed it all into piles.

Still-burning fires hissed at the storm, their tongues taunting the howling wind and lashing water. The once-gleaming buildings of HUB2 were little more than silhouettes of their former glory. Burned and demolished. The ones still intact stood as headstones to a dead city. Lightning flashed, illuminating the splintered remains. Water washed red off the walkway and into the gutter.

HUB2 was a river of red.

"The packs are gathering," Angel said from a crouch. Their palms left perfect prints in the mud and grime.

"What are we walking into?" Dahlia's voice trembled.

Rumor clenched his jaw so his teeth wouldn't chatter as cold wind bit through his wet clothes. Hot fury arced between his ribs.

The rain stung his face, each drop a needle settling under his skin. He didn't want to think about what Angel and Jude had told him below. He couldn't destroy the carefully built path to revenge that culminated in the death of Reaper.

"Rumor." Jude touched his arm.

"Come on, let's go." Rumor headed down the walkway, keeping to what shadows he could and searching for any signs of life—human or otherwise. Sightless corpses stared at him, judging him, accusing him of running away.

"You aren't a coward," Jude said.

He cut Jude a sideways glance. Jude's eyes narrowed, but he said nothing. Did he agree or was it just not something worth arguing about?

Rumor pointed down the street. "Main command spires are at the end of this road. All streets in HUB2 spiral down to the command center and the central plaza. The nearest ring around the center is—was—communication and emergency services. Next out was nonemergency medical and education. Next out" —he gestured to where they stood— "commerce. The outermost ring was residential and arts."

"So when they breached the wall…" Jude said.

"They landed on people's homes." Dahlia put a hand to her mouth. "Stupid design. Stupid, stupid."

Nyx grabbed Dahlia's hand and looked around as if she'd sensed something.

The rain howled in the absence of speech.

Pieces of the wall stood—grand curves of metal and stone and technology encompassing the city and turning it into a giant bowl. Or a pen.

The beginnings of a dome arced up from one side. Cages within cages. What had humans become that they'd wrapped themselves in so many layers of protection just to exist? Next they'd be tying rocks to their feet so they couldn't be carried off.

But they'd stop moving anywhere at that point.

Is that where they were now? Not moving. Not going forward. Not backward. Just trying to make it in the now. Hunkering down until the latest storm passed and they could count their dead. Watching the clock until the next dayside. Until those twin suns peered from behind the giant planet in the sky and something resembling peace counted down to nightside.

Jude looked away, his expression sick. "We should head to the armory. See if we can find a sniper rifle for Nyx. Extra ammunition. Maybe some protection if that's stored there."

They cut across the main street and ducked between two buildings. George followed Rumor and Jude. Angel brought up the back of the group. Every howl or roar had them pausing and melting into shadows until they were certain no one waited just around a corner.

Jude spun in a slow circle, frowning. George nudged Jude's hand with his beak, a low whine rolling out of his chest.

"What?" Rumor asked.

"How many chimera attacked?" Jude asked.

He picked his way over debris. The fires and destruction had pulled vegetation off the buildings, heaping them in great compost piles. The rain made the burned vegetation slimy, and it clung to their skin as they tried to dodge it. "I wasn't counting. A lot."

"How many people lived here?" Jude's voice was distracted.

Rumor tried to think back to his studies and remember the exact number. "Twenty-five thousand maybe? Thirty? We were one of the smaller HUBs. Lots of transitional families because of the military training."

"When we left, it was about twenty-three thousand," Dahlia said.

"How much of that was military?" Jude asked.

"Why?" Rumor stopped under an overhang. The rain pounded around them, excess water cascading over the edges of buildings in waterfalls. The rolling thunder barely masked the sounds of gathering chimera somewhere deeper in the city.

Jude frowned at the cascade. "It doesn't make sense. None of the pack leaders have an army *that big*. Not even one as popular as Reaper. Not even with dragons."

"That you know of?" Rumor ventured.

Jude ran his hands over his face, smearing dirt on his cheek. "How can a single army of chimera take down an entire city this size? I know how they fight, how they swear allegiance. *This*" — he waved a hand around at the darkened, burning city — "doesn't fit."

"Jude is right," Angel said. They couldn't fit under the over-hang but spread their wings to provide more cover. "Our packs are independent."

"But they could be united if there was a common goal?" Rumor asked.

"Like getting Vala back," Jude said.

Angel nodded one head while the other kept a lookout. "Vala is important enough."

A chimera screeched as it flew overhead, going too fast through the storm to notice them. Rumor pressed a hand to his sternum, willing his heart to return to its normal rhythm.

The memories of chimera scaling the walls and carrying guns and ripping people apart would forever be etched onto every wall of his mind.

"How does a pack of chimera, even a large one, take down a city?" Nyx's voice muted as she glanced at her feet with a frown.

Jude chewed on his lower lip. "It happens if there's no resistance. Or very little. How big was the military here?"

Rumor's heart thudded. "Standing army. Several squads of recruits in training."

"How many of them did you see?" Jude asked.

Rumor was already shaking his head at the implication. "They wouldn't abandon us."

"Even under orders?" Jude spoke quieter.

"No." Dahlia's voice was harsh. "I knew these people. They had families here."

"But you didn't see everyone." Jude's expression tightened.

"The city's a hundred and fifty square miles, Jude!" Rumor snapped. "Of course I didn't see everyone." Anger spiked through him, familiar and warm. "Just because you hate colonists—"

"You're right, I do," Jude said. "Because of them, my parents are dead. And because of chimera, your parents are dead. This isn't about who I hate or why. This is about how a single pack of chimera could take down a city in the blink of an eye. And how no one has come to reclaim it since. Do you see anyone around?" Jude flung an arm outward. "Because I sure don't." He backed out from under the awning. "You want to find and kill Reaper, and stop a rally and call it a night, then cool. You do you. But there's more going on here. This doesn't make sense. And I'm not just saying that because I live in the forest."

"Guys." Nyx stepped between them. Her wide eyes stared up at Rumor, pleading with him to swallow his temper, his pride, and do only what they came to do.

Stop this rally.

Save the colonies.

Warn Epsilon. Tell them to warn the others.

Rumor closed his mouth against the words that wanted to fly from it.

Rain fell down Jude's face like tears, smudging the dirt on his cheeks. Rumor shook his head and walked away, the roar of the storm competing with the whoosh of blood in his ears. Jude followed, his silence as loud as his outburst.

Rumor kept to alleyways as they neared the center of the city. He strained his hearing over the storm, trying to figure out how close the chimera were but never able to over the monstrous noises coming from the center of HUB2.

George darted ahead, his sleek dark form blending with shadows as he scouted before beckoning them forward. Block after ravaged block. They kept to cover as much as possible even though it did little good against the swirling storm.

"Everything smells like blood," Nyx said.

Rumor didn't know what to say. He flicked his blade on and stopped at an intersection, holding it up for more light. The others moved ahead, and he glanced right and left, almost like he was waiting for oncoming traffic. A crumbled facade caught his eye, and his heart panged at the destroyed food market he'd gone to even though it was on the other side of town from his residence. They'd had a certain kind of candy bar he couldn't find anywhere else.

Little things. Gone. Changed forever.

Rumor started to turn away, but movement at the end of the block past the market caught his attention. He gripped his blade, waiting for chimera to leap out of the shadows at him. A streetlight flickered twice, the feeble thumps of a dying power grid. In the wavering light a person stood, head bowed, tapping on an illuminated cuff. They were mostly in shadow, but Rumor knew that form. He knew the curly hair that hung in dripping locks around his face.

Rumor nearly dropped his blade. "Dad?" He took two steps forward, squinting through the rain. "Dad!"

The others stopped at his shout and ran back to him.

"What's going on?" Dahlia asked.

"My dad." Rumor turned to her, wide-eyed. "He's right—" He looked back. "There." He stared in confusion at the spot under the light where moments ago, his father had stood.

"Where?" She grabbed his arm.

"End of the block." Rumor pointed. He jogged away.

"Rumor!" Nyx called after him.

Rumor ran to the end of the block, his boots sliding on slick pavement, the rain plastering his hair to his forehead and cheeks. When he reached the corner, no one waited. No footprints, no sign, nothing.

"Maybe it was another block," he said as the others caught up.

"Rumor." Jude tried to grab Rumor's arm, but he took off running again.

He'd seen his dad. He had. He would swear across the entire nebula that his dad was alive. He reached the next corner, panting, his throat stinging with inhaled rainwater. His cheekbone throbbed, and his broken fingers felt three times their normal size.

Nothing.

"Dad!" Rumor shouted.

"Rumor, stop," Jude said. "Stop. The chimera will hear you."

"I saw him," Rumor insisted. "I did."

Dahlia and Nyx exchanged a look. Jude pressed his lips together.

Rumor shook his head. "No, I saw him. He was here. He was…" His voice cracked. "He was here."

"Maybe it was a shadow," Nyx ventured.

"Or a chimera," Dahlia said softly.

"No, it was my dad. He's alive. I saw him. I saw…" Rumor dragged his teeth over his lower lip, sadness balling up in his throat. It wouldn't matter if he cried. Tears. Rain. No one could tell. He tried to speak, but the words lodged in the sadness. He shifted his weight, paced two steps away, and paced back, trying to find his voice again. His eyes burned, and his skin prickled. He wanted to scream and beat his fists bloody on the ground. He wanted to rip the city apart to find his dad, to find Reaper, to find the ones who *did this*.

"Rumor," Dahlia said. "I hope you did see him. I hope he's alive."

Rumor looked past her to Jude, who watched him with an almost anguished expression. Rumor wanted nothing more than to go bury himself in Jude's chest and let everything out. His heart pounded across his entire body, pushing pain to the surface like a spreading bruise.

Rumor took a step toward him. Dahlia screamed.

Searing pain.

Weightlessness.

Rumor gasped and flailed as claws wrapped around his arm and jerked him from the ground. The moon's surface fell away, the air growing cold as a chimera snarled and pulled him toward the nebula. He kicked his legs, fear washing through him as Jude's yell faded the higher they flew. The girls screamed as more chimera swooped in, claws reaching for Rumor's friends.

"No!" he snarled, gripping his blade as he slashed at the chimera's foot, hoping it would drop him before they were too high for survival. They were only a few meters above the ground, but the gargoyle was climbing fast.

The chimera's tail thrashed, snapping like the end of a whip against Rumor's lower back. He screamed as pain jolted up his spine.

Rumor took a deep breath and looked down. Oh gods, they were too high now. He swallowed hard—he was going to die anyway at this point—and wrenched his body sideways, jamming his blade into the beast's shoulder. He used it as leverage to pull himself up as the monster howled, banking in surprise and pain. Rumor used the turn's momentum to scramble up on the creature's bony back. He hunched over, yanking on his trapped arm, and stabbed the chimera again, this time closer to its spine. He ducked the lashing tail and blinked away tears as the cold wind and rain clawed at his face.

"Let me go, you bastard." Rumor finally pulled his arm free and wrapped it around the chimera's neck, slicing its throat open. Black blood sprayed back across his chest, hot and sticky.

The chimera howled and lurched toward the ground, sending Rumor's stomach into his throat as they plummeted.

"Rumor!"

He craned his neck. Angel flew above him, their hands reaching down as they tried to keep up with the free fall. Rumor strained, his fingers brushing Angel's in desperation. The chimera's tail snapped up and smacked Angel in the stomach, sending them lurching upward, blood blooming from a puncture in their gut from the tail spikes. Rumor yelled in frustration and pulled his knees up to either side of the chimera's spine. He gripped with his boots and sat up straight, straining his free hand up. His forearm ran red where he'd been grabbed. His fingertips tingled, and dots crowded the corners of his vision. The air was too thin up here, and the rate of fall almost too much.

Angel's strong hand gripped his wrist and yanked him from the chimera's back. Angel pulled up and banked away, turning from the crashing chimera body as it hit the side of a building with a noise Rumor never wanted to hear again.

His boots scraped the ground, and he collapsed to the street. Angel released him, and Rumor fell to his side, pain throbbing through his body in a steady pulse and his blade clattering away. He rolled to his back, his body shaking with fear and adrenaline and pain.

A chimera roared, and Rumor stared as another dove for him. He fumbled for his blade, but it had slid well out of reach. He lurched for it, slipping through the mud and blood. The chimera bared its teeth, claws extended, bent on maiming—not grabbing.

A low twang and a whistle sounded a split second before an arrow punctured the chimera's neck. It scrabbled at its throat and hit the ground with a thud. Rumor stared, his breath coming out in shallow, sharp pants.

"Look out!" Dahlia screamed.

A third chimera dove for him. Another arrow sped out of the storm and took it down with a head shot. Rumor followed the path back and caught a glimpse of a smaller figure atop a building. They wore a hooded cloak, a large bow in one hand. After a moment, they turned and vanished into the waning storm.

Jude hit the ground next to him and touched Rumor's chest and face and head and shoulders and down to his waist as if he couldn't believe Rumor was still alive.

"I couldn't get a clear shot," Jude was saying over and over. "I'm sorry. I'm so sorry."

"I'm sorry," Rumor gasped. "About before." He twisted his hand in Jude's shirt and pulled until his face was pressed to Jude's chest. Jude's arms swept around him. He tried to catch his breath. "Did you see—"

"The person on the building with the bow, yeah," Jude said in a shaky voice. "I saw them. I promise, I saw them. I saw them earlier in the forest. I promise, they're real."

Rumor shuddered and pushed away from Jude's chest. "Angel."

He scrambled across the ground toward Angel's body, sprawled a few feet from where they'd crash-landed. Blood covered their torso and pooled across the wet ground. "Angel, no." He held his hands on Angel's stomach, but the blood squelched between his fingers. One of Angel's faces turned to him. "No, no, no. You can't die for me. I don't deserve it."

George lay at Angel's heads, his face solemn. A low whine rolled out of his throat as he nudged one of Angel's heads. Nyx knelt next to Rumor, tears running down her face. Dahlia dropped to her knees at Angel's feet, both hands over her mouth and her shoulders shaking.

Long, bloody fingers touched Rumor's cheek. "End this," they said, their voice barely audible over the roars around them. Their fingers drifted down to Rumor's chest and tapped his sternum right over the coin Rumor kept hidden under his shirt. "End this."

Jude sank to his knees on the other side of Angel, stricken, hands cupping Angel's other face, which lay still, eyes closed. "Angel, you can't. Trick isn't here. You can't go without saying good-bye to him." His voice choked. "He'll kill me if you die without him here."

"Mother will tell him," Angel whispered. They touched Jude's cheek, catching a teardrop. "I am better for knowing you." Angel's remaining eyes slid shut. "All of you."

Jude bent over Angel's form, tears streaming down his face. His shoulders shook with quiet sobs. "Not again," he said over and over again.

Rumor's body thrummed with pain and loss and a sudden hopelessness. His chest tingled where Angel had touched him, his necklace heavy and hot. *End this.*

This.

Rumor stared at Angel's body, then gazed into the distance, where the spires towered and beckoned like a giant sign broadcasting revenge. Fires threw moving shadows across buildings as more and more chimera gathered in HUB2 to pledge loyalty to a dictator.

Jude cut several of Angel's jewels from their horns and shoved them in his pocket. He looked around, his lips pressed thin, and scooped up three rocks from the ground. George put one on each forehead and one above the wound that killed Angel, murmuring something so quiet Rumor couldn't make it out. After a moment, Jude scooped up mud and pressed a dot on each of Angel's closed eyes, tears tracking down his face.

Rumor rose and backed away unsteadily, feeling like he was intruding on a sacred moment. He could run now. Slip away while they dealt with this and find Reaper on his own. Stop the rally. Kill the one who'd caused everything tonight.

Because you'd totally survive running into a throng of hundreds of chimeras to attack their leader.

He couldn't make himself take a step. He stood rooted to the spot, watching Dahlia and Nyx cry. Watching Jude and George perform a ritual so simple and yet so heartbreaking. Jude stood and backed away a step, motioning the others to do so as well. George placed his front paws on either side of Angel's heads and closed his eyes. The ground melted as if George had called up quicksand, and Angel sunk slowly into the moon's surface. Rumor watched until all that was left was a slightly disturbed patch of ground a little darker than the rest.

He was hollow. He had chimera blood on his hands.

For the first time in his life, sadness accompanied that realization.

Jude stepped up, shoulder-to-shoulder with Rumor. "I know what you're thinking," he said, his voice shaking with grief.

"Of course you do. What color is doubt and helplessness?" Rumor asked without looking at him.

Jude grasped Rumor's shoulder and turned him so they faced each other. He held up one of Angel's jewels, the smoky stone wrapped in soft braided rope. Without a word, he pressed it into Rumor's hand.

Rumor looked back at Angel's grave, at George sitting next to it like a silent sentry of the dead, at Jude's grief, at Dahlia's tears, at Nyx's frightened eyes.

"Go back," he said.

Jude's eyes narrowed, grief giving way to frustration. "You're not doing this alone."

"I've messed all of this up. I never should've asked anyone to come with me. Too many people are dying." His resolve strengthened with every word. He dug deep for that cold feeling of detachment that'd served him so well in the past. After his mother died. Whenever his dad would drink too much and put him through too many drills until his muscles screamed in agony. "I'll do this on my own."

"*No*," Jude spat.

Rumor stared at him. Jude grabbed Rumor's arm—his damaged one—and squeezed hard. Pain shot up the side of his arm and into his elbow, and Rumor cried out a string of curses, trying to pull away. Jude held on tighter, his eyes angry and hurt.

"You aren't invincible, Rumor. You aren't some lone savior. This isn't your noble quest, so stop acting like everything you touch burns alive." He flung Rumor's arm away with a disgusted noise. "You want to go get yourself killed, fine, but you can go all the way to deep space if you think no one here needs you or wants you."

Rumor opened his mouth, but all that came out was a choked sound.

"You think I'm only here for a quickie in my room?" Jude shook his head, his eyes wet and his mouth in a thin line. "You think I only want you because I can see you want me?"

"Jude," Rumor tried, but his voice cracked. Jude cared about him? Actually cared about *him*.

Jude's jaw flexed. "Don't."

"I'm sorry," he whispered. "I don't know what I'm doing."

He closed his eyes and felt the rain on his face, the jewel in his hand, the hopelessness in his chest, and moments later, Jude's fingers on his cheek.

NYX

Ever since the attack in Azrou, Nyx's heart had beat faster. The rumbling under her feet seemed sharper, more urgent. Almost as if the moon knew something was coming. The growing rumble from the impending rally grew with every minute that ticked toward dayside. She stared at the darkened patch of ground where Angel's grave lay, turning away from Rumor and Jude's private moment.

"This is wrong," she said, not caring who paid attention to her. "Their grave shouldn't be here. Not here."

Dahlia touched her elbow and signed, "Jude says it's not really a grave. Angel is part of the moon now. Their voice is part of the moon."

Great, she was going hear Angel's voice now, too.

Nyx nodded, blinking back tears. Jude squatted next to the grave, his palm pressed to the soil. Rumor stood off to one side, clutching one of Angel's jewels and looking so lost. It was as if someone had sucker punched all the motivation out of him.

"Can I hug you?" she asked.

Surprise flitted through his eyes. After a moment, he nodded, and she wrapped her arms around his middle. He was so tall, she only came up to his chest, but she squeezed him. He stiffened, but relaxed by degrees until his arms wrapped around her shoulders and he returned the hug.

Progress.

"It's not over yet." She looked up at him and forced a small smile.

He nodded, but said nothing. She turned around, meeting Dahlia's red rimmed eyes. The silver in them had dimmed. She seemed so defeated. Nyx wanted to go to her, but something held her rooted to the spot. Fear? Doubt? She didn't know.

Jude frowned at his cuff. He wiped a stray tear off his face as he stood and said something, but Nyx missed it over the moon's thrumming. She glanced at Dahlia, who quickly signed, "He can't send a message to Trick. Something's wrong."

"Have you heard from Braeden?" Nyx asked him. Jude shook his head.

A sliver of fear wormed its way through her system. What if neither of them ever brought help? What if it really was up to the four of them? Five, including George.

Nyx took a deep breath. "I need to find a sniper rifle."

Three sets of human eyes and one set of chimera eyes turned to her at once.

She licked her lips. "We need to get this done. If we can get Reaper before he gets to the rally, it should create enough chaos for us to get out of here. Between George and I, we can even dig a tunnel to get out quickly." She took a deep breath and glanced at Jude before continuing. "How many hours to dayside?"

Jude held up seven fingers.

Only seven.

Nyx swallowed hard, a shudder rolling through her. The rally would start soon, if it hadn't already. She couldn't tell. Any sound her ears picked up was nothing more than a dull roar. She felt as if she were moving through a constant moonquake.

Rumor tucked a stray piece of hair behind his ear. "Armory

is on the northern side of the city. Near the central plaza. Not that far from here."

Dahlia signed quickly.

"What's the roof like?" Nyx asked.

The corner of his mouth ticked up. "Flat. Clear view of the plaza."

She cracked her knuckles. "Perfect."

Rumor tied Angel's jewel around his neck and tucked it under his shirt. Jude watched him with an unreadable expression. Dahlia watched him, too, which twisted something in Nyx's stomach again. She hated that it bothered her. Rumor was so obviously into Jude. Dahlia was in love with her.

Right?

Nyx glanced at George, who nudged her arm with his beak like a cat wanting attention. She ran her hand over the cool, stonelike surface of his skin. They were all hurtling toward an inevitability none of them were ready for. She was only sixteen, and here she was, planning an assassination that could turn the tide of a war that had started before she was born.

Rumor and Jude started walking, and George slipped out from under her fingers to join them. Nyx chewed on the inside of her cheek, wondering if she'd ever see dayside again.

A hand grabbed her arm before she could take a step, familiar fingers curling around her bare skin and sending warmth flooding into her bones.

Dahlia tilted her head. "What's wrong?" she asked.

Nyx frowned and ran her tongue over her teeth. How could she possibly explain everything in her head in a way that would make sense? She didn't even know if any of it made sense to herself, let alone translating it for someone who couldn't feel the moon the way she did.

"When we were attacked just now," she signed, "I was afraid that was it. For you. For us."

Dahlia's eyes filled with understanding. "We made it. You

and me. The others."

When Nyx didn't answer, Dahlia looked around quickly before pulling her out of the rain and under the shallow shelter of a doorway. Nyx almost asked what she was doing, but then Dahlia's lips were on hers and Nyx's words rolled over Dahlia's tongue instead of the cold air, and Nyx fell fell fell into a world where nothing existed but the girl in her arms. Dahlia's lips moved against hers, her voice vibrating Nyx's lips, but Nyx didn't care what she was saying. She just wanted to be closer, ever closer, always closer. She wanted Dahlia wrapped around her, inside her, above her, beneath her, everywhere.

Dahlia pulled away, her eyes wide and nearly black in the shadows. Her lips were wet and curved into a self-satisfied smile. "You back with me now?"

"Always," Nyx managed. Her head swam and her body ached all over with need and frustration. Wrong time, wrong place, wrong everything.

As if Dahlia read her mind, she pressed another soft kiss to Nyx's lips. "When this is done, you and I are locking the door to that bedroom and not coming out for a week."

Nyx nodded, probably a little too fast, but Dahlia's wide, beaming smile was worth it. They could finish this. With Dahlia by her side, at her back, Nyx could do anything. The whole kiss had taken a fraction of a moment, but to her, it'd felt like waking up.

She could do this. "Okay, let's find the armory."

Dahlia grabbed her hand and pulled her into the gentle rain to catch up with the others.

They'd only gone one more block when George stopped, his head straight up and his tail twitching. Jude spoke to him, and George replied, but their voices fell to the ground with the raindrops. Fear streaked across Jude's face as he spun around. His mouth moved, and Dahlia signed.

"Chimera pack behind us."

"Heading for the rally?" Nyx asked.

Dahlia nodded. "This road leads to the plaza."

"We need to hide," Rumor said. "Now."

Jude hesitated. "Hide near the bodies. They won't be able to smell you as well."

Nyx's stomach turned over, but she nodded. They hurried off the main road and to the walkway, which was littered with overturned vehicles, broken glass, burned vegetation, and bodies.

So many bodies. Her shuddering breath tasted like blood and bile. Dahlia grabbed her hand and pulled her into a partially destroyed building. They ducked as far inside the room as they could go, which wasn't far. Most of the building had caved in, turning it into a giant pile of plastic, wiring, glass, stone, and adamantine. Blood smeared the floor and bodies lay scattered as if they'd been thrown or dropped. Nyx put a hand over her mouth and nose to keep from getting sick.

Dahlia's fingers tightened, and her eyes widened. She put a finger over her lips, and Nyx nodded.

Nyx put her hand on the ground and closed her eyes, sending every plea into the moon that the group would pass right by them without stopping. She opened her eyes and pressed closer to Dahlia as vibrations ran underneath them.

Dahlia trembled and held Nyx tightly. A tear slipped out of her eye, and Nyx watched it roll down Dahlia's cheek.

"How many?" Nyx asked.

Dahlia shook her head. "Can't tell. All I can hear is breathing and footsteps."

Nyx swallowed, her throat dry. Dahlia crouched lower, her eyes widening. Nyx crouched with her, staring at her in question. A shadow passed directly in front of the building's blown-out window.

And stopped.

Dahlia put her hand over her mouth to stifle her breathing. Nyx did the same, her eyes on the shadow. She glanced at Dahlia, who fingerspelled, "Sniffing."

Nyx's heart pounded so hard, she was sure the chimera could

hear it. She wished she'd asked Jude how big packs were. Was a pack five or fifty? Were they going to have to hide for a few minutes or a few hours?

More shadows passed, some tall enough to block the faint light that made it through the thinning storm clouds.

Another shadow stopped. Dahlia stiffened, her head bent as if she were concentrating. Nyx could barely see her hands, so Dahlia fingerspelled against Nyx's palm. "Sniffing. Shuffling."

There was a dull, faraway noise to Nyx's ears, but Dahlia cringed and clapped a hand over her mouth again. Her nostrils flared as she tried to control her breathing, and her eyes filled with tears. Fear and confusion filled Nyx, and she shook with all the force of the moon's thrumming. The scent of fresh blood filled the air, metallic and warm.

Finally, the shadows moved away.

"What happened?" Nyx asked in the faint light.

Dahlia's hands shook as she signed. "There was someone alive in the rubble outside. They groaned and called for help and the chimera heard and…"

She stopped signing and shook her head fiercely, tears streaming down her face.

Nyx's stomach rolled, and she wrapped her arms around Dahlia. She couldn't promise they'd make it out of this, because she had no idea if they would.

Dahlia's head snapped up, nearly hitting Nyx in the chin. She pushed to her feet, hauling Nyx up with her. Jude and Rumor ran into the wreckage of the shop, relief on their faces.

"We need to get this done and get out of here," Dahlia said. "Now."

Rumor nodded. "We're close to the armory, and it should position us close enough to the plaza to get him from the roof."

Nyx wiped her sweaty palms on her thighs. "Okay, let's go."

The storm had stopped by the time they reached a series of large silver buildings just outside the center of HUB2. There

were no identifying marks on them other than STORAGE in large
blocky letters. Each building was dark and silver and lined up
in a row like her abuela's dominoes.

Smart. Wouldn't do much good to plaster ARMORY across the
doors. Might as well put up another sign: WE KEEP GUNS HERE.

Nyx's gut twisted with nerves. Every shadow seemed darker,
longer. The clouds closer. What little light filtered through the
storm threw the city in broken streaks of light. She crouched
and pressed her palms to the ground, trying to listen, interpret.
The rolling vibrations coalesced into a hum that ran through her
fingertips and up her arms, tugging and pulling her attention
toward the center of the city.

Buildings blocked their immediate view of the command
spires and central plaza, but even Nyx could hear the roars and
howls as each sound screeched through the air in high decibels.

She stood and touched Rumor's arm. "How do I get to the
roof?"

He was frowning in the direction of the gathering, so she
tapped his arm again. He glanced at her and motioned for her
to follow him. As they walked away, she signed to Dahlia, "Head
inside with Jude and get weapons. Meet us on the roof."

"You're sexy when you take charge," Dahlia signed back.
She mock saluted Nyx and plucked at Jude's shirtsleeve for
him to follow.

The roof of the armory was flat and slick with rain and mud.
All its vegetation had been pulled off, and huge gouge marks
furrowed the middle of the roof. Rumor stared at them, his
fingers twitching toward his blades.

"Dragon?" she asked.

He nodded.

Nyx squeezed his arm as she walked past him. The command
spires rose above the ravaged buildings and blood-soaked streets.
They'd been designed as three twisted prongs scraping at the
sky. The partially completed dome connected to the middle

spire—the tallest of the three. Under any other circumstances, it would be impressive.

Right now, it was haunting.

She scanned the ground. Even without a scope, she had a fairly clean view of the plaza. The emptiness of it all sent shivers across her skin. A city like this was never meant to stand silent.

Rumor touched her elbow. She turned as a hatch opened in the middle of the roof, and Jude climbed up. He turned and grabbed a black duffel that poked through the hole after him. Then he grabbed a black weapons case and looked at her with a smug smile.

"Where's George?" she asked. There was no way he could fit through that tiny hatch.

Jude pointed over the edge of the roof. Nyx peered over the edge and barely made out George in the shadows. She shuddered, glad he was standing guard, but a little unsettled at the thought of a chimera in the bushes.

Dahlia climbed up last. She carried two heartseeker knives and had a chaos pistol strapped to her other thigh. She handed the knives to Rumor as she walked past him to the black case. She glanced at Nyx as she opened it. "Will this work?"

Nyx nodded. "I've used this before."

She settled against the raised lip of the building and tried to get comfortable as she adjusted the focus on the scope. The night vision bathed everything in vivid green, turning the darkened city into a ghoulish landscape. Whatever light Rumor had seen in the towers was gone now. The buildings stood tall and silent, three twisted fingers reaching for the receding storm clouds. She panned even slower across the wide-open plaza in the middle of HUB2. Twice as big, but it was so similar to the one in Epsilon that it made her heart ache and her thoughts skip to Abuela. Gods above and below, Abuela had better be okay.

One of the woven columns was damaged along the bottom like it'd been hit with something heavy, but whatever had damaged it was long gone. No tire tracks or footprints. Other than the damage to the column, the area was pristine. It was like someone had come through with a broom and spray-cleaner.

"I thought you said the rally would be in the center of the city." Nyx pulled away from the scope.

Rumor knelt next to her and scratched at his stubble as he stared at the spires. "Check the mining ravine."

He pointed east, toward the foothills, where the HUB2 wall curved up to the northern edge of the city.

Nyx snugged up to the scope again, panning east. Several buildings blocked her sight line, so she had to move to a different part of the roof to get a clearer view.

"Yep, it's there." She hoped her voice didn't quaver as the scope revealed chimera of all different shapes and sizes covering the sides of the mining crater. They climbed up the machinery. They flew over the area and dove into the sunken shafts. Many perched on the remaining pieces of wall around one edge. "If you ask how many, the answer is I can't count that high."

She rocked back on her heels and looked at the others.

"Did you see Reaper?" Rumor fidgeted with the edge of his shirt.

Nyx shook her head. "There's so many, though. I mean, he could be down there and I'm just not seeing him. But…" She got up and walked back to the other side of the roof. "If the rally is taking place at the mining area instead of the plaza like you thought, we might be able to use the plaza."

She knelt and peered through the scope again. "We lure him to the plaza. I can see the whole thing from up here, so I could take the shot."

She was about to suggest a few ideas for luring him from the chimera crowds when movement across the plaza caught her attention. "Everyone get down."

She moved the scope over, centering it on a group of figures standing in front of the middle tower. She counted eight…no, ten. Mostly chimera, and at least two humans.

Her heart hammered as several chimera moved into her line of sight and stood a full two heads taller than their companions. Their bodies were hidden by long, hooded cloaks, but the impressive glowing scythe one of them held told her all she needed to know.

"Reaper," she breathed. She was about to straighten to show the others when the hooded figure handed the scythe to one of the other hooded figures, who held it for a moment before passing it off to a third. Every minute or so, they passed the scythe around. "Dammit."

Nyx straightened and handed the rifle to Dahlia. "I don't know which one is actually Reaper. There are five down there in hoods, and they keep passing the scythe around. I could guess, but the second one goes down, the others will run and that will blow our chance."

Dahlia pressed the scope to her eye and pointed in the direction Nyx indicated. Rumor and Jude squatted with them. Rumor rocked slightly as he waited, his dark eyes glued to Dahlia. Jude seemed thoughtful and far away.

After a moment, Dahlia pulled back, eyes wide. "The humans. It's the general," she signed, her hands shaking. "And Rumor's dad."

Nyx grabbed Dahlia's hands to stop their trembling. "Are you sure?"

She nodded.

Chills fell down Nyx's body as she and Dahlia both turned to Rumor.

"What?" He straightened.

Dahlia spoke, but Nyx watched him instead of her. Rumor sagged against the lip of the building, his mouth parting and every muscle going still. His hands trembled. Finally, he blinked and held his hand out for the rifle.

Jude put a hand on Rumor's wrist and spoke, facing him.

Nyx picked up snatches of Jude's voice, but she couldn't make anything out.

Dahlia's eyebrows drew together as she signed, "Jude doesn't think it's a good idea if Rumor sees his dad through a scope mounted to a rifle."

"Is he seriously afraid Rumor would shoot his dad?"

Dahlia shrugged. Rumor dropped his hand and rubbed the other over his eyes. Jude glanced at Nyx.

"Why does Reaper have a scythe?" Rumor gaze darted everywhere but them.

Jude hesitated before answering. "That's Reaper. He's obsessed with human death mythology. Loves the idea of reaping humans off his lands."

"In the tunnels, Colt said he saw his father," Rumor said. "I thought he was messed up from the attack."

"Who's his dad?" Jude asked.

"General Stewart," Nyx answered.

Jude didn't answer for a long moment. "I take it he's important."

Rumor snorted. "Forest boy, Stewart's in charge. Like *in charge.*"

"Why is he here?" Dahlia looked toward the spires.

"Do I seem like I would even remotely have that answer?" Rumor snapped.

Dahlia slowly turned to him, her face expressionless.

"What's under the city?" Jude asked. "Besides the chimera tunnels we came through."

Rumor frowned. "Rock, tunnels, sewers…I have no idea."

"How do you not know what's under your own city?"

"Because I'm seventeen and far more concerned with food and getting into your pants than what's under my house."

Nyx coughed to cover a laugh. Dahlia grinned.

Jude rolled his eyes. "You said the chimera had weapons. The ones who attacked."

"Yeah."

"Were they new?" he asked.

Rumor shook his head. "I didn't stop to ask."

Nyx raised an eyebrow. "What are you getting at?"

Jude stood. "Obviously, they're working together, but why?" He ran his hands through his hair. "I wish Trick were here. He's better at figuring this out."

Dahlia stood and held out her hand for Nyx to take. "Still haven't been able to reach him?"

Jude shook his head. "It's garbled."

Nyx brushed off her pant legs. "Would higher elevation work?"

Jude shrugged. "Maybe."

Rumor stood. "This is one of the tallest buildings in the city."

Nyx smiled. "But not *the* tallest."

The other three looked back at the spires at the same time.

"Okay, now what are *you* getting at?" Dahlia asked.

"Me going up as high as I need to be to get a clean shot at Reaper without any of those columns in the way when Rumor lures him back. I can take Jude's cuff up and try to broadcast from there, too." Nyx glanced at Rumor. "Unless there's communication equipment?"

Rumor pointed and Dahlia signed. "The right tower had communications. That would put you closer to the mining ravine, too."

Nyx bit her lip as she stared at the towers. "We need to find another roof to plan this. I can't see the roadways leading from the mining crater to the plaza."

They gathered their things and headed back down. Outside, George rumbled at all of them, butting his head against Jude's chest. It warmed Nyx's insides to see the open affection even as they stood in the middle of a very deadly situation.

They kept to the shadows and alleys as much as they possibly could as they worked their way up the western side of the plaza. They didn't want to risk running into any more packs on their way to the rally. Rumor would occasionally slow, his eyes lingering on a specific building or spot. Nyx's heart hurt for him. A lifetime's worth of memories destroyed in an instant.

She couldn't imagine.

The world grew bright and hot. The ground shook and rumbled under Nyx's feet as an explosion lit up the night in shades of orange. The ground rolled and pitched and, for four heartbeats, Nyx knew what it was like to fly.

RUMOR

Had he died?
Who had done that?
Were the others alive?
And why was he staring at the sky?

Rumor answered the first question as a dull ache rolled through his body, and answered the last as he realized he was lying on his back in a puddle of water and who knew what else. His ears rang, and his throat felt scorched as he breathed in hot air. The world burned around him as fire spread from the explosion, despite the rain-soaked city. He stood, using debris for balance when the everything threatened to spin.

Whoever had set off the explosion could be waiting for him to give himself away. Give the others away. Or they could be waiting for a mass of chimera who'd surely be curious about random explosions.

He curled his still-healing fingers around his blade and drew it, flicking it on as he looked around. The fire cast the city in the brightest almost-sunlike glow, hurting his eyes. He heard a groan and spun around.

Jude lay in the middle of the road. Rumor ran to him. "Jude."

"Ow." Jude grimaced. He opened one eye, the green turning almost gold in the firelight. "Am I alive?"

Rumor helped him sit up. "Mostly." His hands lingered on Jude's body, not letting go immediately. He let his hands slide off Jude's shoulders, feeling the stretch and roll of Jude's muscles as he moved. "Anything broken?"

Jude squinted. "Either I'm in shock or no. You?"

"Same." He didn't see Dahlia or Nyx, and a huge slab of roof lying on its side plus a pile of blown-out wall blocked the roadway. "Dahlia!"

Jude swiveled. "George!"

Rumor kept calling Dahlia's name as he limped for the blockade. His knee hurt every time he put weight on it, but he was fairly sure it wasn't broken. Probably somewhere around ninety-two percent sure.

"Rumor?" Dahlia's voice drifted through a small opening in the rubble.

"Dahl!" He wanted to reach through and grab her hand just to make sure she was okay, but the rubble looked precarious enough. "Are you two okay?"

"Yeah. Some nicks. Nyx is checking the rifle. You guys?"

"Yeah." Rumor looked around, trying to remember how this street had been before all the destruction. "We're at the edge of the merchant district."

"We are?" Dahlia was quiet for a minute. "Prem is still around, right? At the very least, the building? It'd be tall enough for Nyx to see the roadway to the rally."

Rumor blinked back the sudden need to cry over a tiny teahouse on the ground floor of the newer merchant complex. It had barely fit more than ten people at a time, but served the best chai in the city. The name meant *love* in the Gujarati language, which was one of the only links he'd had to his mother. "Yeah, it's still there."

Dahlia was silent again, as if she'd heard his heart skip. "I'm sorry." She cleared her throat. "We'll head for Prem and meet you on the roof. You can take the roofways across the shops."

"If they're all still there," Rumor said.

"Figure it out," she said, a smile in her voice. "Don't you dare die, or I'll resurrect you and beat your ass."

A laugh escaped him before he realized it'd gathered in his throat. "Yes, ma'am." He turned away. Jude stood a few meters away with George, who was shaking dust off his body. "Is he okay?"

Jude nodded. "Where are we going?"

"We need to find a way up," Rumor said. "This is the beginning of the merchant district. All the shops were connected via bridges from rooftop to rooftop for entrances to upper floor shops. Kept people from clogging stairs and lifts. If we can get up top, we can make our way over to a teahouse I went to a lot that was in a taller building."

Jude rolled his shoulder with a grimace. "Lead the way."

It took them two blocks in the opposite direction to maybe find a way up. Jude led the way down the alley. He kicked a bunch of burned vegetation to the side, releasing a bitter stench. Rumor opened his mouth to breathe. "Wow."

Jude turned, a grin on his face, which slipped as he faced Rumor. "Dammit." Fear crept into his voice.

"What?" Rumor froze at the all-too-familiar growls drifting closer behind him. His breath stuttered.

"We need to go." Jude spun around. "There. We get up to the roof and run."

Jude's voice sounded far away. Echoed back and forth and back and forth, the words meaningless as panic rose like a tide.

"Rumor, there are hellhounds, we need to go," Jude said in an even tone, fear in his eyes.

Rumor sucked in a shaky breath and turned. Three hellhounds stood in the entrance to the alleyway, fangs bared and spines arched. The world slid around him, and smoke hit his nostrils.

"Jude, I can't…I can't move," he gasped. The admission of fear sliced through his mental shields, bleeding him into the ground for Jude to see, locking his joints and covering his rain-soaked skin in sweat and ice.

Jude grabbed Rumor's arm and pulled him up the alley as George followed, growling at the hellhounds. Jude scrambled onto a stack of metal crates under a chrome ladder. He turned and knelt, holding out a hand. "Come on," he urged. "Grab onto me. I need you to grab onto me and I'll pull you up."

Rumor stared at him, his breath coming out in sharp pants, his body frozen and his mind churning churning churning.

"Come on, baby. *Please.*"

Jude's words sliced through his panic. Rumor groped through the near darkness, his world pressing in from all sides. His fingers slid across a warm palm.

"Go!" Jude yelled.

Up the ladder and across the slick rooftops, following bridges from roof to roof as hellhounds gave chase. Roaring filled the air behind them, the grinding of teeth and claws sliding down Rumor's brain. He focused on Jude's presence matching him step for step, trying to squeeze out the panic, his mind spinning and icy fingers wrapped around his heart.

They made it five buildings before the bridges ran out. A twisted bit of metal was all that remained. Jude smacked the edge of the roof in frustration as he leaned over. "There's a ladder, but we have to drop to it."

"Great, more ladders to fall from," Rumor muttered.

Jude swung himself over the edge, blew out a breath, and let go. Rumor heard a *clang* and then he swung over the edge. He glanced back the direction they'd come and froze.

George had the hellhounds trapped one roof back, but it was three-to-one.

"Rumor, come on!" Jude yelled.

"What about George?" Rumor's heart pounded and his

fingers hurt from clinging to the edge of the roof.

"He'll move when you drop!" Jude answered.

George surged forward, snapping his beak on the throat of the middle hellhound. The other two darted past him to the bridge.

Rumor dropped.

He fell only a meter or two, hitting the narrow metal ladder with a clang that echoed through the alley and inside his skull. He grabbed the wall until his balance stabilized and looked up. Nothing yet.

He climbed down as quickly as he could, part-sliding, part-dropping. He hit the ground with a thud, sending pain shooting through his bruised knee.

"Rumor, get up," Jude urged.

Rumor scrambled to his feet, pulling his blades as he did. His insides seized.

Hellhounds.

Two of them. One at each entrance of the alley.

Another snarl and a scraping of stone from above pulled their attention up. Rumor cursed and slammed into Jude, rolling out of the way as the third hound landed where they had been. Rumor's knee and elbow banged into a wall, and he scrambled one direction while Jude headed the opposite way. George tore over the edge of the roof after the one that dropped on them, tackling it halfway down the alley with a roar. The other two burst into motion.

Rumor ran at the opposite wall of the alley, using it to bank off. The jump took him out of the snapping jaws of the hound. It howled and spun around as he landed behind it, swiping at Rumor with one massive paw. Rumor's blade came up in a block and he swung the other, aiming for the neck. He hit the jaw instead and hissed as pain shot up his weakened fingers. The hound pulled back and surged forward again, its mouth closing around Rumor's forearm and its bulk pushing him to the ground.

He hit hard, the pavement digging into his spine. White-hot pain twisted around his arm. He shoved the point of the blade under its throat and out the back of its neck.

It went limp.

Rumor yanked his arm free of its jaws and rolled out of the way so it didn't land on him, panting for breath.

"You okay?" Jude blocked out the nebula, also panting hard.

"Yeah. You?" Rumor pulled himself to his feet, holding the gash on his forearm. Blood welled up between his fingers. His arm throbbed, and he hissed as torn nerves sparked and misfired.

"A few scrapes. Is that broken?"

Rumor shook his head. "You're bleeding."

Jude swiped the back of his hand at his cheek. "Bastard slapped me. Let me see your arm."

Rumor pulled his blade from the hound's neck and held out his arm for Jude's inspection. Jude pressed his lips together. "We need to bind this. You're bleeding everywhere."

"Delicate senses?" Rumor asked wryly.

Jude leveled him with a look as he pulled his knife out and sliced at Rumor's sleeve to tie up the wound. "That'll hold until we get back to Azrou. And thank you."

"For what?"

Jude cleared his throat. "You saved my life just now."

Rumor wanted to kiss him. Wanted to sway forward and press their lips together, but he didn't know if he deserved it. Or if Jude even wanted to kiss him anymore. Rumor was dragging him along on this quest and making him kill. He had made Jude break his rules all night for what—so Angel could die and all of them could get hurt and Rumor could *maybe* kill one chimera?

One chimera whose death might not even make a difference in the war. Why was he doing this anymore? Personal vendetta? Revenge for his home?

Revenge for people he didn't know?

What about their revenge? Dahlia had lived here, too.

Rumor broke eye contact and turned away, ignoring how his heart stuttered painfully at his decision. "We don't have much time left. We need to find the girls."

BRAEDEN

T rick laughed, the sound bouncing off the tunnel walls and blending with the far-off rumble of chimera inhabitants. Braeden fell silent as they hurried through the shelter tunnels, listening to the life around him. The faint ticks of claws against stone, the rumbles of chimera talking to each other, higher-pitched sounds that were probably young playing, the flutter of wings. A few hours ago, all those sounds would've sent fear careening through his body and put his gun in his hand in less than a heartbeat.

But now.

"What is it?" Trick asked.

Braeden shook his head. "It hasn't even been a full nightside and everything I've known has just gone..." He made an exploding sound. "I mean, I knew you guys were out here, but I didn't know it was like this. I didn't get it. I don't know if I wanted to get it. And Bailey." He tugged on his hair.

"Hey, don't beat yourself up about Bailey. Her job was to blend in and be one of you guys. I know that probably doesn't make you feel any better, but you're not dumb or anything for not figuring her out." Trick took another tunnel. "Scouts should be back from the other communities by now."

"How many were hit?" Braeden's heart lurched as human voices filtered down the tunnels. Survivors from Azrou. People who'd gotten away when the marines—his people—attacked. Led by his mother.

"As far as we can tell, just Azrou." Trick frowned at his cuff as he typed. "Come on, Jude, let me know you're still alive, bro."

"It would've sent a signal if his heart stopped beating," Braeden offered.

Trick pulled up short, straightening and tilting his head. "Did you hear that?"

Braeden held his breath, listening. Three tunnels branched off from where they stood. He tapped Trick on the arm and motioned back into the tunnel from where they'd come. They pressed back into the shadows. Trick found a spot where the algae wasn't as thick and stood there, silent and listening.

Braeden reached for his knife in the sheath over his shoulder but gripped thin air. He grimaced and thought seriously about punching the wall. He'd walked out on his moms without getting his weapons back. His knife. His father's revolver.

He pulled his jacket tighter as if he were warding off the chill of the tunnels. At least he still had this.

After several moments of waiting, Gideon crept out of one of the other tunnels. Braeden nearly called out to him, but Trick put a finger to his lips and shook his head. Gideon walked a few steps into the junction, looked around then beckoned. Two marines stepped out after him, guns drawn and ready.

Their cuffs were red.

Braeden went cold.

"Which way?" one of them growled.

Gideon pointed then stepped out of the way as they passed, but instead of following, he hurried back up the tunnel he'd come from.

"That son of a bitch," Trick growled in a low whisper.

Rocks skittered again and Gideon returned, this time leading three large chimera with military weapons. Braeden's heart jumped as they headed in the same direction as the marines.

"Come on," Trick whispered when they'd all disappeared. He darted across the junction and into a different tunnel. Braeden followed at a run.

"Here." Trick handed Braeden a small dagger. "Guns will be loud in the tunnels."

"Where are we going?" Braeden asked.

"To warn the others."

The tunnel curved, opening to a series of rooms lining a large cavern. It was like every tunnel in the complex dumped into this central room, which rose several kilometers straight up. Stalactites dangled from the ceiling, their sharpened points staring down the occupants. Algae lit up the space in a soft blue glow, the iridescent adamantine reflecting to create even more light. Trick and Braeden ran through the space as gunshots rang out behind them.

"Marines are here!" Trick bellowed. "Reaper's minions, too! Get the kids out!"

A single heartbeat of pure silence followed his warning.

Then someone screamed, shattering the bubble of peace they'd all so carefully constructed.

A huge, red hand reached out from behind a column and grabbed Braeden's arm in a bruising grip. The chimera's lips curled back from his teeth. "How did they find us?"

"It wasn't me," Braeden gasped, fear freezing his insides. This guy's face could be the last thing he saw, and that wasn't appealing.

"Minotaur! It was Gideon!" Trick tried to break the chimera's hold before he fractured Braeden's arm. "We saw him lead the others in."

"Human lies!" Minotaur hissed.

"No, I swear—" Braeden's protests cut off as a spike of pain lanced through his arm at Minotaur's twisting. "I can help you. Please."

"Don't do this," Trick said in an urgent voice as shouts and gunfire grew louder. "He's on our side."

Minotaur glared at Braeden, and then shifted his attention to Trick. "Why do you trust it?"

"He's my friend," Trick said.

"You would protect its life with your own?" Minotaur asked.

"Yes," Trick said without hesitation, not breaking Minotaur's glare.

Braeden froze, his lips parting in shock, and he momentarily forgot about the pain in his arm. Was Trick just saying that to free him, or did he really mean it? He didn't know Trick well enough to know for sure, but Trick hadn't struck Braeden as someone who'd lie about something like that.

In such a short span of hours, people he'd never met before—people he'd never had a reason to fight alongside—had become as close to him as Nyx and Dahlia were.

Minotaur released him with a growl. "If you are lying, I will bury you alive in the tunnel walls."

He stalked away toward the gunfire without another word.

He rubbed his biceps and flexed his fingers. "Thanks, man, you didn't have to..."

"I meant it." Trick's eyes were bright and serious. "You okay?"

Braeden nodded, his throat suddenly tight. "We should help."

Trick pulled another knife from his boot and spun it over his palm. He held it out. "Go for the head or the belly. Both fatal for them. The chest not so much."

"You say that as if I haven't killed any of them before," Braeden said with a wide grin he didn't feel. He ducked into one of the branching tunnels. If his mental map of the tunnels was right—and it always was—he should loop around and come up on Reaper's chimera.

When I'm good, I'm good. Braeden spun the knife in his hand and crept up behind the shorter of the two chimera who'd lagged behind to reload its stolen pistol. He jammed the knife in the base of its skull and wrapped his other arm around it as it fell. Trick swiped the pistol as he ran by, sliding the clip home and shooting the second chimera in the back of the skull in one fluid motion. The sound blasted up and down the tunnel, sending a whine through Braeden's ears.

"You know, if I were attracted to people, you'd be really high on the list right now." Braeden shook his head to clear it.

Trick laughed as he searched the bodies for more weapons. "I'll take it." He pried a shotgun out of the hand of the one he'd killed and held it out. "Here. The gunshot will bring more of them."

"Whoa." Braeden took the sleek weapon. "Prototype Black Hole MK11." He hefted it. "Nice."

Trick shook his head. "You are such a nerd."

"You think Reaper left HUB2 and is coming here?" he asked instead of responding.

"No, I think he sent a smaller group to root out humans and any chimera he can make an example of at his rally. Join him or else." Trick's expression turned serious. "We need to find my brother now." He pressed a palm to the walls and frowned. "Come on, please."

"Hey, Trick?" Braeden didn't really want to interrupt rock-talking time, but… "What're you doing?"

"Trying to figure out these vibrations." Trick smacked the wall once. "I've never been able to interpret them."

"Nyx can. She can feel them, I mean. She described them as more emotion than anything else."

Trick grunted in response and took off down the tunnel at a run.

"That's great, Braeden," Braeden said in a mimicry of Trick's deeper voice. "Good talk." He headed after Trick with a limping run, following him through a maze of tunnels that felt colder and colder the farther they went. "Where are we going?" he called over the gunfire echoing through the tunnels.

Trick only pointed ahead at the growing pinpoint of green

light. The tunnel sloped upward. An exit. Where would they come out? Near the colonies? Across the forest? The other side of the moon? It would be really great if people would share more information with him, so he could make some decisions instead of always following.

The gunfire faded the closer they got to the exit.

"Where does this dump us out?" Braeden asked. "And why is it so narrow?"

"We'll be about a kilometer from HUB2. It's a human-only exit. Chimera don't come here." Trick slowed, his gun ready.

"Why not?" Fear prickled the hair on his arms.

"Marines made this tunnel with explosives. A lot of people died that day." Trick swallowed hard and wouldn't look at Braeden. "Jude's parents. He was with them."

Braeden cursed softly. Somehow it made him understand Jude a little bit better. Every kid had a story of someone close to them lost because of the war, but every story Braeden heard or told was about gargoyles taking a person—never really a person being killed by another person. Humans weren't supposed to die at the hands of other humans, of people trained and sworn to protect them.

They reached the exit, a jagged hole in the side of a mountain. Streaks of adamantine laced the stone like veins, shiny and bleeding down the stone walls in long, jagged lines. Braeden brushed his fingers over the bare minerals. "No algae."

"This tunnel is cursed," was all Trick said before he disappeared out the exit.

Braeden splayed his hand flat to the wall, trying to feel the same vibrations Trick and Nyx felt. Trying to feel that connection to the moon his friends did. Everyone had a reason for what they were doing but him. Rumor's revenge. Dahlia's dad. Nyx's gift. Trick's leadership. Jude's peace. He didn't even know where he belonged. Commander's son. Rebel's stepson. One foot in each world with nothing to hold onto.

He felt nothing but cold stone. He dropped his hand and took a step out the exit.

"Braeden, no!" Trick shouted right as claws swiped at him.

Braeden dropped to his knees and rolled, coming up with the shotgun raised. A chimera he didn't recognize lunged at him, grabbing the barrel and moving it away as Braeden pulled the trigger. The shot sailed harmlessly into the woods, and the chimera ripped the gun out of his hands and grabbed Braeden's neck, lifting him off the ground.

His lungs went tight and his windpipe compressed. His face tingled all over and went hot. Braeden kicked as hard as he could in the chimera's belly. The chimera groaned in pain and dropped Braeden, who managed to stay on his feet. He pulled the knife Trick had given him and stabbed the chimera in the forehead. He twisted the knife out and kicked the beast in the chest. It fell with a wet sound.

Over his gasping breaths and raging heartbeat, he heard clapping.

"Well done," Gideon said. "Now drop the knife."

Braeden turned slowly, his hammering heart dropping to his toes when he saw Trick on his knees with a gun pressed to his head. Three more chimera stood in a semicircle behind Trick, leering at Braeden with smug expressions.

"You let me kill one of your own?" Braeden asked as another chimera took the knife from his hands and pushed him toward Trick.

Gideon smiled, all teeth. "He wasn't one of ours. He was one of Vala's and needed punishing. We told him he had to kill you to save his pack. He was only too happy to take the deal. Loyalty, you see."

Braeden sank to his knees, cold and numb. He stared at the chimera corpse, at the black blood staining the yellow grass.

"I didn't know," he whispered.

"What are you smiling at?" Gideon snarled at Trick.

Trick ran his tongue across his bottom lip. "That gun you're holding? I'm going to kill you with it."

Gideon backhanded Trick, one of his claws slicing Trick's cheek open. Trick slowly looked back at Gideon, and without breaking eye contact, spat blood into the grass. "I think I've lost two teeth tonight, thanks to these assholes."

Braeden glanced at him, trying to dig up the detached sarcasm he could usually spool out so effortlessly. He managed a weak smile. "Why?" he asked Gideon. "You lived in Azrou."

Gideon shifted his weight on his enormous haunches. "Lived there, yes. Indoctrinated, no. Bailey wasn't the only one spying."

Trick bared his teeth in a snarl, his body tensing.

The sky lit up with orange and red and yellow. For a split second, Braeden thought they'd horribly misjudged the time and dayside was breaking from behind their host planet. But then the moon rumbled, and the crunching boom of an explosion sounded.

The chimera turned at the light and noise, and gunfire rang out from the forest. Trick pushed off his knees and slammed into Gideon, surprise and momentum bowling them over. Marines melted from the trees, guns rattling. Bullets struck the other chimera in the heads, the wings, the torsos.

Braeden put his hands up and remained on his knees as his mother walked out of the trees as well, her expression hard but her face pale at the sight of him. He slowly rose to face her. What would she do? Take them back to Azrou in chains? Order them to be killed?

She didn't even seem fazed at the explosion behind her, or else it was a very good act.

One marine aimed his gun at Gideon.

"No!" Trick yelled as he stumbled to his feet with Gideon's gun in his hand. Blood streamed from his cheek and his nose.

Gideon put up his hands, his expression murderous. "Trick—"

Trick squeezed the trigger twice, dropped the gun, and put his hands up. "Thanks," he said to the marine.

Braeden stared at his mom. She stood haloed by the glimmering orange of the sky. "HUB2 is burning," he said. "We need to go there now. They need our help."

"We know," was all she said. "Where's Vala?"

Braeden frowned before he could school his features. "I left her with you when I stormed out."

"And I'm to believe you haven't seen her since."

"Listen, I'm not lying to you," Braeden snapped. "She's not here. If she is, I haven't seen her."

Trick sniffed once. "I'm done with this." He dropped his hands and swiped the gun from the grass, then stuffed it into the empty holster on his hip. He glanced at Braeden. "You coming?"

Braeden nodded, his eyes still on his mom, who hadn't made a move to stop either of them.

"Braeden," his mom said.

"Nyx and Dahlia are there. Rumor and Jude. My friends are in trouble, and I'm going to go help them." A tremble rolled over him, but he held firm. For the first time in his life, he felt like the right words were rolling out of his mouth. Sure words. Firm words. Words he could notch around him like armor.

"Trick!"

"Oh, thank Mother," Trick whispered as Kai, Bailey, and several other rebels broke the tree line on the other side. He ran for his brother and tackled him in a hug.

"They're my family, Mom. I have to go find them. You can arrest me or shoot me for treason when I get back." Braeden turned his back on her, on his colony life, and headed over to Trick. Trick pulled away from his brother and met Braeden's gaze with an arched eyebrow.

"Rebel?" he asked.

The corner of Braeden's mouth quirked. "Maybe."

"Braeden."

He turned at Bailey's voice. She stood off to the side, holding his gun out to him. "This group will follow you and Trick to

HUB2. I'll be right behind you."

"What about Mom?" He took his weapon and strapped it to his hip. The familiar weight soothed some of his jangling nerves. He kept his hand on it as if to reassure himself no one would take it.

"I'll handle it."

Several marines watched them in confusion, waiting for an order from their commander that hadn't come. Sara watched them, her face unreadable in the shadows. Bailey walked over to her, slowly and deliberately.

Trick wiped off his cheek with the back of his hand. "Kai, I can't get ahold of Jude. None of my messages are going through."

"There's a sailboard back in the trees. You go ahead and try to get in contact. Stay outside the walls. Do not go in until we get there." Kaipo handed Trick a rag. "You look like you went two rounds with a mountain."

Trick wiped his face off. "Gideon sold us out. Was going to turn us over to Reaper."

"He told you that?" Kaipo's face turned murderous.

Trick pressed the rag to his cheek. "I took care of him."

Kaipo nodded, something like pride whispering through his eyes as he watched his younger brother. Braeden's heart lifted a little. Kaipo squeezed Trick's shoulder. "Later, we're going to have a talk about letting four teenagers go off to a chimera-invaded city alone."

Braeden snorted. "You try stopping Rumor."

Trick glanced at him, gratitude in his eyes. Kai shook his head and turned away.

Braeden followed Trick into the trees. "You think they caused the explosion?"

Trick grabbed the colorful sailboard. "Huh. If they did, it was to attract Reaper's attention. In any case, they're probably in trouble."

Braeden's stomach twisted as he stepped onto the board

behind Trick. "Push this thing as fast as it'll go."

Trick grinned over his shoulder, a macabre sight with the bloody streaks he'd missed with the rag. He gunned the engine and pulled up, pushing the board out of the trees and down the path. They passed marines and rebels alike. No one tried to stop them.

The ride to HUB2 took longer than Braeden expected, and by the time they crested the hill to the south of the city, he was antsy and scared. They only had a few hours left to dayside, but nothing else had been attacked yet. Whatever was happening, either someone's information was wrong or Reaper's plan had changed.

Trick pulled to a stop and jumped off the board. "Who's that?"

Braeden hopped off. At the bottom of the hill, a figure in a cloak stood on top of twisted wreckage. They had a bow and were firing arrows into chimera trying to climb up to them.

"Whoever they are, they're in trouble," Braeden said. "Come on, they might've seen the others."

They half ran, half slid through the mud down the hill. Braeden paused as a chimera crawled up the back of the wreckage, its shadowy hide blending in with the twisted metal. The hooded figure was focused on two chimera in front of them and there was no way they'd see the third in time. He sighted and squeezed the trigger, the boom cracking the air. The chimera fell, its body sliding to the ground in a messy heap. The hooded figure turned at the sound, notching a new arrow at them.

"Whoa!" Trick held up his hands. "We're from Azrou! We're looking for our friends!"

"Four of them our age," Braeden added quickly.

The figure stayed silent, then turned away and ran off faster than Braeden had ever seen anyone run on foot.

Braeden stared after them. "What in deep space just happened?"

Trick made a triumphant noise. "There he is!"

"You got a message?"

"No, when I get this close to Jude, I start to tingle all over," Trick said.

Braeden held up his revolver. "I'm going to throw this at your head."

Trick snorted and jerked his head toward the city. "Do you know your way through this place?"

Braeden tapped his temple. "Been here twice. Memorized it."

"You did what?" Trick asked as they ran toward a jagged tear in the wall.

Embarrassment heated Braeden's neck. He slipped through the wall, all senses on alert. "I have a good memory," he muttered. "Aren't we supposed to wait?"

Trick nodded. "We are." He pointed over Braeden's shoulder. "And there they are."

Braeden glanced back. Azrous, marines, and a handful of automaton animals, broke the forest line, led by Kaipo.

The marines' cuffs were green.

"Epsilon," Braeden breathed.

"What?" Trick asked.

Braeden turned to answer but stopped as he got his first full look at HUB2. He stared at the bloody ground and ravaged buildings. Smelled the death and smoke and blood in the air. His skin crawled at the bodies sprawled in unnatural positions down the street. His gut lurched, and all of Rumor's shields and reticence and anger made complete sense. He couldn't even imagine surviving something like this. He didn't even know how he'd react if he'd lost everything and everyone he'd ever known and loved in one unexpected swipe of a monster's claws.

He regretted not hugging his mom.

NYX

The moon shook with fear. The ground beneath Nyx's feet sang a song of terror. It crawled up her legs like a legion of insects, goose bumps raising the coarse hair on her shins and rolling up into her hips before crashing in her stomach like a storm. She didn't know how much of it was her own fear or the moon's fear or both blending into a cacophony in her bones, but her skin felt slicked with ice. She trembled.

"Stop," she said, vibrations in her chest. She coughed, the dust from the explosion still sticking to her throat and lungs like sap.

Dahlia turned, her eyes wide. Dust and blood mottled her beautiful face. Her hair had flattened in places, and her clothes were torn.

But they were alive.

And together.

"Are you okay?" Dahlia's eyes widened in question as she signed.

Nyx nodded and coughed again. She hated that her coughs echoed. "Are we lost?"

Dahlia frowned and spun around, her eyebrows knit and lips pursed. "No. I know where we are. I just can't get to where

I want to go." She stared straight up and bit her lower lip. "We'll go up here instead of at Prem."

Nyx nodded in agreement. She couldn't shake the feeling that something big lurked just under the surface, just on the other side of the clock as it ticked away to dayside.

While Dahlia looked for a door to open, Nyx pressed her hands to the ground. *Tell me*, she pleaded with the moon. *Tell me what's scaring you.*

But for all her pleading, the vibrations and rumblings made no sense. It was as if the moon were hysterical with no one to calm her down. And Nyx didn't have Angel or George or Vala to dampen the thrumming.

Nyx took a deep breath, counting to five like Dahlia had shown her long ago, and then tried again. The vibrations rolled up her arms, but she forced herself to remain calm, to not give in to the hysteria. She closed her eyes and pushed her own words through her fingers and through the building's prefabricated flooring and into the rock below.

Help us.

Foolishness swept through her in the wake of the plea. A telepathic link with the moon was a child's wish. Wishes were stars, and stars were obscured by the terrible beauty of a butterfly nebula.

She could do this. She could do this without Vala. Without George. Without a chimera acting like a muffler. She didn't need help—she just needed to understand. To find the correct wavelength. To find the right emotions.

Help us stay safe.

A tug. Another pull, like someone hooked their finger on the inside of her ribs and yanked ever so gently. A small child tapping on her thigh. A whisper of fingers just around her triceps, pulling, leading.

She stood and pointed to the building next to the one they faced. "That one."

The coffee shop smelled like coffee and sugar, even after

all the rain and killing and fire that'd consumed the city during the night. Nyx stared at the overturned tables and glass on the floor. Cleaning supplies were out, scattered across the counter. A silver mug sat on the counter, lipstick on the rim. A glass-fronted pastry case stood unharmed in the chaos, the pastries still on the shelves.

Tears burned her eyes. So many people gone in a matter of moments. People like her, like Dahlia. People just drinking their coffee before their nightside shift. People cleaning up so they could go home and sleep. People who lived their lives cycle to cycle, who had nothing to do with the war beyond the uncontrollable location of their birth.

"Maybe we never should've come here." Her voice caught on a sob.

Dahlia squeezed her hand. She pulled gently, and Nyx followed, her insides a waterfall of emotion. She couldn't let herself and Dahlia meet the same fate here. They wouldn't become two more tally marks on some chimera's gun.

Stairs in the kitchen led straight to the roof, which was partially burned but intact. Nyx grinned, pride bubbling up in her throat. Being this far from the ground muted the vibrations to almost nothing, but she'd led them through the building with no problems. She could get a hold on whatever this gift was. Maybe she could turn the tide of this war if she could figure out a way to really *talk* to the moon.

Sahara was alive all on its own—Nyx believed that now.

"Do you see Rumor and Jude?" Dahlia signed.

Nyx shook her head. She walked to the edge of the roof and peered over it. Dahlia's hand slid out of hers as she walked away to explore the safer sections of the roof. Nyx watched her move around, mesmerized by the sway of her hips and so glad she could look now. She'd spent so long trying to avoid staring that she'd have to retrain herself, but that wasn't exactly a problem.

After a moment, she followed, eyes on Dahlia. As Nyx passed

her, she squeezed Dahlia's butt and laughed as she dodged her retaliating swat. Warmth surged through Nyx as she turned around and stuck out her tongue.

Dahlia's bright grin dropped, and she ran for Nyx, slamming into her and pushing her out of the way. Dahlia cried out in pain as they landed in a tumble on the roof. Dahlia moved off her and raised her pistol, firing at the chimera crawling over the edge of the roof. She hit it, and it disappeared, but another two scrambled their way to the top and rushed forward.

Nyx brought up her rifle, breathing as evenly as she could after that tackle, and pulled the trigger. The second shot hit it. Dahlia pushed Nyx behind her, shielding her with her body, and raised the gun.

The shot missed.

The chimera's claws didn't.

Dahlia fell back into Nyx, driving them both to the ground. Nyx's head struck the rooftop. Dahlia sprawled atop her and rolled to one side, her body pinning Nyx's hip to the ground. "Dahl, you need to move," Nyx gasped. "Dahlia, please."

Then she saw the blood covering Dahlia's stomach.

The chimera advanced, lips curled back over fangs as long as her forearm. It resembled a giant lizard with its pointed snout and slender body. Nyx squirmed and strained, fingers grappling down Dahlia's arm for the gun. Her fingers closed around it. She lifted the gun and squeezed the trigger.

Again.

And again.

Over.

And over.

Until the gun grew hot, and the trigger clicked with no kickback.

The chimera fell, the stench of its blood mixing with the burned city and singeing her nostrils. Nyx let out a sob as she pulled herself out from under Dahlia and rolled her to her back.

So much blood.

Nyx stripped her shirt off and pressed it to Dahlia's stomach.

High-pitched ringing in her ears. The word was dull and muffled and so far away as the girl she loved moved her bloodstained lips and tried to speak. Nyx splayed her hand on Dahlia's chest and pressed her cheek to her breastbone, straining and praying for a beat beyond the ringing.

"Why did you do that?" she screamed. "Why did you stand in front of me?"

Dahlia was warm despite the chilled night. Her shirt was soaked with blood. All Dahlia's warmth rushed to her core, leaving the hand pressed to Nyx's arm so cold, so fragile.

Tears burned in Nyx's eyes and tingled her nose as she leaned over Dahlia. Her vision warped as they curtained her sight. She blinked them away, and the droplets traced lines down her cheeks.

"Don't die," she pleaded, pushing as much force behind her voice as she could. *Please come back. Don't go.* "Why did you do that? Why?"

Her hand on Dahlia's stomach was stained red, the blood squelching between her fingers and filling the grooves of her skin. It stained Nyx's shirt, the blood eating the fibers row by row by row. Dahlia's hand gripped hers and squeezed. Silver eyes filled with confusion found Nyx's, and she shook her head, bloodstained lips moving, but Nyx couldn't read them.

"Why?" Nyx sobbed. "Please don't die. Don't leave me."

Dahlia's fingers curled into a fist on the top of Nyx's hand and she extended her thumb, index, and pinkie. "I love you."

Nyx didn't know whether to cry or scream. She mimicked the sign, her eyes blurring with tears.

She told Dahlia to hold onto her and to not let go.

She told Dahlia to keep her eyes open and not be afraid.

She told Dahlia to focus on her eyes.

She didn't know what to do.

The moon's thrum wound up the building and across the roof, tapping at Nyx as she knelt there. *Come look come look come look* it almost seemed to say. Could she even trust it right now?

Angel. They were part of the moon now, and they wouldn't lie to her, right?

"I'll be right back. Don't you dare leave," Nyx ordered in a shaky voice. She pressed a kiss to Dahlia's lips, tasting blood and salt. She stumbled to her feet and hurried to the edge of the roof. She collapsed to her knees at what she saw.

"Braeden!" she yelled. "Up here! Dahlia's hurt! Bad!"

At her yell, Braeden and Trick looked up and ran across the street, disappearing into the cafe entrance. A group of five marines followed them, their jackets identifying them as an Epsilon squad. Her heart leaped with hope.

Nyx ran back to Dahlia and cradled her head in her lap, trying to remember a song her abuela used to sing her. A story. Anything. Her mind failed her. It only showed her image after image of Dahlia dead. A funeral pyre.

"No," she whispered. "Please, no. I just got you."

Dahlia managed a smile up at her.

The door flew open, and both boys burst onto the rooftop. Braeden reached them first, peeling off his outer shirt as he hit his knees. He moved Nyx's blood-soaked one and replaced it with his, then peered at Nyx with wide eyes and pointed at her in question.

Nyx shook her head. "I'm not hurt. It's Dahlia's blood."

Braeden leaned over Dahlia, smiling at her and speaking, but Nyx heard none of it. He kept his face open and smiling even though the set of his shoulders and the tremble of his fingers betrayed his fear. He said something as he looked at the others. One of the marines threw him a field bandage, which Braeden used to press against Dahlia's stomach. He flattened his bloody shirt out and sliced up one side with his knife, working as fast as he could. "I need you to help me wrap this," he signed. "Can you do that?"

Nyx nodded, clenching her jaw to keep from crying more. Dahlia needed her to be strong, to help her. "How close is a med clinic?"

"Epsilon set one up right outside the wall," Braeden signed. He started wrapping Dahlia's torso with his shirt. Nyx helped keep it straight and layered.

Trick paced the edge of the roof, gun in hand, jaw set. The five marines who'd come with them kept up a perimeter, occasionally answering something Trick asked them, but Nyx couldn't read their lips. She didn't care.

Another flurry of movement caught her attention. Rumor, Jude, and George ran across the bridge that connected this building with its neighbor. Fresh tears spilled down Nyx's cheeks at seeing them safe.

Rumor froze when he saw. "What happened?"

Nyx explained as briefly as she could, the vibrations of her voice catching and halting as she spoke. Jude moved away to speak to his brother while George nuzzled Dahlia's temple with his beak.

Trick held his arms out for Dahlia when they were done. He and Braeden had a quick, but pointed, conversation which Trick apparently won, because Braeden stepped out of the way.

Nyx raised her eyebrows as Trick gently picked Dahlia up and cradled her to his chest.

"He said it made more sense for him to carry her. He's bigger, I'm a better shot, and I'm the only one here who can sign with you." Braeden rolled the signs off as fast as he could.

Nyx nodded. She grabbed Dahlia's pistol and handed it to Braeden. "It's empty."

Braeden glanced from the gun to the bullet-riddled chimera corpse and took it without question. Trick said something over his shoulder.

"He's going to take Dahlia to the camp outside the walls and get her to a doctor. Then he'll come back and help us."

Nyx pressed her lips together, tears stinging her eyes. Dahlia looked like a limp doll in Trick's arms.

Braeden touched her elbow. "He'll have two marines with him. Three will stay here with us."

Nyx felt her head nodding, but all she could do was watch Trick disappear through the door. Everything in her screamed for her to go after Trick. To go with Dahlia. To be there when she woke up. To make sure she got help.

She put her hands over her mouth as a sob broke loose. She had to stay here. She was needed here. Her skills were needed here. All she could do there would be hold Dahlia's hand and pray she woke up.

Braeden wrapped his arms around her and held her close as she cried. Her tears soaked into his undershirt, mixing with water and blood and whatever else stained their clothes tonight.

"What's the plan?" She sniffed and wiped her eyes over and over.

The boys watched her carefully. Even the marines examined her. She frowned. "I can still shoot."

Braeden gave her a soft smile.

Rumor scratched his wrist. "Reaper wants me, so we give him me."

"No," Jude said. "That never works in movies, and we sure aren't doing it here."

Rumor's smile was brittle. "The rest of you guys and whoever Trick brings back will be spread out around the plaza on rooftops to pick off any groupies."

"So Reaper is yours, then?" Nyx folded her arms.

Rumor met her eyes. "No, I'm going to keep him busy so you can shoot him."

RUMOR

Rumor picked his way over the soaked debris and corpses, on the way to the central pavilion of HUB2. Where Nyx had seen his father alive, with Reaper and General Stewart.

Alive.

Alive.

His hair had fallen from the bun Jude had pulled it into earlier. Had that only been a little while ago? The attack on HUB2 felt like days ago. Years, even. Since then he'd run and fought and escaped and broken bones and kissed a stranger and been reunited with his ex and made new friends.

Friends.

Friends who were now getting into position to help him with his revenge and end a war.

His boots squelched through the mud as he turned that over in his mind. He'd been solitary when he lived in HUB2, partly by choice and partly by design. His father drummed survival training and fighting skills into him daily. And after his boyfriend had died and Dahlia had moved away, he'd pulled within himself. Didn't make many friends beyond school acquaintances. The occasional basketball game at the park. He wasn't the only marine brat around the place. Or the only queer kid.

He'd always thought he had the answers. His dad had answered every question he'd asked. He'd believed in everything his father stood for. Everything he'd been taught to hate. But during the drills and the fighting and surviving, he'd come up with more questions than answers. He'd buried them, content to ignore when things didn't entirely line up or when something beyond his understanding occurred. He'd just never fully understood until tonight. Until Vala and Angel and George.

And Jude.

Back in Jude's room in Azrou, kissing Jude for the first time had felt like something he needed to do or he'd crack apart. He didn't want any of them to suffer because of him. Not anymore.

He retied his hair back out of his face as he stood halfway down the roadway connecting the plaza to the mining ravine.

In plain sight.

He wasn't filled with blind rage toward chimera any longer, but his hatred of Reaper and the havoc he wreaked on HUB2 smoldered in his belly. Angel had died tonight because of what Reaper had started. Because of this never-ending war.

Someone grabbed his arm, slapping a hand over his mouth before he could cry out. Jude spun him around, glaring, his eyes glowing in the green of the nebula light.

"Why are you here?" Rumor asked in shock when Jude removed his hand. "This isn't part of the plan."

"I made you a deal," Jude said.

Rumor was already shaking his head as the words fell from Jude's lips. "No, I never should've done that. I never should've forced you to come kill. You don't…" He flexed his hand around the blade grip. "I'm sorry for threatening Vala. I'm sorry that I lost my temper like that. I don't even have an excuse as to why I did it, but I'm sorry and—"

Jude kissed him.

It was that first fraught and needy kiss in Jude's bedroom.

It was more than that. It was less than that. It was elation and shock and relief. It stole his breath and sent buzzing through his head. It was everything he thought he'd forfeited and didn't deserve. Rumor clutched at him, clawing at him with his free hand while his heart ached.

When Jude finally pulled away, Rumor stared at him, memorizing the way the nebula picked up the flecks of blue in his green eyes. "Thought you were pissed at me."

"I am." Jude smiled. He put a thumb over Rumor's lips. He took a deep breath, as if steeling himself. "I can't let you walk in there alone, even if it's to fake offer yourself up to Reaper. I'm going in there with you. George and I can work on Reaper's bodyguards. At the very least, we can hold them in one place for Nyx."

"Are you sure?" Rumor asked. "You don't kill."

"It's necessary. Reaper isn't going to stop, and he isn't going to listen to reason. I was an idiot to think otherwise."

Rumor shook his head. "No, no you weren't. I should've listened to you. I should've listened to Vala."

Jude didn't answer, his eyes filled with a wealth of emotions Rumor couldn't even begin to untangle.

"What color am I?" Rumor asked, nerves swamping him. He was tired of always being angry.

"Do you really want to know?"

Rumor nodded.

"Red." Jude's eyes squinted at the corners.

"Good or bad?" Rumor whispered.

"Both, and that's okay." Jude carefully extricated himself from Rumor's arms, his eyes determined. He slid a hand around the back of Rumor's neck and tipped their foreheads together. "You're the most beautiful red I've ever seen. Use it and let's get Reaper."

Rumor nodded, his heart in his throat and his blood singing in his ears. He pulled Jude to him for one more kiss. Just in case.

"Okay, which way?"

Jude pulled his revolver and checked it. "Command spires first. That's where we last saw Reaper. Give Trick more time to get back with help. That fails, we'll head to the mining area. We've got three hours."

"Only three hours," Rumor said.

"No, we've got three whole hours," Jude said.

George was sitting off to the side, watching them with what was probably amusement. Rumor's neck went hot, and he turned away.

At the end of the roadway, they paused, staring at the command spires towering above them like a fortress.

"Wow," Jude breathed.

"Where do you suppose they are? If they're here," Rumor asked.

Jude shook his head. "Wherever they'd have the best view of the city."

"Think we can keep Reaper distracted enough for Nyx to get her shot?" Rumor glanced at the spires.

Jude nodded. "If you piss him off enough."

Rumor pointed to himself. "Excels at pissing people off."

Jude switched his gun to his good hand. "Okay, I guess we could just walk to the center and wave. If they're in there—"

The doors to the closest spire opened, and his father stepped out. "Rumor, what are you doing?"

His world collapsed. He'd almost convinced himself that he'd imagined seeing his dad earlier. That somehow Nyx had been mistaken, too. But here, now, staring at that face, his mind went completely blank. A low buzzing started in his ears, and his cheekbones tingled.

"Do you see him?" he whispered.

Jude wrapped his fingers around Rumor's forearm and squeezed. "Yes."

"Hey, Dad. Good to see you." Rumor held his ground despite

wanting to run to him.

Eric Mora jogged down the roadway quickly, his gaze furtive. "You need to leave."

Rumor looked him over, his hands shaking. "You aren't hurt. How are you not hurt? I saw the blood. I saw the hellhounds."

His father didn't answer, just stepped closer. Sweat beaded his temples. He grabbed Rumor's arm and snapped a cuff onto it, shaking his head the entire time. "You aren't supposed to be here. You're supposed to be safe and far away."

"Safe?" Rumor echoed, staring at him instead of the cuff. "You died." The words sounded foreign to his ears. Maybe he was talking to a ghost. Maybe he'd finally snapped, and his waking nightmares had manifested into hallucinations. "Jude, my dad died."

Jude squeezed his arm again, anchoring Rumor to the ground and to reality. "You're not imagining this."

Eric ignored Jude, grabbed Rumor's shoulders and shook him. "Focus, son. You need to leave. You need to get as far away from here as possible. It isn't safe for you here. Not if General Stewart succeeds. Not if Reaper…" He trailed off and ran his hands through wild curly hair, making it stand even more on end.

"What is Reaper doing? What's going on? How are you *alive*?"

Eric ran his hands over his face. "War. Genocide. I don't…" He trailed off with a wave of his hands, his head tilting to one side and back again like a twitch. "This is too big. Bigger than Hector ever told us. This wasn't supposed to—not like this."

"Us?" Rumor repeated.

"You need to keep that safe. Keep it away from colonist leaders." Eric pointed to the cuff on Rumor's wrist and yanked Rumor's sleeve over it to hide it. "It has information. It has all I could get without them knowing."

"How are you alive?" Rumor demanded again as he stared at this person who looked and sounded like his dad, but couldn't be.

Eric paused, blinking at his son. "I never died," he said as if that should've been obvious. His eyes snapped to Jude as if he'd just realized he was there. "I don't know you."

"Hi." Jude's voice was cold.

"Where are they?" a grating voice boomed from the plaza behind Eric.

Anger rose, hot and heavy, pushing every other emotion away in a blink. Rumor would never forget that voice as long as he lived. "Reaper."

"Son, don't." Eric grabbed his arm.

"Let go of me," Rumor growled.

"Rumor," Jude said in a calm voice. "We're surrounded."

Rumor and Eric froze, their eyes darting around. Chimera slunk out of the shadows—big ones, little ones, another hellhound, several humanoid ones, even another gryphon-like one, which George hissed at. Their growls built and overlapped, sending shivers over Rumor's skin.

Rumor turned, his back pressing to Jude's. Rumor reached behind him and curled his hand around Jude's hip. More and more chimera melted out of the shadows, eyes narrowed and teeth bared. They spoke in their native tongue, Jude flinching every so often.

"Even with Nyx's sniper shots, there are too many," Rumor said.

"It wasn't supposed to be like this," Rumor's dad said over and over. "Not like this."

"Dad—" Rumor's voice cracked. He reached for Jude, and Jude reached back, tangling their hands together. Jude, his anchor. Jude squeezed Rumor's hand. His palm was so hot it pulled Rumor's attention. "Jude."

A tremble ran up Jude's back.

Rumor sucked in a breath as all his anger dissipated for a breath, and Jude's hand went ice cold. Was this… No, this wasn't another panic attack. For an inhale, nothing existed in his body but peace. He wanted to cling to that feeling. But it vanished in a blink, and Jude's hand returned to normal temperature as if nothing had happened.

Four shots rang out.

Four chimera fell, each from a bullet to the head.

The city held its breath.

Then let it out in a roar of chaos.

Gunfire burst from the surrounding rooftops. Rumor caught sight of familiar faces in the nebula light as humans slid out of the darkness behind the chimera. Lights clicked on, bathing the ground in white. "Marines."

"Azrou." Jude pointed to another rooftop nearby. "Trick!"

Trick grinned down at them, a tsunami pistol in each hand. "I found some folks who weren't busy. Y'all need help?"

The chimera turned, screeching and howling at the ambush. Several attacked, hurtling toward the lights. Many ran for the plaza.

For Reaper.

"Dad?" Rumor spun around, eyes wide. "Where'd he go?"

"I didn't see him leave," Jude said.

Rumor ran his hands through his hair. Nothing made sense. Nothing that happened tonight made a bit of sense. He was sick and tired of being eighteen steps behind everyone else.

"Reaper's in the plaza!" Trick yelled. "I believe he'd like a word."

"Oh I'll give him a word," Rumor growled as he held up his blades and headed to the plaza. Jude kept pace. Several chimera followed them, keeping their distance as if following some understood order. The crackle of gunfire filled the air behind him. The city burned along the northern edge.

"Reaper!" Rumor yelled.

Four chimera gathered in the plaza, all hooded. As Rumor watched, they passed the scythe around. He snorted. "This is the weirdest version of keep-away I've ever seen."

One of the Reapers hissed at him.

Jude laughed. "That's…so cliché."

A shot rang out, and one of the hooded gargoyles dropped into a messy heap on the ground. The other three moved immediately, heading for the giant woven columns to use as cover.

George lunged out from the shadows, aiming for one of the chimera on the left side. He leaped and slammed into the chimera, tumbling back into the shadows with a crunch of bone and the visceral sounds of tearing flesh.

Jude aimed and fired twice at one of the Reapers, but a humanoid chimera jumped in the way. It roared in anger and pain and hurtled toward Jude, claws extended and mouth wide. Rumor ran for it, driving his shoulder into the chimera's side. Pain shot down his shoulder as they toppled over in a messy tangle of human and monster. Rumor pushed up and drove his blade into the chimera's neck, the tip slicing clean through and crunching into bone. Black blood bubbled up when he wrenched his weapon free.

Jude cursed. "My gun's gone."

"Use a blade." Rumor turned back toward the remaining Reapers. Another guard charged him, a roaring screech setting Rumor's teeth on edge.

Rumor ducked out of the way at the last minute, bringing his blade up toward its ribs. The chimera howled and brought its arm around in a backhand that made Rumor's vision go spotty. He fell, his head hitting the stone with a crack that he felt all the way down to the bones of his legs. He rolled, coming up to a crouch. As he stood slowly, something wet rolled down his neck.

"Rumor!" Jude yelled. "Duck!"

Rumor fell flat to the ground as a scythe whistled where his neck had been and cleaved the head of the remaining chimera. He rolled and pushed to his feet, then backed away from one of the remaining Reapers to give himself some space. "They're still using the columns as cover!" he yelled. "Draw them out!"

Up close, the moniker fit. Reaper's hood covered his face, but the hands sticking out of the sleeves had fingers longer than Vala's and bone-thin. They tapered off into natural points that looked like they could rip open his chest. "So you're Reaper. I mean, you have to be the real one. Those other two are horrible actors."

"And you're the survivor," Reaper's voice grated. It sent shivers over Rumor's skin.

"I am, but I guess I'm not the only one after all, am I?" Rumor backed away and circled, trying to move Reaper better into Nyx's line of fire. More shots rang out, and several of Reaper's minions dropped to the ground.

Reaper didn't move. He kept the column between himself and where Nyx perched. "Your father has been immensely helpful to our efforts."

"Efforts?"

"Humans are a parasite, and you're destroying this land with your mining and your colonization. You came and took with no regard to the life already existing here and, according to your histories, that's fairly standard for your species, isn't it?"

Rumor shrugged. "Not all of us. The forest humans coexist."

"Of course, not all humans. I'll kill them last."

Marines shouted back and forth. Howls grew in volume as more chimera arrived. Rumor had no idea if they were Reaper's chimera or Vala's.

Wherever she was.

Rumor licked his lips, eyeing the scythe that Reaper held as a staff. "What about all the chimera who coexist with humans? Going to kill your own kind?"

"Traitors," Reaper spat. "I'm protecting my race from a disease, and if that means I cut out infected flesh, then so be it."

Nyx's sniper rifle fired almost methodically as she picked off Reaper's chimera rushing at the pavilion one at a time. Other rifles fired, and bodies fell in Rumor's peripheral vision.

But there was nothing Rumor could do about them. He needed to get Reaper to move, to step out from behind the column so Nyx could get him.

Reaper carried the scythe about a third of the way down the shaft. Loosely.

Piss him off.

"Well, you had to get humans to help you take down a city so, honestly, how effective do you really think you're going to be?" Rumor injected as much condescension into the statement as he could. He thought he spotted movement but didn't want to risk turning his head. Hopefully it was George.

Trick's voice rose above the growing cacophony, cursing. More shouting joined Trick's. Rumor's back tensed as several screams rose into the air, then were abruptly cut off.

A roar filled the night, and Jude made a sound somewhere between agony and surprise somewhere behind him. Rumor's blood ran cold, but he kept his focus on Reaper.

Move, you asshole.

Reaper laughed, low and chilling. "There is much you don't know, human."

"I know Angel is dead," Rumor said, loud and clear. "I know that they died saving my life."

"Lies," Reaper snapped. "You spread lies."

"Their stomach was split open by one of your minions when they rescued me." Rumor tightened his grip on his blade. "They were coming here to tell you to stop, to make you pay for what you've done tonight."

Reaper keened. "Murderer! How dare you believe your life is worth that of my nestmate! How dare you kill them."

Anger sparked through him, and he swung at Reaper, aiming for his chest. Reaper moved out of the way, his robes swinging in a tattered display of dead iconography. Rumor smelled blood and smoke.

He straightened and tilted his head at Reaper. "You need humans to take down a city. You need other monsters to kill a couple of humans."

Reaper made a sound somewhere between a growl and

thunderclap. "What did you call my kind?"

Rumor lowered his chin. "*Monster.*"

It felt so good to say. He darted forward, blade sweeping up in an arc as if he was aiming for Reaper's neck. Reaper took a step back and raised his scythe, but Rumor twisted, slashing his blade to the side as he fell to his knees and spun across the rain-slick stone. The homemade heritage blade found home at the joint of Reaper's wrist, severing his hand. The heated blade hissed as it burned through flesh and blood.

Reaper howled, the sound underscored by gunshots. Rumor rose just as Jude limped into his line of sight. Blood stained his pant leg, and his face was a mask of pain and determination. He carried a blade.

Reaper swung at Rumor again, the blade narrowly missing Rumor's face as Rumor bent out of the way.

They had to get the scythe away from him or they'd die here. And Reaper wasn't moving out of the way of the column.

"Rumor!" Jude yelled.

"Jude, move!" Rumor called as the scythe flashed, catching Jude on the hip. "No!"

Jude's scream scraped across Rumor's skin. The boy fell to the ground in a tumble of blood and splayed limbs, and time seemed to move backward. George leaped into the air as the chimera he was chasing threw itself into the weakened column above Jude.

The artistic latticework at the base bent farther, squealing as it tilted. Something else crunched, and Rumor watched, frozen, as the column gave way and slammed to the ground. Onto Jude.

Reaper laughed. A string of curses erupted from Rumor as he brought his blade down with all the anger in his body and severed the scythe handle in two. Reaper dropped the remaining piece and grabbed Rumor instead.

Long, cold fingers wrapped around his throat and jerked him from the ground. Rumor clawed at Reaper's hand, his fingers uselessly scraping dense hide. Reaper spun, slamming him against another column.

"Stupid human! Thinking you can take this ground from us." Up close, Reaper's eyes were too wide and almost hollow, dark pools of nothing swallowing what little light remained.

Spots crowded Rumor's vision, and his chest burned with the need for air.

Not like this. Not when I'm so close.

Rumor's tingling fingers tightened around his blade handle and, using what little energy he had left, he brought it up and plunged it into Reaper's chest.

JUDE

Jude raised his head. One of the columns surrounding the pavilion had fallen and, with it, the decorative latticework, which had all landed on his left leg in a crumbled mass of stone and twisted metal. His knee didn't look right, and he couldn't feel anything beyond that.

Reaper dropped Rumor and stumbled back almost in slow motion, Rumor's blade sticking out of his chest. Rumor fell back against the column, coughing and gasping. Jude shook his head as Rumor shakily ran to Jude without looking back.

"Jude," Rumor said hoarsely, scrambling back over to him. "Oh damn…can you wiggle your toes?" He glanced up as if to call for help.

Jude shook his head and tried to get air. "I can't feel my leg. Rumor, he's not dead. Give me my gun."

"What? No, I got him, it's okay. George!" Rumor yelled.

"Rumor, my gun," Jude pleaded.

Rumor swiped the revolver off the ground and pressed it into Jude's outstretched hand. "It's okay. It's right here. It's not lost. George!"

Jude pushed onto his elbows, trying to get his vision to clear long enough. A shadow grew out of the pavilion. Jude gasped and tried to form words as claws extended toward Rumor's neck.

Jude grabbed Rumor's shirt and yanked him to the side with all his strength as he raised the gun and fired.

One.

Two.

Three.

The gun kicked three times. Three bullets disappeared into Reaper's hood. Reaper stumbled back and fell into a messy heap on the shiny pavilion surface. Jude gulped air, his arm extended, aiming at the spot the chimera leader fell.

The world held its breath.

Jude waited for Reaper to surge up, impossible to kill, like a dark nightmare. His arm shook with the effort to hold the gun steady. After an eternity or a few seconds, Rumor got to his feet and limped over to the body, breathing hard. Reaper's hood had fallen back, exposing his narrow head and curved horns to the nebula above. Rumor yanked his blade from Reaper's chest.

"That was for Angel, you son of a bitch," Jude whispered. With those words, his strength left him. He fell to the ground with a harsh exhale. The sky went fuzzy and darkened around the edges. Shouldn't it be getting lighter? Dayside was soon.

Maybe he was wrong.

Maybe he didn't care.

Rumor appeared in his blurry vision. His fingers pushed through Jude's hair. "Jude. Jude."

He raised shaking fingers and touched Rumor's cheek. His Rumor couldn't go a half hour without injuring himself. "You're bleeding again."

Rumor smiled, his eyes shiny with tears. "I'm fine. I'm okay. We'll get to a medic. We'll both be okay. Trick!"

Jude cracked a weak smile. "Did we win?"

"Yeah, baby, we won." Rumor looked around frantically. "Trick! Jude's hurt!" His necklace slipped out of his shirt, and a single copper coin dangled directly above Angel's stone.

"Tell me about the coin," Jude said softly.

Rumor didn't make any move to hide it. "It was my mother's." He pushed Jude's hair back again, petting him as if he didn't know what to do with his hands. "Earlier, when we were surrounded and you grabbed my hand…"

Jude tried to focus. The world swam, but Rumor's voice kept him anchored. Kept him on this plane instead of floating into the abyss of the nebula with only stars and ice. The sounds of gunfire and shouting seemed so far away.

"…for a moment, I felt…" Rumor ran his fingertips over Jude's cheek. "Peaceful. Just for a second, and then it all came back and I don't know how, but did you do that?"

Jude reached for Rumor's hand, tangling their fingers together. "I don't know," he whispered.

Rumor nodded, swallowed. "When you're better, we'll find out."

Trick's face appeared in Jude's line of sight, anguish and fear coating him in yellow and blue. "Jude. Oh gods, hang on." His face disappeared again, but his voice seemed to echo. "Someone help me get this off him!"

Jude coughed and gasped in pain, his hands twitching toward his leg. "Think they'll give me a badass cyborg leg?"

Rumor lay on the ground next to Jude and pressed his forehead to Jude's shoulder. "Definitely."

"I want it to shoot rockets." His words slurred. Rumor raised his head, his colors turning to pure fear and sadness as Jude's eyes slid shut and darkness overtook him.

RUMOR

R umor kept his hand in Jude's as paramedics loaded Jude onto a hover gurney and pushed him into Azrou's medical center. He kept pace as doctors and nurses jostled him and asked a million questions he had no answers to. He held onto Jude even though every step hurt and words flew around him in a cloud of confusion and worry. Jude's fingers were so pale in his. Too pale. Even against Rumor's brown skin, they were too pale.

Jude's eyes fluttered open, the green glassy and dull with painkillers and who-knew-what-else already sliding through his system.

Rumor pushed blond curls back from Jude's forehead, petting him as if he needed soothing. "Hey, Jude."

Jude's lips quirked in a crooked smile. "That's an old Earth song, I think."

Rumor huffed. "Jackass."

"Son, we need to take him into surgery." A nurse pulled gently at Rumor's arm.

Rumor's heart leaped and his eyes burned. "You come back, okay?"

Jude nodded, squeezing Rumor's hand weakly. "You'll still be here?"

He nodded almost too fast. Everything was going too fast. "Promise."

"You need to move," the nurse said, gently but firmly.

"I really want to kiss you," Rumor whispered.

Jude blinked for far too long, and he nodded. Rumor pressed his lips to Jude's, clutching at him, scared and lost, believing he would spin off into the nebula if he let go. He pulled away and stood rooted to the spot as Jude disappeared behind a set of double doors with no windows.

Numbness stole through Rumor's body. His heart and his head pounded.

"You need a doctor," the nurse said. "Son."

Distant beeping sounded and he looked down at the silver cuff his father had given him. "Dayside. We made it to dayside."

He pulled his hair down out of its tie. His hair tumbled in a mess around his shoulders. He glanced at the double doors again. They'd made it, but at what cost?

"What's your name?" The nurse's hold tightened as the room wavered around the edges.

"Rumor." His name echoed back to him from far away, and he shook his head as the room tipped. "Whoa."

"We need a gurney here!" the nurse called.

Rumor squeezed his eyes shut and opened them wide, trying to clear his vision. Teal eyes met his, and Trick's face split into three copies, then went back together.

"He needs a doctor," the nurse protested as Trick grabbed Rumor's shoulders.

"Where's Jude?" Trick asked.

"Surgery," Rumor managed. "His leg…"

"I know, Rumor, I was there." Trick spoke in soothing tones.

Rumor's cheeks pulled in a smile that felt wrong for the situation but so right for Jude. "Jude shot Reaper. Saved my life."

He stumbled, and Trick slung an arm across his shoulders and held him up.

"I got him." Trick's voice fading as darkness rolled over him swift and fast and sent him crashing.

His awareness came and went in snatches of light and sound as if his body wasn't ready to stop yet. Wasn't ready to let go and sleep. Wasn't ready to admit it was over.

All over.

A bed.

A pinch in his arm.

A bright light in his eyes.

People speaking but sound fading in and out.

He may have called for his dad at one point.

"Rumor," a voice whispered.

"Mom?" he croaked.

"No, babe, it's Dahlia."

Rumor's eyelashes felt laced together as he pried open his eyes. The soft amber glow of the bedside lamp haloed her. She'd bound her hair up in a colorful scarf. Scratches and bruises littered her face and neck.

"You're okay." His words came out somewhere between a statement and a question.

She smiled and held his hand in both of hers—one of them bandaged from elbow to wrist—and pressed it to her cheek. "I am. I'm not supposed to be out of bed yet, but I had to come check on you."

"Jude?" he asked.

"Nothing yet. Hasn't been that long. I came here as soon as I heard where they put you."

"Excuse me, are you family?" A nurse stopped in the doorway.

"Yes." Rumor squeezed Dahlia's hand as if they were going to rip her away from him.

The nurse smiled and left without another word.

Dahlia settled next to his bed. She ran her fingers through

his hair. "You need to sleep. You pushed yourself too far."

"Jude," he mumbled.

"Jude will be fine." She continued petting his curls. Tingles rolled down his body, and his muscles melted into the soft mattress.

"The cuff," he slurred. "Nyx."

She shushed him softly. "I'll give it to Nyx."

"Keep...safe...secret." He couldn't open his eyes anymore. "Stay."

"I'm not going anywhere," she promised. "Sleep. You're safe now. It's over." Her lips pressed to his forehead. They were cool and dry and familiar. "I'll be here when you wake up."

And, trusting her wholly and without reservation, Rumor finally, *finally* slept.

BRAEDEN

The twin suns broke over the mountainous horizon, illuminating a changed moon in streaks of orange and blue. They illuminated the sky, turning it from a cloudy nebula to a bruise to a sigh of light blue. The orange sun rose first, followed by its smaller blue twin only moments later. Sahara's host planet lit up in streaks of gaseous red and brown and yellow, its angry and deadly presence filling a third of the sky.

Braeden watched it unfold outside Azrou's medical center, savoring the warmth on his bare arms. Relief like he'd never felt before filled his body, and it wasn't until this very moment that he realized he hadn't expected to see this. Part of him truly believed he'd never make it through the night. That they would fail and the moon would crack open and swallow everyone.

But they'd won a victory…of sorts. They'd stopped an escalation of the war, but at what cost? Dahlia had been horribly injured. Jude lay in surgery, his survival precarious even as Braeden stood under the open sky.

When they'd returned to Azrou, the Alpha marines were gone, but so were Sara and Vala. All anyone knew was they'd all been taken to Alpha colony. The thought of Vala in the general's hands froze his insides. And who knew what they'd do to his mom.

He rubbed his forehead and took a steadying breath. He wanted to find Trick. Nyx would tell Dahlia everything. Braeden could talk about this with Trick, help him get his mind off Angel.

"Braeden!" Bailey called.

He turned, his eyebrows doing the talking as she walked up. He didn't want to give her much; he didn't owe her anything. But she was his stepmother, unless his mom decided to end that, and he loved her. She'd been there since a little while after his dad had died. She'd taught him fun science experiments and helped him manage his memory abilities.

"I just wanted to make sure you were okay." Bailey's expression was soft and her eyes hopeful.

He'd been taller than her for a long time now, shooting up like a tent pole when he'd hit puberty. But all he wanted right now was to be small again so he could curl up in her lap and listen to her heartbeat and play with the rings on her fingers.

"I'm fine," he said, standing so still his muscles ached.

She nodded. "Listen," she started in a hesitant voice. "I know it will take a while for you to trust me again, and I respect that." She licked her lips, yanked her hair down from its messy knot, and tied it back up again. "I love you, Braeden. That was always real, and that hasn't changed."

Braeden swallowed around the prickly ball of words in his throat and nodded. "Okay."

Bailey nodded, forced a tight smile, and walked away.

He cleared his throat. "Bailey?"

She turned immediately.

"Have you seen Trick?" He pretended not to notice how her shoulders dropped a fraction.

She pointed to the trees behind him. "He's up in one of the lookouts, last I saw."

"Thanks." He hurried away before his resolve broke.

The lookouts were built into the tallest trees, the platforms wrapping around the trunks and weaving between branches in a tangled mass of vines and man-made structure. Braeden loved it. The wind whipped around him as he climbed, carrying the cinnamon scents off the bark and mixing with the gentle perfume of morning flowers opening to the daylight. He pulled himself up and up—away from his moms, away from Rumor and Jude in the medical center, away from Nyx and Dahlia, away from Epsilon, away from HUB2, away from the chimera. The ground dropped from his feet, the chill of the air clearing his head for the first time in hours.

"What's got you so happy?" Trick peered over the railing. He held a hand out.

Braeden took it and swung a leg over the railing onto the platform. He brushed his hands off and shrugged. "Nothing, really. This is cool."

Trick jerked his head to the other side. "Nah, this is better. Come on." He led the way through twists of branches and vines to the far side of the tree—well away from the stability of the trunk. "You're not afraid of heights, are you?"

Braeden shook his head.

Trick gestured to the railing. "Take a look."

He stepped up to the railing, the wind pulling at his clothes and his hair. They stood just above the trees—high enough to see but still low enough to blend in. The forest stretched before him in a carpet of golds and oranges and reds. In the distance, the forest ended as if someone had gouged a line in the dirt, and the foothills began, bulging from the moon in great stony growths.

"How's Jude?" he asked.

Trick cleared his throat. "Surgery. They're…they're trying to save his leg, but they don't know if they can."

"Having a cyborg brother sounds pretty cool," Braeden said.

Trick gave him a weak laugh. He pointed a little north.

"HUB2 is that way. At night, you could see the spires lit up."

Braeden glanced in that direction. The sunlight glinted over what remained of the spires and the jagged edge of a dome that would never be finished.

"How are you holding up?" Braeden asked as he took in the view.

Trick stayed silent so long, Braeden assumed he wouldn't answer.

"Angel was one of the first chimera I met when Kai brought us from the colonies. They were huge, and I'd never seen one with two heads." Trick sniffed and swiped under one eye. He traced an invisible pattern on the railing. "Angel sat on the ground so we were more at eye level and said 'hello.' That was it. Sat there while I touched their wings and horns and fingers and asked a million questions. They were always there. We were like…" He trailed off.

"Partners," Braeden finished.

"Yeah. Nothing romantic but…"

"It doesn't have to be romance to be love," Braeden said quietly, a little lurch in his stomach with the words.

Trick met his gaze for a long time. He seemed like he wanted to say something else, so Braeden waited quietly, fighting the urge to say something else or babble or glance away.

"Are you staying?" Trick asked.

Braeden stared at HUB2. "Like, forever?"

"I mean are you choosing a side," Trick said quietly.

Braeden bowed his head. "Is it officially full-on war between the colonies and the forest now?"

"I don't know." Trick let out a long breath. He turned around and folded his arms over his chest. "But, if you're going to stay, you have to be *with* us. You can't suddenly change your mind and go back."

"And if I want to go rescue my mom from Alpha colony?" Braeden straightened and faced Trick.

"Who says she's a prisoner?"

"My gut," he answered.

Trick rubbed his fingers over his lips. "And if you're wrong and she's working with them still and Vala is her prisoner as well?"

Braeden swallowed, looked at HUB2 again, and couldn't find the words.

NYX

Nyx leaned against the doorframe, a soft smile on her face at Dahlia reclining in her hover chair by Rumor's bed. She had one arm draped across her stomach, the other along the edge of Rumor's mattress, her fingers twined with his. The shirt she'd been given rode up a little, exposing the bandage taped to her midsection.

The medics had stopped the bleeding with knitting gel and quick thinking. They'd saved her life. Technically, she shouldn't even be out of bed, but when had Dahlia ever listened to directions?

Dahlia looked up, her eyes widening a fraction as if Nyx finding her with Rumor would upset her. Nyx shook her head. "It's okay. How is he?" she signed.

Dahlia carefully extracted her hand from his so she could sign. "Exhausted. Doc said his body just shut down. His voice is a little screwed up from Reaper choking him, but he'll recover. He needs rest."

"You going to stay here with him?"

Dahlia nodded. "Is that okay? I told him I'd be here when he wakes up."

Nyx smiled and walked over to her girlfriend. She leaned over and kissed her softly, lingering an extra beat or ten.

"Go back to bed soon and rest. I love you," she whispered against Dahlia's lips.

Dahlia's lips moved against hers, and Nyx knew she'd said it back. As she straightened, she glanced at Rumor. Bruises ringed his throat, and his skin had lost a lot of its luster. But he slept, his chest rising and falling in a gentle rhythm, and that was what he needed most. "Do you need anything? A blanket? Pillow?"

"I'm okay right now," Dahlia signed.

"I'm going to find Braeden and Trick. See if I can find out how Jude's doing." Nyx kissed Dahlia one more time and ran her fingertips over the uninjured cheek. Her heart did a little dance when Dahlia smiled up at her, as tired as it was. She didn't know if it was possible to love anyone more than how much she loved this girl. Tonight had reshaped and rewoven and torn apart everything she'd known about life and her existence. Pieces of herself scattered across the moon and back.

But telling Dahlia she loved her in that little room in that little treehouse was something that had stitched her whole last night, and Nyx curled her fingers around it, protecting it with every molecule of her being. She had no idea what would happen as the clock ticked onward and the ripples of last night grew larger the further they spread. She felt as though she stood on the precipice of something vast and unknowable. Something that would eat them alive if they leaned too far in.

The moon rumbled under her boots as she left the medical center. The trees towered above her, shafts of orange and blue dawn slicing through the leaves and branches and bathing the limping community in dappled patterns.

She stared up at the sky, watching it lighten by degrees, when a movement caught her peripheral vision. At first, it looked like a bird, but the bird turned out to be Braeden, high in the treetops on a platform. She gauged the stairs and ladders. Yeah, she could climb that.

And climb she did, the hum of the moon under her fingertips as it traveled up the tree with her, licking at her senses and giving her the energy to make the climb.

As she neared the top, she looked up into Braeden's smiling face.

"What are you doing here?" he signed, his grin wide and welcoming.

She crawled onto the platform. "Came to see how you were doing."

"You're not tired, either?"

She shook her head. He held out a hand and led her across the platform to the far side, where Trick waited. His smile was gentle, but his eyes held sadness and worry about Jude, with the grief over Angel's death still too close to the surface. Trick had to mourn in his own way since he hadn't been there, and Nyx couldn't imagine the pain of that. She let go of Braeden's hand and hugged Trick. After a moment's hesitation, he wrapped his arms around her and squeezed her gently. When she pulled away, he spoke quickly to Braeden, who nodded and held up an open palm, touched his fingertips to his chin, and pulled it away in one smooth motion.

Trick turned to her. "Thank you," he signed, mimicking what Braeden showed him.

Nyx smiled, warmed by the attempt, and turned toward the view.

"This is amazing," she said, not caring whether they answered. The wind cut across the trees, rustling the colorful leaves in great waves. She smelled cinnamon and flowers and life swirling around her.

Braeden stepped up beside her, his shoulder brushing hers, and she could almost imagine this as it was before—as it was yesterday before everything turned upside down. Her and Braeden up high, picking out random colonists and making up stories about them. Dahlia down below waiting, since she didn't like heights. Nyx could almost imagine.

Almost.

"Which way are the colonies?"

Trick pointed, and she shaded her eyes against the growing sunlight as she tried to pick out the glints of cities and colonies in the distance. She frowned. "What is that?"

She pointed in the direction of HUB—the original city built when the colonists first landed.

Braeden shaded his eyes with both hands, frowning hard. After a minute he looked around, speaking to Trick while he did. Trick rummaged in a box near a branch and pulled out a pair of binoculars. He tossed them to Braeden, who put them to his face immediately. His lips parted in shock and he handed the lenses to Nyx, his eyes hard and almost scared.

Nyx put the lenses to her face, adjusted the clarity, and pointed them toward HUB. They didn't let her see all the way to the gleaming dome of the city, but close enough to identify precisely what she'd seen drifting down from the morning clouds like specks of falling ash.

Ships.

Battle cruisers like the ones that had arrived in '64 with guns and troops.

Four of them.

Landing on Sahara's surface.

ACKNOWLEDGMENTS

27 Hours is a book of journeys. When Rumor Mora formed in my imagination back in 2005, I had no idea that path he would take, the incarnations he'd undergo, or how the final story would shape around him. Over the past twelve years, so many people have read drafts, given advice, and encouraged me. I've scribbled your names on scraps of paper, in the margins of drafts, and in my heart. I could never thank everyone enough for your time, energy, ideas, and love for this story and these characters.

To Cassandra Graham, Vickie Peterson, Michael Waters, Tamara Mataya, HE Griffin, and Amber Tuscan-Clites, you were some of my very first readers through the ups and downs of draft after draft and queries galore. This story wouldn't exist without your tireless encouragement.

Ami Rose, Melody Timpani, and Abi Roux, the four of us are my favorite dumpster fire.

Leah Karge, you are light and love and everything I wish to be and more. Thank you for loving these characters as much as I do.

To my many betas and sensitivity readers who helped me with the nuances of groups I don't belong to and my own internal biases regarding the groups I do call home: Shannon Walsh, Natalie Peltier, Maya Bernau, Camryn Garrett, Corinne Duyvis, Shveta Thakrar, Keiko Furukawa, Jenn Fitzpatrick, Tehlor Kay Mejia, Maria Mora, Nicole Tersigni, Cam Montgomery, Kristin Andrews, and Andrea Shettle. Thank you. Thank you for your knowledge, your time, your energy, and for calling me out on my mistakes. I will forever be in your debt.

To Katherine Locke, "Hey Jude" will always be yours.

Laura Lam, you were the first to ever offer to blurb anything I've ever written, and coming from a woman and author I admire so much, it was one of the best moments of my career.

Nita Tyndall, Tara Sim, and Erica Cameron, I love you three more than you'll ever know. Your friendship and love and unwavering belief in me made this book happen. Thank you.

There are those who say social media is empty calories. That you can't form anything meaningful via tubes and wires. To my pocket friends in my phone, Sarah Hollowell, Ali Trotta, Chelsea Cameron, Paul Krueger, Sangu Mandanna, Sarah Gailey, AdriAnne Strickland, Meredith Russo, Ashley Blake, you read my little story and then had the amazing audacity to brag to the world you'd done so. As if my little tale was something worth bragging about. Thank you for bolstering a new author's ego. I will never forget that warmth or your friendship.

To my Patreon backers, especially Katie Spina, Chanie Beckham, d+tee, and Katharine Meyers, thank you for your continuing generosity and support. I'm able to write because of you, and I'm honored you chose me.

To my agent, Danielle Chiotti, thank you for never wavering with this story. We went through so many drafts, so many versions, until we found the right story for this cast. You never told me to stop, and I will always be grateful for your support.

To my editor, Kate Brauning, you took my little space story and made it into something incredible. Your guidance and suggestions and respect have meant the world to me. You not only get this story, but you love it, and it shows in every conversation, every note, every comment. Thank you.

And to the rest of the Entangled Publishing crew, Bethany Robison, Jessie Devine, Mark O'Brien, Alex Ott, Tammy Subia, and Melissa Montovani, thank you for your work, your energy, your time, and your excitement for this book and what it could add to the world of young adult science fiction.

Also to my cover designer Fiona Jayde, that is one amazing, badass work of art. Thank you. Your talent is incredible, and I'm so lucky.

To my parents, Cathy and Andy, thank you for never refusing to buy me a book and for taking me to the library anytime I wanted to go. I love to read because of you, and I will always be grateful for that gift.

Finally, to Stephen. The past twelve years have been some of the greatest of my life so far, and that's not an exaggeration. You've stuck with me through mental and physical diagnoses you didn't understand. You've been there on my best days and seen me on my absolute worst days. I love you with my whole heart, and I'm so grateful I woke up the night you and Rebecca threw rocks at my window.

Also, we make some cute kids, dude.

GRAB THE ENTANGLED TEEN RELEASES READERS ARE TALKING ABOUT!

BLACK BIRD OF THE GALLOWS
BY MEG KASSEL

A simple but forgotten truth: Where harbingers of death appear, the morgues will soon be full.

Angie Dovage can tell there's more to Reece Fernandez than just the tall, brooding athlete who has her classmates swooning, but she can't imagine his presence signals a tragedy that will devastate her small town. When something supernatural tries to attack her, Angie is thrown into a battle between good and evil she never saw coming. Right in the center of it is Reece—and he's not human.

What's more, she knows something most don't. That the secrets her town holds could kill them all. But that's only half as dangerous as falling in love with a harbinger of death.

ISLAND OF EXILES
BY ERICA CAMERON

On the isolated desert island of Shiara, every breath is a battle.

The clan comes before self, and protecting her home means Khya is a warrior above all else. But when obeying the clan leaders could cost her brother his life, Khya's home becomes a deadly trap. The council she hoped to join has betrayed her, and their secrets, hundreds of years deep, reach around a world she's never seen.

To save her brother's life and her island home, her only choice is to turn against her clan and go on the run—a betrayal and a death sentence.

entangled teen

an imprint of Entangled Publishing LLC

AL

Relocating to A
For Leda Lindg
size of her form
as it sounds. Unt

Unfortunately, n
secrets as unnerv

Roar shouldn't be
him weak in the k
and survives, Roa
exactly what he w
capable of saving

She just doesn't kr

"We all hold a beas
when freed."

Something's not rig
surface, it's a frienc
lurks underneath the
something—especial
laid eyes on. Rain's
him...and it just migh

Ancient magic and i
romance perfect for i
proves sometimes be